Terry Pratchett is one of the most popular authors writing today. He lives behind a keyboard in Wiltshire and says he 'doesn't want to get a life, because it feels as though he's trying to lead three already'. He was appointed OBE in 1998 and his first Discworld novel for children, *The Amazing Maurice and His Educated Rodents*, was awarded the 2001 Carnegie Medal.

The Colour of Magic and *The Light Fantastic* are the first two novels in his phenomenally successful Discworld series.

BOOKS BY TERRY PRATCHETT

For Younger Readers

TRUCKERS ✤
DIGGERS ✤
WINGS ✤
THE BROMELIAD TRILOGY
(containing *Truckers, Diggers* and *Wings*)
THE CARPET PEOPLE ✤
ONLY YOU CAN SAVE MANKIND ✤
JOHNNY AND THE DEAD ✤
JOHNNY AND THE BOMB ✤
THE JOHNNY MAXWELL TRILOGY
(containing *Only You Can Save Mankind, Johnny and the Dead* and *Johnny and the Bomb*)
JOHNNY AND THE DEAD playscript (adapted by Stephen Briggs) ★

Discworld for Younger Readers

THE AMAZING MAURICE AND HIS EDUCATED RODENTS ✤
THE AMAZING MAURICE AND HIS EDUCATED RODENTS playscript (adapted by Stephen Briggs) ★
THE WEE FREE MEN ✤
THE ILLUSTRATED WEE FREE MEN
(illustrated by Stephen Player)
A HAT FULL OF SKY ✤
WINTERSMITH ✤

For Adults of All Ages

The Discworld® series

THE COLOUR OF MAGIC ✤
THE LIGHT FANTASTIC ✤
EQUAL RITES ✤
MORT ✤
SOURCERY ✤
WYRD SISTERS ✤
PYRAMIDS ✤
GUARDS! GUARDS! ✤
ERIC
(illustrated by Josh Kirby) ✤ ●
MOVING PICTURES ✤
REAPER MAN ✤
WITCHES ABROAD ✤
SMALL GODS ✤
LORDS AND LADIES ✤
MEN AT ARMS ✤
SOUL MUSIC ✤
INTERESTING TIMES ✤
MASKERADE ✤
FEET OF CLAY ✤
HOGFATHER ✤
JINGO ✤
THE LAST CONTINENT ✤
CARPE JUGULUM ✤
THE FIFTH ELEPHANT ✤
THE TRUTH ✤
THIEF OF TIME ✤
NIGHT WATCH ✤
MONSTROUS REGIMENT ✤
GOING POSTAL ✤
THUD! ✤
MAKING MONEY ✤

THE FIRST DISCWORLD NOVELS
(containing *The Colour of Magic* and *The Light Fantastic*)
THE COLOUR OF MAGIC – GRAPHIC NOVEL
THE LIGHT FANTASTIC – GRAPHIC NOVEL
MORT: A DISCWORLD BIG COMIC
(illustrated by Graham Higgins) ●
GUARDS! GUARDS!: A DISCWORLD BIG COMIC
(adapted by Stephen Briggs, illustrated by Graham Higgins) ●

SOUL MUSIC: THE ILLUSTRATED SCREENPLAY
WYRD SISTERS: THE ILLUSTRATED SCREENPLAY
HOGFATHER: THE ILLUSTRATED SCREENPLAY (with Vadim Jean)
MORT – THE PLAY (adapted by Stephen Briggs)
WYRD SISTERS – THE PLAY (adapted by Stephen Briggs)
GUARDS! GUARDS! – THE PLAY (adapted by Stephen Briggs)
MEN AT ARMS – THE PLAY (adapted by Stephen Briggs)
MASKERADE (adapted for the stage by Stephen Briggs) ■
CARPE JUGULUM (adapted for the stage by Stephen Briggs) ■
LORDS AND LADIES (adapted for the stage by Irana Brown) ■
INTERESTING TIMES (adapted for the stage by Stephen Briggs) ◆
THE FIFTH ELEPHANT (adapted for the stage by Stephen Briggs) ◆
THE TRUTH (adapted for the stage by Stephen Briggs) ◆
JINGO (adapted for the stage by Stephen Briggs) ◆
NIGHTWATCH (adapted for the stage by Stephen Briggs) ◆
MONSTROUS REGIMENT (adapted for the stage by Stephen Briggs) ◆
GOING POSTAL (adapted for the stage by Stephen Briggs) ◆

THE SCIENCE OF DISCWORLD (with Ian Stewart and Jack Cohen) ✪
THE SCIENCE OF DISCWORLD II: THE GLOBE
(with Ian Stewart and Jack Cohen) ✪
THE SCIENCE OF DISCWORLD III: DARWIN WATCH
(with Ian Stewart and Jack Cohen) ✪
THE NEW DISCWORLD COMPANION (with Stephen Briggs) ●
THE STREETS OF ANKH-MORPORK (with Stephen Briggs)
THE DISCWORLD MAPP (with Stephen Briggs)
A TOURIST GUIDE TO LANCRE – A DISCWORLD MAPP
(with Stephen Briggs and Paul Kidby)
DEATH'S DOMAIN (with Paul Kidby)
NANNY OGG'S COOKBOOK
(with Stephen Briggs, Tina Hannan and Paul Kidby)
THE PRATCHETT PORTFOLIO (with Paul Kidby) ●
THE LAST HERO (with Paul Kidby) ●
THE CELEBRATED DISCWORLD ALMANAK (with Bernard Pearson)
THE UNSEEN UNIVERSITY CUT-OUT BOOK
(with Alan Batley and Bernard Pearson)
WHERE'S MY COW? (illustrated by Melvyn Grant)
THE WIT AND WISDOM OF DISCWORLD (edited by Stephen Briggs)
GOOD OMENS (with Neil Gaiman)
STRATA
THE DARK SIDE OF THE SUN
THE UNADULTERATED CAT (cartoons by Gray Jolliffe) ●

(With Stephen Briggs, illustrated by Paul Kidby)
DISCWORLD'S UNSEEN UNIVERSITY DIARY 1998 ✦
DISCWORLD'S ANKH-MORPORK CITY WATCH DIARY 1999 ✦
DISCWORLD ASSASSINS' GUILD YEARBOOK AND DIARY 2000 ✦
DISCWORLD FOOLS' GUILD YEARBOOK AND DIARY 2002 ✦
DISCWORLD (REFORMED) VAMPYRE'S DIARY 2003 ✦
DISCWORLD ANKH-MORPORK POST OFFICE HANDBOOK DIARY 2007 ✦
LU-TSE'S YEARBOOK OF ENLIGHTENMENT 2008 ✦

✤ also available in audio/CD ● published by Victor Gollancz
■ published by Samuel French ◆ published by Methuen Drama
✪ published by Ebury Press ★ published by Oxford University Press
✦ published by Colin Smythe

The Colour of Magic

and

The Light Fantastic

Terry Pratchett

TRANSWORLD PUBLISHERS
61-63 Uxbridge Road, London W5 5SA
A Random House Group Company
www.rbooks.co.uk

THE COLOUR OF MAGIC and THE LIGHT FANTASTIC
A CORGI BOOK: 9780552157278

THE COLOUR OF MAGIC
Originally published in Great Britain in 1983 by Colin Smythe Ltd
Corgi edition published 1985

THE LIGHT FANTASTIC
Originally published in Great Britain in 1986 by Colin Smythe Ltd
Corgi edition published 1986

A CIP catalogue record for this book is available from the British Library.

Addresses for Random House Group Ltd companies outside the UK
can be found at: www.randomhouse.co.uk
The Random House Group Ltd Reg. No. 954009

The Random House Group Limited supports The Forest Stewardship Council (FSC), the leading international forest certification organisation. All our titles that are printed on Greenpeace approved FSC certified paper carry the FSC logo.
Our paper procurement policy can be found at
www.rbooks.co.uk/environment

Typeset in Minion by Falcon Oast Graphic Art Ltd

Printed in the UK by CPI Cox & Wyman, Reading, RG1 8EX.

2 4 6 8 10 9 7 5 3 1

The Colour of Magic

Terry Pratchett

CORGI BOOKS

Contents

The Colour of Magic

· Prologue ·

IN A DISTANT AND second-hand set of dimensions, in an astral plane that was never meant to fly, the curling star-mists waver and part . . .

See . . .

Great A'Tuin the Turtle comes, swimming slowly through the interstellar gulf, hydrogen frost on his ponderous limbs, his huge and ancient shell pocked with meteor craters. Through sea-sized eyes that are crusted with rheum and asteroid dust He stares fixedly at the Destination.

In a brain bigger than a city, with geological slowness, He thinks only of the Weight.

Most of the weight is of course accounted for by Berilia, Tubul, Great T'Phon and Jerakeen, the four giant elephants upon whose broad and star-tanned shoulders the disc of the World rests, garlanded by the long waterfall at its vast circumference and domed by the baby-blue vault of Heaven.

Astropsychology has been, as yet, unable to establish what they think about.

The Great Turtle was a mere hypothesis until the day the small and secretive kingdom of Krull, whose rim-most mountains project out over the Rimfall, built a gantry and pulley arrangement at the tip of the most precipitous crag and lowered several observers over the Edge in a quartz-windowed brass vessel to peer through the mist veils.

The early astrozoologists, hauled back from their long dangle by enormous teams of slaves, were able to bring back much information about the shape and nature of A'Tuin and the elephants but this did not resolve fundamental questions about the nature and purpose of the universe.

For example, what was A'Tuin's actual sex? This vital question, said the astrozoologists with mounting authority, would not be answered until a larger and more powerful gantry was constructed for a deep-space vessel. In the meantime, they could only speculate about the revealed cosmos.

There was, for example, the theory that A'Tuin had come from nowhere and would continue at a uniform crawl, or steady gait, into nowhere, for all time. This theory was popular among academics.

An alternative, favoured by those of a religious persuasion, was that A'Tuin was crawling from the Birthplace to the Time of Mating, as were all the stars in the sky which were, obviously, also carried by giant turtles. When they arrived they would briefly and passionately mate, for the first and only time, and from that fiery union new turtles would be born to carry a new pattern of worlds. This was known as the Big Bang hypothesis.

Thus it was that a young cosmochelonian of the Steady Gait faction, testing a new telescope with which he hoped to make measurements of the precise albedo of Great A'Tuin's right eye, was on this eventful evening the first outsider to see the smoke rise hubward from the burning of the oldest city in the world.

Later that night he became so engrossed in his studies he completely forgot about it. Nevertheless, he was the first.

There were others . . .

The Colour of Magic

FIRE ROARED THROUGH THE bifurcated city of Ankh-Morpork. Where it licked the Wizards' Quarter it burned blue and green and was even laced with strange sparks of the eighth colour, octarine; where its outriders found their way into the vats and oil stores all along Merchants Street it progressed in a series of blazing fountains and explosions; in the streets of the perfume blenders it burned with a sweetness; where it touched bundles of rare and dry herbs in the storerooms of the drugmasters it made men go mad and talk to God.

By now the whole of downtown Morpork was alight, and the richer and worthier citizens of Ankh on the far bank were bravely responding to the situation by feverishly demolishing the bridges. But already the ships in the Morpork docks – laden with grain, cotton and timber, and coated with tar – were blazing merrily and, their moorings burnt to ashes, were breasting the river Ankh on the ebb tide, igniting riverside palaces and bowers as they drifted like drowning fireflies towards the sea. In any case, sparks were riding the breeze and touching down far across the river in hidden gardens and remote rickyards.

The smoke from the merry burning rose miles

high, in a wind-sculpted black column that could be seen across the whole of the discworld.

It was certainly impressive from the cool, dark hilltop a few leagues away, where two figures were watching with considerable interest.

The taller of the pair was chewing on a chicken leg and leaning on a sword that was only marginally shorter than the average man. If it wasn't for the air of wary intelligence about him it might have been supposed that he was a barbarian from the Hubland wastes.

His partner was much shorter and wrapped from head to toe in a brown cloak. Later, when he has occasion to move, it will be seen that he moves lightly, cat-like.

The two had barely exchanged a word in the last twenty minutes except for a short and inconclusive argument as to whether a particularly powerful explosion had been the oil bond store or the workshop of Kerible the Enchanter. Money hinged on the fact.

Now the big man finished gnawing at the bone and tossed it into the grass, smiling ruefully.

'There go all those little alleyways,' he said. 'I liked them.'

'All the treasure houses,' said the small man. He added thoughtfully, 'Do gems burn, I wonder? 'Tis said they're kin to coal.'

'All the gold, melting and running down the gutters,' said the big one, ignoring him. 'And all the wine, boiling in the barrels.'

'There were rats,' said his brown companion.

'Rats, I'll grant you.'

'It was no place to be in high summer.'

'That, too. One can't help feeling, though, a – well, a momentary—'

He trailed off, then brightened. 'We owed old Fredor at the Crimson Leech eight silver pieces,' he added. The little man nodded.

They were silent for a while as a whole new series of explosions carved a red line across a hitherto dark section of the greatest city in the world. Then the big man stirred.

'Weasel?'

'Yes?'

'I wonder who started it?'

The small swordsman known as the Weasel said nothing. He was watching the road in the ruddy light. Few had come that way since the Deosil Gate had been one of the first to collapse in a shower of white-hot embers.

But two were coming up it now. The Weasel's eyes, always at their sharpest in gloom and half-light, made out the shapes of two mounted men and some sort of low beast behind them. Doubtless a rich merchant escaping with as much treasure as he could lay frantic hands on. The Weasel said as much to his companion, who sighed.

'The status of footpad ill suits us,' said the barbarian, 'but as you say, times are hard and there are no soft beds tonight.'

He shifted his grip on his sword and, as the leading rider drew near, stepped out onto the road with a hand held up and his face set in a grin nicely calculated to reassure yet threaten.

'Your pardon, sir—' he began.

The rider reined in his horse and drew back his hood. The big man looked into a face blotched with superficial burns and punctuated by tufts of singed beard. Even the eyebrows had gone.

'Bugger off,' said the face. 'You're Bravd the Hublander,[1] aren't you?'

Bravd became aware that he had fumbled the initiative.

'Just go away, will you?' said the rider. 'I just haven't got time for you, do you understand?'

He looked around and added: 'That goes for your shadow-loving fleabag partner too, wherever he's hiding.'

The Weasel stepped up to the horse and peered at the dishevelled figure.

'Why, it's Rincewind the wizard, isn't it?' he said in

[1] The shape and cosmology of the disc system are perhaps worthy of note at this point.

There are, of course, two major directions on the disc: Hubward and Rimward. But since the disc itself revolves at the rate of once every eight hundred days (in order to distribute the weight fairly upon its supportive pachyderms, according to Reforgule of Krull) there are also two lesser directions, which are Turnwise and Widdershins.

Since the disc's tiny orbiting sunlet maintains a fixed orbit while the majestic disc turns slowly beneath it, it will be readily deduced that a disc year consists of not four but eight seasons. The summers are those times when the sun rises or sets at the nearest point on the Rim, the winters those occasions when it rises or sets at a point around ninety degrees along the circumference.

Thus, in the lands around the Circle Sea, the year begins on Hogs' Watch Night, progresses through a Spring Prime to its first mid-summer (Small Gods' Eve) which is followed by Autumn Prime and, tones of delight, meanwhile filing the wizard's description of him in his memory for leisurely vengeance. 'I thought I recognized the voice.'

Bravd spat and sheathed his sword. It was seldom worth tangling with wizards, they so rarely had any treasure worth speaking of.

'He talks pretty big for a gutter wizard,' he muttered.

'You don't understand at all,' said the wizard wearily. 'I'm so scared of you my spine has turned to jelly, it's just that I'm suffering from an overdose of terror right now. I mean, when I've got over that then I'll have time to be decently frightened of you.'

The Weasel pointed towards the burning city.

'You've been through that?' he asked.

The wizard rubbed a red-raw hand across his eyes. 'I was there when it started. See him? Back there?' He pointed back down the road to where his travelling

straddling the half-year point of Crueltide, Winter Secundus (also known as the Spindlewinter, since at this time the sun rises in the direction of spin). Then comes Secundus Spring with Summer Two on its heels, the three quarter mark of the year being the night of Alls Fallow – the one night of the year, according to legend, when witches and warlocks stay in bed. Then drifting leaves and frosty nights drag on towards Backspindlewinter and a new Hogs' Watch Night nestling like a frozen jewel at its heart.

Since the Hub is never closely warmed by the weak sun the lands there are locked in permafrost. The Rim, on the other hand, is a region of sunny islands and balmy days.

There are, of course, eight days in a disc week and eight colours in its light spectrum. Eight is a number of some considerable occult significance on the disc and must never, ever, be spoken by a wizard.

Precisely why all the above should be so is not clear, but goes some way to explain why, on the disc, the Gods are not so much worshipped as blamed.

companion was still approaching, having adopted a method of riding that involved falling out of the saddle every few seconds.

'Well?' said Weasel.

'He started it,' said Rincewind simply.

Bravd and Weasel looked at the figure, now hopping across the road with one foot in a stirrup.

'Fire-raiser, is he?' said Bravd at last.

'No,' said Rincewind. 'Not precisely. Let's just say that if complete and utter chaos was lightning, then he'd be the sort to stand on a hilltop in a thunderstorm wearing wet copper armour and shouting "All gods are bastards". Got any food?'

'There's some chicken,' said Weasel. 'In exchange for a story.'

'What's his name?' said Bravd, who tended to lag behind in conversations.

'Twoflower.'

'Twoflower?' said Bravd. 'What a funny name.'

'You,' said Rincewind, dismounting, 'do not know the half of it. Chicken, you say?'

'Devilled,' said Weasel. The wizard groaned.

'That reminds me,' added the Weasel, snapping his fingers, 'there was a really big explosion about, oh, half an hour ago—'

'That was the oil bond store going up,' said Rincewind, wincing at the memory of the burning rain.

Weasel turned and grinned expectantly at his companion, who grunted and handed over a coin from his pouch. Then there was a scream from the roadway, cut off abruptly. Rincewind did not look up from his chicken.

'One of the things he can't do, he can't ride a horse,' he said. Then he stiffened as if sandbagged by a sudden recollection, gave a small yelp of terror and dashed into the gloom. When he returned, the being called Twoflower was hanging limply over his shoulder. It was small and skinny, and dressed very oddly in a pair of knee length britches and a shirt in such a violent and vivid conflict of colours that Weasel's fastidious eye was offended even in the half-light.

'No bones broken, by the feel of things,' said Rincewind. He was breathing heavily. Bravd winked at the Weasel and went to investigate the shape that they assumed was a pack animal.

'You'd be wise to forget it,' said the wizard, without looking up from his examination of the unconscious Twoflower. 'Believe me. A power protects it.'

'A spell?' said Weasel, squatting down.

'No-oo. But magic of a kind, I think. Not the usual sort. I mean, it can turn gold into copper while at the same time it is still gold, it makes men rich by destroying their possessions, it allows the weak to walk fearlessly among thieves, it passes through the strongest doors to leach the most protected treasuries. Even now it has me enslaved – so that I must follow this madman willynilly and protect him from harm. It's stronger than you, Bravd. It is, I think, more cunning even than you, Weasel.'

'What is it called then, this mighty magic?'

Rincewind shrugged. 'In our tongue it is called

reflected-sound-as-of-underground-spirits. Is there any wine?'

'You must know that I am not without artifice where magic is concerned,' said Weasel. 'Only last year did I – assisted by my friend there – part the notoriously powerful Archmage of Ymitury from his staff, his belt of moon jewels and his life, in that approximate order. I do not fear this *reflected-sound-of-underground-spirits* of which you speak. However,' he added, 'you engage my interest. Perhaps you would care to tell me more?'

Bravd looked at the shape on the road. It was closer now, and clearer in the pre-dawn light. It looked for all the world like a—

'A box on legs?' he said.

'I'll tell you about it,' said Rincewind. 'If there's any wine, that is.'

Down in the valley there was a roar and a hiss. Someone more thoughtful than the rest had ordered to be shut the big river gates that were at the point where the Ankh flowed out of the twin city. Denied its usual egress, the river had burst its banks and was pouring down the fire-ravaged streets. Soon the continent of flame became a series of islands, each one growing smaller as the dark tide rose. And up from the city of fumes and smoke rose a broiling cloud of steam, covering the stars. Weasel thought that it looked like some dark fungus or mushroom.

The twin city of proud Ankh and pestilent Morpork, of which all the other cities of time and space are, as it were, mere reflections, has stood many assaults in its long and crowded history and has always risen to flourish again. So the fire and its subsequent flood, which destroyed everything left that was not flammable and added a particularly noisome flux to the survivors' problems, did not mark its end. Rather it was a fiery punctuation mark, a coal-like comma, or salamander semi-colon, in a continuing story.

Several days before these events a ship came up the Ankh on the dawn tide and fetched up, among many others, in the maze of wharves and docks on the Morpork shore. It carried a cargo of pink pearls, milknuts, pumice, some official letters for the Patrician of Ankh-Morpork, and a man.

It was the man who engaged the attention of Blind Hugh, one of the beggars on early duty at Pearl Dock. He nudged Cripple Wa in the ribs, and pointed wordlessly.

Now the stranger was standing on the quayside, watching several straining seamen carry a large brass-bound chest down the gangplank. Another man, obviously the captain, was standing beside him. There was about the seaman – every nerve in Blind Hugh's body, which tended to vibrate in the presence of even a small amount of impure gold at fifty paces, screamed into his brain – the air of one anticipating imminent enrichment.

Sure enough, when the chest had been deposited on the cobbles, the stranger reached into a pouch and there was the flash of a coin. Several coins. Gold. Blind Hugh, his body twanging like a hazel rod in the presence of water, whistled to himself. Then he nudged Wa again, and sent him scurrying off down a nearby alley into the heart of the city.

When the captain walked back onto his ship, leaving the newcomer looking faintly bewildered on the quayside, Blind Hugh snatched up his begging cup and made his way across the street with an ingratiating leer. At the sight of him the stranger started to fumble urgently with his money pouch.

'Good day to thee, sire,' Blind Hugh began, and found himself looking up into a face with four eyes in it. He turned to run.

'!' said the stranger, and grabbed his arm. Hugh was aware that the sailors lining the rail of the ship were laughing at him. At the same time his specialized senses detected an overpowering impression of money. He froze. The stranger let go and quickly thumbed through a small black book he had taken from his belt. Then he said 'Hallo'.

'What?' said Hugh. The man looked blank.

'Hallo?' he repeated, rather louder than necessary and so carefully that Hugh could hear the vowels tinkling into place.

'Hallo yourself,' Hugh riposted. The stranger smiled widely then fumbled yet again in the pouch. This time his hand came out holding a large gold coin. It was in fact slightly larger than an 8,000-dollar Ankhian crown and the design on it was unfamiliar, but it spoke inside Hugh's mind in a language he understood perfectly. My current owner, it said, is in need of succour and assistance; why not give it to him, so you and me can go off somewhere and enjoy ourselves?

Subtle changes in the beggar's posture made the

stranger feel more at ease. He consulted the small book again.

'I wish to be directed to an hotel, tavern, lodging house, inn, hospice, caravanserai,' he said.

'What, all of them?' said Hugh, taken aback.

'?' said the stranger.

Hugh was aware that a small crowd of fishwives, shellfish diggers and freelance gawpers were watching them with interest.

'Look,' he said, 'I know a good tavern, is that enough?' He shuddered to think of the gold coin escaping from his life. He'd keep that one, even if Ymor confiscated all the rest. And the big chest that comprised most of the newcomer's luggage looked to be full of gold, Hugh decided.

The four-eyed man looked at his book.

'I would like to be directed to an hotel, place of repose, tavern, a—'

'Yes, all right. Come on then,' said Hugh hurriedly. He picked up one of the bundles and walked away quickly. The stranger, after a moment's hesitation, strolled after him.

A train of thought shunted its way through Hugh's mind. Getting the newcomer to the Broken Drum so easily was a stroke of luck, no doubt of it, and Ymor would probably reward him. But for all his new acquaintance's mildness there was something about him that made Hugh uneasy, and for the life of him he couldn't figure out what it was. Not the two extra eyes, odd though they were. There was something else. He glanced back.

The little man was ambling along in the middle of

the street, looking around him with an expression of keen interest.

Something else Hugh saw nearly made him gibber.

The massive wooden chest, which he had last seen resting solidly on the quayside, was following on its master's heels with a gentle rocking gait. Slowly, in case a sudden movement on his part might break his fragile control over his own legs, Hugh bent slightly so that he could see under the chest.

There were lots and lots of little legs.

Very deliberately, Hugh turned around and walked very carefully towards the Broken Drum.

'Odd,' said Ymor.

'He had this big wooden chest,' added Cripple Wa.

'He'd have to be a merchant or a spy,' said Ymor. He pulled a scrap of meat from the cutlet in his hand and tossed it into the air. It hadn't reached the zenith of its arc before a black shape detached itself from the shadows in the corner of the room and swooped down, taking the morsel in mid-air.

'A merchant or a spy,' repeated Ymor. 'I'd prefer a spy. A spy pays for himself twice, because there's always the reward when we turn him in. What do you think, Withel?'

Opposite Ymor the second greatest thief in Ankh-Morpork half-closed his one eye and shrugged.

'I've checked on the ship,' he said. 'It's a freelance trader. Does the occasional run to the Brown Islands. People there are just savages. They don't understand about spies and I expect they eat merchants.'

'He looked a bit like a merchant,' volunteered Wa. 'Except he wasn't fat.'

There was a flutter of wings at the window. Ymor shifted his bulk out of the chair and crossed the room, coming back with a large raven. After he'd unfastened the message capsule from its leg it flew up to join its fellows lurking among the rafters. Withel regarded it without love. Ymor's ravens were notoriously loyal to their master, to the extent that Withel's one attempt to promote himself to the rank of greatest thief in Ankh-Morpork had cost their master's right-hand man his left eye. But not his life, however. Ymor never grudged a man his ambitions.

'B12,' said Ymor, tossing the little phial aside and unrolling the tiny scroll within.

'Gorrin the Cat,' said Withel automatically. 'On station up in the gong tower at the Temple of Small Gods.'

'He says Hugh has taken our stranger to the Broken Drum. Well, that's good enough. Broadman is a – friend of ours, isn't he?'

'Aye,' said Withel. 'If he knows what's good for trade.'

'Among his customers has been your man Gorrin,' said Ymor pleasantly, 'for he writes here about a box on legs, if I read this scrawl correctly.' He looked at Withel over the top of the paper.

Withel looked away. 'He will be disciplined,' he said flatly. Wa looked at the man leaning back in his chair, his black-clad frame resting as nonchalantly as a Rimland puma on a jungle branch, and decided that Gorrin atop Small Gods temple would soon be joining those little deities in the multifold dimensions of Beyond. And he owed Wa three copper pieces.

Ymor crumpled the note and tossed it into a corner. 'I think we'll wander along to the Drum later on, Withel. Perhaps, too, we may try this beer that your men find so tempting.'

Withel said nothing. Being Ymor's right-hand man was like being gently flogged to death with scented bootlaces.

The twin city of Ankh-Morpork, foremost of all the cities bounding the Circle Sea, was as a matter of course the home of a large number of gangs, thieves' guilds, syndicates and similar organizations. This was one of the reasons for its wealth. Most of the humbler folk on the widdershins side of the river, in Morpork's mazy alleys, supplemented their meagre incomes by filling some small role for one or other of the competing gangs. So it was that by the time Hugh and Twoflower entered the courtyard of the Broken Drum the leaders of a number of them were aware that someone had arrived in the city who appeared to have much treasure. Some reports from the more observant spies included details about a book that told the stranger what to say, and a box that walked by itself. These facts were immediately discounted. No magician capable of such enchantments ever came within a mile of Morpork docks.

It still being that hour when most of the city was just rising or about to go to bed there were few people in the Drum to watch Twoflower descend the stairs. When the Luggage appeared behind him and started to lurch confidently down the steps the customers at the rough wooden tables, as one man, looked suspiciously at their drinks.

Broadman was browbeating the small troll who swept the bar when the trio walked past him. 'What in hell's that?' he said.

'Just don't talk about it,' hissed Hugh. Twoflower was already thumbing through his book.

'What's he doing?' said Broadman, arms akimbo.

'It tells him what to say. I know it sounds ridiculous,' muttered Hugh.

'How can a book tell a man what to say?'

'I wish for an accommodation, a room, lodgings, the lodging house, full board, are your rooms clean, a room with a view, what is your rate for one night?' said Twoflower in one breath.

Broadman looked at Hugh. The beggar shrugged.

'He's got plenty money,' he said.

'Tell him it's three copper pieces, then. And that Thing will have to go in the stable.'

'?' said the stranger. Broadman held up three thick red fingers and the man's face was suddenly a sunny display of comprehension. He reached into his pouch and laid three large gold pieces in Broadman's palm.

Broadman stared at them. They represented about four times the worth of the Broken Drum, staff included. He looked at Hugh. There was no help there. He looked at the stranger. He swallowed.

'Yes,' he said, in an unnaturally high voice. 'And then there's meals, o'course. Uh. You understand, yes? Food. You eat. No?' He made the appropriate motions.

'Fut?' said the little man.

'Yes,' said Boardman, beginning to sweat. 'Have a look in your little book, I should.'

The man opened the book and ran a finger down one page. Broadman, who could read after a fashion, peered over the top of the volume. What he saw made no sense.

'Fooood,' said the stranger. 'Yes. Cutlet, hash, chop, stew, ragout, fricassee, mince, collops, souffle, dumpling, blancmange, sorbet, gruel, sausage, not to have a sausage, beans, without a bean, kickshaws, jelly, jam. Giblets.' He beamed at Broadman.

'All that?' said the innkeeper weakly.

'It's just the way he talks,' said Hugh. 'Don't ask me why. He just does.'

All eyes in the room were watching the stranger – except for a pair belonging to Rincewind the wizard, who was sitting in the darkest corner nursing a mug of very small beer.

He was watching the Luggage.

Watch Rincewind.

Look at him. Scrawny, like most wizards, and clad in a dark red robe on which a few mystic sigils were embroidered in tarnished sequins. Some might have taken him for a mere apprentice enchanter who had run away from his master out of defiance, boredom, fear and a lingering taste for heterosexuality. Yet around his neck was a chain bearing the bronze octagon that marked him as an alumnus of Unseen University, the high school of magic whose time-and-space transcendent campus is never precisely Here or There. Graduates were usually destined for mageship at least, but Rincewind – after an unfortunate event – had left knowing only one spell and made a living of sorts around the town by capitalizing on an innate gift for languages. He avoided work as a rule, but had a quickness of wit that put his acquaintances in mind of a bright rodent. And he knew sapient pearwood when he saw it. He was seeing it now, and didn't quite believe it.

An archmage, by dint of great effort and much expenditure of time, might eventually obtain a small staff made from the timber of the sapient peartree. It grew only on the sites of ancient magic. There were probably no more than two such staffs in all the cities of the Circle Sea. A large chest of it . . . Rincewind tried to work it out, and decided that even if the box were crammed with star opals and sticks of auricholatum the contents would not be worth one-tenth the price of the container. A vein started to throb in his forehead.

He stood up and made his way to the trio.

'May I be of assistance?' he ventured.

'Shove off, Rincewind,' snarled Broadman.

'I only thought it might be useful to address this gentleman in his own tongue,' said the wizard gently.

'He's doing all right on his own,' said the innkeeper, but took a few steps backward.

Rincewind smiled politely at the stranger and tried a few words of Chimeran. He prided himself on his fluency in the tongue, but the stranger only looked bemused.

'It won't work,' said Hugh knowledgeably. 'It's the book, you see. It tells him what to say. Magic.'

Rincewind switched to High Borogravian, to Vanglemesht, Sumtri and even Black Oroogu, the language with no nouns and only one adjective, which is obscene. Each was met with polite incomprehension. In desperation he tried heathen Trob, and the little man's face split into a delighted grin.

'At last!' he said. 'My good sir! This is remarkable!' (Although in Trob the last word in fact became 'a thing which may happen but once in the usable lifetime of a canoe hollowed diligently by axe and fire from the tallest diamondwood tree that grows in the noted diamondwood forests on the lower slopes of Mount Awayawa, home of the firegods or so it is said.')

'What was all that?' said Broadman suspiciously.

'What did the innkeeper say?' said the little man.

Rincewind swallowed. 'Broadman,' he said. 'Two mugs of your best ale, please.'

'You can understand him?'

'Oh, sure.'

'Tell him – tell him he's very welcome. Tell him breakfast is – uh – one gold piece.' For a moment Broadman's face looked as though some vast internal struggle was going on, and then he added with a burst of generosity, 'I'll throw in yours, too.'

'Stranger,' said Rincewind levelly. 'If you stay here you will be knifed or poisoned by nightfall. But don't stop smiling, or so will I.'

'Oh, come now,' said the stranger, looking around. 'This looks like a delightful place. A genuine Morporkian tavern. I've heard so much about them, you know. All these quaint old beams. And so reasonable, too.'

Rincewind glanced around quickly, in case some leakage of enchantment from the Magicians' Quarter across the river had momentarily transported them to some other place. No – this was still the interior of the Drum, its walls stained with smoke, its floor a compost of old rushes and nameless beetles, its sour beer not so much purchased as merely hired for a while. He tried to fit the image around the word 'quaint', or rather the nearest Trob equivalent, which was 'that pleasant oddity of design found in the little coral houses of the sponge-eating pygmies on the Orohai peninsula'.

His mind reeled back from the effort. The visitor went on, 'My name is Twoflower,' and extended his hand. Instinctively, the other three looked down to see if there was a coin in it.

'Pleased to meet you,' said Rincewind. 'I'm Rincewind. Look, I wasn't joking. This is a tough place.'

'Good! Exactly what I wanted!'

'Eh?'

'What is this stuff in the mugs?'

'This? Beer. Thanks, Broadman. Yes. Beer. You know. Beer.'

'Ah. The so-typical drink. A small gold piece will be sufficient payment, do you think? I do not want to cause offence.'

It was already half out of his purse.

'Yarrt,' croaked Rincewind. 'I mean, no, it won't cause offence.'

'Good. You say this is a tough place. Frequented, you mean, by heroes and men of adventure?'

Rincewind considered this. 'Yes?' he managed.

'Excellent. I would like to meet some.'

An explanation occurred to the wizard. 'Ah,' he said. 'You've come to hire mercenaries ("warriors who fight for the tribe with the most milknut-meal")?'

'Oh no. I just want to meet them. So that when I get home I can say that I did it.'

Rincewind thought that a meeting with most of the Drum's clientele would mean that Twoflower never went home again, unless he lived downriver and happened to float past.

'Where is your home?' he enquired. Broadman had slipped away into some back room, he noticed. Hugh was watching them suspiciously from a nearby table.

'Have you heard of the city of Bes Pelargic?'

'Well, I didn't spend much time in Trob. I was just passing through, you know—'

'Oh, it's not in Trob. I speak Trob because there are many beTrobi sailors in our ports. Bes Pelargic is the major seaport of the Agatean Empire.'

'Never heard of it, I'm afraid.'

Twoflower raised his eyebrows. 'No? It is quite big. You sail turnwise from the Brown Islands for about a week and there it is. Are you all right?'

He hurried around the table and patted the wizard on the back. Rincewind choked on his beer.

The Counterweight Continent!

Three streets away an old man dropped a coin into a saucer of acid and swirled it gently. Broadman waited impatiently, ill at ease in a room made noisome by vats and bubbling beakers and lined with shelves containing shadowy shapes suggestive of skulls and stuffed impossibilities.

'Well?' he demanded.

'One cannot hurry these things,' said the old alchemist peevishly. 'Assaying takes time. Ah.' He prodded the saucer, where the coin now lay in a swirl of green colour. He made some calculations on a scrap of parchment.

'Exceptionally interesting,' he said at last.

'*Is it genuine?*'

The old man pursed his lips. 'It depends on how you define the term,' he said. 'If you mean: is this coin the same as, say, a fifty-dollar piece, then the answer is no.'

'I *knew* it,' screamed the innkeeper, and started towards the door.

'I'm not sure that I'm making myself clear,' said the alchemist. Broadman turned round angrily.

'What do you mean?'

'Well, you see, what with one thing and another our coinage has been somewhat watered, over the years. The gold content of the average coin is barely four parts in twelve, the balance being made up of silver, copper—'

'What of it?'

'I said this coin isn't like ours. It is *pure* gold.'

After Broadman had left, at a run, the alchemist spent some time staring at the ceiling. Then he drew out a very small piece of thin parchment, rummaged for a pen amongst the debris on his workbench, and wrote a very short, small message. Then he went over to his cages of white doves, black cockerels and other laboratory animals. From one cage he removed a glossy coated rat, rolled the parchment into the phial attached to a hind leg, and let the animal go.

It sniffed around the floor for a moment, then disappeared down a hole in the far wall.

At about this time a hitherto unsuccessful fortune-teller living on the other side of the block chanced to glance into her scrying bowl, gave a small scream and, within the hour, had sold her jewellery, various magical accoutrements, most of her clothes and almost all her other possessions that could not be conveniently carried on the fastest horse she could buy. The fact that later on, when her house collapsed in flames, she herself died in a freak landslide in the Morpork Mountains, proves that Death, too, has a sense of humour.

Also at about the same moment as the homing rat disappeared into the maze of runs under the city, scurrying along in faultless obedience to an ancient instinct, the Patrician of Ankh-Morpork picked up the letters delivered that morning by albatross. He looked pensively at the topmost one again, and summoned his chief of spies.

And in the Broken Drum Rincewind was listening open-mouthed as Twoflower talked.

'So I decided to see for myself,' the little man was saying. 'Eight years' saving up, this has cost me. But worth every half-*rhinu*. I mean, here I am. In Ankh-Morpork. Famed in song and story, I mean. In the streets that have known the tread of Heric Whiteblade, Hrun the Barbarian, and Bravd the

Hublander and the Weasel . . . It's all just like I imagined, you know.'

Rincewind's face was a mask of fascinated horror.

'I just couldn't stand it any more back in Bes Pelargic,' Twoflower went on blithely, 'sitting at a desk all day, just adding up columns of figures, just a pension to look forward to at the end of it . . . where's the romance in that? Twoflower, I thought, it's now or never. You don't just have to listen to stories. You can go there. Now's the time to stop hanging around the docks listening to sailors' tales. So I compiled a phrase book and bought a passage on the next ship to the Brown Islands.'

'No guards?' murmured Rincewind.

'No. Why? What have I got that's worth stealing?'

Rincewind coughed. 'You have, uh, gold,' he said.

'Barely two thousand *rhinu.* Hardly enough to keep a man alive for more than a month or two. At home, that is. I imagine they might stretch a bit further here.'

'Would a *rhinu* be one of those big gold coins?' said Rincewind.

'Yes.' Twoflower looked worriedly at the wizard over the top of his strange seeing-lenses. 'Will two thousand be sufficient, do you think?'

'Yarrrt,' croaked Rincewind. 'I mean, yes – sufficient.'

'Good.'

'Um. Is everyone in the Agatean Empire as rich as you?'

'Me? Rich? Bless you, whatever put that idea into your head? I am but a poor clerk! Did I pay the innkeeper too much, do you think?' Twoflower added.

'Uh. He might have settled for less,' Rincewind conceded.

'Ah. I shall know better next time. I can see I have a lot to learn. An idea occurs to me. Rincewind, would you perhaps consent to be employed as a, I don't know, perhaps the word "guide" would fit the circumstances? I think I could afford to pay you a *rhinu* a day.'

Rincewind opened his mouth to reply but felt the words huddle together in his throat, reluctant to emerge in a world that was rapidly going mad. Twoflower blushed.

'I have offended you,' he said. 'It was an impertinent request to make of a professional man such as yourself. Doubtless you have many projects you wish to return to – some works of high magic, no doubt . . .'

'No,' said Rincewind faintly. 'Not just at present. A *rhinu*, you say? One a day. Every day?'

'I think perhaps in the circumstances I should make it one and one-half *rhinu* per day. Plus any out-of-pocket expenses, of course.'

The wizard rallied magnificently. 'That will be fine,' he said. 'Great.'

Twoflower reached into his pouch and took out a large round gold object, glanced at it for a moment, and slipped it back. Rincewind didn't get a chance to see it properly.

'I think,' said the tourist, 'that I would like a little rest now. It was a long crossing. And then perhaps you would care to call back at noon and we can take a look at the city.'

'Sure.'

'Then please be good enough to ask the innkeeper to show me to my room.'

Rincewind did so, and watched the nervous Broadman, who had arrived at a gallop from some back room, lead the way up the wooden steps behind the bar. After a few seconds the Luggage got up and pattered across the floor after them.

Then the wizard looked down at the six big coins in his hand. Twoflower had insisted on paying his first four days' wages in advance.

Hugh nodded and smiled encouragingly. Rincewind snarled at him.

As a student wizard Rincewind had never achieved high marks in precognition, but now unused circuits in his brain were throbbing and the future might as well have been engraved in bright colours on his eyeballs. The space between his shoulder-blades began to itch. The sensible thing to do, he knew, was to buy a horse. It would have to be a fast one, and expensive – offhand, Rincewind couldn't think of any horsedealer he knew who was rich enough to give change out of almost a whole ounce of gold.

And then, of course, the other five coins would help him set up a useful practice at some safe distance, say two hundred miles. That would be the sensible thing.

But what would happen to Twoflower, all alone in a city where even the cockroaches had an unerring instinct for gold? A man would have to be a real heel to leave him.

* * *

The Patrician of Ankh-Morpork smiled, but with his mouth only.

'The Hub Gate, you say?' he murmured.

The guard captain saluted smartly. 'Aye, lord. We had to shoot the horse before he would stop.'

'Which, by a fairly direct route, brings you here,' said the Patrician, looking down at Rincewind. 'And what have you got to say for yourself?'

It was rumoured that an entire wing of the Patrician's palace was filled with clerks who spent their days collating and updating all the information collected by their master's exquisitely organized spy system. Rincewind didn't doubt it. He glanced towards the balcony that ran down one side of the audience room. A sudden run, a nimble jump – a sudden hail of crossbow quarrels. He shuddered.

The Patrician cradled his chins in a beringed hand, and regarded the wizard with eyes as small and hard as beads.

'Let me see,' he said. 'Oathbreaking, the theft of a horse, uttering false coinage – yes, I think it's the Arena for you, Rincewind.'

This was too much.

'I didn't steal the horse! I bought it fairly!'

'But with false coinage. Technical theft, you see.'

'But those *rhinu* are solid gold!'

'*Rhinu?*' The Patrician rolled one of them around in his thick fingers. 'Is that what they are called? How interesting. But, as you point out, they are not very similar to dollars . . .'

'Well, of course they're not—'

'Ah! you admit it, then?'

Rincewind opened his mouth to speak, thought better of it, and shut it again.

'Quite so. And on top of these there is, of course, the moral obloquy attendant on the cowardly betrayal of a visitor to this shore. For shame, Rincewind!'

The Patrician waved a hand vaguely. The guards behind Rincewind backed away, and their captain took a few paces to the right. Rincewind suddenly felt very alone.

It is said that when a wizard is about to die Death himself turns up to claim him (instead of delegating the task to a subordinate, such as Disease or Famine, as is usually the case). Rincewind looked around nervously for a tall figure in black (wizards, even failed wizards, have in addition to rods and cones in their eyeballs the tiny octagons that enable them to see into the far octarine, the basic colour of which all other colours are merely pale shadows impinging on normal four-dimensional space. It is said to be a sort of fluorescent greenish-yellow purple).

Was that a flickering shadow in the corner?

'Of course,' said the Patrician, 'I could be merciful.'

The shadow disappeared. Rincewind looked up, an expression of insane hope on his face.

'Yes?' he said.

The Patrician waved a hand again. Rincewind saw the guards leave the chamber. Alone with the overlord of the twin cities, he almost wished they would come back.

'Come hither, Rincewind,' said the Patrician. He indicated a bowl of savouries on a low onyx table by the throne. 'Would you care for a crystallized jellyfish? No?'

'Um,' said Rincewind, 'no.'

'Now I want you to listen very carefully to what I am about to say,' said the Patrician amiably, 'otherwise you will die. In an interesting fashion. Over a period. Please stop fidgeting like that.

'Since you are a wizard of sorts, you are of course aware that we live upon a world shaped, as it were, like a disc? And that there is said to exist, towards the far rim, a continent which though small is equal in weight to all the mighty landmasses in this hemicircle? And that this, according to ancient legend, is because it is largely made of gold?'

Rincewind nodded. Who hadn't heard of the Counterweight Continent? Some sailors even believed the childhood tales and sailed in search of it. Of course, they returned either empty handed or not at all. Probably eaten by giant turtles, in the opinion of more serious mariners. Because, of course, the Counterweight Continent was nothing more than a solar myth.

'It does, of course, exist,' said the Patrician. 'Although it is not made of gold, it is true that gold is a very common metal there. Most of the mass is made up by vast deposits of octiron deep within the crust. Now it will be obvious to an incisive mind like yours that the existence of the Counterweight Continent poses a deadly threat to our people here—' he paused, looking at Rincewind's open mouth. He sighed. He said, 'Do you by some chance fail to follow me?'

'Yarrg,' said Rincewind. He swallowed, and licked his lips. 'I mean, no. I mean – well, gold . . .'

'I see,' said the Patrician sweetly. 'You feel, perhaps,

that it would be a marvellous thing to go to the Counterweight Continent and bring back a shipload of gold?'

Rincewind had a feeling that some sort of trap was being set.

'Yes?' he ventured.

'And if every man on the shores of the Circle Sea had a mountain of gold of his own? Would that be a good thing? What would happen? Think carefully.'

Rincewind's brow furrowed. He thought. 'We'd all be rich?'

The way the temperature fell at his remark told him that it was not the correct one.

'I may as well tell you, Rincewind, that there is some contact between the Lords of the Circle Sea and the Emperor of the Agatean Empire, as it is styled,' the Patrician went on. 'It is only very slight. There is little common ground between us. We have nothing they want, and they have nothing we can afford. It is an old Empire, Rincewind. Old and cunning and cruel and very, very rich. So we exchange fraternal greetings by albatross mail. At infrequent intervals.

'One such letter arrived this morning. A subject of the Emperor appears to have taken it into his head to visit our city. It appears he wishes to look at it. Only a madman would possibly undergo all the privations of crossing the Turnwise Ocean in order to merely *look* at anything. However.

'He landed this morning. He might have met a great hero, or the cunningest of thieves, or some wise and great sage: he met you. He has employed you as a guide. You will be a guide, Rincewind, to this *looker*, this Twoflower. You will see that he returns home with a good report of our little homeland. What do you say to that?'

'Er. Thank you, lord,' said Rincewind miserably.

'There is another point, of course. It would be a tragedy should anything untoward happen to our little visitor. It would be dreadful if he were to die, for example. Dreadful for the whole of our land, because the Agatean Emperor looks after his own and could certainly extinguish us at a nod. A mere nod. And that would be dreadful for you, Rincewind, because in the weeks that remained before the Empire's huge mercenary fleet arrived certain of my servants would occupy themselves about your person in the hope that the avenging captains, on their arrival, might find their anger tempered by the sight of your still-living body. There are certain spells that can prevent the life departing from a body, be it never so abused, and – I see by your face that understanding dawns?'

'Yarrg.'

'I beg your pardon?'

'Yes, lord. I'll, er, see to it, I mean, I'll endeavour to see, I mean, well, I'll try to look after him and see he comes to no harm.' And after that I'll get a job juggling snowballs through Hell, he added bitterly in the privacy of his own skull.

'Capital! I gather already that you and Twoflower are on the best of terms. An excellent beginning. When he returns safely to his homeland you will not find me ungrateful. I shall probably even dismiss the charges against you. Thank you, Rincewind. You may go.'

Rincewind decided not to ask for the return of his five remaining *rhinu*. He backed away, cautiously.

'Oh, and there is one other thing,' the Patrician said, as the wizard groped for the door handles.

'Yes, lord?' he replied, with a sinking heart.

'I'm sure you won't dream of trying to escape from your obligations by fleeing the city. I judge you to be a born city person. But you may be sure that the lords of the other cities will be apprised of these conditions by nightfall.'

'I assure you the thought never even crossed my mind, lord.'

'Indeed? Then if I were you I'd sue my face for slander.'

Rincewind reached the Broken Drum at a dead run, and was just in time to collide with a man who came out backwards, fast. The stranger's haste was in part accounted for by the spear in his chest. He bubbled noisily and dropped dead at the wizard's feet.

Rincewind peered around the doorframe and jerked back as a heavy throwing axe whirred past like a partridge.

It was probably a lucky throw, a second cautious glance told him. The dark interior of the Drum was a broil of fighting men, quite a number of them – a third and longer glance confirmed – in bits. Rincewind swayed back as a wildly thrown stool sailed past and smashed on the far side of the street. Then he dived in.

He was wearing a dark robe, made darker by constant wear and irregular washings. In the raging gloom no-one appeared to notice a shadowy shape that shuffled desperately from table to table. At one point a fighter, staggering back, trod on what felt like fingers. A number of what felt like teeth bit his ankle. He yelped shrilly and dropped his guard just sufficiently for a sword, swung by a surprised opponent, to skewer him.

Rincewind reached the stairway, sucking his bruised hand and running with a curious, bent-over gait. A crossbow quarrel thunked into the banister rail above him, and he gave a whimper.

He made the stairs in one breathless rush, expecting at any moment another, more accurate shot.

In the corridor above he stood upright, gasping, and saw the floor in front of him scattered with bodies. A big black-bearded man, with a bloody sword in one hand, was trying a door handle.

'Hey!' screamed Rincewind. The man looked around and then, almost absent-mindedly, drew a short throwing knife from his bandolier and hurled it. Rincewind ducked. There was a brief scream behind him as the crossbow man, sighting down his weapon, dropped it and clutched at his throat.

The big man was already reaching for another knife. Rincewind looked around wildly, and then with wild improvisation drew himself up into a wizardly pose.

His hand was flung back. 'Asoniti! Kyorucha! Beazleblor!'

The man hesitated, his eyes flicking nervously from side to side as he waited for the magic. The conclusion that there was not going to be any hit him at the same time as Rincewind, whirring wildly down the passage, kicked him sharply in the groin.

As he screamed and clutched at himself the wizard dragged open the door, sprang inside, slammed it behind him and threw his body against it, panting.

It was quiet in here. There was Twoflower, sleeping peacefully on the low bed. And there, at the foot of the bed, was the Luggage.

Rincewind took a few steps forward, cupidity moving him as easily as if he were on little wheels. The chest was open. There were bags inside, and in one of them he caught the gleam of gold. For a moment greed overcame caution, and he reached out gingerly . . . but what was the use? He'd never live to enjoy it. Reluctantly he drew his hand back, and was surprised to see a slight tremor in the chest's open lid. Hadn't it shifted slightly, as though rocked by the wind?

Rincewind looked at his fingers, and then at the lid. It looked heavy, and was bound with brass bands. It was quite still now.

What wind?

'Rincewind!'

Twoflower sprang off the bed. The wizard jumped back, wrenching his features into a smile.

'My dear chap, right on time! We'll just have lunch, and then I'm sure you've got a wonderful programme lined up for this afternoon!'

'Er—'

'That's great!'

Rincewind took a deep breath. 'Look,' he said desperately, 'let's eat somewhere else. There's been a bit of a fight down below.'

'A tavern brawl? Why didn't you wake me up?'

'Well, you see, I – *what*?'

'I thought I made myself clear this morning, Rincewind. I want to see genuine Morporkian life – the slave market, the Whore Pits, the Temple of Small Gods, the Beggars' Guild . . . and a genuine tavern brawl.' A faint note of suspicion entered Twoflower's voice. 'You *do* have them, don't you? You know, people swinging on chandeliers, swordfights over the table, the sort of thing Hrun the Barbarian and the Weasel are always getting involved in. You know – *excitement*.'

Rincewind sat down heavily on the bed.

'You *want* to see a fight?' he said.

'Yes. What's wrong with that?'

'For a start, people get hurt.'

'Oh, I wasn't suggesting we get involved. I just want to see one, that's all. And some of your famous heroes. You do have some, don't you? It's not all dockside talk?' And now, to the wizard's astonishment, Twoflower was almost pleading.

'Oh, yeah. We have them all right,' said Rincewind hurriedly. He pictured them in his mind, and recoiled from the thought.

All the heroes of the Circle Sea passed through the gates of Ankh-Morpork sooner or later. Most of them were from the barbaric tribes nearer the frozen Hub, which had a sort of export trade in heroes. Almost all of them had crude magic swords, whose unsuppressed harmonics on the astral plane played hell with any delicate experiments in applied sorcery for miles around, but Rincewind didn't object to them on that score. He knew himself to be a magical dropout, so it didn't bother him that the mere appearance of a hero at the city gates was enough to cause retorts to explode and demons to materialize all through the Magical Quarter. No, what he didn't like about heroes was that they were usually suicidally gloomy when sober and homicidally insane when drunk. There were too many of them, too. Some of the most notable questing grounds near the city were a veritable hub-bub in the season. There was talk of organizing a rota.

He rubbed his nose. The only heroes he had much time for were Bravd and the Weasel, who were out of town at the moment, and Hrun the Barbarian, who was practically an academic by Hub standards in that he could think without moving his lips. Hrun was said to be roving somewhere Turnwise.

'Look,' he said at last. 'Have you ever met a barbarian?'

Twoflower shook his head.

'I was afraid of that,' said Rincewind. 'Well, they're—'

There was a clatter of running feet in the street outside and a fresh uproar from downstairs. It was followed by a commotion on the stairs. The door was flung open before Rincewind could collect himself sufficiently to make a dash for the window.

But instead of the greed-crazed madman he expected, he found himself looking into the round red face of a Sergeant of the Watch. He breathed again. Of course. The Watch were always careful not to intervene too soon in any brawl where the odds were not heavily stacked in their favour. The job carried a pension, and attracted a cautious, thoughtful kind of man.

The sergeant glowered at Rincewind, and then peered at Twoflower with interest.

'Everything all right here, then?' he said.

'Oh, fine,' said Rincewind. 'Got held up, did you?'

The sergeant ignored him. 'This the foreigner, then?' he enquired.

'We were just leaving,' said Rincewind quickly, and switched to Trob. 'Twoflower, I think we ought to get lunch somewhere else. I know some places.'

He marched out into the corridor with as much aplomb as he could muster. Twoflower followed, and a few seconds later there was a strangling sound from the sergeant as the Luggage closed its lid with a snap, stood up, stretched, and marched after them.

Watchmen were dragging bodies out of the room downstairs. There were no survivors. The Watch had ensured this by giving them ample time to escape via the back door, a neat compromise between caution and justice that benefited all parties.

'Who are all these men?' said Twoflower.

'Oh, you know. Just men,' said Rincewind. And before he could stop himself some part of his brain that had nothing to do took control of his mouth and added, 'Heroes, in fact.'

'Really?'

When one foot is stuck in the Grey Miasma of H'rull it is much easier to step right in and sink rather than prolong the struggle. Rincewind let himself go.

'Yes, that one over there is Erig Stronginthearm, over there is Black Zenell—'

'Is Hrun the Barbarian here?' said Twoflower, looking around eagerly. Rincewind took a deep breath.

'That's him behind us,' he said.

The enormity of this lie was so great that its ripples did in fact spread out on one of the lower astral planes as far as the Magical Quarter across the river, where it picked up tremendous velocity from the huge standing wave of power that always hovered there and bounced wildly across the Circle Sea. A harmonic got as far as Hrun himself, currently fighting a couple of gnolls on a crumbling ledge high in the Caderack Mountains, and caused him a moment's unexplained discomfort.

Twoflower, meanwhile, had thrown back the lid of the Luggage and was hastily pulling out a heavy black cube.

'This is fantastic!' he said. 'They're never going to believe this at home!'

'What's he going on about?' said the sergeant doubtfully.

'He's pleased you rescued us,' said Rincewind. He looked sidelong at the black box, half expecting it to explode or emit strange musical tones.

'Ah,' said the sergeant. He was staring at the box, too.

Twoflower smiled brightly at them.

'I'd like a record of the event,' he said. 'Do you think you could ask them all to stand over by the window, please? This won't take a moment. And, er, Rincewind?'

'Yes?'

Twoflower stood on tiptoe to whisper.

'I expect you know what this is, don't you?'

Rincewind stared down at the box. It had a round

glass eye protruding from the centre of one face, and a lever at the back.

'Not wholly,' he said.

'It's a device for making pictures quickly,' said Twoflower. 'Quite a new invention. I'm rather proud of it but, look, I don't think these gentlemen would – well, I mean they might be – sort of apprehensive? Could you explain it to them? I'll reimburse them for their time, of course.'

'He's got a box with a demon in it that draws pictures,' said Rincewind shortly. 'Do what the madman says and he will give you gold.'

The Watch smiled nervously.

'I'd like you in the picture, Rincewind. That's fine.' Twoflower took out the golden disc that Rincewind had noticed before, squinted at its unseen face for a moment, muttered, 'Thirty seconds should about do it,' and said brightly, 'Smile please!'

'Smile,' rasped Rincewind. There was a whirr from the box.

'Right!'

High above the disc the second albatross soared; so high in fact that its tiny mad orange eyes could see the whole of the world and the great, glittering, girdling Circle Sea. There was a yellow message capsule strapped to one leg. Far below it, unseen in the clouds, the bird that had brought the earlier message to the Patrician of Ankh-Morpork flapped gently back to its home.

Rincewind looked at the tiny square of glass in astonishment. There he was, all right – a tiny figure, in perfect colour, standing in front of a group of Watchmen whose faces were each frozen in a terrified rictus. A buzz of wordless terror went up from the men around him as they craned over his shoulder to look.

Grinning, Twoflower produced a handful of the smaller coins Rincewind now recognized as quarter-*rhinu*. He winked at the wizard.

'I had similar problems when I stopped over in the Brown Islands,' he said. 'They thought the iconograph steals a bit of their souls. Laughable, isn't it?'

'Yarg,' said Rincewind and then, because somehow that was hardly enough to keep up his side of the conversation, added, 'I don't think it looks *very* like me, though.'

'It's easy to operate,' said Twoflower, ignoring him. 'Look, all you have to do is press this button. The iconograph does the rest. Now, I'll just stand over here next to Hrun, and you can take the picture.'

The coins quietened the men's agitation in the way that gold can, and Rincewind was amazed to find, half a minute later, that he was holding a little glass portrait of Twoflower wielding a huge notched sword and smiling as though all his dreams had come true.

They lunched at a small eating-house near the Brass Bridge, with the Luggage nestling under the table. The food and wine, both far superior to Rincewind's normal fare, did much to relax him. Things weren't going to be too bad, he decided. A bit of invention and some quick thinking, that was all that was needed.

Twoflower seemed to be thinking too. Looking

reflectively into his wine cup he said, 'Tavern fights are pretty common around here, I expect?'

'Oh, fairly.'

'No doubt fixtures and fittings get damaged?'

'Fixt— oh, I see. You mean like benches and whatnot. Yes, I suppose so.'

'That must be upsetting for the innkeepers.'

'I've never really thought about it. I suppose it must be one of the risks of the job.'

Twoflower regarded him thoughtfully.

'I might be able to help there,' he said. 'Risks are my business. I say, this food is a bit greasy, isn't it?'

'You did say you wanted to try some typical Morporkian food,' said Rincewind. 'What was that about risks?'

'Oh, I know all about risks. They're my business.'

'I thought that's what you said. I didn't believe it the first time either.'

'Oh, I don't *take* risks. About the most exciting thing that happened to me was knocking some ink over. I *assess* risks. Day after day. Do you know what the odds are against a house catching fire in the Red Triangle district of Bes Pelargic? Five hundred and thirty-eight to one. I calculated that,' he added with a trace of pride.

'What—' Rincewind tried to suppress a burp – 'what for? 'Scuse me.' He helped himself to some more wine.

'For—' Twoflower paused. 'I can't say it in Trob,' he said. 'I don't think the beTrobi have a word for it. In my language we call it—' he said a collection of outlandish syllables.

'*Inn-sewer-ants*,' repeated Rincewind. 'That's a funny word. Wossit mean?'

'Well, suppose you have a ship loaded with, say, gold bars. It might run into storms or be taken by pirates. You don't want that to happen, so you take out an *inn-sewer-ants-polly-sea*. I work out the odds against the cargo being lost, based on weather reports and piracy records for the last twenty years, then I add a bit, then you pay me some money based on those odds—'

'—and the bit—' Rincewind said, waggling a finger solemnly.

'—and then, if the cargo *is* lost, I reimburse you.'

'Reeburs?'

'Pay you the value of your cargo,' said Twoflower patiently.

'I get it. It's like a bet, right?'

'A wager? In a way, I suppose.'

'And you make money at this *inn-sewer-ants*?'

'It offers a return on investment, certainly.'

Wrapped in the warm yellow glow of the wine, Rincewind tried to think of *inn-sewer-ants* in Circle Sea terms.

'I don't think I unnerstan' this *inn-sewer-ants*,' he said firmly, idly watching the world spin by. 'Magic, now. Magic I unnerstan'.'

Twoflower grinned. 'Magic is one thing, and *reflected-sound-of-underground-spirits* is another,' he said.

'Wha'?'

'What?'

'That funny wor' you used,' said Rincewind impatiently.

'*Reflected-sound-of-underground-spirits*?'

'Never heard o' it.'

Twoflower tried to explain.

Rincewind tried to understand.

In the long afternoon they toured the city turnwise of the river. Twoflower led the way, with the strange picturebox slung on a strap round his neck. Rincewind trailed behind, whimpering at intervals and checking to see that his head was still there.

A few others followed, too. In a city where public executions, duels, fights, magical feuds and strange events regularly punctuated the daily round, the inhabitants had brought the profession of interested bystander to a peak of perfection. They were, to a man, highly skilled gawpers. In any case, Twoflower was delightedly taking picture after picture of people engaged in what he described as typical activities, and since a quarter-*rhinu* would subsequently change hands 'for their trouble' a tail of bemused and happy *nouveaux-riches* was soon following him in case this madman exploded in a shower of gold.

At the Temple of the Seven-Handed Sek a hasty convocation of priests and ritual heart-transplant artisans agreed that the hundred-span-high statue of Sek was altogether too holy to be made into a magic picture, but a payment of two *rhinu* left them astoundedly agreeing that perhaps He wasn't as holy as all that.

A prolonged session at the Whore Pits produced a number of colourful and instructive pictures, a number of which Rincewind concealed about his person for detailed perusal in private. As the fumes cleared from his brain he began to speculate seriously as to how the iconograph worked.

Even a failed wizard knew that some substances were sensitive to light. Perhaps the glass plates were treated by some arcane process that froze the light that passed through them? Something like that, anyway. Rincewind often suspected that there was something, somewhere, that was better than magic. He was usually disappointed.

However, he soon took every opportunity to operate the box. Twoflower was only too pleased to allow this, since that enabled the little man to appear in his own pictures. It was at this point that Rincewind noticed something strange. Possession of the box conferred a kind of power on the wielder – which was that anyone, confronted with the hypnotic glass eye, would submissively obey the most peremptory orders about stance and expression.

It was while he was thus engaged in the Plaza of Broken Moons that disaster struck.

Twoflower had posed alongside a bewildered charm-seller, his crowd of new-found admirers watching him with interest in case he did something humorously lunatic.

Rincewind got down on one knee, the better to arrange the picture, and pressed the enchanted lever.

The box said, 'It's no good. I've run out of pink.'

A hitherto unnoticed door opened in front of his eyes. A small, green and hideously warty humanoid figure leaned out, pointed at a colour-encrusted palette in one clawed hand, and screamed at him.

'No pink! See?' screeched the homunculus. 'No good you going on pressing the lever when there's no pink, is there? If you wanted pink you shouldn't of took all those pictures of young ladies, should you? It's monochrome from now on, friend. Alright?'

'Alright. Yeah, sure,' said Rincewind. In one dim corner of the little box he thought he could see an easel, and a tiny unmade bed. He hoped he couldn't.

'So long as that's understood,' said the imp, and shut the door. Rincewind thought he could hear the muffled sound of grumbling and the scrape of a stool being dragged across the floor.

'Twoflower—' he began, and looked up.

Twoflower had vanished. As Rincewind stared at the crowd, with sensations of prickly horror travelling up his spine, there came a gentle prod in the small of his back.

'Turn without haste,' said a voice like black silk. 'Or kiss your kidneys goodbye.'

The crowd watched with interest. It was turning out to be quite a good day.

Rincewind turned slowly, feeling the point of the sword scrape along his ribs. At the other end of the blade he recognized Stren Withel – thief, cruel swordsman, disgruntled contender for the title of worst man in the world.

'Hi,' he said weakly. A few yards away he noticed a couple of unsympathetic men raising the lid of the Luggage and pointing excitedly at the bags of gold. Withel smiled. It made an unnerving effect on his scar-crossed face.

'I know you,' he said. 'A gutter wizard. What is that *thing*?'

Rincewind became aware that the lid of the Luggage was trembling slightly, although there was no wind. And he was still holding the picturebox.

'This? It makes pictures,' he said brightly. 'Hey, just hold that smile, will you?' He backed away quickly and pointed the box.

For a moment Withel hesitated. '*What*?' he said.

'That's fine, hold it just like that . . .' said Rincewind.

The thief paused, then growled and swung his sword back.

There was a *snap*, and a duet of horrible screams. Rincewind did not glance around for fear of the terrible things he might see, and by the time Withel looked for him again he was on the other side of the Plaza, and still accelerating.

The albatross descended in wide, slow sweeps that ended in an undignified flurry of feathers and a thump as it landed heavily on its platform in the Patrician's bird garden.

The custodian of the birds, dozing in the sun and hardly expecting a long-distance message so soon after this morning's arrival, jerked to his feet and looked up.

A few moments later he was scuttling through the palace's corridors holding the message capsule and – owing to carelessness brought on by surprise – sucking at the nasty beak wound on the back of his hand.

* * *

Rincewind pounded down an alley, paying no heed to the screams of rage coming from the picturebox, and cleared a high wall with his frayed robe flapping around him like the feathers of a dishevelled jackdaw. He landed in the forecourt of a carpet shop, scattering the merchandise and customers, dived through its rear exit trailing apologies, skidded down another alley and stopped, teetering dangerously, just as he was about to plunge unthinkingly into the Ankh.

There are said to be some mystic rivers one drop of which can steal a man's life away. After its turbid passage through the twin cities the Ankh could have been one of them.

In the distance the cries of rage took on a shrill note of terror. Rincewind looked around desperately for a boat, or a handhold up the sheer walls on either side of him.

He was trapped.

Unbidden, the spell welled up in his mind. It was perhaps untrue to say that he had learned it; it had learned him. The episode had led to his expulsion from Unseen University, because, for a bet, he had dared to open the pages of the last remaining copy of the Creator's own grimoire, the Octavo (while the University librarian was otherwise engaged). The spell had leapt out of the page and instantly burrowed deeply into his mind, from whence even the combined talents of the Faculty of Medicine had been unable to coax it. Precisely which one it was they were also unable to ascertain, except that it was one of the eight basic spells that were intricately interwoven with the very fabric of time and space itself.

Since then it had been showing a worrying tendency, when Rincewind was feeling rundown or especially threatened, to try to get itself said.

He clenched his teeth together but the first syllable forced itself around the corner of his mouth. His left hand raised involuntarily and, as the magical force whirled him round, began to give off octarine sparks . . .

The Luggage hurtled around the corner, its several hundred knees moving like pistons.

Rincewind gaped. The spell died, unsaid.

The box didn't appear to be hampered in any way by the ornamental rug draped roguishly over it, nor by the thief hanging by one arm from the lid. It was, in a very real sense, a dead weight. Further along the lid were the remains of two fingers, owner unknown.

The Luggage halted a few feet from the wizard and, after a moment, retracted its legs. It had no eyes that Rincewind could see, but he was nevertheless sure that it was staring at him. Expectantly.

'Shoo,' he said weakly. It didn't budge, but the lid creaked open, releasing the dead thief.

Rincewind remembered about the gold. Presumably the box had to have a master. In the absence of Twoflower, had it adopted him?

The tide was turning and he could see debris drifting downstream in the yellow afternoon light towards the River Gate, a mere hundred yards downstream. It was the work of a moment to let the dead thief join them. Even if it was found later it would hardly cause comment. And the sharks in the estuary were used to solid, regular meals.

Rincewind watched the body drift away, and considered his next move. The Luggage would probably float. All he had to do was wait until dusk, and then go out with the tide. There were plenty of wild places downstream where he could wade ashore, and then – well, if the Patrician really *had* sent out word about him then a change of clothing and a shave should take care of that. In any case, there were other lands and he had a facility for languages. Let him but get to Chimera or Gonim or Ecalpon and half a dozen armies couldn't bring him back. And then – wealth, comfort, security . . .

There was, of course, the problem of Twoflower. Rincewind allowed himself a moment's sadness.

'It could be worse,' he said by way of farewell. 'It could be *me*.'

It was when he tried to move that he found his robe was caught on some obstruction.

By craning his neck he found that the edge of it was being gripped firmly by the Luggage's lid.

'Ah, Gorphal,' said the Patrician pleasantly. 'Come in. Sit down. Can I press you to a candied starfish?'

'I am yours to command, master,' said the old man calmly. 'Save, perhaps, in the matter of preserved echinoderms.'

The Patrician shrugged, and indicated the scroll on the table.

'Read that,' he said.

Gorphal picked up the parchment and raised one eyebrow slightly when he saw the familiar ideograms of the Golden Empire. He read in silence for perhaps a minute, and then turned the scroll over to examine minutely the seal on the obverse.

'You are famed as a student of Empire affairs,' said the Patrician. 'Can you explain this?'

'Knowledge in the matter of the Empire lies less in noting particular events than in studying a certain cast of mind,' said the old diplomat. 'The message is curious, yes, but not surprising.'

'This morning the Emperor *instructed*,' the Patrician allowed himself the luxury of a scowl, '*instructed* me, Gorphal, to protect this Two Flower person. Now it seems I must have him killed. You don't find that surprising?'

'No. The Emperor is no more than a boy. He is – idealistic. Keen. A god to his people. Whereas this afternoon's letter is, unless I am very much mistaken, from Nine Turning Mirrors, the Grand Vizier. He has grown old in the service of several Emperors. He regards them as a necessary but tiresome ingredient in the successful running of the Empire. He does not like things out of place. The Empire was not built by allowing things to get out of place. That is his view.'

'I begin to see—' said the Patrician.

'Quite so.' Gorphal smiled into his beard. 'This tourist is a thing that is out of place. After acceding to his master's wishes Nine Turning Mirrors would, I am quite sure, make his own arrangements with a view to ensuring that one wanderer would not be allowed to return home bringing, perhaps, the disease of dissatisfaction. The Empire likes people to stay where it puts them. So much more convenient, then, if this

Two Flower disappears for good in the barbarian lands. Meaning here, master.'

'And your advice?' said the Patrician.

Gorphal shrugged.

'Merely that you should do nothing. Matters will undoubtedly resolve themselves. However,' he scratched an ear thoughtfully, 'perhaps the Assassins' Guild . . . ?'

'Ah yes,' said the Patrician. 'The Assassins' Guild. Who is their president at the moment?'

'Zlorf Flannelfoot, master.'

'Have a word with him, will you?'

'Quite so, master.'

The Patrician nodded. It was all rather a relief. He agreed with Nine Turning Mirrors – life was difficult enough. People ought to stay where they were put.

Brilliant constellations shone down on the discworld. One by one the traders shuttered their shops. One by one the gonophs, thieves, finewirers, whores, illusionists, backsliders and second-storey men awoke and breakfasted. Wizards went about their poly-dimensional affairs. Tonight saw the conjunction of two powerful planets, and already the air over the Magical Quarter was hazy with early spells.

'Look,' said Rincewind, 'this isn't getting us any-where.' He inched sideways. The Luggage followed faithfully, lid half open and menacing. Rincewind briefly considered making a desperate leap to safety. The lid smacked in anticipation.

In any case, he told himself with sinking heart, the damn thing would only follow him again. It had that dogged look about it. Even if he managed to get to a horse, he had a nasty suspicion that it would follow him at its own pace. Endlessly. Swimming rivers and oceans. Gaining slowly every night, while he had to stop to sleep. And then one day, in some exotic city and years hence, he'd hear the sound of hundreds of tiny feet accelerating down the road behind him . . .

'You've got the wrong man!' he moaned. 'It's not my fault! I didn't kidnap him!'

The box moved forward slightly. Now there was just a narrow strip of greasy jetty between Rincewind's heels and the river. A flash of precognition told him that the box would be able to swim faster than he could. He tried not to imagine what it would be like to drown in the Ankh.

'It won't stop until you give in, you know,' said a small voice conversationally.

Rincewind looked down at the iconograph, still hanging around his neck. Its trapdoor was open and the homunculus was leaning against the frame, smoking a pipe and watching the proceedings with amusement.

'I'll take you in with me, at least,' said Rincewind through gritted teeth.

The imp took the pipe out of his mouth. 'What did you say?' he said.

'I said I'll take you in with me, dammit!'

'Suit yourself.' The imp tapped the side of the box meaningfully. 'We'll see who sinks first.'

The Luggage yawned, and moved forward a fraction of an inch.

'Oh all right,' said Rincewind irritably. 'But you'll have to give me time to think.'

The Luggage backed off slowly. Rincewind edged his way back onto reasonably safe land and sat down with his back against a wall. Across the river the lights of Ankh city glowed.

'You're a wizard,' said the picture imp. 'You'll think of some way to find him.'

'Not much of a wizard, I'm afraid.'

'You can just jump down on everyone and turn them into worms,' the imp added encouragingly, ignoring his last remark.

'No. Turning to Animals is an Eighth Level spell. I never even completed my training. I only know one spell.'

'Well, that'll do.'

'I doubt it,' said Rincewind hopelessly.

'What does it do, then?'

'Can't tell you. Don't really want to talk about it. But frankly,' he sighed, 'no spells are much good. It takes three months to commit even a simple one to memory, and then once you've used it, pouf! it's gone. That's what's so stupid about the whole magic thing, you know. You spend twenty years learning the spell that makes nude virgins appear in your bedroom, and then you're so poisoned by quicksilver fumes and half-blind from reading old grimoires that you can't remember what happens next.'

'I never thought of it like that,' said the imp.

'Hey, look – this is all wrong. When Twoflower said they'd got a better kind of magic in the Empire I thought – I thought . . .'

The imp looked at him expectantly. Rincewind cursed to himself.

'Well, if you must know, I thought he didn't *mean* magic. Not as such.'

'What else is there, then?'

Rincewind began to feel really wretched. 'I don't know,' he said. 'A better way of doing things, I suppose. Something with a bit of sense in it. Harnessing – harnessing the lightning, or something.'

The imp gave him a kind but pitying look.

'Lightning is the spears hurled by the thunder giants when they fight,' it said gently. 'Established meteorological fact. You can't *harness* it.'

'I know,' said Rincewind miserably. 'That's the flaw in the argument, of course.'

The imp nodded, and disappeared into the depths of the iconograph. A few moments later Rincewind smelled bacon frying. He waited until his stomach couldn't stand the strain any more, and rapped on the box. The imp reappeared.

'I've been thinking about what you said,' it said before Rincewind could open his mouth. 'And even if you could get a harness on it, how could you get it to pull a cart?'

'What the hell are you talking about?'

'Lightning. It just goes up and down. You'd want it to go along, not up and down. Anyway, it'd probably burn through the harness.'

'I don't care about the lightning! How can I think on an empty stomach?'

'Eat something, then. That's logic.'

'How? Every time I move that damn box flexes its hinges at me!'

The Luggage, on cue, gaped widely.

'See?'

'It's not trying to bite you,' said the imp. 'There's food in there. You're no use to it starved.'

Rincewind peered into the dark recesses of the Luggage. There were indeed, among the chaos of boxes and bags of gold, several bottles and packages in oiled paper. He gave a cynical laugh, mooched around the abandoned jetty until he found a piece of wood about the right length, wedged it as politely as possible in the gap between the lid and the box, and pulled out one of the flat packages.

It held biscuits that turned out to be as hard as diamond-wood.

' 'loody 'ell,' he muttered, nursing his teeth.

'Captain Eightpanther's Travellers' Digestives, them,' said the imp from the doorway to his box. 'Saved many a life at sea, they have.'

'Oh, sure. Do you use them as a raft, or just throw them to the sharks and sort of watch them sink? What's in the bottles? Poison?'

'Water.'

'But there's water everywhere! Why'd he want to bring water?'

'Trust.'

'Trust?'

'Yes. That's what he didn't, the water here. See?'

Rincewind opened a bottle. The liquid inside might have been water. It had a flat, empty flavour, with no trace of life. 'Neither taste nor smell,' he grumbled.

The Luggage gave a little creak, attracting his attention. With a lazy air of calculated menace it shut its lid slowly, grinding Rincewind's impromptu wedge like a dry loaf.

'All right, all right,' he said. 'I'm thinking.'

Ymor's headquarters were in the Leaning Tower at the junction of Rime Street and Frost Alley. At midnight the solitary guard leaning in the shadows looked up at the conjoining planets and wondered idly what change in his fortunes they might herald.

There was the faintest of sounds, as of a gnat yawning.

The guard glanced down the deserted street, and now caught the glimmer of moonlight on something lying in the mud a few yards away. He picked it up. The lunar light gleamed on gold, and his intake of breath was almost loud enough to echo down the alleyway.

There was a slight sound again, and another coin rolled into the gutter on the other side of the street.

By the time he had picked it up there was another one, a little way off and still spinning. Gold was, he remembered, said to be formed from the crystallized light of stars. Until now he had never believed it to be true, that something as heavy as gold could fall naturally from the sky.

As he drew level with the opposite alley mouth some more fell. It was still in its bag, there was an awful lot of it, and Rincewind brought it down heavily onto his head.

When the guard came to he found himself looking up into the wild-eyed face of a wizard, who was menacing his throat with a sword. In the darkness, too, something was gripping his leg.

It was the disconcerting sort of grip that suggested that the gripper could grip a whole lot harder, if he wanted to.

'Where is he, the rich foreigner?' hissed the wizard. 'Quickly!'

'What's holding my leg?' said the man, with a note of terror in his voice. He tried to wriggle free. The pressure increased.

'You wouldn't want to know,' said Rincewind. 'Pay attention, please. Where's the foreigner?'

'Not here! They've got him at Broadman's place! Everyone's looking for him! You're Rincewind, aren't you? The box – the box that bites people – ononono . . . pleasssse . . .'

Rincewind had gone. The guard felt the unseen leg-gripper release his – or, as he was beginning to fear, *its* – hold. Then, as he tried to pull himself to his feet, *something* big and heavy and square cannoned into him out of the dark and plunged off after the wizard. Something with hundreds of tiny feet.

With only his home-made phrase book to help him, Twoflower was trying to explain the mysteries of *inn-sewer-ants* to Broadman. The fat innkeeper was listening intently, his little black eyes glittering.

From the other end of the table Ymor watched with mild amusement, occasionally feeding one of his ravens with scraps from his plate. Beside him Withel paced up and down.

'You fret too much,' said Ymor, without taking his eyes from the two men opposite him. 'I can feel it, Stren. Who would dare attack us here? And the gutter wizard will come. He's too much of a coward not to. And he'll try to bargain. And we shall have him. And the gold. And the chest.'

Withel's one eye glared, and he smacked a fist into the palm of a black-gloved hand.

'Who would have thought there was so much sapient pearwood in the whole of the disc?' he said. 'How could we have known?'

'You fret too much, Stren. I'm sure you can do better this time,' said Ymor pleasantly.

The lieutenant snorted in disgust, and strode off around the room to bully his men. Ymor carried on watching the tourist.

It was strange, but the little man didn't seem to realize the seriousness of his position. Ymor had on several occasions seen him look around the room with an expression of deep satisfaction. He had also been talking for ages to Broadman and Ymor had seen a piece of paper change hands. And Broadman had given the foreigner some coins. It was strange.

When Broadman got up and waddled past Ymor's chair the thiefmaster's arm shot out like a steel spring and grabbed the fat man by his apron.

'What was that all about, friend?' asked Ymor quietly.

'N-nothing, Ymor. Just private business, like.'

'There are no secrets between friends, Broadman.'

'Yar. Well, I'm not sure about it myself, really. It's a sort of bet, see?' said the innkeeper nervously. '*Inn-sewer-ants*, it's called. It's like a bet that the Broken Drum won't get burned down.'

Ymor held the man's gaze until Broadman twitched

in fear and embarrassment. Then the thiefmaster laughed.

'This worm-eaten old tinder pile?' he said. 'The man must be mad!'

'Yes, but mad with money. He says now he's got the – can't remember the word, begins with a P, it's what you might call the stake money – the people he works for in the Agatean Empire will pay up. If the Broken Drum burns down. Not that I hope it does. Burn down. The Broken Drum, I mean. I mean, it's like a home to me, is the Drum . . .'

'Not entirely stupid, are you?' said Ymor, and pushed the innkeeper away.

The door slammed back on its hinges and thudded into the wall.

'Hey, that's my door!' screamed Broadman. Then he realized who was standing at the top of the steps, and ducked behind the table a mere shaving of time before a short black dart sped across the room and thunked into the woodwork.

Ymor moved his hand carefully, and poured out another flagon of beer.

'Won't you join me, Zlorf?' he said levelly. 'And put that sword away, Stren. Zlorf Flannelfoot is our friend.'

The president of the Assassins' Guild spun his short blowgun dexterously and slotted it into its holster in one smooth movement.

'Stren!' said Ymor.

The black-clad thief hissed, and sheathed his sword. But he kept his hand on the hilt, and his eyes on the assassin.

That wasn't easy. Promotion in the Assassins' Guild was by competitive examination, the Practical being the most important – indeed, the only – part. Thus Zlorf's broad, honest face was a welter of scar tissue, the result of many a close encounter. It probably hadn't been all that good-looking in any case – it was said that Zlorf had chosen a profession in which dark hoods, cloaks and nocturnal prowlings figured largely because there was a day-fearing trollish streak in his parentage. People who said this in earshot of Zlorf tended to carry their ears home in their hats.

He strolled down the stairs, followed by a number of assassins. When he was directly in front of Ymor he said: 'I've come for the tourist.'

'Is it any of your business, Zlorf?'

'Yes. Grinjo, Urmond – take him.'

Two of the assassins stepped forward. Then Stren was in front of them, his sword appearing to materialize an inch from their throats without having to pass through the intervening air.

'Possibly I could only kill one of you,' he murmured, 'but I suggest you ask yourselves – which one?'

'Look up, Zlorf,' said Ymor.

A row of yellow, baleful eyes looked down from the darkness among the rafters.

'One step more and you'll leave here with fewer eyeballs than you came with,' said the thiefmaster. 'So sit down and have a drink, Zlorf, and let's talk about this sensibly. *I* thought we had an agreement. You don't rob – I don't kill. Not for payment, that is,' he added after a pause.

Zlorf took the proffered beer.

'So?' he said. 'I'll kill him. Then you rob him. Is he that funny looking one over there?'

'Yes.'

Zlorf stared at Twoflower, who grinned at him. He shrugged. He seldom wasted time wondering why people wanted other people dead. It was just a living.

'Who is your client, may I ask?' said Ymor.

Zlorf held up a hand. 'Please!' he protested. 'Professional etiquette.'

'Of course. By the way—'

'Yes?'

'I believe I have a couple of guards outside—'

'Had.'

'And some others in the doorway across the street—'

'Formerly.'

'And two bowmen on the roof.'

A flicker of doubt passed across Zlorf's face, like the last shaft of sunlight over a badly ploughed field.

The door flew open, badly damaging the assassin who was standing beside it.

'Stop doing that!' shrieked Broadman, from under his table.

Zlorf and Ymor stared up at the figure on the threshold. It was short, fat and richly dressed. Very richly dressed. There were a number of tall, big shapes looming behind it. Very big, *threatening* shapes.

'Who's that?' said Zlorf.

'I know him,' said Ymor. 'His name's Rerpf. He runs the Groaning Platter tavern down by Brass Bridge. Stren – remove him.'

Rerpf held up a beringed hand. Stren Withel

hesitated halfway to the door as several very large trolls ducked under the doorway and stood on either side of the fat man, blinking in the light. Muscles the size of melons bulged in forearms like floursacks. Each troll held a double-headed axe. Between thumb and forefinger.

Broadman erupted from cover, his face suffused with rage.

'Out!' he screamed. 'Get those trolls out of here!'

No-one moved. The room was suddenly quiet. Broadman looked around quickly. It began to dawn on him just what he had said, and to whom. A whimper escaped from his lips, glad to be free.

He reached the doorway to his cellars just as one of the trolls, with a lazy flick of one ham-sized hand, sent his axe whirling across the room. The slam of the door and its subsequent splitting as the axe hit it merged into one sound.

'Bloody hell!' exclaimed Zlorf Flannelfoot.

'What do you want?' said Ymor.

'I am here on behalf of the Guild of Merchants and Traders,' said Rerpf evenly. 'To protect our interests, you might say. Meaning the little man.'

Ymor wrinkled his brows.

'I'm sorry,' he said. 'I thought I heard you say the Guild of Merchants?'

'And traders,' agreed Rerpf. Behind him now, in addition to more trolls, were several humans that Ymor vaguely recognized. He had seen them, maybe, behind counters and bars. Shadowy figures, usually – easily ignored, easily forgotten. At the back of his mind a bad feeling began to grow. He thought about how it might be to be, say, a fox confronted with an angry sheep. A sheep, moreover, that could afford to employ wolves.

'How long has this – Guild – been in existence, may I ask?' he said.

'Since this afternoon,' said Rerpf. 'I'm vice-guildmaster in charge of tourism, you know.'

'What is this tourism of which you speak?'

'Uh – we are not quite sure . . .' said Rerpf. An old bearded man poked his head over the guildmaster's shoulder and cackled, 'Speaking on behalf of the wine-sellers of Morpork, Tourism means Business. See?'

'Well?' said Ymor coldly.

'Well,' said Rerpf, 'we're protecting our interests, like I said.'

'Thieves OUT, Thieves OUT!' cackled his elderly companion. Several others took up the chant. Zlorf grinned. 'And assassins,' chanted the old man. Zlorf growled.

'Stands to reason,' said Rerpf. 'People robbing and murdering all over the place, what sort of impression are visitors going to take away? You come all the way to see our fine city with its many points of historical and civic interest, also many quaint customs, and you wake up dead in some back alley or as it might be floating down the Ankh, how are you going to tell all your friends what a great time you're having? Let's face it, you've got to move with the times.'

Zlorf and Ymor met each other's gaze.

'We have, have we?' said Ymor.

'Then let us move, brother,' agreed Zlorf. In one movement he brought his blowgun to his mouth and sent a dart hissing towards the nearest troll. It spun around, hurling its axe, which whirred over the assassin's head and buried itself in a luckless thief behind him.

Rerpf ducked, allowing a troll behind him to raise its huge iron crossbow and fire a spear-length quarrel into the nearest assassin. That was the start . . .

It has been remarked before that those who are sensitive to radiations in the far octarine – the eighth colour, the pigment of the Imagination – can see things that others cannot.

Thus it was that Rincewind, hurrying through the crowded, flare-lit evening bazaars of Morpork with the Luggage trundling behind him, jostled a tall dark figure, turned to deliver a few suitable curses, and beheld Death.

It had to be Death. No-one else went around with empty eye sockets and, of course, the scythe over one shoulder was another clue. As Rincewind stared in horror a courting couple, laughing at some private joke, walked straight through the apparition without appearing to notice it.

Death, insofar as it was possible in a face with no movable features, looked surprised.

RINCEWIND? Death said, in tones as deep and heavy as the slamming of leaden doors, far underground.

'Um,' said Rincewind, trying to back away from that eyeless stare.

BUT WHY ARE YOU HERE? (Boom, boom went crypt lids, in the worm-haunted fastnesses under old mountains . . .)

'Um, why not?' said Rincewind. 'Anyway, I'm sure you've got lots to do, so if you'll just—'

I WAS SURPRISED THAT YOU JOSTLED ME, RINCEWIND, FOR I HAVE AN APPOINTMENT WITH THEE THIS VERY NIGHT.

'Oh no, not—'

OF COURSE, WHAT'S SO BLOODY VEXING ABOUT THE WHOLE BUSINESS IS THAT I WAS EXPECTING TO MEET THEE IN PSEPHOPOLOLIS.

'But that's five hundred miles away!'

YOU DON'T HAVE TO TELL ME, THE WHOLE SYSTEM'S GOT SCREWED UP AGAIN, I CAN SEE THAT. LOOK, THERE'S NO CHANCE OF YOU—?

Rincewind backed away, hands spread protectively in front of him. The dried fish salesman on a nearby stall watched this madman with interest.

'Not a chance!'

I COULD LEND YOU A VERY FAST HORSE.

'No!'

IT WON'T HURT A BIT.

'No!' Rincewind turned and ran. Death watched him go, and shrugged bitterly.

SOD YOU, THEN, Death said. He turned, and noticed the fish salesman. With a snarl Death reached out a bony finger and stopped the man's heart, but He didn't take much pride in it.

Then Death remembered what was due to happen later that night. It would not be true to say that Death smiled, because in any case His features were perforce frozen in a calcareous grin. But He hummed a little tune, cheery as a plague pit, and – pausing only to extract the life from a passing mayfly, and one-ninth of the lives from a cat cowering under the fish stall (all cats can see into the octarine) – Death turned on His heel and set off towards the Broken Drum.

Short Street, Morpork, is in fact one of the longest in the city. Filigree Street crosses its turnwise end in the manner of the crosspiece of a T, and the Broken Drum is so placed that it looks down the full length of the street.

At the furthermost end of Short Street a dark oblong rose on hundreds of tiny legs, and started to run. At first it moved at no more than a lumbering trot, but by the time it was halfway up the street it was moving arrow-fast . . .

A darker shadow inched its way along one of the walls of the Drum, a few yards from the two trolls who were guarding the door. Rincewind was sweating. If they heard the faint clinking of the specially prepared bags at his belt . . .

One of the trolls tapped his colleague on the shoulder, producing a noise like two pebbles being knocked together. He pointed down the starlit street . . .

Rincewind darted from his hiding place, turned, and hurled his burden through the Drum's nearest window.

Withel saw it arrive. The bag arced across the room, turning slowly in the air, and burst on the edge of a table. A moment later gold coins were rolling across the floor, spinning, glittering.

The room was suddenly silent, save for the tiny

noises of gold and the whimpers of the wounded. With a curse Withel despatched the assassin he had been fighting. 'It's a trick!' he screamed. 'No-one move!'

Threescore men and a dozen trolls froze in mid-grope.

Then, for the third time, the door burst open. Two trolls hurried through it, slammed it behind them, dropped the heavy bar across it and fled down the stairs.

Outside there was a sudden crescendo of running feet. And, for the last time, the door opened. In fact it exploded, the great wooden bar being hurled far across the room and the frame itself giving way.

Door and frame landed on a table, which flew into splinters. It was then that the frozen fighters noticed that there was something else in the pile of wood. It was a box, shaking itself madly to free itself of the smashed timber around it.

Rincewind appeared in the ruined doorway, hurling another of his gold grenades. It smashed into a wall, showering coins.

Down in the cellar Broadman looked up, muttered to himself, and carried on with his work. His entire spindlewinter's supply of candles had already been strewn on the floor, mixed with his store of kindling wood. Now he was attacking a barrel of lamp oil.

'*Inn-sewer-ants*,' he muttered. Oil gushed out and swirled around his feet.

Withel stormed across the floor, his face a mask of rage. Rincewind took careful aim and caught the thief full in the chest with a bag of gold.

But now Ymor was shouting, and pointing an accusing finger. A raven swooped down from its perch in the rafters and dived at the wizard, talons open and gleaming.

It didn't make it. At about the halfway point the Luggage leapt from its bed of splinters, gaped briefly in mid-air, and snapped shut.

It landed lightly. Rincewind saw its lid open again, slightly. Just far enough for a tongue, large as a palm leaf, red as mahogany, to lick up a few errant feathers.

At the same moment the giant candlewheel fell from the ceiling, plunging the room into gloom. Rincewind, coiling himself like a spring, gave a standing jump and grasped a beam, swinging himself up into the relative safety of the roof with a strength that amazed him.

'Exciting, isn't it!' said a voice by his ear.

Down below, thieves, assassins, trolls and merchants all realized at about the same moment that they were in a room made treacherous of foothold by gold coins and containing something, among the suddenly menacing shapes in the semi-darkness, that was absolutely horrible. As one they made for the door, but had two dozen different recollections of its exact position.

High above the chaos Rincewind stared at Twoflower.

'Did you cut the lights down?' he hissed.

'Yes.'

'How come you're up here?'

'I thought I'd better not get in everyone's way.'

Rincewind considered this. There didn't seem to be much he could say. Twoflower added: 'A real brawl! Better than anything I'd imagined! Do you think I ought to thank them? Or did you arrange it?'

Rincewind looked at him blankly. 'I think we ought to be getting down now,' he said hollowly. 'Everyone's gone.'

He dragged Twoflower across the littered floor and up the steps. They burst out into the tail end of the night. There were still a few stars but the moon was down, and there was a faint grey glow to rimward. Most important, the street was empty.

Rincewind sniffed.

'Can you smell oil?' he said.

Then Withel stepped out of the shadows and tripped him up.

At the top of the cellar steps Broadman knelt down and fumbled in his tinderbox. It turned out to be damp.

'I'll kill that bloody cat,' he muttered, and groped for the spare box that was normally on the ledge by the door. It was missing. Broadman said a bad word.

A lighted taper appeared in mid-air, right beside him.

HERE, TAKE THIS.

'Thanks,' said Broadman.

DON'T MENTION IT.

Broadman went to throw the taper down the steps. His hand paused in mid-air. He looked at the taper, his brow furrowing. Then he turned around and held the taper up to illuminate the scene. It didn't shed much light, but it did give the darkness a shape . . .

'Oh, no—' he breathed.

BUT YES, said Death.

Rincewind rolled.

For a moment he thought Withel was going to spit him where he lay. But it was worse than that. He was waiting for him to get up.

'I see you have a sword, wizard,' he said quietly. 'I suggest you rise, and we shall see how well you use it.'

Rincewind stood up as slowly as he dared, and drew from his belt the short sword he had taken from the guard a few hours and a hundred years ago. It was a short blunt affair compared to Withel's hair-thin rapier.

'But I don't know how to use a sword,' he wailed.

'Good.'

'You know that wizards can't be killed by edged weapons?' said Rincewind desperately.

Withel smiled coldly. 'So I have heard,' he said. 'I look forward to putting it to the test.' He lunged.

Rincewind caught the thrust by sheer luck, jerked his hand away in shock, deflected the second stroke by coincidence, and took the third one through his robe at heart-height.

There was a clink.

Withel's snarl of triumph died in his throat. He drew the sword out and prodded again at the wizard, who was rigid with terror and guilt. There was another clink, and gold coins began to drop out of the hem of the wizard's robe.

'So you bleed gold, do you?' hissed Withel. 'But

have you got gold concealed in that raggedy beard, you little—'

As his sword went back for his final sweep the sullen glow that had been growing in the doorway of the Broken Drum flickered, dimmed, and erupted into a roaring fireball that sent the walls billowing outward and carried the roof a hundred feet into the air before bursting through it, in a gout of red-hot tiles.

Withel stared at the boiling flames, unnerved. And Rincewind leapt. He ducked under the thief's sword arm and brought his own blade around in an arc so incompetently misjudged that it hit the man flat-first and jolted out of the wizard's hand. Sparks and droplets of flaming oil rained down as Withel reached out with both gauntleted hands and grabbed Rincewind's neck, forcing him down.

'You did this!' he screamed. 'You and your box of trickery!'

His thumb found Rincewind's windpipe. This is it, the wizard thought. Wherever I'm going, it can't be worse than here . . .

'Excuse me,' said Twoflower.

Rincewind felt the grip lessen. And now Withel was slowly getting up, a look of absolute hatred on his face.

A glowing ember landed on the wizard. He brushed it off hurriedly, and scrambled to his feet.

Twoflower was behind Withel, holding the man's own needle-sharp sword with the point resting in the small of the thief's back. Rincewind's eyes narrowed. He reached into his robe, then withdrew his hand bunched into a fist.

'Don't move,' he said.

'Am I doing this right?' asked Twoflower anxiously.

'He says he'll skewer your liver if you move,' Rincewind translated freely.

'I doubt it,' said Withel.

'Bet?'

'No.'

As Withel tensed himself to turn on the tourist Rincewind lashed out and caught the thief on the jaw. Withel stared at him in amazement for a moment, and then quietly toppled into the mud.

The wizard uncurled his stinging fist and the roll of gold coins slipped between his throbbing fingers. He looked down at the recumbent thief.

'Good grief,' he gasped.

He looked up and yelled as another ember landed on his neck. Flames were racing along the rooftops on either side of the street. All around him people were hurling possessions from windows and dragging horses from smoking stables. Another explosion in the white-hot volcano that was the Drum sent a whole marble mantelpiece scything overhead.

'The Widdershins Gate's the nearest!' Rincewind shouted above the crackle of collapsing rafters. 'Come on!'

He grabbed Twoflower's reluctant arm and dragged him down the street.

'My Luggage—'

'Blast your luggage! Stay here much longer and you'll go where you don't need luggage! Come on!' screamed Rincewind.

They jogged on through the crowd of frightened people leaving the area, while the wizard took great mouthfuls of cool dawn air. Something was puzzling him.

'I'm sure all the candles went out,' he said. 'So how did the Drum catch fire?'

'I don't know,' moaned Twoflower. 'It's terrible, Rincewind. We were getting along so well, too.'

Rincewind stopped in astonishment, so that another refugee cannoned into him and spun away with an oath.

'*Getting on?*'

'Yes, a great bunch of fellows, I thought – language was a bit of a problem, but they were so keen for me to join their party, they just wouldn't take no for an answer – really friendly people, I thought . . .'

Rincewind started to correct him, then realized he didn't know how to begin.

'It'll be a blow for old Broadman,' Twoflower continued. 'Still, he was wise. I've still got the *rhinu* he paid as his first premium.'

Rincewind didn't know the meaning of the word premium, but his mind was working fast.

'You *inn-sewered* the Drum?' he said. 'You bet Broadman it wouldn't catch fire?'

'Oh yes. Standard valuation. Two hundred *rhinu*. Why do you ask?'

Rincewind turned and stared at the flames racing towards them, and wondered how much of Ankh-Morpork could be bought for two hundred *rhinu*. Quite a large piece, he decided. Only not now, not the way those flames were moving . . .

He glanced down at the tourist.

'You—' he began, and searched his memory for the

worst word in the Trob tongue; the happy little beTrobi didn't really know how to swear properly.

'You,' he repeated. Another hurrying figure bumped into him, narrowly missing him with the blade over its shoulder. Rincewind's tortured temper exploded.

'You little (such a one who, while wearing a copper nose ring, stands in a footbath atop Mount Raruaruaha during a heavy thunderstorm and shouts that Alohura, Goddess of Lightning, has the facial features of a diseased uloruaha root)!'

JUST DOING MY JOB, said the figure, stalking away.

Every word fell as heavily as slabs of marble; moreover, Rincewind was certain that he was the only one who heard them.

He grabbed Twoflower again.

'Let's get out of here!' he suggested.

One interesting side-effect of the fire in Ankh-Morpork concerns the *inn-sewer-ants* policy, which left the city through the ravaged roof of the Broken Drum, was wafted high into the discworld's atmosphere on the ensuing thermal, and came to earth several days and a few thousand miles away on an uloruaha bush in the beTrobi islands. The simple, laughing islanders subsequently worshipped it as a god, much to the amusement of their more sophisticated neighbours. Strangely enough the rainfall and harvests in the next few years were almost supernaturally abundant, and this led to a research team being despatched to the islands by the Minor Religions faculty of Unseen University. Their verdict was that it only went to show.

* * *

The fire, driven by the wind, spread out from the Drum faster than a man could walk. The timbers of the Widdershins Gate were already on fire when Rincewind, his face blistered and reddened from the flames, reached them. By now he and Twoflower were on horseback – mounts hadn't been that hard to obtain. A wily merchant had asked fifty times their worth, and had been left gaping when one thousand times their worth had been pressed into his hands.

They rode through just before the first of the big gate timbers descended in an explosion of sparks. Morpork was already a cauldron of flame.

As they galloped up the red-lit road Rincewind glanced sideways at his travelling companion, currently trying hard to learn to ride a horse.

'Bloody hell,' he thought. 'He's alive! Me too. Who'd have thought it? Perhaps there is something in this *reflected-sound-of-underground-spirits*?' It was a cumbersome phrase. Rincewind tried to get his tongue round the thick syllables that were the word in Twoflower's own language.

'Ecolirix?' he tried. 'Ecro-gnothics? Echo-gnomics?'

That would do. That sounded about right.

Several hundred yards downriver from the last smouldering suburb of the city a strangely rectangular and apparently heavily waterlogged object touched the mud on the widdershins bank. Immediately it sprouted numerous legs and scrabbled for a purchase.

Hauling itself to the top of the bank the Luggage – streaked with soot, stained with water and very, very angry – shook itself and took its bearings. Then it moved away at a brisk trot, the small and incredibly ugly imp that was perching on its lid watching the scenery with interest.

Bravd looked at the Weasel and raised his eyebrows.

'And that's it,' said Rincewind. 'The Luggage caught up with us, don't ask me how. Is there any more wine?'

The Weasel picked up the empty wineskin.

'I think you have had just about enough wine this night,' he said.

Bravd's forehead wrinkled.

'Gold is gold,' he said finally. 'How can a man with plenty of gold consider himself poor? You're either poor or rich. It stands to reason.'

Rincewind hiccupped. He was finding Reason rather difficult to hold on to. 'Well,' he said, 'what I think is, the point is, well, you know octiron?'

The two adventurers nodded. The strange iridescent metal was almost as highly valued in the lands around the Circle Sea as sapient pearwood, and was about as rare. A man who owned a needle made of octiron would never lose his way, since it always pointed to the Hub of the discworld, being acutely sensitive to the disc's magical field; it would also miraculously darn his socks.

'Well, my point is, you see, that gold also has its sort of magical field. Sort of financial wizardry. Echo-gnomics.' Rincewind giggled.

The Weasel stood up and stretched. The sun was well up now, and the city below them was wreathed in mists and full of foul vapours. Also gold, he decided. Even a citizen of Morpork would, at the very point of death, desert his treasure to save his skin. Time to move.

The little man called Twoflower appeared to be asleep. The Weasel looked down at him and shook his head.

'The city awaits, such as it is,' he said. 'Thank you for a pleasant tale, Wizard. What will you do now?' He eyed the Luggage, which immediately backed away and snapped its lid at him.

'Well, there are no ships leaving the city now,' giggled Rincewind. 'I suppose we'll take the coast road to Chirm. I've got to look after him, you see. But look, I didn't make it—'

'Sure, sure,' said the Weasel soothingly. He turned away and swung himself into the saddle of the horse that Bravd was holding. A few moments later the two heroes were just specks under a cloud of dust, heading down towards the charcoal city.

Rincewind stared muzzily at the recumbent tourist. At two recumbent tourists. In his somewhat defenceless state a stray thought, wandering through the dimensions in search of a mind to harbour it, slid into his brain.

'Here's another fine mess you've got me into,' he moaned, and slumped backwards.

'Mad,' said the Weasel. Bravd, galloping along a few feet away, nodded.

'All wizards get like that,' he said. 'It's the quicksilver fumes. Rots their brains. Mushrooms, too.'

'However—' said the brown-clad one. He reached into his tunic and took out a golden disc on a short chain. Bravd raised his eyebrows.

'The wizard said that the little man had some sort of golden disc that told him the time,' said the Weasel.

'Arousing your cupidity, little friend? You always were an expert thief, Weasel.'

'Aye,' agreed the Weasel modestly. He touched the knob at the disc's rim, and it flipped open.

The very small demon imprisoned within looked up from its tiny abacus and scowled. 'It lacks but ten minutes to eight of the clock,' it snarled. The lid slammed shut, almost trapping the Weasel's fingers.

With an oath the Weasel hurled the time-teller far out into the heather, where it possibly hit a stone. Something, in any event, caused the case to split; there was a vivid octarine flash and a whiff of brimstone as the time being vanished into whatever demonic dimension it called home.

'What did you do that for?' said Bravd, who hadn't been close enough to hear the words.

'Do what?' said the Weasel. 'I didn't do anything. Nothing happened at all. Come on – we're wasting opportunities!'

Bravd nodded. Together they turned their steeds and galloped towards ancient Ankh, and honest enchantments.

The Sending of Eight

· Prologue ·

THE DISCWORLD OFFERS SIGHTS FAR more impressive than those found in universes built by Creators with less imagination but more mechanical aptitude.

Although the disc's sun is but an orbiting moonlet, its prominences hardly bigger than croquet hoops, this slight drawback must be set against the tremendous sight of Great A'Tuin the Turtle, upon Whose ancient and meteor-riddled shell the disc ultimately rests. Sometimes, in His slow journey across the shores of Infinity, He moves His country-sized head to snap at a passing comet.

But perhaps the most impressive sight of all – if only because most brains, when faced with the sheer galactic enormity of A'Tuin, refuse to believe it – is the endless Rimfall, where the seas of the disc boil ceaselessly over the Edge into space. Or perhaps it is the Rimbow, the eight-coloured, world-girdling rainbow that hovers in the mist-laden air over the Fall. The eighth colour is octarine, caused by the scatter-effect of strong sunlight on an intense magical field.

Or perhaps, again, the most magnificent sight is the Hub. There, a spire of green ice ten miles high rises through the clouds and supports at its peak the realm of Dunmanifestin, the abode of the disc gods. The disc gods themselves, despite the splendour of the world below them, are seldom satisfied. It is embarrassing to know that one is a god of a world that only exists because every improbability curve must have its far end; especially when one can peer into other dimensions at worlds whose Creators had more mechanical aptitude than imagination. No wonder, then, that the disc gods spend more time in bickering than in omnicognizance.

On this particular day Blind Io, by dint of constant vigilance the chief of the gods, sat with his chin on his hand and looked at the gaming board on the red marble table in front of him. Blind Io had got his name because, where his eye sockets should have been, there were nothing but two areas of blank skin. His eyes, of which he had an impressively large number, led a semi-independent life of their own. Several were currently hovering above the table.

The gaming board was a carefully carved map of the discworld, overprinted with squares. A number of beautifully modelled playing pieces were now occupying some of the squares. A human onlooker would, for example, have recognized in two of them the likenesses of Bravd and the Weasel. Others represented yet more heroes and champions, of which the disc had a more than adequate supply.

Still in the game were Io, Offler the Crocodile God, Zephyrus the god of slight breezes, Fate, and the Lady. There was an air of concentration around the board now that the lesser players had been removed from the Game. Chance had been an early casualty, running her hero into a full house of armed gnolls (the result of a lucky throw by Offler) and shortly afterwards Night had cashed his chips, pleading an appointment with Destiny. Several minor deities had drifted up and were kibitzing over the shoulders of the players.

Side bets were made that the Lady would be the next to leave the board. Her last champion of any standing was now a pinch of potash in the ruins of still-smoking Ankh-Morpork, and there were hardly any pieces that she could promote to first rank.

Blind Io took up the dice-box, which was a skull whose various orifices had been stoppered with rubies, and with several of his eyes on the Lady he rolled three fives.

She smiled. This was the nature of the Lady's eyes: they were bright green, lacking iris or pupil, and they glowed from within.

The room was silent as she scrabbled in her box of pieces and, from the very bottom, produced a couple that she set down on the board with two decisive clicks. The rest of the players, as one God, craned forward to peer at them.

'A wenegade wiffard and fome fort of clerk,' said Offler the Crocodile God, hindered as usual by his tusks. 'Well, weally!' With one claw he pushed a pile of bone-white tokens into the centre of the table.

The Lady nodded slightly. She picked up the dice-cup and held it as steady as a rock, yet all the Gods could hear the three cubes rattling about inside. And then she sent them bouncing across the table.

A six. A three. A five.

Something was happening to the five, however. Battered by the chance collision of several billion molecules, the die flipped onto a point, spun gently and came down a seven.

Blind Io picked up the cube and counted the sides.

'Come *on*,' he said wearily. 'Play fair.'

The Sending of Eight

THE ROAD FROM ANKH-MORPORK to Quirm is high, white and winding, a thirty-league stretch of potholes and half-buried rocks that spirals around mountains and dips into cool green valleys of citrus trees, crosses liana-webbed gorges on creaking rope bridges and is generally more picturesque than useful.

Picturesque. That was a new word to Rincewind the wizard (BMgc, Unseen University [failed]). It was one of a number he had picked up since leaving the charred ruins of Ankh-Morpork. Quaint was another one. Picturesque meant – he decided after careful observation of the scenery that inspired Twoflower to use the word – that the landscape was horribly precipitous. Quaint, when used to describe the occasional village through which they passed, meant fever-ridden and tumbledown.

Twoflower was a tourist, the first ever seen on the discworld. Tourist, Rincewind had decided, meant 'idiot'.

As they rode leisurely through the thyme-scented, bee-humming air, Rincewind pondered on the experiences of the last few days. While the little foreigner was obviously insane, he was also generous and considerably less lethal than half the people the wizard had mixed with in the city. Rincewind rather liked him. Disliking him would be like kicking a puppy.

Currently Twoflower was showing a great interest

in the theory and practice of magic.

'It all seems, well, rather useless to me,' he said. 'I always thought that, you know, a wizard just said the magic words and that was that. Not all this tedious memorizing.'

Rincewind agreed moodily. He tried to explain that magic had indeed once been wild and lawless, but had been tamed back in the mists of time by the Olden Ones, who had bound it to obey among other things the Law of Conservation of Reality; this demanded that the effort needed to achieve a goal should be the same regardless of the means used. In practical terms this meant that, say, creating the illusion of a glass of wine was relatively easy, since it involved merely the subtle shifting of light patterns. On the other hand, lifting a genuine wineglass a few feet in the air by sheer mental energy required several hours of systematic preparation if the wizard wished to prevent the simple principle of leverage flicking his brain out through his ears.

He went on to add that some of the ancient magic could still be found in its raw state, recognizable – to the initiated – by the eightfold shape it made in the crystalline structure of space-time. There was the metal octiron, for example, and the gas octogen. Both radiated dangerous amounts of raw enchantment.

'It's all very depressing,' he finished.

'Depressing?'

Rincewind turned in his saddle and glanced at Twoflower's Luggage, which was currently ambling along on its little legs, occasionally snapping its lid at butterflies. He sighed.

'Rincewind thinks he ought to be able to harness the lightning,' said the picture-imp, who was observing the passing scene from the tiny doorway of the box slung around Twoflower's neck. He had spent the morning painting picturesque views and quaint scenes for his master, and had been allowed to knock off for a smoke.

'When I said *harness* I didn't mean harness,' snapped Rincewind. 'I meant, well I just meant that – I dunno, I just can't think of the right words. I just think the world ought to be more sort of organized.'

'That's just fantasy,' said Twoflower.

'I know. That's the trouble.' Rincewind sighed again. It was all very well going on about pure logic and how the universe was ruled by logic and the harmony of numbers, but the plain fact of the matter was that the disc was manifestly traversing space on the back of a giant turtle and the gods had a habit of going round to atheists' houses and smashing their windows.

There was a faint sound, hardly louder than the noise of the bees in the rosemary by the road. It had a curiously bony quality, as of rolling skulls or a whirling dice-box. Rincewind peered around. There was no-one nearby.

For some reason that worried him.

Then came a slight breeze, that grew and went in the space of a few heartbeats. It left the world unchanged save in a few interesting particulars.

There was now, for example, a five-metre-tall mountain troll standing in the road. It was exceptionally angry. This was partly because trolls generally are, in any case, but it was exacerbated by the fact that the sudden and instantaneous teleportation from its lair in the Rammerorck Mountains three thousand miles away and a thousand yards closer to the Rim had raised its internal temperature to a dangerous level, in accordance with the laws of conservation of energy. So it bared its fangs and charged.

'What a strange creature,' Twoflower remarked. 'Is it dangerous?'

'Only to people!' shouted Rincewind. He drew his sword and, with a smooth overarm throw, completely failed to hit the troll. The blade plunged on into the heather at the side of the track.

There was the faintest of sounds, like the rattle of old teeth.

The sword struck a boulder concealed in the heather – concealed, a watcher might have considered, so artfully that a moment before it had not appeared to be there at all. It sprang up like a leaping salmon and in mid-ricochet plunged deeply into the back of the troll's grey neck.

The creature grunted, and with one swipe of a claw gouged a wound in the flank of Twoflower's horse, which screamed and bolted into the trees at the roadside. The troll spun around and made a grab for Rincewind.

Then its sluggish nervous system brought it the message that it was dead. It looked surprised for a moment, and then toppled over and shattered into gravel (trolls being silicaceous lifeforms, their bodies reverted instantly to stone at the moment of death).

'Aaargh,' thought Rincewind as his horse reared in

terror. He hung on desperately as it staggered two-legged across the road and then, screaming, turned and galloped into the woods.

The sound of hoofbeats died away, leaving the air to the hum of bees and the occasional rustle of butterfly wings. There was another sound, too, a strange noise for the bright time of noonday.

It sounded like dice.

'Rincewind?'

The long aisles of trees threw Twoflower's voice from side to side and eventually tossed it back to him, unheeded. He sat down on a rock and tried to think.

Firstly, he was lost. That was vexing, but it did not worry him unduly. The forest looked quite interesting and probably held elves or gnomes, perhaps both. In fact on a couple of occasions he had thought he had seen strange green faces peering down at him from the branches. Twoflower had always wanted to meet an elf. In fact what he really wanted to meet was a dragon, but an elf would do. Or a real goblin.

His Luggage was missing, and that was annoying. It was also starting to rain. He squirmed uncomfortably on the damp stone, and tried to look on the bright side. For example, during its mad dash his plunging horse had burst through some bushes and disturbed a she-bear with her cubs, but had gone on before the bear could react. Then it had suddenly been galloping over the sleeping bodies of a large wolf pack and, again, its mad speed had been such that the furious yelping had been left far behind. Nevertheless, the day was wearing on and perhaps it would be a good idea

– Twoflower thought – not to hang about in the open. Perhaps there was a . . . he racked his brains trying to remember what sort of accommodation forests traditionally offered . . . perhaps there was a gingerbread house or something?

The stone really *was* uncomfortable. Twoflower looked down and, for the first time, noticed the strange carving.

It looked like a spider. Or was it a squid? Moss and lichens rather blurred the precise details. But they didn't blur the runes carved below it. Twoflower could read them clearly, and they said: Traveller, the hospitable temple of Bel-Shamharoth lies one thousand paces Hubwards. Now this was strange, Twoflower realized, because although he could read the message the actual letters were completely unknown to him. Somehow the message was arriving in his brain without the tedious necessity of passing through his eyes.

He stood up and untied his now-biddable horse from a sapling. He wasn't sure which way the Hub lay, but there seemed to be an old track of sorts leading away between the trees. This Bel-Shamharoth seemed prepared to go out of his way to help stranded travellers. In any case, it was that or the wolves. Twoflower nodded decisively.

It is interesting to note that, several hours later, a couple of wolves who were following Twoflower's scent arrived in the glade. Their green eyes fell on the strange eight-legged carving – which may indeed have been a spider, or an octopus, or may yet again have been something altogether more strange – and they immediately decided that they weren't so hungry, at that.

About three miles away a failed wizard was hanging by his hands from a high branch in a beech tree.

This was the end result of five minutes of crowded activity. First, an enraged she-bear had barged through the undergrowth and taken the throat out of his horse with one swipe of her paw. Then, as Rincewind had fled the carnage, he had run into a glade in which a number of irate wolves were milling about. His instructors at Unseen University, who had despaired of Rincewind's inability to master levitation, would have then been amazed at the speed with which he reached and climbed the nearest tree, without apparently touching it.

Now there was just the matter of the snake.

It was large and green, and wound itself along the branch with reptilian patience. Rincewind wondered if it was poisonous, then chided himself for asking such a silly question. Of course it would be poisonous.

'What are you grinning for?' he asked the figure on the next branch.

I CAN'T HELP IT, said Death. NOW WOULD YOU BE SO KIND AS TO LET GO? I CAN'T HANG AROUND ALL DAY.

'I can,' said Rincewind defiantly.

The wolves clustered around the base of the tree looked up with interest at their next meal talking to himself.

IT WON'T HURT, said Death. If words had weight, a single sentence from Death would have anchored a ship.

Rincewind's arms screamed their agony at him. He scowled at the vulture-like, slightly transparent figure.

'Won't hurt?' he said. 'Being torn apart by wolves won't hurt?'

He noticed another branch crossing his dangerously narrowing one a few feet away. If he could just reach it . . .

He swung himself forward, one hand outstretched.

The branch, already bending, did not break. It simply made a wet little sound and twisted.

Rincewind found that he was now hanging on to the end of a tongue of bark and fibre, lengthening as it peeled away from the tree. He looked down, and with a sort of fatal satisfaction realized that he would land right on the biggest wolf.

Now he was moving slowly as the bark peeled back in a longer and longer strip. The snake watched him thoughtfully.

But the growing length of bark held. Rincewind began to congratulate himself until, looking up, he saw what he had hitherto not noticed. There was the largest hornets' nest he had ever seen, hanging right in his path.

He shut his eyes tightly.

Why the troll? he asked himself. Everything else is just my usual luck, but why the troll? What the hell is going on?

Click. It might have been a twig snapping, except that the sound appeared to be inside Rincewind's head. Click, click. And a breeze that failed to set a single leaf atremble.

The hornets' nest was ripped from the branch as

the strip passed by. It shot past the wizard's head and he watched it grow smaller as it plummeted towards the circle of upturned muzzles.

The circle suddenly closed.

The circle suddenly expanded.

The concerted yelp of pain as the pack fought to escape the furious cloud echoed among the trees. Rincewind grinned inanely.

Rincewind's elbow nudged something. It was the tree trunk. The strip had carried him right to the end of the branch. But there were no other branches. The smooth bark beside him offered no handholds.

It offered hands, though. Two were even now thrusting through the mossy bark beside him; slim hands, green as young leaves. Then a shapely arm followed, and then the hamadryad leaned right out and grasped the astonished wizard firmly and, with that vegetable strength that can send roots questing into rock, drew him into the tree. The solid bark parted like a mist, closed like a clam.

Death watched impassively.

He glanced at the cloud of mayflies that were dancing their joyful zigzags near His skull. He snapped His fingers. The insects fell out of the air. But, somehow, it wasn't quite the same.

Blind Io pushed his stack of chips across the table, glowered through such of his eyes as were currently in the room, and strode out. A few demigods tittered. At least Offler had taken the loss of a perfectly good troll with precise, if somewhat reptilian, grace.

The Lady's last opponent shifted his seat until he faced her across the board.

'Lord,' she said, politely.

'Lady,' he acknowledged. Their eyes met.

He was a taciturn god. It was said that he had arrived in the discworld after some terrible and mysterious incident in another Eventuality. It is of course the privilege of gods to control their apparent outward form, even to other gods; the Fate of the discworld was currently a kindly man in late middle age, greying hair brushed neatly around features that a maiden would confidently proffer a glass of small beer to, should they appear at her back door. It was a face a kindly youth would gladly help over a stile. Except for his eyes, of course.

No deity can disguise the manner and nature of his eyes. The nature of the two eyes of the Fate of the discworld was this: that while at a mere glance they were simply dark, a closer look would reveal – too late! – that they were but holes opening on to a blackness so remote, so deep that the watcher would feel himself inexorably drawn into the twin pools of infinite night and their terrible, wheeling stars . . .

The Lady coughed politely, and laid twenty-one white chips on the table. Then from her robe she took another chip, silvery and translucent and twice the size of the others. The soul of a true Hero always finds a better rate of exchange, and is valued highly by the gods.

Fate raised an eyebrow.

'And no cheating, Lady,' he said.

'But who could cheat Fate?' she asked. He shrugged.

'No-one. Yet everyone tries.'

'And yet, again, I believe I felt you giving me a little assistance against the others?'

'But of course. So that the endgame could be the sweeter, Lady. And now . . .'

He reached into his gaming box and brought forth a piece, setting it down on the board with a satisfied air. The watching deities gave a collective sigh. Even the Lady was momentarily taken aback.

It was certainly ugly. The carving was uncertain, as if the craftsman's hands were shaking in horror of the thing taking shape under his reluctant fingers. It seemed to be all suckers and tentacles. And mandibles, the Lady observed. And one great eye.

'I thought such as He died out at the beginning of Time,' she said.

'Mayhap our necrotic friend was loath even to go near this one,' laughed Fate. He was enjoying himself.

'It should never have been spawned.'

'Nevertheless,' said Fate gnomically. He scooped the dice into their unusual box, and then glanced up at her.

'Unless,' he added, 'you wish to resign . . . ?'

She shook her head.

'Play,' she said.

'You can match my stake?'

'*Play*.'

Rincewind knew what was inside trees: wood, sap, possibly squirrels. Not a palace.

Still – the cushions underneath him were definitely softer than wood, the wine in the wooden cup beside him was much tastier than sap, and there could be absolutely no comparison between a squirrel and the girl sitting before him, clasping her knees and watching him thoughtfully, unless mention was made of certain hints of furriness.

The room was high, wide and lit with a soft yellow light which came from no particular source that Rincewind could identify. Through gnarled and knotted archways he could see other rooms, and what looked like a very large winding staircase. And it had looked a perfectly normal tree from the outside, too.

The girl was green – flesh green. Rincewind could be absolutely certain about that, because all she was wearing was a medallion around her neck. Her long hair had a faintly mossy look about it. Her eyes had no pupils and were a luminous green. Rincewind wished he had paid more attention to anthropology lectures at University.

She had said nothing. Apart from indicating the couch and offering him the wine she had done no more than sit watching him, occasionally rubbing a deep scratch on her arm.

Rincewind hurriedly recalled that a dryad was so linked to her tree that she suffered wounds in sympathy—

'Sorry about that,' he said quickly. 'It was just an accident. I mean, there were these wolves, and—'

'You had to climb my tree, and I rescued you,' said the dryad smoothly. 'How lucky for you. And for your friend, perhaps?'

'Friend?'

'The little man with the magic box,' said the dryad.

'Oh, sure, him,' said Rincewind vaguely. 'Yeah. I hope he's OK.'

'He needs your help.'

'He usually does. Did he make it to a tree too?'

'He made it to the Temple of Bel-Shamharoth.'

Rincewind choked on his wine. His ears tried to crawl into his head in terror of the syllables they had just heard. The Soul Eater! Before he could stop them the memories came galloping back. Once, while a student of practical magic at Unseen University, and for a bet, he'd slipped into the little room off the main library – the room with walls covered in protective lead pentagrams, the room no-one was allowed to occupy for more than four minutes and thirty-two seconds, which was a figure arrived at after two hundred years of cautious experimentation . . .

He had gingerly opened the Book, which was chained to the octiron pedestal in the middle of the rune-strewn floor not lest someone steal it, but lest it escape; for it was the Octavo, so full of magic that it had its own vague sentience. One spell had indeed leapt from the crackling pages and lodged itself in the dark recesses of his brain. And, apart from knowing that it was one of the Eight Great Spells, no-one would know which one until he said it. Even Rincewind did not. But he could feel it sometimes, sidling out of sight behind his Ego, biding its time . . .

On the front of the Octavo had been a representation of Bel-Shamharoth. He was not Evil, for even Evil has a certain vitality – Bel-Shamharoth was the flip side of the coin of which Good and Evil are but one side.

'The Soul Eater. His number lyeth between seven and nine; it is twice four,' Rincewind quoted, his mind frozen with fear. '*Oh no.* Where's the Temple?'

'Hubwards, towards the centre of the forest,' said the dryad. 'It is very old.'

'But who would be so stupid as to worship Bel—him? I mean, devils *yes*, but he's the Soul Eater—'

'There were – certain advantages. And the race that used to live in these parts had strange notions.'

'What happened to them, then?'

'I did say they *used* to live in these parts.' The dryad stood up and stretched out her hand. 'Come. I am Druellae. Come with me and watch your friend's fate. It should be interesting.'

'I'm not sure that—' began Rincewind.

The dryad turned her green eyes on him.

'Do you believe you have a choice?' she asked.

A staircase broad as a major highway wound up through the tree, with vast rooms leading off at every landing. The sourceless yellow light was everywhere. There was also a sound like – Rincewind concentrated, trying to identify it – like far off thunder, or a distant waterfall.

'It's the tree,' said the dryad shortly.

'What's it doing?' said Rincewind.

'Living.'

'I wondered about that. I mean, are we really in a tree? Have I been reduced in size? From outside it looked narrow enough for me to put my arms around.'

'It is.'

'Um, but here I am inside it?'

'You are.'

'Um,' said Rincewind.

Druellae laughed.

'I can see into your mind, false wizard! Am I not a dryad? Do you not know that what you belittle by the name *tree* is but the mere four-dimensional analogue of a whole multidimensional universe which – no, I can see you do not. I should have realized that you weren't a real wizard when I saw you didn't have a staff.'

'Lost it in a fire,' lied Rincewind automatically.

'No hat with magic sigils embroidered on it.'

'It blew off.'

'No familiar.'

'It died. Look, thanks for rescuing me, but if you don't mind I think I ought to be going. If you could show me the way out—'

Something in her expression made him turn around. There were three he-dryads behind him. They were as naked as the woman, and unarmed. That last fact was irrelevant, however. They didn't look as though they would need weapons to fight Rincewind. They looked as though they could shoulder their way through solid rock and beat up a regiment of trolls into the bargain. The three handsome giants looked down at him with wooden menace. Their skins were the colour of walnut husks, and under it muscles bulged like sacks of melons.

He turned around again and grinned weakly at Druellae. Life was beginning to take on a familiar shape again.

'I'm not rescued, am I?' he said. 'I'm captured, right?'

'Of course.'

'And you're not letting me go?' It was a statement.

Druellae shook her head. '*You hurt the Tree.* But you are lucky. Your friend is going to meet Bel-Shamharoth. *You* will only die.'

From behind two hands gripped his shoulders in much the same way that an old tree root coils relentlessly around a pebble.

'With a certain amount of ceremony, of course,' the dryad went on. 'After the Sender of Eight has finished with your friend.'

All Rincewind could manage to say was, 'You know, I never imagined there were he-dryads. Not even in an oak tree.'

One of the giants grinned at him.

Druellae snorted. 'Stupid! Where do you think acorns come from?'

There was a vast empty space like a hall, its roof lost in the golden haze. The endless stair ran right through it.

Several hundred dryads were clustered at the other end of the hall. They parted respectfully when Druellae approached, and stared through Rincewind as he was propelled firmly along behind.

Most of them were females, although there were a few of the giant males among them. They stood like god-shaped statues among the small, intelligent females. Insects, thought Rincewind. The Tree is like a hive.

But why were there dryads at all? As far as he could recall, the tree people had died out centuries before.

They had been out-evolved by humans, like most of the other Twilight Peoples. Only elves and trolls had survived the coming of Man to the discworld; the elves because they were altogether too clever by half, and the trollen folk because they were at least as good as humans at being nasty, spiteful and greedy. Dryads were supposed to have died out, along with gnomes and pixies.

The background roar was louder here. Sometimes a pulsing golden glow would race up the translucent walls until it was lost in the haze overhead. Some power in the air made it vibrate.

'O incompetent wizard,' said Druellae, 'see some magic. Not your weasel-faced tame magic, but root-and-branch magic, the old magic. Wild magic. Watch.'

Fifty or so of the females formed a tight cluster, joined hands and walked backwards until they formed the circumference of a large circle. The rest of the dryads began a low chant. Then, at a nod from Druellae, the circle began to spin widdershins.

As the pace began to quicken and the complicated threads of the chant began to rise Rincewind found himself watching fascinated. He had heard about the Old Magic at University, although it was forbidden to wizards. He knew that when the circle was spinning fast enough against the standing magical field of the discworld itself in its slow turning, the resulting astral friction would build up a vast potential difference which would earth itself by a vast discharge of the Elemental Magical Force.

The circle was a blur now, and the walls of the Tree rang with the echoes of the chant—

Rincewind felt the familiar sticky prickling in the scalp that indicated the build-up of a heavy charge of raw enchantment in the vicinity, and so he was not utterly amazed when, a few seconds later, a shaft of vivid octarine light speared down from the invisible ceiling and focused, crackling, in the centre of the circle.

There it formed an image of a storm-swept, tree-girt hill with a temple on its crest. Its shape did unpleasant things to the eye. Rincewind knew that if it was a temple to Bel-Shamharoth it would have eight sides. (Eight was also the Number of Bel-Shamharoth, which was why a sensible wizard would never mention the number if he could avoid it. Or you'll be eight alive, apprentices were jocularly warned. Bel-Shamharoth was especially attracted to dabblers in magic who, by being as it were beachcombers on the shores of the unnatural, were already half-enmeshed in his nets. Rincewind's room number in his hall of residence had been 7a. He hadn't been surprised.)

Rain streamed off the black walls of the temple. The only sign of life was the horse tethered outside, and it wasn't Twoflower's horse. For one thing, it was too big. It was a white charger with hooves the size of meat dishes and leather harness aglitter with ostentatious gold ornamentation. It was currently enjoying a nosebag.

There was something familiar about it. Rincewind tried to remember where he had seen it before.

It looked as though it was capable of a fair turn of speed, anyway. A speed which, once it had lumbered up to it, it could maintain for a long time. All Rincewind had to do was shake off his guards, fight his way out of the Tree, find the temple and steal the horse out from under whatever it was that Bel-Shamharoth used for a nose.

'The Sender of Eight has two for dinner, it seems,' said Druellae, looking hard at Rincewind. 'Who does that steed belong to, false wizard?'

'I've no idea.'

'No? Well, it does not matter. We shall see soon enough.'

She waved a hand. The focus of the image moved inwards, darted through a great octagonal archway and sped along the corridor within.

There was a figure there, sidling along stealthily with its back against one wall. Rincewind saw the gleam of gold and bronze.

There was no mistaking that shape. He'd seen it many times. The wide chest, the neck like a tree trunk, the surprisingly small head under its wild thatch of black hair looking like a tomato on a coffin . . . he could put a name to the creeping figure, and that name was Hrun the Barbarian.

Hrun was one of the Circle Sea's more durable heroes: a fighter of dragons, a despoiler of temples, a hired sword, the kingpost of every street brawl. He could even – and unlike many heroes of Rincewind's acquaintance – speak words of more than two syllables, if given time and maybe a hint or two.

There was a sound on the edge of Rincewind's hearing. It sounded like several skulls bouncing down the steps of some distant dungeon. He looked sideways at his guards to see if they had heard it.

They had all their limited attention focused on Hrun, who was admittedly built on the same lines as themselves. Their hands were resting lightly on the wizard's shoulders.

Rincewind ducked, jerked backwards like a tumbler, and came up running. Behind him he heard Druellae shout, and he redoubled his speed.

Something caught the hood of his robe, which tore off. A he-dryad waiting at the stairs spread his arms wide and grinned woodenly at the figure hurtling towards him. Without breaking his stride Rincewind ducked again, so low that his chin was on a level with his knees, while a fist like a log sizzled through the air by his ear.

Ahead of him a whole spinney of the tree men awaited. He spun around, dodged another blow from the puzzled guard, and sped back towards the circle, passing on the way the dryads who were pursuing him and leaving them as disorganized as a set of skittles.

But there were still more in front, pushing their way through the crowds of females and smacking their fists into the horny palms of their hands with anticipatory concentration.

'Stand still, false wizard,' said Druellae, stepping forward. Behind her the enchanted dancers spun on; the focus of the circle was now drifting along a violet-lit corridor.

Rincewind cracked.

'Will you knock that off!' he snarled. 'Let's just get this straight, right? I *am* a real wizard!' He stamped a foot petulantly.

'Indeed?' said the dryad. 'Then let us see you pass a spell.'

'Uh—' began Rincewind. The fact was that, since the ancient and mysterious spell had squatted in his mind, he had been unable to remember even the simplest cantrap for, say, killing cockroaches or scratching the small of his back without using his hands. The mages at Unseen University had tried to explain this by suggesting that the involuntary memorizing of the spell had, as it were, tied up all his spell-retention cells. In his darker moments Rincewind had come up with his own explanation as to why even minor spells refused to stay in his head for more than a few seconds.

They were scared, he decided.

'Um—' he repeated.

'A small one would do,' said Druellae, watching him curl his lips in a frenzy of anger and embarrassment. She signalled, and a couple of he-dryads closed in.

The Spell chose that moment to vault into the temporarily abandoned saddle of Rincewind's consciousness. He felt it sitting there, leering defiantly at him.

'I do know a spell,' he said wearily.

'Yes? Pray tell,' said Druellae.

Rincewind wasn't sure that he dared, although the spell was trying to take control of his tongue. He fought it.

'You thed you could read by bind,' he said indistinctly. 'Read it.'

She stepped forward, looking mockingly into his eyes.

Her smile froze. Her hands raised protectively, she crouched back. From her throat came a sound of pure terror.

Rincewind looked around. The rest of the dryads were also backing away. What had he done? Something terrible, apparently.

But in his experience it was only a matter of time before the normal balance of the universe restored itself and started doing the usual terrible things to him. He backed away, ducked between the still-spinning dryads who were creating the magic circle, and watched to see what Druellae would do next.

'Grab him,' she screamed. 'Take him a long way from the Tree and kill him!'

Rincewind turned and bolted.

Across the focus of the circle.

There was a brilliant flash.

There was a sudden darkness.

There was a vaguely Rincewind-shaped violet shadow, dwindling to a point and winking out.

There was nothing at all.

Hrun the Barbarian crept soundlessly along the corridors, which were lit with a light so violet that it was almost black. His earlier confusion was gone. This was obviously a magical temple, and that explained everything.

It explained why, earlier in the afternoon, he had espied a chest by the side of the track while riding through this benighted forest. Its top was invitingly open, displaying much gold. But when he had leapt off his horse to approach it the chest had sprouted legs and had gone trotting off into the forest, stopping again a few hundred yards away.

Now, after several hours of teasing pursuit, he had lost it in these hell-lit tunnels. On the whole, the unpleasant carvings and occasional disjointed skeletons he passed held no fears for Hrun. This was partly because he was not exceptionally bright while being at the same time exceptionally unimaginative, but it was also because odd carvings and perilous tunnels were all in a day's work. He spent a great deal of time in similar situations, seeking gold or demons or distressed virgins and relieving them respectively of their owners, their lives and at least one cause of their distress.

Observe Hrun, as he leaps cat-footed across a suspicious tunnel mouth. Even in this violet light his skin gleams coppery. There is much gold about his person, in the form of anklets and wristlets, but otherwise he is naked except for a leopardskin loincloth. He took that in the steaming forests of Howondaland, after killing its owner with his teeth.

In his right hand he carried the magical black sword Kring, which was forged from a thunderbolt and has a soul but suffers no scabbard. Hrun had stolen it only three days before from the impregnable palace of the Archmandrite of B'Ituni, and he was already regretting it. It was beginning to get on his nerves.

'I tell you it went down that last passage on the right,' hissed Kring in a voice like the scrape of a blade over stone.

'Be silent!'

'All I said was—'

'Shut up!'

* * *

And Twoflower . . .

He was lost, he knew that. Either the building was much bigger than it looked, or he was now on some wide underground level without having gone down any steps, or – as he was beginning to suspect – the inner dimensions of the place disobeyed a fairly basic rule of architecture by being bigger than the outside. And why all these strange lights? They were eight-sided crystals set at regular intervals in the walls and ceiling, and they shed a rather unpleasant glow that didn't so much illuminate as outline the darkness.

And whoever had done those carvings on the wall, Twoflower thought charitably, had probably been drinking too much. For years.

On the other hand, it was certainly a fascinating building. Its builders had been obsessed with the number eight. The floor was a continuous mosaic of eight-sided tiles, the corridor walls and ceilings were angled to give the corridors eight sides if the walls and ceilings were counted and, in those places where part of the masonry had fallen in, Twoflower noticed that even the stones themselves had eight sides.

'I don't like it,' said the picture imp, from his box around Twoflower's neck.

'Why not?' enquired Twoflower.

'It's weird.'

'But you're a demon. Demons can't call things weird. I mean, what's weird to a demon?'

'Oh, you know,' said the demon cautiously, glancing around nervously and shifting from claw to claw. 'Things. Stuff.'

Twoflower looked at him sternly. 'What things?'

The demon coughed nervously (demons do not breathe; however, every intelligent being, whether it breathes or not, coughs nervously at some time in its life. And this was it as far as the demon was concerned).

'Oh, things,' it said wretchedly. 'Evil things. Things we don't talk about is the point I'm broadly trying to get across, master.'

Twoflower shook his head wearily. 'I wish Rincewind was here,' he said. 'He'd know what to do.'

'*Him?*' sneered the demon. 'Can't see a wizard coming here. They can't have anything to do with the number eight.' The demon slapped a hand across his mouth guiltily.

Twoflower looked up at the ceiling.

'What was that?' he asked. 'Didn't you hear something?'

'Me? Hear? No! Not a thing!' the demon insisted. It jerked back into its box and slammed the door. Twoflower tapped on it. The door opened a crack.

'It sounded like a stone moving,' he explained. The door banged shut. Twoflower shrugged.

'The place is probably falling to bits,' he said to himself. He stood up.

'I say!' he shouted. 'Is anyone there?'

AIR, Air, air, replied the dark tunnels.

'Hallo?' he tried.

LO, Lo, lo.

'I know there's someone here, I just heard you playing dice!'

ICE, Ice, ice.

'Look, I had just—'

Twoflower stopped. The reason for this was the bright point of light that had popped into existence a few feet from his eyes. It grew rapidly, and after a few seconds was the tiny bright shape of a man. At this stage it began to make a noise, or, rather, Twoflower started to hear the noise it had been making all along. It sounded like a sliver of a scream, caught in one long instant of time.

The iridescent man was doll-sized now, a tortured shape tumbling in slow motion while hanging in mid-air. Twoflower wondered why he had thought of the phrase 'a sliver of a scream' . . . and began to wish he hadn't.

It was beginning to look like Rincewind. The wizard's mouth was open, and his face was brilliantly lit by the light of – what? Strange suns, Twoflower found himself thinking. Suns men don't usually see. He shivered.

Now the turning wizard was half man-size. At that point the growth was faster, there was a sudden crowded moment, a rush of air, and an explosion of sound. Rincewind tumbled out of the air, screaming. He hit the floor hard, choked, then rolled over with his head cradled in his arms and his body curled up tightly.

When the dust had settled Twoflower reached out gingerly and tapped the wizard on the shoulder. The human ball rolled up tighter.

'It's me,' explained Twoflower helpfully. The wizard unrolled a fraction.

'What?' he said.

'Me.'

In one movement Rincewind unrolled and bounced up in front of the little man, his hands gripping his shoulders desperately. His eyes were wild and wide.

'Don't say it!' he hissed. 'Don't say it and we might get out!'

'Get out? How did you get in? Don't you know—'

'Don't say it!'

Twoflower backed away from this madman.

'Don't say it!'

'Don't say what?'

'The number!'

'Number?' said Twoflower. 'Hey, Rincewind—'

'Yes, number! Between seven and nine. Four plus four!'

'What, ei—'

Rincewind's hands clapped over the man's mouth. 'Say it and we're doomed. Just don't think about it, right. Trust me!'

'I don't understand!' wailed Twoflower. Rincewind relaxed slightly, which was to say that he still made a violin string look like a bowl of jelly.

'Come on,' he said. 'Let's try and get out. And I'll try and tell you.'

After the first Age of Magic the disposal of grimoires began to become a severe problem on the discworld. A spell is still a spell even when imprisoned temporarily in parchment and ink. It has potency. This is not a problem while the book's owner still lives, but on his death the spell book becomes a source of uncontrolled power that cannot easily be defused.

In short, spell books leak magic. Various solutions have been tried. Countries near the Rim simply loaded down the books of dead mages with leaden pentalphas and threw them over the Edge. Near the Hub less satisfactory alternatives were available. Inserting the offending books in canisters of negatively polarized octiron and sinking them in the fathomless depths of the sea was one (burial in deep caves on land was earlier ruled out after some districts complained of walking trees and five-headed cats) but before long the magic seeped out and eventually fishermen complained of shoals of invisible fish or psychic clams.

A temporary solution was the construction, in various centres of magical lore, of large rooms made of denatured octiron, which is impervious to most forms of magic. Here the more critical grimoires could be stored until their potency had attenuated.

That was how there came to be at Unseen University the Octavo, greatest of all grimoires, formerly owned by the Creator of the Universe. It was this book that Rincewind had once opened for a bet. He had only a second to stare at a page before setting off various alarm spells, but that was time enough for one spell to leap from it and settle in his memory like a toad in a stone.

'Then what?' said Twoflower.

'Oh, they dragged me out. Thrashed me, of course.'

'And no-one knows what the spell *does*?'

Rincewind shook his head.

'It'd vanished from the page,' he said. 'No-one will know until I say it. Or until I die, of course. Then it will sort of say itself. For all I know it stops the universe, or ends Time, or anything.'

Twoflower patted him on the shoulder.

'No sense in brooding,' he said cheerfully. 'Let's have another look for a way out.'

Rincewind shook his head. All the terror had been spent now. He had broken through the terror barrier, perhaps, and was in the dead calm state of mind that lies on the other side. Anyway, he had ceased to gibber.

'We're doomed,' he stated. 'We've been walking around all night. I tell you, this place is a spiderweb. It doesn't matter which way we go, we'll end up in the centre.'

'It was kind of you to come looking for me, anyway,' said Twoflower. 'How did you manage it exactly? It was very impressive.'

'Oh, well,' began the wizard awkwardly. 'I just thought "I can't leave old Twoflower there" and—'

'So what we've got to do now is find this Bel-Shamharoth person and explain things to him and perhaps he'll let us out,' said Twoflower.

Rincewind ran a finger around his ear.

'It must be the funny echoes in here,' he said. 'I thought I heard you use words like *find* and *explain*.'

'That's right.'

Rincewind glared at him in the hellish purple glow.

'*Find* Bel-Shamharoth?' he said.

'Yes. We don't have to get involved.'

'Find the Soul Render and not get involved? Just give him a nod, I suppose, and ask the way to the exit?

Explain things to the Sender of Eignnnngh,' Rincewind bit off the end of the word just in time and finished, 'You're *insane*! Hey! *Come back!*'

He darted down the passage after Twoflower, and after a few moments came to a halt with a groan.

The violet light was intense here, giving everything new and unpleasant colours. This wasn't a passage, it was a wide room with walls to a number that Rincewind didn't dare to contemplate, and ei— and 7a passages radiating from it.

Rincewind saw, a little way off, a low altar with the same number of sides as four times two. It didn't occupy the centre of the room, however. The centre was occupied by a huge stone slab with twice as many sides as a square. It looked massive. In the strange light it appeared to be slightly tilted, with one edge standing proud of the slabs around it.

Twoflower was standing on it.

'Hey. Rincewind! Look what's here!'

The Luggage came ambling down one of the other passages that radiated from the room.

'That's great,' said Rincewind. 'Fine. It can lead us out of here. Now.'

Twoflower was already rummaging in the chest.

'Yes,' he said. 'After I've taken a few pictures. Just let me fit the attachment—'

'I said *now*—'

Rincewind stopped. Hrun the Barbarian was standing in the passage mouth directly opposite him, a great black sword held in one ham-sized fist.

'You?' said Hrun uncertainly.

'Ahaha. Yes,' said Rincewind. 'Hrun, isn't it?

Long time no see. What brings you here?'

Hrun pointed to the Luggage.

'That,' he said. This much conversation seemed to exhaust Hrun. Then he added, in a tone that combined statement, claim, threat and ultimatum: 'Mine.'

'It belongs to Twoflower here,' said Rincewind. 'Here's a tip. Don't touch it.'

It dawned on him that this was precisely the wrong thing to say, but Hrun had already pushed Twoflower away and was reaching for the Luggage . . .

. . . which sprouted legs, backed away, and raised its lid threateningly. In the uncertain light Rincewind thought he could see rows of enormous teeth, white as bleached beechwood.

'Hrun,' he said quickly, 'there's something I ought to tell you.'

Hrun turned a puzzled face to him.

'What?' he said.

'It's about numbers. Look, you know if you add seven and one, or three and five, or take two from ten, you get a number. While you're here don't say it, and we might all stand a chance of getting out of here alive. Or merely just dead.'

'Who is he?' asked Twoflower. He was holding a cage in his hands, dredged from the bottom-most depths of the Luggage. It appeared to be full of sulking pink lizards.

'I am Hrun,' said Hrun proudly. Then he looked at Rincewind.

'What?' he said.

'Just don't say it, OK?' said Rincewind.

He looked at the sword in Hrun's hand. It was

black, the sort of black that is less a colour than a graveyard of colours, and there was a highly ornate runic inscription up the blade. More noticeable still was the faint octarine glow that surrounded it. The sword must have noticed him, too, because it suddenly spoke in a voice like a claw being scraped across glass.

'Strange,' it said. 'Why can't he say eight?'

EIGHT, Hate, ate, said the echoes. There was the faintest of grinding noises, deep under the earth.

And the echoes, although they became softer, refused to die away. They bounced from wall to wall, crossing and recrossing, and the violet light flickered in time with the sound.

'You did it!' screamed Rincewind. 'I said you shouldn't say eight!'

He stopped, appalled at himself. But the word was out now, and joined its colleagues in the general susurration.

Rincewind turned to run, but the air suddenly seemed to be thicker than treacle. A charge of magic bigger than he had ever seen was building up; when he moved, in painful slow motion, his limbs left trails of golden sparks that traced their shape in the air.

Behind him there was a rumble as the great octagonal slab rose into the air, hung for a moment on one edge, and crashed down on the floor.

Something thin and black snaked out of the pit and wrapped itself around his ankle. He screamed as he landed heavily on the vibrating flagstones. The tentacle started to pull him across the floor.

Then Twoflower was in front of him, reaching out

for his hands. He grasped the little man's arms desperately and they lay looking into each other's faces. Rincewind slid on, even so.

'What's holding you?' he gasped.

'N-nothing!' said Twoflower. 'What's happening?'

'I'm being dragged into this pit, what do you think?'

'Oh Rincewind, I'm sorry—'

'*You're* sorry—'

There was a noise like a singing saw and the pressure on Rincewind's legs abruptly ceased. He turned his head and saw Hrun crouched by the pit, his sword a blur as it hacked at the tentacles racing out towards him.

Twoflower helped the wizard to his feet and they crouched by the altar stone, watching the manic figure as it battled the questing arms.

'It won't work,' said Rincewind. 'The Sender can materialize tentacles. *What are you doing?*'

Twoflower was feverishly attaching the cage of subdued lizards to the picturebox, which he had mounted on a tripod.

'I've just got to get a picture of this,' he muttered. 'It's stupendous! Can you hear me, imp?'

The picture imp opened his tiny hatch, glanced momentarily at the scene around the pit, and vanished into the box. Rincewind jumped as something touched his leg, and brought his heel down on a questing tentacle.

'Come on,' he said. 'Time to go zoom.' He grabbed Twoflower's arm, but the tourist resisted.

'Run away and leave Hrun with that thing?' he said.

Rincewind looked blank. 'Why not?' he said. 'It's his job.'

'But it'll kill him!'

'It could be worse,' said Rincewind.

'What?'

'It could be *us*,' Rincewind pointed out logically. 'Come on!'

Twoflower pointed. 'Hey!' he said. 'It's got my Luggage!'

Before Rincewind could restrain him Twoflower ran around the edge of the pit to the box, which was being dragged across the floor while its lid snapped ineffectually at the tentacle that held it. The little man began to kick at the tentacle in fury.

Another one snapped out of the mêlée around Hrun and caught him around the waist. Hrun himself was already an indistinct shape amid the tightening coils. Even as Rincewind stared in horror the Hero's sword was wrenched from his grasp and hurled against a wall.

'Your spell!' shouted Twoflower.

Rincewind did not move. He was looking at the Thing rising out of the pit. It was an enormous eye, and it was staring directly at him. He whimpered as a tentacle fastened itself around his waist.

The words of the spell rose unbidden in his throat. He opened his mouth as in a dream, shaping it around the first barbaric syllable.

Another tentacle shot out like a whip and coiled around his throat, choking him. Staggering and gasping, Rincewind was dragged across the floor.

One flailing arm caught Twoflower's picturebox as

it skittered past on its tripod. He snatched it up instinctively, as his ancestors might have snatched up a stone when faced with a marauding tiger. If only he could get enough room to swing it against the Eye . . .

. . . the Eye filled the whole universe in front of him. Rincewind felt his will draining away like water from a sieve.

In front of him the torpid lizards stirred in their cage on the picturebox. Irrationally, as a man about to be beheaded notices every scratch and stain on the executioner's block, Rincewind saw that they had overlarge tails that were bluish-white and, he realized, throbbing alarmingly.

As he was drawn towards the Eye the terror-struck Rincewind raised the box protectively, and at the same time heard the picture imp say, 'They're about ripe now, can't hold them any longer. Everyone smile, please.'

There was a—

—flash of light so white and so bright—

—it didn't seem like light at all.

Bel-Shamharoth screamed, a sound that started in the far ultrasonic and finished somewhere in Rincewind's bowels. The tentacles went momentarily as stiff as rods, hurling their various cargoes around the room, before bunching up protectively in front of the abused Eye. The whole mass dropped into the pit and a moment later the big slab was snatched up by several dozen tentacles and slammed into place, leaving a number of thrashing limbs trapped around the edge.

Hrun landed rolling, bounced off a wall and came

up on his feet. He found his sword and started to chop methodically at the doomed arms. Rincewind lay on the floor, concentrating on not going mad. A hollow wooden noise made him turn his head.

The Luggage had landed on its curved lid. Now it was rocking angrily and kicking its little legs in the air.

Warily, Rincewind looked around for Twoflower. The little man was in a crumpled heap against the wall, but at least he was groaning.

The wizard pulled himself across the floor, painfully, and whispered, 'What the hell was that?'

'Why were they so bright?' muttered Twoflower. 'Gods, my head . . .'

'So bright?' said Rincewind. He looked across the floor to the cage on the picturebox. The lizards inside, now noticeably thinner, were watching him with interest.

'The salamanders,' moaned Twoflower. 'The picture'll be over-exposed, I know it . . .'

'They're salamanders?' asked Rincewind incredulously.

'Of course. Standard attachment.'

Rincewind staggered across to the box and picked it up. He'd seen salamanders before, of course, but they had been small specimens. They had also been floating in a jar of pickle in the curiobiological museum down in the cellars of Unseen University, since live salamanders were extinct around the Circle Sea.

He tried to remember the little he knew about them. They were magical creatures. They also had no mouths, since they subsisted entirely on the nourishing quality of the octarine wavelength in the discworld's sunlight, which they absorbed through their skins. Of course, they also absorbed the rest of the sunlight as well, storing it in a special sac until it was excreted in the normal way. A desert inhabited by discworld salamanders was a veritable lighthouse at night.

Rincewind put them down and nodded grimly. With all the octarine light in this magical place the creatures had been gorging themselves, and then nature had taken its course.

The picturebox sidled away on its tripod. Rincewind aimed a kick at it, and missed. He was beginning to dislike sapient pearwood.

Something small stung his cheek. He brushed it away irritably.

He looked around at a sudden grinding noise, and a voice like a carving knife cutting through silk said, 'This is very undignified.'

'Shuddup,' said Hrun. He was using Kring to lever the top off the altar. He looked up at Rincewind and grinned. Rincewind hoped that rictus-strung grimace was a grin.

'Mighty magic,' commented the barbarian, pushing down heavily on the complaining blade with a hand the size of a ham. 'Now we share the treasure, eh?'

Rincewind grunted as something small and hard struck his ear. There was a gust of wind, hardly felt.

'How do you know there's treasure in there?' he said.

Hrun heaved, and managed to hook his fingers under the stone. 'You find chokeapples under a chokeapple tree,' he said. 'You find treasure under altars. Logic.'

He gritted his teeth. The stone swung up and landed heavily on the floor.

This time something struck Rincewind's hand, heavily. He clawed at the air and looked at the thing he had caught. It was a piece of stone with five-plus-three sides. He looked up at the ceiling. Should it be sagging like that? Hrun hummed a little tune as he began to pull crumbling leather from the desecrated altar.

The air crackled, fluoresced, hummed. Intangible winds gripped the wizard's robe, flapping it out in eddies of blue and green sparks. Around Rincewind's head mad, half-formed spirits howled and gibbered as they were sucked past.

He tried raising a hand. It was immediately surrounded by a glowing octarine corona as the rising magical wind roared past. The gale raced through the room without stirring one iota of dust, yet it was blowing Rincewind's eyelids inside out. It screamed along the tunnels, its banshee-wail bouncing madly from stone to stone.

Twoflower staggered up, bent double in the teeth of the astral gale.

'What the hell is *this*?' he shouted.

Rincewind half-turned. Immediately the howling wind caught him, nearly pitching him over. Poltergeist eddies, spinning in the rushing air, snatched at his feet.

Hrun's arm shot out and caught him. A moment later he and Twoflower had been dragged into the lee of the ravaged altar, and lay panting on the floor. Beside them the talking sword Kring sparkled, its magical field boosted a hundredfold by the storm.

'Hold on!' screamed Rincewind.

'The wind!' shouted Twoflower. 'Where's it coming from? Where's it blowing *to*?' He looked into Rincewind's mask of sheer terror, which made him redouble his own grip on the stones.

'We're doomed,' murmured Rincewind, while overhead the roof cracked and shifted. 'Where do shadows come from? *That's* where the wind is blowing!'

What was in fact happening, as the wizard knew, was that as the abused spirit of Bel-Shamharoth sank through the deeper chthonic planes his brooding spirit was being sucked out of the very stones into the region which, according to the discworld's most reliable priests, was both under the ground and Somewhere Else. In consequence his temple was being abandoned to the ravages of Time, who for thousands of shamefaced years had been reluctant to go near the place. Now the suddenly released, accumulated weight of all those pent-up seconds was bearing down heavily on the unbraced stones.

Hrun glanced up at the widening cracks and sighed. Then he put two fingers into his mouth and whistled.

Strangely the real sound rang out loudly over the pseudosound of the widening astral whirlpool that was forming in the middle of the great octagonal slab. It was followed by a hollow echo which sounded, Rincewind fancied, strangely like the bouncing of strange bones. Then came a noise with no hint of strangeness. It was hollow hoofbeats.

Hrun's warhorse cantered through a creaking

archway and reared up by its master, its mane streaming in the gale. The barbarian pulled himself to his feet and slung his treasure bags into a sack that hung from the saddle, then hauled himself onto the beast's back. He reached down and grabbed Twoflower by the scruff of his neck, dragging him across the saddle tree. As the horse turned around Rincewind took a desperate leap and landed behind Hrun, who raised no objection.

The horse pounded surefooted along the tunnels, leaping sudden slides of rubble and adroitly side-stepping huge stones as they thundered down from the straining roof. Rincewind, clinging on grimly, looked behind them.

No wonder the horse was moving so swiftly. Close behind, speeding through the flickering violet light, were a large ominous-looking chest and a picturebox that skittered along dangerously on its three legs. So great was the ability of sapient pearwood to follow its master anywhere, the grave-goods of dead emperors had traditionally been made of it . . .

They reached the outer air a moment before the octagonal arch finally broke and smashed into the flags.

The sun was rising. Behind them a column of dust rose as the temple collapsed in on itself, but they did not look back. That was a shame, because Twoflower might have been able to obtain pictures unusual even by discworld standards.

There was movement in the smoking ruins. They seemed to be growing a green carpet. Then an oak tree spiralled up, branching out like an exploding green rocket, and was in the middle of a venerable copse even before the tips of its aged branches had stopped quivering. A beech burst out like a fungus, matured, rotted, and fell in a cloud of tinder dust amid its struggling offspring. Already the temple was a half-buried heap of mossy stones.

But Time, having initially gone for the throat, was now setting out to complete the job. The boiling interface between decaying magic and ascendant entropy roared down the hill and overtook the galloping horse, whose riders, being themselves creatures of Time, completely failed to notice it. But it lashed into the enchanted forest with the whip of centuries.

'Impressive, isn't it?' observed a voice by Rincewind's knee as the horse cantered through the haze of decaying timber and falling leaves.

The voice had an eerie metallic ring to it. Rincewind looked down at Kring the sword. It had a couple of rubies set in the pommel. He got the impression they were watching him.

From the moorland rimwards of the wood they watched the battle between the trees and Time, which could only have one ending. It was a sort of cabaret to the main business of the halt, which was the consumption of quite a lot of a bear which had incautiously come within bowshot of Hrun.

Rincewind watched Hrun over the top of his slab of greasy meat. Hrun going about the business of being a hero, he realized, was quite different to the wine-bibbing, carousing Hrun who occasionally came to Ankh-Morpork. He was cat-cautious, lithe as a panther, and thoroughly at home.

And I've survived Bel-Shamharoth, Rincewind reminded himself. Fantastic.

Twoflower was helping the hero sort through the treasure stolen from the temple. It was mostly silver set with unpleasant purple stones. Representations of spiders, octopi and the tree-dwelling octarsier of the hubland wastes figured largely in the heap.

Rincewind tried to shut his ears to the grating voice beside him. It was no use.

'—and then I belonged to the Pasha of Re'durat and played a prominent part in the battle of the Great Nef, which is where I received the slight nick you may have noticed some two-thirds of the way up my blade,' Kring was saying from its temporary home in a tussock. 'Some infidel was wearing an octiron collar, most unsporting, and of course I was a lot sharper in those days and my master used to use me to cut silk handkerchiefs in mid-air and – am I boring you?'

'Huh? Oh, no, no, not at all. It's all very interesting,' said Rincewind, with his eyes still on Hrun. How trustworthy would he be? Here they were, out in the wilds, there were trolls about . . .

'I could see you were a cultured person,' Kring went on. 'So seldom do I get to meet really interesting people, for any length of time, anyway. What I'd really like is a nice mantelpiece to hang over, somewhere nice and quiet. I spent a couple of hundred years on the bottom of a lake once.'

'That must have been fun,' said Rincewind absently.

'Not really,' said Kring.

'No, I suppose not.'

'What I'd *really* like is to be a ploughshare. I don't

know what that is, but it sounds like an existence with some point to it.'

Twoflower hurried over to the wizard.

'I had a great idea,' he burbled.

'Yah,' said Rincewind, wearily. 'Why don't we get Hrun to accompany us to Quirm?'

Twoflower looked amazed. 'How did you know?' he said.

'I just thought you'd think it,' said Rincewind.

Hrun ceased stuffing silverware into his saddlebags and grinned encouragingly at them. Then his eyes strayed back to the Luggage.

'If we had him with us, who'd attack us?' said Twoflower.

Rincewind scratched his chin. 'Hrun?' he suggested.

'But we saved his life in the Temple!'

'Well, if by *attack* you mean *kill*,' said Rincewind, 'I don't think he'd do that. He's not that sort. He'd just rob us and tie us up and leave us for the wolves, I expect.'

'Oh, come *on*.'

'Look, this is real life,' snapped Rincewind. 'I mean, here you are, carrying around a box full of gold, don't you think anyone in their right minds would jump at the chance of pinching it?' I would, he added mentally – if I hadn't seen what the Luggage does to prying fingers.

Then the answer hit him. He looked from Hrun to the picturebox. The picture imp was doing its laundry in a tiny tub, while the salamanders dozed in their cage.

'I've got an idea,' he said. 'I mean, what is it heroes

really want?'

'Gold?' said Twoflower.

'No. I mean *really* want.'

Twoflower frowned. 'I don't quite understand,' he said. Rincewind picked up the picturebox.

'Hrun,' he said. 'Come over here, will you?'

The days passed peacefully. True, a small band of bridge trolls tried to ambush them on one occasion, and a party of brigands nearly caught them unawares one night (but unwisely tried to investigate the Luggage before slaughtering the sleepers). Hrun demanded, and got, double pay for both occasions.

'If any harm comes to us,' said Rincewind, 'then there will be no-one to operate the magic box. No more pictures of Hrun, you understand?'

Hrun nodded, his eyes fixed on the latest picture. It showed Hrun striking a heroic pose, with one foot on a heap of slain trolls.

'Me and you and little friend Two Flowers, we all get on hokay,' he said. 'Also tomorrow, may we get a better profile, hokay?'

He carefully wrapped the picture in trollskin and stowed it in his saddlebag, along with the others.

'It seems to be working,' said Twoflower admiringly, as Hrun rode ahead to scout the road.

'Sure,' said Rincewind. 'What heroes like best is themselves.'

'You're getting quite good at using the picturebox, you know that?'

'Yar.'

'So you might like to have this.' Twoflower held out

a picture.

'What is it?' asked Rincewind.

'Oh, just the picture you took in the temple.'

Rincewind looked in horror. There, bordered by a few glimpses of tentacle, was a huge, whorled, calloused, potion-stained and unfocused thumb.

'That's the story of my life,' he said wearily.

'You win,' said Fate, pushing the heap of souls across the gaming table. The assembled gods relaxed. 'There will be other games,' he added.

The Lady smiled into two eyes that were like holes in the universe.

And then there was nothing but the ruin of the forests and a cloud of dust on the horizon, which drifted away on the breeze. And, sitting on a pitted and moss-grown milestone, a black and raggedy figure. His was the air of one who is unjustly put upon, who is dreaded and feared, yet who is the only friend of the poor and the best doctor for the mortally wounded.

Death, although of course completely eyeless, watched Rincewind disappearing with what would, had His face possessed any mobility at all, have been a frown. Death, although exceptionally busy at all times, decided that He now had a hobby. There was something about the wizard that irked Him beyond measure. He didn't keep appointments for one thing.

I'LL GET YOU YET, CULLY, said Death, in the voice like the slamming of leaden coffin lids, SEE IF I DON'T.

The Lure of the Wyrm

IT WAS CALLED THE WYRMBERG and it rose almost one half of a mile above the green valley; a mountain huge, grey and upside down.

At its base it was a mere score of yards across. Then it rose through clinging cloud, curving gracefully outward like an upturned trumpet until it was truncated by a plateau fully a quarter of a mile across. There was a tiny forest up there, its greenery cascading over the lip. There were buildings. There was even a small river, tumbling over the edge in a waterfall so wind-whipped that it reached the ground as rain.

There were also a number of cave mouths, a few yards below the plateau. They had a crudely carved, regular look about them, so that on this crisp autumn morning the Wyrmberg hung over the clouds like a giant's dovecote.

This would mean that the 'doves' had a wingspan slightly in excess of forty yards.

'I knew it,' said Rincewind. 'We're in a strong magical field.'

Twoflower and Hrun looked around the little hollow where they had made their noonday halt. Then they looked at each other.

The horses were quietly cropping the rich grass by the stream. Yellow butterflies skittered among the bushes. There was a smell of thyme and a buzzing of bees. The wild pig on the spit sizzled gently.

Hrun shrugged and went back to oiling his biceps. They gleamed.

'Looks alright to me,' he said.

'Try tossing a coin,' said Rincewind.

'What?'

'Go on. Toss a coin.'

'Hokay,' said Hrun. 'If it gives you any pleasure.' He reached into his pouch and withdrew a handful of loose change plundered from a dozen realms. With some care he selected a Zchloty leaden quarter-iotum and balanced it on a purple thumbnail.

'You call,' he said. 'Heads or—' he inspected the reverse with an air of intense concentration, 'some sort of a fish with legs.'

'When it's in the air,' said Rincewind. Hrun grinned and flicked his thumb.

The iotum rose, spinning.

'Edge,' said Rincewind, without looking at it.

Magic never dies. It merely fades away.

Nowhere was this more evident on the wide blue expanse of the discworld than in those areas that had been the scene of the great battles of the Mage Wars, which had happened very shortly after Creation. In those days magic in its raw state had been widely available, and had been eagerly utilized by the First Men in their war against the Gods.

The precise origins of the Mage Wars have been lost in the fogs of Time, but disc philosophers agree that the First Men, shortly after their creation, understandably lost their temper. And great and pyrotechnic were the battles that followed – the sun wheeled across the sky, the seas boiled, weird storms ravaged the land, small white pigeons mysteriously appeared in people's clothing, and the very stability of the disc (carried as it was through space on the backs of four giant turtle-riding elephants) was threatened. This resulted in stern action by the Old High Ones, to whom even the Gods themselves are answerable. The Gods were banished to high places, men were re-created a good deal smaller, and much of the old wild magic was sucked out of the earth.

That did not solve the problem of those places on the disc which, during the wars, had suffered a direct hit by a spell. The magic faded away – slowly, over the millennia, releasing as it decayed myriads of sub-astral particles that severely distorted the reality around it . . .

Rincewind, Twoflower and Hrun stared at the coin.

'Edge it is,' said Hrun. 'Well, you're a wizard. So what?'

'I don't do – that sort of spell.'

'You mean you can't.'

Rincewind ignored this, because it was true. 'Try it again,' he suggested.

Hrun pulled out a fistful of coins.

The first two landed in the usual manner. So did the fourth. The third landed on its edge and balanced there. The fifth turned into a small yellow caterpillar and crawled away. The sixth, upon reaching its zenith, vanished with a sharp 'spang!' A moment later there was a small thunder clap.

'Hey, that one was silver!' exclaimed Hrun, rising to his feet and staring upwards. 'Bring it back!'

'I don't know where it's gone,' said Rincewind wearily. 'It's probably still accelerating. The ones I tried this morning didn't come down, anyway.'

Hrun was still staring into the sky.

'What?' said Twoflower.

Rincewind sighed. He had been dreading this.

'We've strayed into a zone with a high magical index,' he said. 'Don't ask me how. Once upon a time a really powerful magic field must have been generated here, and we're feeling the after-effects.'

'Precisely,' said a passing bush.

Hrun's head jerked down.

'You mean this is one of *those* places?' he asked. 'Let's get out of here!'

'Right,' agreed Rincewind. 'If we retrace our steps we might make it. We can stop every mile or so and toss a coin.'

He stood up urgently and started stuffing things into his saddlebags.

'What?' said Twoflower.

Rincewind stopped. 'Look,' he snapped. 'Just don't argue. Come *on*.'

'It looks alright,' said Twoflower. 'Just a bit underpopulated that's all . . .'

'Yes,' said Rincewind. 'Odd, isn't it? Come *on*!'

There was a noise high above them, like a strip of leather being slapped on a wet rock. Something glassy and indistinct passed over Rincewind's head, throwing up a cloud of ashes from the fire, and the pig carcass took off from the spit and rocketed into the sky.

It banked to avoid a clump of trees, righted itself, roared around in a tight circle, and headed hubwards leaving a trail of hot pork-fat droplets.

'What are they doing now?' asked the old man.

The young woman glanced at the scrying glass.

'Heading rimwards at speed,' she reported. 'By the way – they've still got that box on legs.'

The old man chuckled, an oddly disturbing sound in the dark and dusty crypt. 'Sapient pearwood,' he said. 'Remarkable. Yes, I think we will have that. Please see to it, my dear – before they go beyond your power, perhaps?'

'Silence! Or—'

'Or what, Liessa?' said the old man (in this dim light there was something odd about the way he was slumped in the stone chair). 'You killed me once already, remember?'

She snorted and stood up, tossing back her hair scornfully. It was red, flecked with gold. Erect, Liessa Wyrmbidder was entirely a magnificent sight. She was also almost naked, except for a couple of mere scraps of the lightest chain mail and riding boots of iridescent dragonhide. In one boot was thrust a riding crop, unusual in that it was as long as a spear and tipped with tiny steel barbs.

'My power will be quite sufficient,' she said coldly.

The indistinct figure appeared to nod, or at least to wobble. 'As you keep assuring me,' he said. Liessa snorted, and strode out of the hall.

Her father did not bother to watch her go. One reason for this was, of course, that since he had been dead for three months his eyes were in any case not in the best of condition. The other was that as a wizard – even a dead wizard of the fifteenth grade – his optic nerves had long since become attuned to seeing into levels and dimensions far removed from common reality, and were therefore somewhat inefficient at observing the merely mundane. (During his life they had appeared to others to be eight-faceted and eerily insectile.) Besides, since he was now suspended in the narrow space between the living world and the dark shadow-world of Death he could survey the whole of Causality itself. That was why, apart from a mild hope that this time his wretched daughter would get herself killed, he did not devote his considerable powers to learning more about the three travellers galloping desperately out of his realm.

Several hundred yards away, Liessa was in a strange humour as she strode down the worn steps that led into the hollow heart of the Wyrmberg, followed by half a dozen Riders. Would this be the opportunity? Perhaps here was the key to break the deadlock, the key to the throne of the Wyrmberg. It was rightfully hers, of course; but tradition said that only a man could rule the Wyrmberg. That irked Liessa, and when she was angry the Power flowed stronger and the dragons were especially big and ugly.

If she had a man, things would be different. Someone who, for preference, was a big strapping lad but short on brains. Someone who would do what he was told.

The biggest of the three now fleeing the dragonlands might do. And if it turned out that he wouldn't, then dragons were always hungry and needed to be fed regularly. She could see to it that they got ugly.

Uglier than usual, anyway.

The stairway passed through a stone arch and ended in a narrow ledge near the roof of the great cavern where the Wyrms roosted.

Sunbeams from the myriad entrances around the walls criss-crossed the dusty gloom like amber rods in which a million golden insects had been preserved. Below, they revealed nothing but a thin haze. Above . . .

The walking rings started so close to Liessa's head that she could reach up and touch one. They stretched away in their thousands across the upturned acres of the cavern roof. It had taken a score of masons a score of years to hammer the pitons for all those, hanging from their work as they progressed. Yet they were as nothing compared to the eighty-eight major rings that clustered near the apex of the dome. A further fifty had been lost in the old days, as they were swung into place by teams of sweating slaves (and there had been slaves aplenty, in the first days of the Power) and the great rings had gone crashing into the depths, dragging their unfortunate manipulators with them.

But eighty-eight had been installed, huge as rainbows, rusty as blood. From them . . .

The dragons sense Liessa's presence. Air swishes around the cavern as eighty-eight pairs of wings unfold like a complicated puzzle. Great heads with green, multi-faceted eyes peer down at her.

The beasts are still faintly transparent. While the men around her take their hookboots from the rack, Liessa bends her mind to the task of full visualization; above her in the musty air the dragons become fully visible, bronze scales dully reflecting the sunbeam shafts. Her mind throbs, but now that the Power is flowing fully she can, with barely a waver of concentration, think of other things.

Now she too buckles on the hookboots and turns a graceful cartwheel to bring their hooks, with a faint clang, against a couple of the walking rings in the ceiling.

Only now it is the floor. The world has changed. Now she is standing on the edge of a deep bowl or crater, floored with the little rings across which the dragon-riders are already strolling with a pendulum gait. In the centre of the bowl their huge mounts wait among the herd. Far above are the distant rocks of the cavern floor, discoloured by centuries of dragon droppings.

Moving with the easy gliding movement that is second nature Liessa sets off towards her own dragon, Laolith, who turns his great horsey head towards her. His jowls are greasy with pork fat.

It was very enjoyable, he says in her mind.

'I thought I said there were to be no unaccompanied flights?' she snaps.

I was hungry, Liessa.

'Curb your hunger. Soon there will be horses to eat.'

The reins stick in our teeth. Are there any warriors? We like warriors.

Liessa swings down the mounting ladder and lands with her legs locked around Laolith's leathery neck.

'The warrior is mine. There are a couple of others you

can have. One appears to be a wizard of sorts,' she adds by way of encouragement.

Oh, you know how it is with wizards. Half an hour afterwards you could do with another one, the dragon grumbles.

He spreads his wings and drops.

'They're gaining!' screamed Rincewind. He bent even lower over his horse's neck and groaned. Twoflower was trying to keep up while at the same time craning round to look at the flying beasts.

'You don't understand!' screamed the tourist, above the terrible noise of the wingbeats. 'All my life I've wanted to see dragons!'

'From the inside?' shouted Rincewind. 'Shut up and ride!' He whipped at his horse with the reins and stared at the wood ahead, trying to drag it closer by sheer willpower. Under those trees they'd be safe. Under those trees no dragons could fly . . .

He heard the clap of wings before shadows folded around him. Instinctively he rolled in the saddle and felt the white-hot stab of pain as something sharp scored a line across his shoulders.

Behind him Hrun screamed, but it sounded more like a bellow of rage than a cry of pain. The barbarian had vaulted down into the heather and had drawn the black sword, Kring. He flourished it as one of the dragons curved in for another low pass.

'No bloody lizard does that to me!' he roared.

Rincewind leaned over and grabbed Twoflower's reins.

'Come *on*!' he hissed.

'But, the dragons—' said Twoflower, entranced.

'Blast the—' began the wizard, and froze. Another dragon had peeled off from the circling dots overhead and was gliding towards them. Rincewind let go of Twoflower's horse, swore bitterly, and spurred his own mount towards the trees, alone. He didn't look back at the sudden commotion behind him and, when a shadow passed over him, merely gibbered weakly and tried to burrow into the horse's mane.

Then, instead of the searing, piercing pain he had expected, there was a series of stinging blows as the terrified animal passed under the eaves of the wood. The wizard tried to hang on but another low branch, stouter than the others, knocked him out of the saddle. The last thing he heard before the flashing blue lights of unconsciousness closed in was a high reptilian scream of frustration, and the thrashing of talons in the treetops.

When he awoke a dragon was watching him; at least, it was staring in his general direction. Rincewind groaned and tried to dig his way into the moss with his shoulder-blades, then gasped as the pain hit him.

Through the mists of agony and fear he looked back at the dragon.

The creature was hanging from a branch of a large dead oak tree, several hundred feet away. Its bronze-gold wings were tightly wrapped around its body but the long equine head turned this way and that at the end of a remarkably prehensile neck. It was scanning the forest.

It was also semi-transparent. Although the sun

glinted off its scales, Rincewind could clearly make out the outlines of the branches behind it.

On one of them a man was sitting, dwarfed by the hanging reptile. He appeared to be naked except for a pair of high boots, a tiny leather holdall in the region of his groin, and a high-crested helmet. He was swinging a short sword back and forth idly, and stared out across the tree-tops with the air of one carrying out a tedious and unglamorous assignment.

A beetle began to crawl laboriously up Rincewind's leg.

The wizard wondered how much damage a half-solid dragon could do. Would it only half-kill him? He decided not to stay and find out.

Moving on heels, fingertips and shoulder muscles, Rincewind wriggled sideways until foliage masked the oak and its occupants. Then he scrambled to his feet and hared off between the trees.

He had no destination in mind, no provisions, and no horse. But while he still had legs he could run. Ferns and brambles whipped at him, but he didn't feel them at all.

When he had put about a mile between him and the dragon he stopped and collapsed against a tree, which then spoke to him.

'Psst,' it said.

Dreading what he might see, Rincewind let his gaze slide upwards. It tried to fasten on innocuous bits of bark and leaf, but the scourge of curiosity forced it to leave them behind. Finally it fixed on a black sword thrust straight through the branch above Rincewind's head.

'Don't just stand there,' said the sword (in a voice like the sound of a finger dragged around the rim of a large empty wineglass). 'Pull me out.'

'What?' said Rincewind, his chest still heaving.

'Pull me out,' repeated Kring. 'It's either that or I'll be spending the next million years in a coal measure. Did I ever tell you about the time I was thrown into a lake up in the—'

'What happened to the others?' said Rincewind, still clutching the tree desperately.

'Oh, the dragons got them. And the horses. And that box thing. Me too, except that Hrun dropped me. What a stroke of luck for you.'

'Well—' began Rincewind. Kring ignored him.

'I expect you'll be in a hurry to rescue them,' it added.

'Yes, well—'

'So if you'll just pull me out we can be off.'

Rincewind squinted up at the sword. A rescue attempt had hitherto been so far at the back of his mind that, if some advanced speculations on the nature and shape of the many-dimensioned multiplexity of the universe were correct, it was right at the front; but a magic sword was a valuable item . . .

And it would be a long trek back home, wherever that was . . .

He scrambled up the tree and inched along the branch. Kring was buried very firmly in the wood. He gripped the pommel and heaved until lights flashed in front of his eyes.

'Try again,' said the sword encouragingly.

Rincewind groaned and gritted his teeth.

'Could be worse,' said Kring. 'This could have been an anvil.'

'Yaargh,' hissed the wizard, fearing for the future of his groin.

'I have had a multidimensional existence,' said the sword.

'Ungh?'

'I have had many names, you know.'

'Amazing,' said Rincewind. He swayed backwards as the blade slid free. It felt strangely light.

Back on the ground again he decided to break the news.

'I really don't think rescue is a good idea,' he said. 'I think we'd better head back to a city, you know. To raise a search party.'

'The dragons headed hubwards,' said Kring. 'However, I suggest we start with the one in the trees over there.'

'Sorry, but—'

'You can't leave them to their fate!'

Rincewind looked surprised. 'I can't?' he said.

'No. You can't. Look, I'll be frank. I've worked with better material than you, but it's either that or – have you ever spent a million years in a coal measure?'

'Look, I—'

'So if you don't stop arguing I'll chop your head off.'

Rincewind saw his own arm snap up until the shimmering blade was humming a mere inch from his throat. He tried to force his fingers to let go. They wouldn't.

'I don't know how to be a hero!' he shouted.

'I propose to teach you.'

* * *

Bronze Psepha rumbled deep in his throat.

K!sdra the dragonrider leaned forward and squinted across the clearing.

'I see him,' he said. He swung himself down easily from branch to branch and landed lightly on the tussocky grass, drawing his sword.

He took a long look at the approaching man, who was obviously not keen on leaving the shelter of the trees. He was armed, but the dragonrider observed with some interest the strange way in which the man held the sword in front of him at arm's length, as though embarrassed to be seen in its company.

K!sdra hefted his own sword and grinned expansively as the wizard shuffled towards him. Then he leapt.

Later, he remembered only two things about the fight. He recalled the uncanny way in which the wizard's sword curved up and caught his own blade with a shock that jerked it out of his grip. The other thing – and it was this, he averred, that led to his downfall – was that the wizard was covering his eyes with one hand.

K!sdra jumped back to avoid another thrust and fell full length on the turf. With a snarl Psepha unfolded his great wings and launched himself from his tree.

A moment later the wizard was standing over him, shouting, 'Tell it that if it singes me I'll let the sword go! I will! I'll let it go! So tell it!' The tip of the black sword was hovering over K!sdra's throat. What was odd was that the wizard was obviously struggling with it, and it appeared to be singing to itself.

'Psepha!' K!sdra shouted.

The dragon roared in defiance, but pulled out of the dive that would have removed Rincewind's head, and flapped ponderously back to the tree.

'Talk!' screamed Rincewind.

K!sdra squinted at him up the length of the sword.

'What would you like me to say?' he asked.

'What?'

'I said what would you like me to say?'

'Where are my friends? The barbarian and the little man is what I mean!'

'I expect they have been taken back to the Wyrmberg.'

Rincewind tugged desperately against the surge of the sword, trying to shut his mind to Kring's blood-thirsty humming.

'What's a Wyrmberg?' he said.

'*The* Wyrmberg. There is only one. It is Dragonhome.'

'And I suppose you were waiting to take me there, eh?'

K!sdra yelped involuntarily as the tip of the sword pricked a bead of blood from his Adam's apple.

'Don't want people to know you've got dragons here, eh?' snarled Rincewind. The dragonrider forgot himself enough to nod, and came within a quarter-inch of cutting his own throat.

Rincewind looked around desperately, and realized that this was something he was really going to have to go through with.

'Right then,' he said as diffidently as he could

manage. 'You'd better take me to this Wyrmberg of yours, hadn't you?'

'I was supposed to take you in dead,' muttered K!sdra sullenly.

Rincewind looked down at him and grinned slowly. It was a wide, manic and utterly humourless rictus. It was the sort of grin that is normally accompanied by small riverside birds wandering in and out, picking scraps out of the teeth.

'Alive will do,' said Rincewind. 'If we're talking about anyone being *dead*, remember whose sword is in which hand.'

'If you kill me nothing will prevent Psepha killing you!' shouted the prone dragonrider.

'So what I'll do is, I'll chop bits off,' agreed the wizard. He tried the effect of the grin again.

'Oh, all right,' said K!sdra sulkily. 'Do you think I've got no imagination?'

He wriggled out from under the sword and waved at the dragon, which took wing again and glided in towards them. Rincewind swallowed.

'You mean we've got to go on that?' he said. K!sdra looked at him scornfully, the point of Kring still aimed at his neck.

'How else would anyone get to the Wyrmberg?'

'I don't know,' said Rincewind. 'How else?'

'I mean, there is no other way. It's flying or nothing.'

Rincewind looked again at the dragon before him. He could quite clearly see through it to the crushed grass on which it lay but, when he gingerly touched a scale that was a mere golden sheen on thin air, it felt solid enough. Either dragons should exist completely or fail to exist at all, he felt. A dragon only half-existing was worse than the extremes.

'I didn't know dragons could be seen through,' he said.

K!sdra shrugged. 'Didn't you?' he said.

He swung himself astride the dragon awkwardly, because Rincewind was hanging on to his belt. Once uncomfortably aboard the wizard moved his white-knuckle grip to a convenient piece of harness and prodded K!sdra lightly with the sword.

'Have you ever flown before?' said the dragonrider, without looking round.

'Not as such, no.'

'Would you like something to suck?'

Rincewind stared at the back of the man's head, then dropped his gaze to the bag of red and yellow sweets that was being proffered.

'Is it necessary?' he asked.

'It is traditional,' said K!sdra. 'Please yourself.'

The dragon stood up, lumbered heavily across the meadow, and fluttered into the air.

Rincewind occasionally had nightmares about teetering on some intangible but enormously high place, and seeing a blue-distanced, cloud-punctuated landscape reeling away below him (this usually woke him up with his ankles sweating; he would have been even more worried had he known that the nightmare was not, as he thought, just the usual discworld vertigo. It was a backwards memory of an event in his future so terrifying that it had generated harmonics of fear all the way along his lifeline).

This was not that event, but it was good practice for it.

Psepha clawed its way into the air with a series of vertebrae-shattering bounds. At the top of its last leap the wide wings unfolded with a snap and spread out with a thump which shook the trees.

Then the ground was gone, dropping away in a series of gentle jerks. Psepha was suddenly rising gracefully, the afternoon sunlight gleaming off wings that were still no more than a golden film. Rincewind made the mistake of glancing downwards, and found himself looking through the dragon to the treetops below. Far below. His stomach shrank at the sight.

Closing his eyes wasn't much better, because it gave his imagination full rein. He compromised by gazing fixedly into the middle distance, where moorland and forest drifted by and could be contemplated almost casually.

Wind snatched at him. K!sdra half turned and shouted into his ear.

'Behold the Wyrmberg!'

Rincewind turned his head slowly, taking care to keep Kring resting lightly on the dragon's back. His streaming eyes saw the impossibly inverted mountain rearing out of the deep forested valley like a trumpet in a tub of moss. Even at this distance he could make out the faint octarine glow in the air that must be indicating a stable magic aura of at least – he gasped – several milliPrime? At least!

'Oh no,' he said.

Even looking at the ground was better than that. He averted his eyes quickly, and realized that he could now no longer see the ground *through* the dragon. As they glided around in a wide circle towards the Wyrmberg it was definitely taking on a more solid form, as if the creature's body was filling with a gold mist. By the time the Wyrmberg was in front of them, swinging wildly across the sky, the dragon was as real as a rock.

Rincewind thought he could see a faint streak in the air, as if something from the mountain had reached out and touched the beast. He got the strange feeling that the dragon was being made more *genuine.*

Ahead of it the Wyrmberg turned from a distant toy to several billion tons of rock poised between heaven and earth. He could see small fields, woods and a lake up there, and from the lake a river spilled out and over the edge . . .

He made the mistake of following the thread of foaming water with his eyes, and jerked himself back just in time.

The flared plateau of the upturned mountain drifted towards them. The dragon didn't even slow.

As the mountain loomed over Rincewind like the biggest fly-swatter in the universe he saw a cave mouth. Psepha skimmed towards it, shoulder muscles pumping.

The wizard screamed as the dark spread and enfolded him. There was a brief vision of rock flashing past, blurred by speed. Then the dragon was in the open again.

It was inside a cave, but bigger than any cave had a right to be. The dragon, gliding across its vast emptiness, was a mere gilded fly in a banqueting hall.

There were other dragons – gold, silver, black, white – flapping across the sun-shafted air on errands of their own or perched on outcrops of rock. High in the domed roof of the cavern scores of others hung from huge rings, their wings wrapped bat-like around their bodies. There were men up there, too. Rincewind swallowed hard when he saw them, because they were walking on that broad expanse of ceiling like flies.

Then he made out the thousands of tiny rings that studded the ceiling. A number of inverted men were watching Psepha's flight with interest. Rincewind swallowed again. For the life of him he couldn't think of what to do next.

'Well?' he asked, in a whisper. 'Any suggestions?'

'Obviously you attack,' said Kring scornfully.

'Why didn't I think of that?' said Rincewind. 'Could it be because they all have crossbows?'

'You're a defeatist.'

'Defeatist! That's because I'm going to be defeated!'

'You're your own worst enemy, Rincewind,' said the sword.

Rincewind looked up at grinning men.

'Bet?' he said wearily.

Before Kring could reply Psepha reared in mid-air and alighted on one of the large rings, which rocked alarmingly.

'Would you like to die now, or surrender first?' asked K!sdra calmly.

Men were converging on the ring from all directions, walking with a swaying motion as their hooked boots engaged the ceiling rings.

There were more boots on a rack that hung in a

small platform built on the side of the perch-ring. Before Rincewind could stop him the dragonrider had leapt from the creature's back to land on the platform, where he stood grinning at the wizard's discomfiture.

There was a small expressive sound made by a number of crossbows being cocked. Rincewind looked up at a number of impassive, upside down faces. The dragonfolk's taste in clothing didn't run to anything much more imaginative than a leather harness, studded with bronze ornaments. Knives and sword sheaths were worn inverted. Those who were not wearing helmets let their hair flow freely, so that it moved like seaweed in the ventilation breeze near the roof. There were several women among them. The inversion did strange things to their anatomy. Rincewind stared.

'Surrender,' said K!sdra again.

Rincewind opened his mouth to do so. Kring hummed a warning, and agonizing waves of pain shot up his arm. 'Never,' he squeaked. The pain stopped.

'Of course he won't!' boomed an expansive voice behind him. 'He's a hero, isn't he?'

Rincewind turned and looked into a pair of hairy nostrils. They belonged to a heavily built young man, hanging nonchalantly from the ceiling by his boots.

'What is your name, hero?' said the man. 'So that we know who you were.'

Agony shot up Rincewind's arm. 'I-I'm Rincewind of Ankh,' he managed to gasp.

'And I am Lio!rt Dragonlord,' said the hanging man, pronouncing the word with the harsh click in the back of the throat that Rincewind could only think of as a kind of integral punctuation. 'You have come to challenge me in mortal combat.'

'Well, no, I didn't—'

'You are mistaken. K!sdra, help our hero into a pair of hookboots. I am sure he is anxious to get started.'

'No, look, I just came here to find my friends. I'm sure there's no—' Rincewind began, as the dragon-rider guided him firmly onto the platform, pushed him onto a seat, and proceeded to strap hookboots to his feet.

'Hurry up, K!sdra. We mustn't keep our hero from his destiny,' said Lio!rt.

'Look, I expect my friends are happy enough here, so if you could just, you know, set me down somewhere—'

'You will see your friends soon enough,' said the dragonlord airily. 'If you are religious, I mean. None who enter the Wyrmberg ever leave again. Except metaphorically, of course. Show him how to reach the rings, K!sdra.'

'Look what you've got me into!' Rincewind hissed.

Kring vibrated in his hand. 'Remember that I am a *magic* sword,' it hummed.

'How can I forget?'

'Climb the ladder and grab a ring,' said the dragon-rider, 'then bring your feet up until the hooks catch.' He helped the protesting wizard climb until he was hanging upside down, robe tucked into his britches, Kring dangling from one hand. At this angle the dragonfolk looked reasonably bearable but the dragons themselves, hanging from their perches, loomed over the scene like immense gargoyles. Their eyes glowed with interest.

'Attention, please,' said Lio!rt. A dragonrider handed him a long shape, wrapped in red silk.

'We fight to the death,' he said. 'Yours.'

'And I suppose I earn my freedom if I win?' said Rincewind, without much hope.

Lio!rt indicated the assembled dragonriders with a tilt of his head.

'Don't be naïve,' he said.

Rincewind took a deep breath. 'I suppose I should warn you,' he said, his voice hardly quavering at all, 'that this is a *magic* sword.'

Lio!rt let the red silk wrapping drop away into the gloom and flourished a jet-black blade. Runes glowed on its surface.

'What a coincidence,' he said, and lunged.

Rincewind went rigid with fright, but his arm swung out as Kring shot forward. The swords met in an explosion of octarine light.

Lio!rt swung himself backwards, his eyes narrowing. Kring leapt past his guard and, although the dragonlord's sword jerked up to deflect most of the force, the result was a thin red line across its master's torso.

With a growl he launched himself at the wizard, boots clattering as he slid from ring to ring. The swords met again in another violent discharge of magic and, at the same time, Lio!rt brought his other hand down against Rincewind's head, jarring him so hard that one foot jerked out of its ring and flailed desperately.

* * *

Rincewind knew himself to be almost certainly the worst wizard on the discworld since he knew but one spell; yet for all that he was still a wizard, and thus by the inexorable laws of magic this meant that upon his demise it would be Death himself who appeared to claim him (instead of sending one of his numerous servants, as is usually the case).

Thus it was that, as a grinning Lio!rt swung back and brought his sword around in a lazy arc, time ran into treacle.

To Rincewind's eyes the world was suddenly lit by a flickering octarine light, tinged with violet as photons impacted on the sudden magical aura. Inside it the dragonlord was a ghastly-hued statue, his sword moving at a snail's pace in the glow.

Beside Lio!rt was another figure, visible only to those who can see into the extra four dimensions of magic. It was tall and dark and thin and, against a sudden night of frosty stars, it swung two-handed a scythe of proverbial sharpness . . .

Rincewind ducked. The blade hissed coldly through the air beside his head and entered the rock of the cavern roof without slowing. Death screamed a curse in his cold crypt voice. The scene vanished. What passed for reality on the discworld reasserted itself with a rush of sound. Lio!rt gasped at the sudden turn of speed with which the wizard had dodged his killing stroke and, with that desperation only available to the really terrified, Rincewind uncoiled like a snake and launched himself across the space between them. He locked both hands around the dragonlord's sword arm, and wrenched.

It was at that moment that Rincewind's one remaining ring, already overburdened, slid out of the rock with a nasty little metal sound.

He plunged down, swung wildly, and ended up dangling over a bone-splintering death with his hands gripping the dragonlord's arm so tightly that the man screamed.

Lio!rt looked up at his feet. Small flakes of rock were dropping out of the roof around the ring pitons.

'Let go, damn you!' he screamed. 'Or we'll both die!'

Rincewind said nothing. He was concentrating on maintaining his grip and keeping his mind closed to the pressing images of his fate on the rocks below.

'Shoot him!' bellowed Lio!rt.

Out of the corner of his eye Rincewind saw several crossbows levelled at him. Lio!rt chose that moment to flail down with his free hand, and a fistful of rings stabbed into the wizard's fingers.

He let go.

Twoflower grabbed the bars and pulled himself up.

'See anything?' said Hrun, from the region of his feet.

'Just clouds.'

Hrun lifted him down again, and sat on the edge of one of the wooden beds that were the only furnishings in the cell. 'Bloody hell,' he said.

'Don't despair,' said Twoflower.

'I'm not despairing.'

'I expect it's all some sort of misunderstanding. I expect they'll release us soon. They seem very civilized.'

Hrun stared at him from under bushy eyebrows. He started to say something, then appeared to think better of it. He sighed instead.

'And when we get back we can say we've seen dragons!' Twoflower continued. 'What about that, eh?'

'Dragons don't exist,' said Hrun flatly. 'Codice of Chimeria killed the last one two hundred years ago. I don't know what we're seeing, but they aren't dragons.'

'But they carried us up in the air! In that hall there must have been hundreds—'

'I expect it was just magic,' said Hrun, dismissively.

'Well, they looked like dragons,' said Twoflower, an air of defiance about him. 'I always wanted to see dragons, ever since I was a little lad. Dragons flying around in the sky, breathing flames . . .'

'They just used to crawl around in swamps and stuff, and all they breathed was stink,' said Hrun, lying down in the bunk. 'They weren't very big, either. They used to collect firewood.'

'*I* heard they used to collect treasure,' said Twoflower.

'*And* firewood. Hey,' Hrun added, brightening up, 'did you notice all those rooms they brought us through? Pretty impressive, I thought. Lot of good stuff about, plus some of those tapestries have got to be worth a fortune.' He scratched his chin thoughtfully, making a noise like a porcupine shouldering its way through gorse.

'What happens next?' asked Twoflower.

Hrun screwed a finger in his ear and inspected it absently.

'Oh,' he said, 'I expect in a minute the door will be flung back and I'll be dragged off to some sort of temple arena where I'll fight maybe a couple of giant spiders and an eight-foot slave from the jungles of Klatch and then I'll rescue some kind of a princess from the altar and then kill off a few guards or whatever and then this girl will show me the secret passage out of the place and we'll liberate a couple of horses and escape with the treasure.' Hrun leaned his head back on his hands and looked at the ceiling, whistling tunelessly.

'All that?' said Twoflower.

'Usually.'

Twoflower sat down on his bunk and tried to think. This proved difficult, because his mind was awash with dragons.

Dragons!

Ever since he was two years old he had been captivated by the pictures of the fiery beasts in *The Octarine Fairy Book*. His sister had told him they didn't really exist, and he recalled the bitter disappointment. If the world didn't contain those beautiful creatures, he'd decided, it wasn't half the world it ought to be. And then later he had been bound apprentice to Ninereeds the Masteraccount, who in his grey-mindedness was everything that dragons were not, and there was no time for dreaming.

But there was something wrong with these dragons. They were too small and sleek, compared to the ones in his mind's eye. Dragons ought to be big and green and clawed and exotic and fire-breathing – big and green with long sharp . . .

Something moved at the edge of his vision, in the furthest, darkest corner of the dungeon. When he turned his head it vanished, although he thought he heard the faintest of noises that might have been made by claws scrabbling on stone.

'Hrun?' he said.

There was a snore from the other bunk.

Twoflower padded over to the corner, poking gingerly at the stones in case there was a secret panel. At that moment the door was flung back, thumping against the wall. Half a dozen guards hurtled through it, spread out and flung themselves down on one knee. Their weapons were aimed exclusively at Hrun. When he thought about this later, Twoflower felt quite offended.

Hrun snored.

A woman strode into the room. Not many women can stride convincingly, but she managed it. She glanced briefly at Twoflower, as one might look at a piece of furniture, then glared down at the man on the bed.

She was wearing the same sort of leather harness that the dragonriders had been wearing, but in her case it was much briefer. That, and the magnificent mane of chestnut-red hair that fell to her waist, was her only concession to what even on the discworld passed for decency. She was also wearing a thoughtful expression.

Hrun made a glubbing noise, turned over, and slept on.

With a careful movement, as though handling some instrument of rare delicacy, the woman drew a slim black dagger from her belt and stabbed downward.

Before it was halfway through its arc Hrun's right hand moved so fast that it appeared to travel between two points in space without at any time occupying the intervening air. It closed around the woman's wrist with a dull smack. His other hand groped feverishly for a sword that wasn't there . . .

Hrun awoke.

'Gngh?' he said, looking up at the woman with a puzzled frown. Then he caught sight of the bowmen.

'Let go,' said the woman, in a voice that was calm and quiet and edged with diamonds. Hrun released his grip slowly.

She stepped back, massaging her wrist and looking at Hrun in much the same way that a cat watches a mousehole.

'So,' she said at last. 'You pass the first test. What is your name, barbarian?'

'Who are you calling a barbarian?' snarled Hrun.

'That is what I want to know.'

Hrun counted the bowmen slowly and made a brief calculation. His shoulders relaxed.

'I am Hrun of Chimeria. And you?'

'Liessa Dragonlady.'

'You are the lord of this place?'

'That remains to be seen. You have the look about you of a hired sword, Hrun of Chimeria. I could use you – if you pass the tests, of course. There are three of them. You have passed the first.'

'What are the other—' Hrun paused, his lips moved soundlessly and then he hazarded, 'two?'

'Perilous.'

'And the fee?'

'Valuable.'

'Excuse me,' said Twoflower.

'And if I fail these tests?' said Hrun, ignoring him. The air between Hrun and Liessa crackled with small explosions of charisma as their gazes sought for a hold.

'If you had failed the first test you would now be dead. This may be considered a typical penalty.'

'Um, look,' began Twoflower. Liessa spared him a brief glance, and appeared actually to notice him for the first time.

'Take that away,' she said calmly, and turned back to Hrun. Two of the guards shouldered their bows, grasped Twoflower by the elbows and lifted him off the ground. Then they trotted smartly through the doorway.

'Hey,' said Twoflower, as they hurried down the corridor outside, 'where' (as they stopped in front of another door) 'is my' (as they dragged the door open) 'Luggage?' He landed in a heap of what might once have been straw. The door banged shut, its echoes punctuated by the sound of bolts being slammed home.

In the other cell Hrun had barely blinked.

'OK,' he said, 'what is the second test?'

'You must kill my two brothers.' Hrun considered this.

'Both at the same time, or one after the other?' he said.

'Consecutively or concurrently,' she assured him.

'What?'

'Just kill them,' she said sharply.

'Good fighters, are they?'

'Renowned.'

'So in return for all this . . . ?'

'You will wed me and become Lord of the Wyrmberg.'

There was a long pause. Hrun's eyebrows twisted themselves in unaccustomed calculation.

'I get you and this mountain?' he said at last.

'Yes.' She looked him squarely in the eye, and her lips twitched. 'The fee is worthwhile, I assure you.'

Hrun dropped his gaze to the rings on her hand. The stones were large, being the incredibly rare blue milk diamonds from the clay basins of Mithos. When he managed to turn his eyes from them he saw Liessa glaring down at him in fury.

'So calculating?' she rasped. 'Hrun the Barbarian, who would boldly walk into the jaws of Death Himself?'

Hrun shrugged. 'Sure,' he said, 'the only reason for walking into the jaws of Death is so's you can steal His gold teeth.' He brought one arm around expansively, and the wooden bunk was at the end of it. It cannoned into the bowmen and Hrun followed it joyously, felling one man with a blow and snatching the weapon from another. A moment later it was all over.

Liessa had not moved.

'Well?' she said.

'Well what?' said Hrun, from the carnage.

'Do you intend to kill me?'

'What? Oh no. No, this is just, you know, kind of a habit. Just keeping in practice. So where are these brothers?' He grinned.

Twoflower sat on his straw and stared into the darkness. He wondered how long he had been there. Hours, at least. Days, probably. He speculated that perhaps it had been years, and he had simply forgotten.

No, that sort of thinking wouldn't do. He tried to think of something else – grass, trees, fresh air, dragons. Dragons . . .

There was the faintest of scrabblings in the darkness. Twoflower felt the sweat prickle on his forehead.

Something was in the cell with him. Something that made small noises, but even in the pitch blackness gave the impression of hugeness. He felt the air move.

When he lifted his arm there was the greasy feel and faint shower of sparks that betokened a localized magical field. Twoflower found himself fervently wishing for light.

A gout of flame rolled past his head and struck the far wall. As the rocks flashed into furnace heat he looked up at the dragon that now occupied more than half the cell.

I obey, lord, said a voice in his head.

By the glow of the crackling, spitting stone Twoflower looked into his own reflection in two enormous green eyes. Beyond them the dragon was as multi-hued, horned, spiked and lithe as the one in his memory – a *real* dragon. Its folded wings were nevertheless still wide enough to scrape the wall on both sides of the room. It lay with him between its talons.

'Obey?' he said, his voice vibrating with terror and delight.

Of course, lord.

The glow faded away. Twoflower pointed a trembling finger at where he remembered the door to be and said, 'Open it!'

The dragon raised its huge head. Again the ball of flame rolled out but this time, as the dragon's neck muscles contracted, its colour faded from orange to yellow, from yellow to white, and finally to the faintest of blues. By that time the flame was also very thin, and where it touched the wall the molten rock spat and ran. When it reached the door the metal exploded into a shower of hot droplets.

Black shadows arced and jiggered over the walls. The metal bubbled for an eye-aching moment, and then the door fell in two pieces in the passage beyond. The flame winked out with a suddenness that was almost as startling as its arrival.

Twoflower stepped gingerly over the cooling door and looked up and down the corridor. It was empty.

The dragon followed. The heavy door frame caused it some minor difficulty, which it overcame with a swing of its shoulders that tore the timber out and tossed it to one side. The creature looked expectantly at Twoflower, its skin rippling and twitching as it sought to open its wings in the confines of the passage.

'How did you get in there?' said Twoflower.

You summoned me, master.

'I don't remember doing that.'

In your mind. You called me up, in your mind, thought the dragon, patiently.

'You mean I just thought of you and there you were?'

Yes.

'It was magic?'

Yes.

'But I've thought about dragons all my life!'

In this place the frontier between thought and reality is probably a little confused. All I know is that once I was not, and then you thought me, and then I was. Therefore, of course, I am yours to command.

'Good grief!'

Half a dozen guards chose that moment to turn the bend in the corridor. They stopped, open-mouthed. Then one remembered himself sufficiently to raise his crossbow and fire.

The dragon's chest heaved. The quarrel exploded into flaming fragments in mid-air. The guards scurried out of sight. A fraction of a second later a wash of flame played over the stones where they had been standing.

Twoflower looked up in admiration.

'Can you fly too?' he said.

Of course.

Twoflower glanced up and down the corridor, and decided against following the guards. Since he knew himself to be totally lost already, any direction was probably an improvement. He edged past the dragon and hurried away, the huge beast turning with difficulty to follow him.

They padded down a series of passages that criss-crossed like a maze. At one point Twoflower thought he heard shouts, a long way behind them, but they soon faded away. Sometimes the dark arch of a crumbling doorway loomed past them in the gloom. Light filtered through dimly from various shafts and, here and there, bounced off big mirrors that had been mortared into angles of the passage. Sometimes there was a brighter glow from a distant light-well.

What was odd, thought Twoflower as he strolled down a wide flight of stairs and kicked up billowing clouds of silver dust motes, was that the tunnels here were much wider. And better constructed, too. There were statues in niches set in the walls, and here and there faded but interesting tapestries had been hung. They mainly showed dragons – dragons by the hundred, in flight or hanging from their perch rings, dragons with men on their backs hunting down deer and, sometimes, other men. Twoflower touched one tapestry gingerly. The fabric crumbled instantly in the hot dry air, leaving only a dangling mesh where some threads had been plaited with fine gold wire.

'I wonder why they left all this?' he said.

I don't know, said a polite voice in his head.

He turned and looked up into the scaly horse face above him.

'What is your name, dragon?' said Twoflower.

I don't know.

'I think I shall call you Ninereeds.'

That is my name, then.

They waded through the all-encroaching dust in a series of huge, dark-pillared halls which had been carved out of the solid rock. With some cunning too: from floor to ceiling the walls were a mass of statues, gargoyles, bas-reliefs and fluted columns that cast weirdly moving shadows when the dragon gave an obliging illumination at Twoflower's request. They crossed the lengthy galleries and vast carven amphitheatres, all awash with deep soft dust and completely uninhabited. No-one had come to these dead caverns in centuries.

Then he saw the path, leading away into yet another dark tunnel mouth. Someone had been using it regularly, and recently. It was a deep narrow trail in the grey blanket.

Twoflower followed it. It led through still more lofty halls and winding corridors quite big enough for a dragon (and dragons had come this way once, it seemed; there was a room full of rotting harness, dragon-sized, and another room containing plate armour and chain mail big enough for elephants). They ended in a pair of green bronze doors, each so high that they disappeared into the gloom. In front of Twoflower, at chest height, was a small handle shaped like a brass dragon.

When he touched it the doors swung open instantly and with a disconcerting noiselessness.

Instantly sparks crackled in Twoflower's hair and there was a sudden gust of hot dry wind that didn't disturb the dust in the way that ordinary wind should but, instead, whipped it up momentarily into unpleasantly half-living shapes before it settled again.

In Twoflower's ears came the strange shrill twittering of the Things locked in the distant dungeon Dimensions, out beyond the fragile lattice of time and space. Shadows appeared where there was nothing to cause them. The air buzzed like a hive.

In short, there was a vast discharge of magic going on around him.

The chamber beyond the door was lit by a pale green glow. Stacked around the walls, each on its own marble shelf, were tier upon tier of coffins. In the centre of the room was a stone chair on a raised dais, and it contained a slumped figure which did not move but said, in a brittle old voice, 'Come in, young man.'

Twoflower stepped forward. The figure in the seat was human, as far as he could make out in the murky light, but there was something about the awkward way it was sprawled in the chair that made him glad he couldn't see it any clearer.

'I'm dead, you know,' came a voice from what Twoflower fervently hoped was a head, in conversational tones. 'I expect you can tell.'

'Um,' said Twoflower. 'Yes.' He began to back away.

'Obvious, isn't it?' agreed the voice. 'You'd be Twoflower, wouldn't you? Or is that later?'

'Later?' said Twoflower. 'Later than what?' He stopped.

'Well,' said the voice. 'You see, one of the disadvantages of being dead is that one is released as it were from the bonds of time and therefore I can see everything that has happened or will happen, all at the same time except that of course I now know that Time does not, for all practical purposes, exist.'

'That doesn't sound like a disadvantage,' said Twoflower.

'You don't think so? Imagine every moment being at one and the same time a distant memory and a nasty surprise and you'll see what I mean. Anyway, I now recall what it was I am about to tell you. Or have I already done so? That's a fine looking dragon, by the way. Or don't I say that yet?'

'It is rather good. It just turned up,' said Twoflower.

'It turned up?' said the voice. 'You summoned it!'

'Yes, well, all I did—'

'You have the Power!'

'All I did was think of it.'

'That's what the Power is! Have I already told you that I am Greicha the First? Or is that next? I'm sorry, but I haven't had too much experience of transcendence. Anyway, yes – the Power. It summons dragons, you know.'

'I think you already told me that,' said Twoflower.

'Did I? I certainly intended to,' said the dead man.

'But *how* does it? I've been thinking about dragons all my life, but this is the first time one has turned up.'

'Oh well, you see, the truth of the matter is that dragons have never existed as you (and, until I was poisoned some three months ago, *I*) understand existence. I'm talking about the true dragon, *draconis nobilis*, you understand; the swamp dragon, *draconis vulgaris*, is a base creature and not worth our consideration. The *true* dragon, on the other hand, is a creature of such refinement of spirit that they can only take on form in this world if they are conceived by the most skilled imagination. And even then the said imagination must be in some place heavily impregnated with magic, which helps to weaken the walls between the world of the seen and unseen. Then the dragons pop through, as it were, and impress their form on this world's possibility matrix. I was very good at it when I was alive. I could imagine up to, oh, five hundred dragons at a time. Now Liessa, the most skilled of my children, can barely imagine fifty rather nondescript creatures. So much for a progressive education. She doesn't really *believe* in them. That's why her dragons are rather boring – while yours,' said the voice of Greicha, 'is almost as good as some of mine used to be. A sight for sore eyes, not that I have any to speak of now.'

Twoflower said hurriedly, 'You keep saying you're dead . . .'

'Well?'

'Well, the dead, er, they, you know, don't talk much. As a rule.'

'I used to be an exceptionally powerful wizard. My daughter poisoned me, of course. It is the generally accepted method of succession in our family, but,' the corpse sighed, or at least a sigh came from the air a few feet above it, 'it soon became obvious that none of my three children is sufficiently powerful to wrest the lordship of the Wyrmberg from the other two. A most unsatisfactory arrangement. A kingdom like ours has to have one ruler. So I resolved to remain alive in an unofficial capacity, which of course annoys them all immensely. I won't give my children the satisfaction of burying me until there is only one of them left to perform the ceremony.' There was a nasty wheezing noise. Twoflower decided that it was meant to be a chuckle.

'So it was one of them that kidnapped us?' said Twoflower.

'Liessa,' said the dead wizard's voice. 'My daughter. Her power is strongest, you know. My sons' dragons are incapable of flying more than a few miles before they fade.'

'Fade? I did notice that we could see through the one that brought us here,' said Twoflower. 'I thought that was a bit odd.'

'Of course,' said Greicha. 'The Power only works near the Wyrmberg. It's the inverse square law, you know. At least, I think it is. As the dragons fly further away they begin to *dwindle.* Otherwise my little Liessa would be ruling the whole world by now, if I know anything about it. But I can see I mustn't keep you. I expect you'll be wanting to rescue your friend.'

Twoflower gaped. 'Hrun?' he said.

'Not him. The skinny wizard. My son Lio!rt is trying to hack him to pieces. I admired the way you rescued him. Will, I mean.'

Twoflower drew himself up to his full height, an easy task. 'Where is he?' he said, heading towards the door with what he hoped was an heroic stride.

'Just follow the pathway in the dust,' said the voice. 'Liessa comes to see me sometimes. She still comes to see her old dad, my little girl. She was the only one with the strength of character to murder me. A chip off the old block. Good luck, by the way. I seem to recall I said that. Will say it now, I mean.'

The rambling voice got lost in a maze of tenses as Twoflower ran along the dead tunnels, with the dragon loping along easily behind him. But soon he was leaning against a pillar, completely out of breath. It seemed ages since he'd had anything to eat.

Why don't you fly? said Ninereeds, inside his head. The dragon spread its wings and gave an experimental flap, which lifted it momentarily off the ground. Twoflower stared for a moment, then ran forward and clambered quickly on to the beast's neck. Soon they were airborne, the dragon skimming along easily a few feet from the floor and leaving a billowing cloud of dust in its wake.

Twoflower hung on as best he could as Ninereeds swooped through a succession of caverns and soared around a spiral staircase that could easily have accommodated a retreating army. At the top they emerged into the more inhabited regions, the mirrors at every corridor corner brightly polished and reflecting a pale light.

I smell other dragons.

The wings became a blur and Twoflower was jerked back as the dragon veered and sped off down a side corridor like a gnat-crazed swallow. Another sharp turn sent them soaring out of a tunnel mouth in the side of a vast cavern. There were rocks far below, and up above were broad shafts of light from great holes near the roof. A lot of activity on the ceiling, too . . . as Ninereeds hovered, thumping the air with his wings, Twoflower peered up at the shapes of roosting beasts and tiny man-shaped dots that were somehow walking upside down.

This is a roosting hall, said the dragon in a satisfied tone.

As Twoflower watched, one of the shapes far above detached itself from the roof and began to grow larger . . .

Rincewind watched as Lio!rt's pale face dropped away from him. This is funny, gibbered a small part of his mind, why am I rising?

Then he began to tumble in the air and reality took over. He was dropping to the distant, guano-speckled rocks.

His brain reeled with the thought. The words of the spell picked just that moment to surface from the depths of his mind, as they always did in time of crisis. Why not say us, they seemed to urge. What have you got to lose?

Rincewind waved a hand in the gathering slip-stream.

'Ashonai,' he called. The word formed in front of him in a cold blue flame that streamed in the wind.

He waved the other hand, drunk with terror and magic.

'Ebiris,' he intoned. The sound froze into a flickering orange word that hung beside its companion.

'Urshoring, Kvanti. Pythan. N'gurad. Feringomalee.' As the words blazed their rainbow colours around him he flung his hands back and prepared to say the eighth and final word that would appear in coruscating octarine and seal the spell. The imminent rocks were forgotten.

'—' he began.

The breath was knocked out of him, the spell scattered and snuffed out. A pair of arms locked around his waist and the whole world jerked sideways as the dragon rose out of its long dive, claws grazing just for a moment the topmost rock on the Wyrmberg's noisome floor. Twoflower laughed triumphantly.

'Got him!'

And the dragon, curving gracefully at the top of his flight, gave a lazy flip of his wings and soared through a cavemouth into the morning air.

At noon, in a wide green meadow on the lush tableland that was the top of the impossibly balanced Wyrmberg, the dragons and their riders formed a wide circle. There was room beyond them for a rabble of servants and slaves and others who scratched a living here on the roof of the world, and they were all watching the figures clustered in the centre of the grassy arena.

The group contained a number of senior dragonlords, and among them were Lio!rt and his brother Liartes. The former was still rubbing his legs, with small grimaces of pain. Slightly to one side stood Liessa and Hrun, with some of the woman's own followers. Between the two factions stood the Wyrmberg's hereditary Loremaster.

'As you know,' he said uncertainly, 'the not-fully-late Lord of the Wyrmberg, Greicha the First, has stipulated that there will be no succession until one of his children feels himself – or as it might be, herself – powerful enough to challenge and defeat his or her siblings in mortal combat.'

'Yes, yes, we know all that. Get on with it,' said a thin peevish voice from the air beside him.

The Loremaster swallowed. He had never come to terms with his former master's failure to expire properly. Is the old buzzard dead or isn't he? he wondered.

'It is not certain,' he quavered, 'whether it is allowable to issue a challenge by proxy—'

'It is, it is,' snapped Greicha's disembodied voice. 'It shows intelligence. Don't take all day about it.'

'I challenge you,' said Hrun, glaring at the brothers, 'both at once.'

Lio!rt and Liartes exchanged looks.

'You'll fight us both together?' said Liartes, a tall, wiry man with long black hair.

'Yah.'

'That's pretty uneven odds, isn't it?'

'Yah. I outnumber you one to two.'

Lio!rt scowled. 'You arrogant barbarian—'

'That just about does it!' growled Hrun. 'I'll—'

The Loremaster put out a blue-veined hand to restrain him.

'It is forbidden to fight on the Killing Ground,' he said, and paused while he considered the sense of this. 'You know what I mean, anyway,' he hazarded, giving up, and added: 'As the challenged parties my lords Lio!rt and Liartes have choice of weapons.'

'Dragons,' they said together. Liessa snorted.

'Dragons can be used offensively, therefore they are weapons,' said Lio!rt firmly. 'If you disagree we can fight over it.'

'Yah,' said his brother, nodding at Hrun.

The Loremaster felt a ghostly finger prod him in the chest.

'Don't stand there with your mouth open,' said Greicha's graveyard voice. 'Just hurry up, will you?'

Hrun stepped back, shaking his head.

'Oh no,' he said. 'Once was enough. I'd rather be dead than fight on one of those things.'

'Die, then,' said the Loremaster, as kindly as he could manage.

Lio!rt and Liartes were already striding back across the turf to where the servants stood waiting with their mounts. Hrun turned to Liessa. She shrugged.

'Don't I even get a sword?' he pleaded. 'A knife, even?'

'No,' she said. 'I didn't expect this.' She suddenly looked smaller, all defiance gone. 'I'm sorry.'

'*You're* sorry?'

'Yes. I'm sorry.'

'Yes, I thought you said you're sorry.'

'Don't glare at me like that! I can imagine you the finest dragon to ride—'

'No!'

The Loremaster wiped his nose on a handkerchief, held the little silken square aloft for a moment, then let it fall.

A boom of wings made Hrun spin around. Lio!rt's dragon was already airborne and circling around towards them. As it swooped low over the turf a billow of flame shot from its mouth, scoring a black streak across the grass that rushed towards Hrun.

At the last minute he pushed Liessa aside, and felt the wild pain of the flame on his arm as he dived for safety. He rolled as he hit the ground, and flipped on to his feet again while he looked around frantically for the other dragon. It came in from one side, and Hrun was forced to take a badly judged standing jump to escape the flame. The dragon's tail whipped around as it passed and caught him a stinging blow across the forehead. He pushed himself upright, shaking his head to make the wheeling stars go away. His blistered back screamed pain at him.

Lio!rt came in for a second run, but slower this time to allow for the big man's unexpected agility. As the ground drifted up he saw the barbarian standing stock still, chest heaving, arms hanging loosely by his sides. An easy target.

As his dragon swooped away Lio!rt turned his head, expecting to see a dreadfully big cinder.

There was nothing there. Puzzled, Lio!rt turned back.

Hrun, heaving himself over the dragon's shoulder scales with one hand and beating out his flaming hair with the other, presented himself to his view. Lio!rt's hand flew to his dagger, but pain had sharpened Hrun's normally excellent reflexes to needle point. A backhand blow hammered into the dragonlord's wrist, sending the dagger arcing away towards the ground, and another caught the man full on the chin.

The dragon, carrying the weight of two men, was only a few yards above the grass. This turned out to be fortunate, because at the moment Lio!rt lost consciousness the dragon winked out of existence.

Liessa hurried across the grass and helped Hrun stagger to his feet. He blinked at her.

'What happened? What happened?' he said thickly.

'That was really fantastic!' she said. 'The way you turned that somersault in mid-air and everything!'

'Yah, but what *happened*?'

'It's rather difficult to explain—'

Hrun peered up at the sky. Liartes, by far the more cautious of the two brothers, was circling high above them.

'Well, you've got about ten seconds to try,' he said.

'The dragons—'

'Yah?'

'They're imaginary.'

'Like all these imaginary burns on my arm, you mean?'

'Yes. No!' she shook her head violently. 'I'll have to tell you later!'

'Fine, if you can find a really good medium,' snapped Hrun. He glared up at Liartes, who was beginning to descend in wide sweeps.

'Just *listen*, will you? Unless my brother is conscious his dragon can't exist, it's got no pathway through to this—'

'Run!' shouted Hrun. He threw her away from him and flung himself flat on the ground as Liartes' dragon thundered by, leaving another smoking scar across the turf.

While the creature sought height for another sweep Hrun scrambled to his feet and set off at a dead run for the woods at the edge of the arena. They were sparse, little more than a wide and overgrown hedge, but at least no dragon would be able to fly through them.

It didn't try. Liartes brought his mount in to land on the turf a few yards away and dismounted casually. The dragon folded its wings and poked its head in among the greenery, while its master leaned against a tree and whistled tunelessly.

'I can burn you out,' said Liartes, after a while.

The bushes remained motionless.

'Perhaps you're in that holly bush over there?'

The holly bush became a waxy ball of flame.

'I'm sure I can see movement in those ferns.'

The ferns became mere skeletons of white ash.

'You're only prolonging it, barbarian. Why not give in now? I've burned lots of people; it doesn't hurt a bit,' said Liartes, looking sideways at the bushes.

The dragon continued through the spinney, incinerating every likely-looking bush and clump of ferns. Liartes drew his sword and waited.

Hrun dropped from a tree and landed running. Behind him the dragon roared and crashed through the bushes as it tried to turn around, but Hrun was running, running, with his gaze fixed on Liartes and a dead branch in his hands.

It is a little known but true fact that a two-legged creature can usually beat a four-legged creature over a short distance, simply because of the time it takes the quadruped to get its legs sorted out. Hrun heard the scrabble of claws behind him and then an ominous thump. The dragon had half-opened its wings and was trying to fly.

As Hrun bore down on the dragonlord Liartes' sword came up wickedly, to be caught on the branch.

Then Hrun cannoned into him and the two men sprawled on the ground.

The dragon roared.

Liartes screamed as Hrun brought a knee upwards with anatomical precision, but managed a wild blow that rebroke the barbarian's nose for him.

Hrun kicked away and scrambled to his feet, to find himself looking up into the wild horse-face of the dragon, its nostrils distended.

He lashed out with a foot and caught Liartes, who was trying to stand up, on the side of his head. The man slumped.

The dragon vanished. The ball of fire that was billowing towards Hrun faded until, when it reached him, it was no more than a puff of warm air. Then there was no sound but the crackle of burning bushes.

Hrun slung the unconscious dragonlord over his shoulder and set off at a trot back to the arena. Halfway there he found Lio!rt sprawled on the ground, one leg bent awkwardly. He stooped and, with a grunt, hoisted the man on to his vacant shoulder.

Liessa and the Loremaster were waiting on a raised dais at one end of the meadow. The dragonwoman had quite recovered her composure now, and looked levelly at Hrun as he threw the two men down on the steps before her. The people around her were standing in deferential poses, like a court.

'Kill them,' she said.

'I kill in my own time,' he said. 'In any case, killing unconscious people isn't right.'

'I can't think of a more opportune time,' said the Loremaster. Liessa snorted.

'Then I shall banish them,' she said. 'Once they are beyond the reach of the Wyrmberg's magic then they'll have no Power. They'll be simply brigands. Will that satisfy you?'

'Yes.'

'I am surprised that you are so merciful, ba—Hrun.'

Hrun shrugged. 'A man in my position, he can't afford to be anything else, he's got to consider his image.' He looked around. 'Where's the next test, then?'

'I warn you that it is perilous. If you wish, you may leave now. If you pass the test, however, you will become Lord of the Wyrmberg and, of course, my lawful husband.'

Hrun met her gaze. He thought about his life, to date. It suddenly seemed to him to have been full of long damp nights sleeping under the stars, desperate fights with trolls, city guards, countless bandits and evil priests and, on at least three occasions, actual demigods – and for what? Well, for quite a lot of treasure, he had to admit – but where had it all gone? Rescuing beleaguered maidens had a certain passing reward, but most of the time he'd finished up by setting them up in some city somewhere with a handsome dowry, because after a while even the most agreeable ex-maiden became possessive and had scant sympathy for his efforts to rescue her sister sufferers. In short, life had really left him with little more than a reputation and a network of scars. Being a lord might be fun. Hrun grinned. With a base like this, all these dragons and a good bunch of fighting men, a man could really be a contender.

Besides, the wench was not uncomely.

'The third test?' she said.

'Am I to be weaponless again?' said Hrun.

Liessa reached up and removed her helmet, letting the coils of red hair tumble out. Then she unfastened the brooch of her robe. Underneath, she was naked.

As Hrun's gaze swept over her his mind began to operate two notional counting machines. One assessed the gold in her bangles, the tiger-rubies that ornamented her toe-rings, the diamond spangle that adorned her navel, and two highly individual whirligigs of silver filigree. The other was plugged straight into his libido. Both produced tallies that pleased him mightily.

As she raised a hand and proffered a glass of wine she smiled, and said, 'I think not.'

'He didn't attempt to rescue you,' Rincewind pointed out as a last resort.

He clung desperately to Twoflower's waist as the dragon circled slowly, tilting the world at a dangerous angle. The new knowledge that the scaly back he was astride only existed as a sort of three-dimensional daydream did not, he had soon realized, do anything at all for his ankle-wrenching sensations of vertigo. His mind kept straying towards the possible results of Twoflower losing his concentration.

'Not even Hrun could have prevailed against those crossbows,' said Twoflower stoutly.

As the dragon rose higher above the patch of woodland, where the three of them had slept a damp and uneasy sleep, the sun rose over the edge of the disc.

Instantly the gloomy blues and greys of pre-dawn were transformed into a bright bronze river that flowed across the world, flaring into gold where it struck ice or water or a light-dam. (Owing to the density of the magical field surrounding the disc, light itself moved at sub-sonic speeds; this interesting property was well utilized by the Sorca people of the Great Nef, for example, who over the centuries had constructed intricate and delicate dams, and valleys walled with polished silica, to catch the slow sunlight and sort of *store* it. The scintillating reservoirs of the Nef, overflowing after several weeks of uninterrupted sunlight, were a truly magnificent sight from the air and it is therefore unfortunate that Twoflower and Rincewind did not happen to glance in that direction.)

In front of them the billion-ton impossibility that was the magic-wrought Wyrmberg hung against the sky and that was not too bad, until Rincewind turned his head and saw the mountain's shadow slowly unroll itself across the cloudscape of the world . . .

'What can you see?' said Twoflower to the dragon.

I see fighting on the top of the mountain came the gentle reply.

'See?' said Twoflower. 'Hrun's probably fighting for his life at this very moment.'

Rincewind was silent. After a moment Twoflower looked around. The wizard was staring intently at nothing at all, his lips moving soundlessly.

'Rincewind?'

The wizard made a small croaking noise.

'I'm sorry,' said Twoflower. 'What did you say?'

'... all the way ... the great fall ...' muttered Rincewind. His eyes focused, looked puzzled for a moment, then widened in terror. He made the mistake of looking down.

'Aargh,' he opined, and began to slide. Twoflower grabbed him.

'What's the matter?'

Rincewind tried shutting his eyes, but there were no eyelids to his imagination and it was staring widely.

'Don't you get scared of heights?' he managed to say.

Twoflower looked down at the tiny landscape, mottled with cloud shadows. The thought of fear hadn't actually occurred to him.

'No,' he said. 'Why should I? You're just as dead if you fall from forty feet as you are from four thousand fathoms, that's what I say.'

Rincewind tried to consider this dispassionately, but couldn't see the logic of it. It wasn't the actual falling, it was the *hitting* he ...

Twoflower grabbed him quickly.

'Steady on,' he said cheerfully. 'We're nearly there.'

'I wish I was back in the city,' moaned Rincewind. 'I wish I was back on the ground!'

'I wonder if dragons can fly all the way to the stars?' mused Twoflower. 'Now *that* would be something ...'

'You're mad,' said Rincewind flatly. There was no reply from the tourist, and when the wizard craned around he was horrified to see Twoflower looking up at the paling stars with an odd smile on his face.

'Don't you even think about it,' added Rincewind, menacingly.

The man you seek is talking to the dragonwoman said the dragon.

'Hmm?' said Twoflower, still looking at the paling stars.

'What?' said Rincewind urgently.

'Oh yes. Hrun,' said Twoflower. 'I hope we're in time. Dive now! Go low!'

Rincewind opened his eyes as the wind increased to a whistling gale. Perhaps they were blown open – the wind certainly made them impossible to shut.

The flat summit of the Wyrmberg rose up at them, lurched alarmingly, then somersaulted into a green blur that flashed by on either side. Tiny woods and fields blurred into a rushing patchwork. A brief silvery flash in the landscape may have been the little river that overflowed into the air at the plateau's rim. Rincewind tried to force the memory out of his mind, but it was rather enjoying itself there, terrorizing the other occupants and kicking over the furniture.

'I think not,' said Liessa.

Hrun took the wine cup, slowly. He grinned like a pumpkin.

Around the arena the dragons started to bay. Their riders looked up. And something like a green blur flashed across the arena, and Hrun had gone.

The wine cup hung momentarily in the air, then crashed down on the steps. Only then did a single drop spill.

This was because, in the instant of enfolding Hrun gently in his claws, Ninereeds the dragon had momentarily synchronized their bodily rhythms.

Since the dimension of the imagination is much more complex than those of time and space, which are very junior dimensions indeed, the effect of this was to instantly transform a stationary and priapic Hrun into a Hrun moving sideways at eighty miles an hour with no ill-effects whatsoever, except for a few wasted mouthfuls of wine. Another effect was to cause Liessa to scream with rage and summon her dragon. As the gold beast materialized in front of her she leapt astride it, still naked, and snatched a crossbow from one of the guards. Then she was airborne, while the other dragonriders swarmed towards their own beasts.

The Loremaster, watching from the pillar he had prudently slid behind in the mad scramble, happened at that moment to catch the cross-dimensional echoes of a theory being at the same instant hatched in the mind of an early psychiatrist in an adjacent universe, possibly because the dimension-leak was flowing both ways, and for a moment the psychiatrist saw the girl on the dragon. The Loremaster smiled.

'Want to bet that she won't catch him?' said Greicha, in a voice of worms and sepulchres, right by his ear.

The Loremaster shut his eyes and swallowed hard.

'I thought that my Lord would now be residing fully in the Dread Land,' he managed.

'I am a wizard,' said Greicha. 'Death Himself must claim a wizard. And, aha, He doesn't appear to be in the neighbourhood . . .'

SHALL WE GO? asked Death.

He was on a white horse, a horse of flesh and blood

but red of eye and fiery of nostril, and He stretched out a bony hand and took Greicha's soul out of the air and rolled it up until it was a point of painful light, and then He swallowed it.

Then He clapped spurs to his steed and it sprang into the air, sparks coruscating from its hooves.

'Lord Greicha!' whispered the old Loremaster, as the universe flickered around him.

'That was a mean trick,' came the wizard's voice, a mere speck of sound disappearing into the infinite black dimensions.

'My Lord . . . what is Death like?' called the old man tremulously.

'When I have investigated it fully, I will let you know,' came the faintest of modulations on the breeze.

'Yes,' murmured the Loremaster. A thought struck him. 'During daylight, please,' he added.

'You clowns,' screamed Hrun, from his perch on Ninereeds' foreclaws.

'What did he say?' roared Rincewind, as the dragon ripped its way through the air in the race for the heights.

'Didn't hear!' bellowed Twoflower, his voice torn away by the gale. As the dragon banked slightly he looked down at the little toy spinning top that was the mighty Wyrmberg and saw the swarm of creatures rising in pursuit. Ninereeds' wings pounded and flicked the air away contemptuously. Thinner air, too. Twoflower's ear popped for the third time.

Ahead of the swarm, he noticed, was a golden dragon. Someone on it, too.

'Hey, are you all right?' said Rincewind urgently. He had to drink in several lungfuls of the strangely distilled air in order to get the words out.

'I could have been a lord, and you clowns had to go and—' Hrun gasped, as the chill thin air drew the life even out of his mighty chest.

'Wass happnin to the air?' muttered Rincewind. Blue lights appeared in front of his eyes.

'Unk,' said Twoflower, and passed out.

The dragon vanished.

For a few seconds the three men continued upwards, Twoflower and the wizard presenting an odd picture as they sat one in front of the other with their legs astride something that wasn't there. Then what passed for gravity on the disc recovered from the surprise, and claimed them.

At that moment Liessa's dragon flashed by, and Hrun landed heavily across its neck. Liessa leaned over and kissed him.

This detail was lost to Rincewind as he dropped away, with his arms still clasped around Twoflower's waist. The disc was a little round map pinned against the sky. It didn't appear to be moving, but Rincewind knew that it was. The whole world was coming towards him like a giant custard pie.

'Wake up!' he shouted, above the roar of the wind. 'Dragons! Think of dragons!'

There was a flurry of wings as they plummeted through the host of pursuing creatures, which fell away and up. Dragons screamed and wheeled across the sky.

No answer came from Twoflower. Rincewind's robe whipped around him, but he did not wake.

Dragons, thought Rincewind in a panic. He tried to concentrate his mind, tried to envisage a really lifelike dragon. If he can do it, he thought, then so can I. But nothing happened.

The disc was bigger now, a cloud-swirled circle rising gently underneath them.

Rincewind tried again, screwing up his eyes and straining every nerve in his body. A dragon. His imagination, a somewhat battered and over-used organ, reached out for a dragon . . . any dragon.

IT WON'T WORK, laughed a voice like the dull tolling of a funereal bell, YOU DON'T BELIEVE IN THEM.

Rincewind looked at the terrible mounted apparition grinning at him, and his mind bolted in terror.

There was a brilliant flash.

There was utter darkness.

There was a soft floor under Rincewind's feet, a pink light around him, and the sudden shocked cries of many people.

He looked around wildly. He was standing in some kind of tunnel, which was mostly filled with seats in which outlandishly dressed people had been strapped. They were all shouting at him.

'Wake up!' he hissed. 'Help me!'

Dragging the still-unconscious tourist with him he backed away from the mob until his free hand found an oddly shaped door handle. He twisted it and ducked through, then slammed it hard.

He stared around the new room in which he found himself and met the terrified gaze of a young woman who dropped the tray she was holding and screamed.

It sounded like the sort of scream that brings muscular help. Rincewind, awash with fear-distilled adrenalin, turned and barged past her. There were more seats here, and the people in them ducked as he dragged Twoflower urgently along the central gangway. Beyond the rows of seats were little windows. Beyond the windows, against a background of fleecy clouds, was a dragon's wing. It was silver.

I've been eaten by a dragon, he thought. That's ridiculous, he replied, you can't see out of dragons. Then his shoulder hit the door at the far end of the tunnel, and he followed it through into a cone-shaped room that was even stranger than the tunnel.

It was full of tiny glittering lights. Among the lights, in contoured chairs, were four men who were now staring at him open-mouthed. As he stared back he saw their gazes dart sideways.

Rincewind turned slowly. Beside him was a fifth man – youngish, bearded, as swarthy as the nomad folk of the Great Nef.

'Where am I?' said the wizard. 'In the belly of a dragon?'

The young man crouched back and shoved a small black box in the wizard's face. The men in the chairs ducked down.

'What is it?' said Rincewind. 'A picturebox?' He reached out and took it, a movement which appeared to surprise the swarthy man, who shouted and tried to snatch it back. There was another shout, this time from one of the men in the chairs. Only now he wasn't sitting. He was standing up, pointing something small and metallic at the young man.

It had an amazing effect. The man crouched back with his hands in the air.

'Please give me the bomb, sir,' said the man with the metallic thing. 'Carefully, please.'

'This thing?' said Rincewind. 'You have it! I don't want it!' The man took it very carefully and put it on the floor. The seated men relaxed, and one of them started speaking urgently to the wall. The wizard watched him in amazement.

'*Don't move!*' snapped the man with the metal – an amulet, Rincewind decided, it must be an amulet. The swarthy man backed into the corner.

'That was a very brave thing you did,' said Amulet-holder to Rincewind. 'You know that?'

'What?'

'What's the matter with your friend?'

'Friend?'

Rincewind looked down at Twoflower, who was still slumbering peacefully. That was no surprise. What was *really* surprising was that Twoflower was wearing new clothes. Strange clothes. His britches now ended just above his knees. Above that he wore some sort of vest of brightly striped material. On his head was a ridiculous little straw hat. With a feather in it.

An awkward feeling around the leg regions made Rincewind look down. *His* clothes had changed too. Instead of the comfortable old robe, so marvellously well adapted for speed into action in all possible contingencies, his legs were encased in cloth tubes. He was wearing a jacket of the same grey material . . .

Until now he'd never heard the language the man

with the amulet was using. It was uncouth and vaguely Hublandish – so why could he understand every word?

Let's see, they'd suddenly appeared in this dragon after, they'd materialized in this drag, they'd sudd, they'd, they'd – *they had struck up a conversation in the airport so naturally they had chosen to sit together on the plane, and he'd promised to show Jack Zweiblumen around when they got back to the States.* Yes, that was it. And then Jack had been taken ill and he'd panicked and come through here and surprised this hijacker. Of course. What on earth was 'Hublandish'?

Dr Rjinswand rubbed his forehead. What he could do with was a drink.

Ripples of paradox spread out across the sea of causality.

Possibly the most important point that would have to be borne in mind by anyone outside the sum totality of the multiverse was that although the wizard and the tourist had indeed only recently appeared in an aircraft in mid-air, they had also at one and the same time been riding on that aeroplane in the normal course of things. That is to say: while it was true that they had just appeared in this particular set of dimensions, it was also true that they had been living in them all along. It is at this point that normal language gives up, and goes and has a drink.

The point is that several quintillion atoms had just materialized (however, they had not. See below) in a universe where they should not strictly have been. The usual upshot of this sort of thing is a vast explosion but, since universes are fairly resilient things, this particular universe had saved itself by instantaneously unravelling its space-time continuum back to a point where the surplus atoms could safely be accommodated and then rapidly rewinding back to that circle of firelight which for want of a better term its inhabitants were wont to call The Present. This had of course changed history – there had been a few less wars, a few extra dinosaurs and so on – but on the whole the episode passed remarkably quietly.

Outside of this particular universe, however, the repercussions of the sudden double-take bounced to and fro across the face of The Sum of Things, bending whole dimensions and sinking galaxies without a trace.

All this was however totally lost on Dr Rjinswand, 33, a bachelor, born in Sweden, raised in New Jersey, and a specialist in the breakaway oxidation phenomena of certain nuclear reactors. Anyway, he probably would not have believed any of it.

Zweiblumen still seemed to be unconscious. The stewardess, who had helped Rjinswand to his seat to the applause of the rest of the passengers, was bending over him anxiously.

'We've radioed ahead,' she told Rjinswand. 'There'll be an ambulance waiting when we land. Uh, it says on the passenger list that you're a doctor—'

'I don't know what's wrong with him,' said Rjinswand hurriedly. 'It might be a different matter if he was a Magnox reactor of course. Is it shock of some kind?'

'I've never—'

Her sentence terminated in a tremendous crash from the rear of the plane. Several passengers screamed. A sudden gale of air swept every loose magazine and newspaper into a screaming whirlwind that twisted madly down the aisle.

Something else was coming *up* the aisle. Something big and oblong and wooden and brass-bound. It had hundreds of legs. If it was what it seemed – a walking chest of the kind that appeared in pirate stories brim full of ill-gotten gold and jewels – then what would have been its lid suddenly gaped open.

There were no jewels. But there *were* lots of big square teeth, white as sycamore, and a pulsating tongue, red as mahogany.

An ancient suitcase was coming to eat him.

Rjinswand clutched at the unconscious Zweiblumen for what little comfort there was there, and gibbered. He wished fervently that he was somewhere else . . .

There was a sudden darkness.

There was a brilliant flash.

The sudden departure of several quintillion atoms from a universe that they had no right to be in anyway caused a wild imbalance in the harmony of the Sum Totality which it tried frantically to retrieve, wiping out a number of sub-realities in the process. Huge surges of raw magic boiled uncontrolled around the very foundations of the multiverse itself, welling up through every crevice into hitherto peaceful dimensions and causing novas, supernovas, stellar collisions, wild flights of geese and drowning of imaginary continents. Worlds as far away as the other end of time experienced brilliant sunsets of coruscating octarine as highly charged magical particles roared through the atmosphere. In the cometary halo around the fabled Ice System of Zeret a noble comet died as a prince flamed across the sky.

All this was however lost on Rincewind as, clutching the inert Twoflower around the waist, he plunged towards the Disc's sea several hundred feet below. Not even the convulsions of all the dimensions could break the iron Law of the Conservation of Energy, and Rjinswand's brief journey in the plane had sufficed to carry him several hundred miles horizontally and seven thousand feet vertically.

The world 'plane' flamed and died in Rincewind's mind.

Was that a ship down there?

The cold waters of the Circle Sea roared up at him and sucked him down into their green, suffocating embrace. A moment later there was another splash as the Luggage, still bearing a label carrying the powerful travelling rune TWA, also hit the sea.

Later on, they used it as a raft.

Close to the Edge

IT HAD BEEN A LONG time in the making. Now it was almost completed, and the slaves hacked away at the last clay remnants of the mantle.

Where other slaves were industriously rubbing its metal flanks with silver sand it was already beginning to gleam in the sun with the silken, organic sheen of young bronze. It was still warm, even after a week of cooling in the casting pit.

The Arch-astronomer of Krull motioned lightly with his hand and his bearers set the throne down in the shadow of the hull.

Like a fish, he thought. A great flying fish. And of what seas?

'It is indeed magnificent,' he whispered. 'A work of true art.'

'Craft,' said the thickset man by his side. The Arch-astronomer turned slowly and looked up at the man's impassive face. It isn't particularly hard for a face to look impassive when there are two golden spheres where the eyes should be. They glowed disconcertingly.

'Craft, indeed,' said the astronomer, and smiled. 'I would imagine that there is no greater craftsman on the entire disc than you, Goldeneyes. Would I be right?'

The craftsman paused, his naked body – naked, at

least, were it not for a toolbelt, a wrist abacus and a deep tan – tensing as he considered the implications of this last remark. The golden eyes appeared to be looking into some other world.

'The answer is both yes and no,' he said at last. Some of the lesser astronomers behind the throne gasped at this lack of etiquette, but the Arch-astronomer appeared not to have noticed it.

'Continue,' he said.

'There are some essential skills that I lack. Yet I am Goldeneyes Silverhand Dactylos,' said the craftsman. 'I made the Metal Warriors that guard the Tomb of Pitchiu, I designed the Light Dams of the Great Nef, I built the Palace of the Seven Deserts. And yet—' he reached up and tapped one of his eyes, which rang faintly, 'when I built the golem army for Pitchiu he loaded me down with gold and then, so that I would create no other work to rival my work for him, he had my eyes put out.'

'Wise but cruel,' said the Arch-astronomer sympathetically.

'Yah. So I learned to *hear* the temper of metals and to see with my fingers. I learned how to distinguish ores by taste and smell. I made these eyes, but I cannot make them see.

'Next I was summoned to build the Palace of the Seven Deserts, as a result of which the Emir showered me with silver and then, not entirely to my surprise, had my right hand cut off.'

'A grave hindrance in your line of business,' nodded the Arch-astronomer.

'I used some of the silver to make myself this new

hand, putting to use my unrivalled knowledge of levers and fulcrums. It suffices. After I created the first great Light Dam, which had a capacity of 50,000 day-light hours, the tribal councils of the Nef loaded me down with fine silks and then hamstrung me so that I could not escape. As a result I was put to some inconvenience to use the silk and some bamboo to build a flying machine from which I could launch myself from the top-most turret of my prison.'

'Bringing you, by various diversions, to Krull,' said the Arch-astronomer. 'And one cannot help feeling that some alternative occupation – lettuce farming, say – would offer somewhat less of a risk of being put to death by instalments. Why do you persist in it?'

Goldeneyes Dactylos shrugged.

'I'm good at it,' he said.

The Arch-astronomer looked up again at the bronze fish, shining now like a gong in the noontime sun.

'Such beauty,' he murmured. 'And unique. Come, Dactylos. Recall to me what it was that I promised should be your reward?'

'You asked me to design a fish that would swim through the seas of space that lie between the worlds,' intoned the master craftsman. 'In return for which – in return—'

'Yes? My memory is not what it used to be,' purred the Arch-astronomer, stroking the warm bronze.

'In return,' continued Dactylos, without much apparent hope, 'you would set me free, and refrain from chopping off any appendages. I require no treasure.'

'Ah, yes. I recall now.' The old man raised a blue-veined hand, and added, 'I lied.'

There was the merest whisper of sound, and the goldeneyed man rocked on his feet. Then he looked down at the arrowhead protruding from his chest, and nodded wearily. A speck of blood bloomed on his lips.

There was no sound in the entire square (save for the buzzing of a few expectant flies) as his silver hand came up, very slowly, and fingered the arrowhead.

Dactylos grunted.

'Sloppy workmanship,' he said, and toppled backwards.

The Arch-astronomer prodded the body with his toe, and sighed.

'There will be a short period of mourning, as befits a master craftsman,' he said. He watched a bluebottle alight on one golden eye and fly away puzzled . . . 'That would seem to be long enough,' said the Arch-astronomer, and beckoned a couple of slaves to carry the corpse away.

'Are the chelonauts ready?' he asked.

The Master Launchcontroller bustled forward.

'Indeed, your prominence,' he said.

'The correct prayers are being intoned?'

'Quite so, your prominence.'

'How long to the doorway?'

'The launch window,' corrected the Master Launch-controller carefully. 'Three days, your prominence. Great A'Tuin's tail will be in an unmatched position.'

'Then all that remains,' concluded the Arch-astronomer, 'is to find the appropriate sacrifices.'

The Master Launchcontroller bowed.

'The ocean shall provide,' he said.

The old man smiled. 'It always does,' he said.

'If only you could navigate—'

'If only you could steer—'

A wave washed over the deck. Rincewind and Twoflower looked at each other. 'Keep bailing!' they screamed in unison, and reached for the buckets.

After a while Twoflower's peevish voice filtered up from the waterlogged cabin.

'I don't see how it's my fault,' he said. He handed up another bucket, which the wizard tipped over the side.

'You were supposed to be on watch,' snapped Rincewind.

'I saved us from the slavers, remember,' said Twoflower.

'I'd rather be a slave than a corpse,' replied the wizard. He straightened up and looked out to sea. He appeared puzzled.

He was a somewhat different Rincewind from the one that had escaped the fire of Ankh-Morpork some six months before. More scarred, for one thing, and much more travelled. He had visited the Hublands, discovered the curious folkways of many colourful peoples – invariably obtaining more scars in the process – and had even, for a never-to-be-forgotten few days, sailed on the legendary Dehydrated Ocean at the heart of the incredibly dry desert known as the Great Nef. On a colder and wetter sea he had seen floating mountains of ice. He had ridden on an imaginary dragon. He had very nearly said the most powerful spell on the disc. He had—

There was *definitely* less horizon than there ought to be.

'Hmm?' said Rincewind.

'I said nothing's worse than slavery,' said Twoflower. His mouth opened as the wizard flung his bucket far out to sea and sat down heavily on the waterlogged deck, his face a grey mask.

'Look, I'm sorry I steered us into the reef, but this boat doesn't seem to want to sink and we're bound to strike land sooner or later,' said Twoflower comfortingly. 'This current must go somewhere.'

'Look at the horizon,' said Rincewind, in a monotone.

Twoflower squinted.

'It looks all right,' he said after a while. 'Admittedly, there seems to be *less* than there usually is, but—'

'That's because of the Rimfall,' said Rincewind. 'We're being carried over the edge of the world.'

There was a long silence, broken only by the lapping of the waves as the foundering ship spun slowly in the current. It was already quite strong.

'That's probably why we hit that reef,' Rincewind added. 'We got pulled off course during the night.'

'Would you like something to eat?' asked Twoflower. He began to rummage through the bundle that he had tied to the rail, out of the damp.

'Don't you understand?' snarled Rincewind. 'We are going over the *Edge*, godsdammit!'

'Can't we do anything about it?'

'No!'

'Then I can't see the sense in panicking,' said Twoflower calmly.

'I *knew* we shouldn't have come this far Edgewise,' complained Rincewind to the sky, 'I wish—'

'I wish I had my picturebox,' said Twoflower, 'but it's back on that slaver ship with the rest of the Luggage and—'

'You won't need luggage where we're going,' said Rincewind. He sagged, and stared moodily at a distant whale that had carelessly strayed into the rimward current and was now struggling against it.

There was a line of white on the foreshortened horizon, and the wizard fancied he could hear a distant roaring.

'What happens after a ship goes over the Rimfall?' said Twoflower.

'Who knows?'

'Well, in that case perhaps we'll just sail on through space and land on another world.' A faraway look came into the little man's eyes. 'I'd like that,' he said.

Rincewind snorted.

The sun rose in the sky, looking noticeably bigger this close to the Edge. They stood with their backs against the mast, busy with their own thoughts. Every so often one or other would pick up a bucket and do a bit of desultory bailing, for no very intelligent reason.

The sea around them seemed to be getting crowded. Rincewind noticed several tree trunks keeping station with them, and just below the surface the water was alive with fish of all sorts. Of course – the current must be teeming with food washed from the continents near the Hub. He wondered what kind of life it would be, having to keep swimming all the time to stay exactly in the same place. Pretty similar to his own, he decided. He spotted a small green frog which was paddling desperately in the grip of the inexorable current. To Twoflower's amazement he found a paddle and carefully extended it towards the little amphibian, which scrambled onto it gratefully. A moment later a pair of jaws broke the water and snapped impotently at the spot where it had been swimming.

The frog looked up at Rincewind from the cradle of his hands, and then bit him thoughtfully on the thumb. Twoflower giggled. Rincewind tucked the frog away in a pocket, and pretended he hadn't heard.

'All very humanitarian, but why?' said Twoflower. 'It'll all be the same in an hour.'

'Because,' said Rincewind vaguely, and did a bit of bailing. Spray was being thrown up now and the current was so strong that waves were forming and breaking all around them. It all seemed unnaturally warm. There was a hot golden haze on the sea.

The roaring was louder now. A squid bigger than anything Rincewind had seen before broke the surface a few hundred yards away and thrashed madly with its tentacles before sinking away. Something else that was large and fortunately unidentifiable howled in the mist. A whole squadron of flying fish tumbled up in a cloud of rainbow-edged droplets and managed to gain a few yards before dropping back and being swept in an eddy.

They were running out of world. Rincewind

dropped his bucket and snatched at the mast as the roaring, final end of everything raced towards them.

'I must see this—' said Twoflower, half falling and half diving towards the prow.

Something hard and unyielding smacked into the hull, which spun ninety degrees and came side-on to the invisible obstacle. Then it stopped suddenly and a wash of cold sea foam cascaded over the deck, so that for a few seconds Rincewind was under several feet of boiling green water. He began to scream and then the underwater world became the deep clanging purple colour of fading consciousness, because it was at about this point that Rincewind started to drown.

He awoke with his mouth full of burning liquid and, when he swallowed, the searing pain in his throat jerked him into full consciousness.

The boards of a boat pressed into his back and Twoflower was looking down at him with an expression of deep concern. Rincewind groaned, and sat up.

This turned out to be a mistake. The edge of the world was a few feet away.

Beyond it, at a level just below that of the lip of the endless Rimfall, was something altogether *magical.*

Some seventy miles away, and well beyond the tug of the rim current, a dhow with the red sails typical of a freelance slaver drifted aimlessly through the velvety twilight. The crew – such as remained – were clustered on the foredeck, surrounding the men working feverishly on the raft.

The captain, a thickset man who wore the elbow-turbans typical of a Great Nef tribesman, was much travelled and had seen many strange peoples and curious things, many of which he had subsequently enslaved or stolen. He had begun his career as a sailor on the Dehydrated Ocean in the heart of the disc's driest desert. (Water on the disc has an uncommon fourth state, caused by intense heat combined with the strange desiccating effects of octarine light: it dehydrates, leaving a silvery residue like free-flowing sand through which a well-designed hull can glide with ease. The Dehydrated Ocean is a strange place, but not so strange as its fish.) The captain had never before been really frightened. Now he was terrified.

'I can't hear anything,' he muttered to the first mate.

The mate peered into the gloom.

'Perhaps it fell overboard?' he suggested hopefully. As if in answer there came a furious pounding from the oar deck below their feet, and the sound of splintering wood. The crewmen drew together fearfully, brandishing axes and torches.

They probably wouldn't dare to use them, even if the Monster came rushing towards them. Before its terrible nature had been truly understood several men had attacked it with axes, whereupon it had turned aside from its single-minded searching of the ship and had either chased them overboard or had – *eaten* them? The captain was not quite certain. The Thing looked like an ordinary wooden sea chest. A bit larger than usual, maybe, but not suspiciously so. But while it sometimes seemed to contain things like old socks and miscellaneous luggage, at other times – and he shuddered – it seemed to be, seemed to *have* . . . He tried not to think about it. It was just that the men who had been drowned overboard had probably been more fortunate than those it had caught. He tried not to think about it. There had been *teeth*, teeth like white wooden gravestones, and a tongue red as mahogany . . .

He tried not to think about it. It didn't work.

But he thought bitterly about one thing. This was going to be the last time he rescued ungrateful drowning men in mysterious circumstances. Slavery was better than sharks, wasn't it? And then they had escaped and when his sailors had investigated their big chest – how had they appeared in the middle of an untroubled ocean sitting on a big chest, anyway? – it had bitt . . . He tried not to think about it again, but he found himself wondering what would happen when the damned thing realized that its owner wasn't on board any longer . . .

'Raft's ready, lord,' said the first mate.

'Into the water with it,' shouted the captain, and 'Get aboard!' and 'Fire the ship!'

After all, another ship wouldn't be too hard to come by, he philosophized, but a man might have to wait a long time in that Paradise the mullahs advertised before he was granted another life. Let the magical box eat lobsters.

Some pirates achieved immortality by great deeds of cruelty or derring-do. Some achieved immortality by amassing great wealth. But the captain had long ago decided that he would, on the whole, prefer to achieve immortality by not dying.

* * *

'What the hell is that?' demanded Rincewind.

'It's beautiful,' said Twoflower beatifically.

'I'll decide about that when I know what it is,' said the wizard.

'It is the Rimbow,' said a voice immediately behind his left ear, 'and you are fortunate indeed to be looking at it. From above, at any rate.'

The voice was accompanied by a gust of cold, fishy breath. Rincewind sat quite still.

'Twoflower?' he said.

'Yes?'

'If I turn around, what will I see?'

'His name is Tethis. He says he's a sea troll. This is his boat. He rescued us,' explained Twoflower. 'Will you look around now?'

'Not just at the moment, thank you. So why aren't we going over the Edge, then?' asked Rincewind with glassy calmness.

'Because your boat hit the Circumfence,' said the voice behind him (in tones that made Rincewind imagine submarine chasms and lurking Things in coral reefs).

'The Circumfence?' he repeated.

'Yes. It runs along the edge of the world,' said the unseen troll. Above the roar of the waterfall Rincewind thought he could make out the splash of oars. He *hoped* they were oars.

'Ah. You mean the *circumference*,' said Rincewind. 'The circumference makes the edge of things.'

'So does the Circumfence,' said the troll.

'He means this,' said Twoflower, pointing down.

Rincewind's eyes followed the finger, dreading what they might see . . .

Hubwards of the boat was a rope suspended a few feet above the surface of the white water. The boat was attached to it, moored yet mobile, by a complicated arrangement of pulleys and little wooden wheels. They ran along the rope as the unseen rower propelled the craft along the very lip of the Rimfall. That explained one mystery – but what supported the rope?

Rincewind peered along its length and saw a stout wooden post sticking up out of the water a few yards ahead. As he watched the boat neared it and then passed it, the little wheels clacking neatly around it in a groove obviously cut for the purpose.

Rincewind also noticed that smaller ropes hung down from the main rope at intervals of a yard or so.

He turned back to Twoflower.

'I can see what it *is*,' he said, 'but *what* is it?'

Twoflower shrugged. Behind Rincewind the sea troll said, 'Up ahead is my house. We will talk more when we are there. Now I must row.'

Rincewind found that looking ahead meant that he would have to turn and find out what a sea troll actually looked like, and he wasn't sure he wanted to do that yet. He looked at the Rimbow instead.

It hung in the mists a few lengths beyond the edge of the world, appearing only at morning and evening when the light of the disc's little orbiting sun shone past the massive bulk of Great A'Tuin the World Turtle and struck the disc's magical field at exactly the right angle.

A double rainbow coruscated into being. Close into the lip of the Rimfall were the seven lesser colours, sparkling and dancing in the spray of the dying seas.

But they were pale in comparison to the wider band that floated beyond them, not deigning to share the same spectrum.

It was the King Colour, of which all the lesser colours are merely partial and wishy-washy reflections. It was octarine, the colour of magic. It was alive and glowing and vibrant and it was the undisputed pigment of the imagination, because wherever it appeared it was a sign that mere matter was a servant of the powers of the magical mind. It was enchantment itself.

But Rincewind always thought it looked a sort of greenish-purple.

After a while a small speck on the rim of the world resolved itself into a eyot or crag, so perilously perched that the waters of the fall swirled around it at the start of their long drop. A driftwood shanty had been built on it, and Rincewind saw that the top rope of the Circumfence climbed over the rocky island on a number of iron stakes and actually passed through the shack by a small round window. He learned later that this was so that the troll could be alerted to the arrival of any salvage on his stretch of the Circumfence by means of a series of small bronze bells, balanced delicately on the rope.

A crude floating stockade had been built out of rough timber on the hubward side of the island. It contained one or two hulks and quite a large amount of floating wood in the form of planks, baulks and even whole natural tree trunks, some still sporting green leaves. This close to the Edge the disc's magical field was so intense that a hazy corona flickered across everything as raw illusion spontaneously discharged itself.

With a last few squeaky jerks the boat slid up against a small driftwood jetty. As it grounded itself and formed a circuit Rincewind felt all the familiar sensations of a huge occult aura – oily, bluish-tasting, and smelling of tin. All around them pure, unfocused magic was sleeting soundlessly into the world.

The wizard and Twoflower scrambled onto the planking and for the first time Rincewind saw the troll.

It wasn't half so dreadful as he had imagined.

Umm, said his imagination after a while.

It wasn't that the troll was *horrifying*. Instead of the rotting, betentacled monstrosity he had been expecting Rincewind found himself looking at a rather squat but not particularly ugly old man who would quite easily have passed for normal on any city street, always provided that other people on the street were *used* to seeing old men who were apparently composed of water and very little else. It was as if the ocean had decided to create life without going through all that tedious business of evolution, and had simply formed a part of itself into a biped and sent it walking squishily up the beach. The troll was a pleasant translucent blue colour. As Rincewind stared a small shoal of silver fish flashed across its chest.

'It's rude to stare,' said the troll. Its mouth opened

with a little crest of foam, and shut again in exactly the same way that water closes over a stone.

'Is it? Why?' said Rincewind. How does he hold himself together, his mind screamed at him. Why doesn't he spill?

'If you will follow me to my house I will find you food and a change of clothing,' said the troll solemnly. He set off over the rocks without turning to see if they would follow him. After all, where else could they go? It was getting dark, and a chilly damp breeze was blowing over the edge of the world. Already the transient Rimbow had faded and the mists above the waterfall were beginning to thin.

'Come on,' said Rincewind, grabbing Twoflower's elbow. But the tourist didn't appear to want to move.

'Come on,' the wizard repeated.

'When it gets really dark, do you think we'll be able to look down and see Great A'Tuin the World Turtle?' asked Twoflower, staring at the rolling clouds.

'I hope not,' said Rincewind, 'I really do. Now let's go, shall we?'

Twoflower followed him reluctantly into the shack. The troll had lit a couple of lamps and was sitting comfortably in a rocking chair. He got to his feet as they entered and poured two cups of a green liquid from a tall pitcher. In the dim light he appeared to phosphoresce, in the manner of warm seas on velvety summer nights. Just to add a baroque gloss to Rincewind's dull terror he seemed to be several inches taller, too.

Most of the furniture in the room appeared to be boxes.

'Uh. Really great place you've got here,' said Rincewind. 'Ethnic.'

He reached for a cup and looked at the green pool shimmering inside it. It'd better be drinkable, he thought. Because I'm going to drink it. He swallowed.

It was the same stuff Twoflower had given him in the rowing boat but, at the time, his mind had ignored it because there were more pressing matters. Now it had the leisure to savour the taste.

Rincewind's mouth twisted. He whimpered a little. One of his legs came up convulsively and caught him painfully in the chest.

Twoflower swirled his own drink thoughtfully while he considered the flavour.

'Ghlen Livid,' he said. 'The fermented *vul* nut drink they freeze-distil in my home country. A certain smokey quality . . . Piquant. From the western plantations in, ah, Rehigreed Province, yes? Next year's harvest, I fancy, from the colour. May I ask how you came by it?'

(Plants on the disc, while including the categories known commonly as *annuals*, which were sown this year to come up later this year, *biennials*, sown this year to grow next year, and *perennials*, sown this year to grow until further notice, also included a few rare *re-annuals* which, because of an unusual four-dimensional twist in their genes, could be planted this year to come up *last year*. The *vul* nut vine was particularly exceptional in that it could flourish as many as eight years prior to its seed actually being sown. *Vul* nut wine was reputed to give certain drinkers an insight into the future which was, from the nut's point of view, the past. Strange but true.)

'All things drift into the Circumfence in time,' said the troll, gnomically, gently rocking in his chair. 'My job is to recover the flotsam. Timber, of course, and ships. Barrels of wine. Bales of cloth. You.'

Light dawned inside Rincewind's head.

'It's a net, isn't it? You've got a net right on the edge of the sea!'

'The Circumfence,' nodded the troll. Ripples ran across his chest.

Rincewind looked out into the phosphorescent darkness that surrounded the island, and grinned inanely.

'Of course,' he said. 'Amazing! You could sink piles and attach it to reefs and – good grief! The net would have to be *very* strong.'

'It is,' said Tethis.

'It could be extended for a couple of miles, if you found enough rocks and things,' said the wizard.

'Ten thousands of miles. I just patrol this league.'

'That's a third of the way around the disc!'

Tethis sloshed a little as he nodded again. While the two men helped themselves to some more of the green wine, he told them about the Circumfence, the great effort that had been made to build it, and the ancient and wise Kingdom of Krull which had constructed it several centuries before, and the seven navies that patrolled it constantly to keep it in repair and bring its salvage back to Krull, and the manner in which Krull had become a land of leisure ruled by the most learned seekers after knowledge, and the way in which they sought constantly to understand in every possible particular the wondrous complexity of the universe, and the way in which sailors marooned on the Circumfence were turned into slaves, and usually had their tongues cut out. After some interjections at this point he spoke, in a friendly way, on the futility of force, the impossibility of escaping from the island except by boat to one of the other three hundred and eighty isles that lay between the island and Krull itself, or by leaping over the Edge, and the high merit of muteness in comparison to, for example, death.

There was a pause. The muted night-roar of the Rimfall only served to give the silence a heavier texture.

Then the rocking chair started to creak again. Tethis seemed to have grown alarmingly during the monologue.

'There is nothing personal in all this,' he added. 'I too am a slave. If you try to overpower me I shall have to kill you, of course, but I won't take any particular pleasure in it.'

Rincewind looked at the shimmering fists that rested lightly in the troll's lap. He suspected they could strike with all the force of a tsunami.

'I don't think you understand,' explained Two-flower. 'I am a citizen of the Golden Empire. I'm sure Krull would not wish to incur the displeasure of the Emperor.'

'How will the Emperor know?' asked the troll. 'Do you think you're the first person from the Empire who has ended up on the Circumfence?'

'I won't be a slave!' shouted Rincewind. 'I'd – I'd jump over the Edge first!' He was amazed at the sound in his own voice.

'Would you, though?' asked the troll. The rocking chair flicked back against the wall and one blue arm caught the wizard around the waist. A moment later the troll was striding out of the shack with Rincewind gripped carelessly in one fist.

He did not stop until he came to the rimward edge of the island. Rincewind squealed.

'Stop that or I really will throw you over the edge,' snapped the troll. 'I'm holding you, aren't I? Look.'

Rincewind looked.

In front of him was a soft black night whose mist-muted stars glowed peacefully. But his eyes turned downwards, drawn by some irresistible fascination.

It was midnight on the disc and so, therefore, the sun was far, far below, swinging slowly under Great A'Tuin's vast and frosty plastron. Rincewind tried a last attempt to fix his gaze on the tips of his boots, which were protruding over the rim of the rock, but the sheer drop wrenched it away.

On either side of him two glittering curtains of water hurtled towards infinity as the sea swept around the island on its way to the long fall. A hundred yards below the wizard the largest sea salmon he had ever seen flicked itself out of the foam in a wild, jerky and ultimately hopeless leap. Then it fell back, over and over, in the golden underworld light.

Huge shadows grew out of that light like pillars supporting the roof of the universe. Hundreds of miles below him the wizard made out the shape of something, the edge of something—

Like those curious little pictures where the silhouette of an ornate glass suddenly becomes the outline of two faces, the scene beneath him flipped into a whole new, terrifying perspective. Because down there was the head of an elephant as big as a reasonably sized continent. One mighty tusk cut like a mountain against the golden light, trailing a widening shadow towards the stars. The head was slightly tilted, and a huge ruby eye might almost have been a red supergiant that had managed to shine at noonday.

Below the elephant—

Rincewind swallowed and tried not to think—

Below the elephant there was nothing but the distant, painful disc of the sun. And, sweeping slowly past it, was something that for all its city-sized scales, its crater-pocks, its lunar cragginess, was indubitably a flipper.

'Shall I let go?' suggested the troll.

'Gnah,' said Rincewind, straining backwards.

'I have lived *here on the Edge* for five years and I have not had the courage,' boomed Tethis. 'Nor have you, if I'm any judge.' He stepped back, allowing Rincewind to fling himself onto the ground.

Twoflower strolled up to the rim and peered over.

'Fantastic,' he said. 'If only I had my picturebox . . . What else is down there? I mean, if you jumped off, what would you see?'

Tethis sat down on an outcrop. High over the disc the moon came out from behind a cloud, giving him the appearance of ice.

'My home is down there, perhaps,' he said slowly. 'Beyond your silly elephants and that ridiculous turtle. A real world. Sometimes I come out here and look, but somehow I can never bring myself to take that extra step . . . A real world, with real people. I have wives and little ones, somewhere down there . . .' He stopped, and blew his nose. 'You soon learn what you're made of, *here on the Edge*.'

'Stop saying that. Please,' moaned Rincewind. He turned over and saw Twoflower standing unconcernedly at the very lip of the rock. 'Gnah,' he said, and tried to burrow into the stone.

'There's another world down there?' said Twoflower, peering over. 'Where, exactly?'

The troll waved an arm vaguely. 'Somewhere,' he said. 'That's all I know. It was quite a small world. Mostly blue.'

'So why are you here?' said Twoflower.

'Isn't it obvious?' snapped the troll. 'I fell off the edge!'

He told them of the world of Bathys, somewhere among the stars, where the seafolk had built a number of thriving civilizations in the three large oceans that sprawled across its disc. He had been a meatman, one of the caste which earned a perilous living in large, sail-powered land yachts that ventured far out to land and hunted the shoals of deer and buffalo that abounded in the storm-haunted continents. His particular yacht had been blown into uncharted lands by a freak gale. The rest of the crew had taken the yacht's little rowing trolley and had struck out for a distant lake, but Tethis, as master, had elected to remain with his vessel. The storm had carried it right over the rocky rim of the world, smashing it to matchwood in the process.

'At first I fell,' said Tethis, 'but falling isn't so bad, you know. It's only the landing that hurts, and there was nothing below me. As I fell I saw the world spin off into space until it was lost against the stars.'

'What happened next?' said Twoflower breathlessly, glancing towards the misty universe.

'I froze solid,' said Tethis simply. 'Fortunately it is something my race can survive. But I thawed out occasionally when I passed near other worlds. There was one, I think it was the one with what I thought was this strange ring of mountains around it that turned out to be the biggest dragon you could ever imagine, covered in snow and glaciers and holding its tail in its mouth – well, I came within a few leagues of that, I shot over the landscape like a comet, in fact, and then I was off again. Then there was a time I woke up and there was your world coming at me like a custard pie thrown by the Creator and, well, I landed in the sea not far from the Circumfence widdershins of Krull. All sorts of creatures get washed up against the Fence, and at the time they were looking for slaves to man the way stations, and I ended up here.' He stopped and stared intently at Rincewind. 'Every night I come out here and look down,' he finished, 'and I never jump. Courage is hard to come by, *here on the Edge.*'

Rincewind began to crawl determinedly towards the shack. He gave a little scream as the troll picked him up, not unkindly, and set him on his feet.

'Amazing,' said Twoflower, and leaned further out over the Edge. 'There are lots of other worlds out there?'

'Quite a number, I imagine,' said the troll.

'I suppose one could contrive some sort of, I don't know, some sort of a *thing* that could preserve one against the cold,' said the little man thoughtfully. 'Some sort of a ship that one could sail over the Edge and sail to far-off worlds, too. I wonder . . .'

'Don't even think about it!' moaned Rincewind. 'Stop talking like that, do you hear?'

'They all talk like that in Krull,' said Tethis. 'Those with tongues, of course,' he added.

'Are you awake?'

Twoflower snored on. Rincewind jabbed him viciously in the ribs.

'I said, are you awake?' he snarled.

'Scrdfngh . . .'

'We've got to get out of here before this salvage fleet comes!'

The dishwater light of dawn oozed through the shack's one window, slopping across the piles of salvaged boxes and bundles that were strewn around the interior. Twoflower grunted again and tried to burrow into the pile of furs and blankets that Tethis had given them.

'Look, there's all kinds of weapons and stuff in here,' said Rincewind. 'He's gone out somewhere. When he comes back we could overpower him and – and – well, then we can think of something. How about it?'

'That doesn't sound like a very good idea,' said Twoflower. 'Anyhow, it's a bit ungracious isn't it?'

'Tough buns,' snapped Rincewind. 'This is a rough universe.'

He rummaged through the piles around the walls and selected a heavy, wavy-bladed scimitar that had probably been some pirate's pride and joy. It looked the sort of weapon that relied as much on its weight as its edge to cause damage. He raised it awkwardly.

'Would he leave that sort of thing around if it could hurt him?' Twoflower wondered aloud.

Rincewind ignored him and took up a position beside the door. When it opened some ten minutes later he moved unhesitatingly, swinging it across the opening at what he judged was the troll's head height. It swished harmlessly through nothing at all and struck the doorpost, jerking him off his feet and on to the floor.

There was a sigh above him. He looked up into Tethis' face, which was shaking sadly from side to side.

'It wouldn't have harmed me,' said the troll, 'but nevertheless I am hurt. Deeply hurt.' He reached over the wizard and jerked the sword out of the wood. With no apparent effort he bent its blade into a circle and sent it bowling away over the rocks until it hit a stone and sprang, still spinning, in a silver arc that ended in the mists forming over the Rimfall.

'*Very* deeply hurt,' he concluded. He reached down beside the door and tossed a sack towards Twoflower.

'It's the carcass of a deer that is just about how you humans like it, and a few lobsters, and a sea salmon. The Circumfence provides,' he said casually.

He looked hard at the tourist, and then down again at Rincewind.

'What are you staring at?' he said.

'It's just that—' said Twoflower.

'—compared to last night—' said Rincewind.

'You're so *small*,' finished Twoflower.

'I *see*,' said the troll carefully. 'Personal remarks now.' He drew himself up to his full height, which was currently about four feet. 'Just because I'm made of water doesn't mean I'm made of wood, you know.'

'I'm sorry,' said Twoflower, climbing hastily out of the furs.

'You're made of *dirt*,' said the troll, 'but I didn't pass comments about things you can't help, did I? Oh, no. We can't help the way the Creator made us, that's my view. But if you must know, your moon here is rather more powerful than the ones around my own world.'

'The moon?' said Twoflower. 'I don't under—'

'If I've got to spell it out,' said the troll, testily, 'I'm suffering from chronic tides.'

A bell jangled in the darkness of the shack. Tethis strode across the creaking floor to the complicated device of levers, strings and bells that was mounted on the Circumfence's topmost strand where it passed through the hut.

The bell rang again, and then started to clang away in an odd jerky rhythm for several minutes. The troll stood with his ear pressed close to it.

When it stopped he turned slowly and looked at them with a worried frown.

'You're more important than I thought,' he said. 'You're not to wait for the salvage fleet. You're to be collected by a flyer. That's what they say in Krull.' He shrugged. 'And I hadn't even sent a message that you're here, yet. Someone's been drinking *vul* nut wine again.'

He picked up a large mallet that hung on a pillar beside the bell and used it to tap out a brief carillon.

'That'll be passed from lengthman to lengthman all the way back to Krull,' he said. 'Marvellous really, isn't it?'

It came speeding across the sea, floating a manlength above it, but still leaving a foaming wake as whatever power that held it up smacked brutally into the water. Rincewind *knew* what power held it up. He was, he would be the first to admit, a coward, an incompetent, and not even very good at being a failure; but he was still a wizard of sorts, he knew one of the Eight Great Spells, he would be claimed by Death himself when he died, and he recognized really finely honed magic when he saw it.

The lens skimming towards the island was perhaps twenty feet across, and totally transparent. Sitting around its circumference were a large number of black-robed men, each one strapped securely to the disc by a leather harness and each one staring down at the waves with an expression so tormented, so agonizing, that the transparent disc seemed to be ringed with gargoyles.

Rincewind sighed with relief. This was such an unusual sound that it made Twoflower take his eyes off the approaching disc and turn them on him.

'We're important, no lie,' explained Rincewind. 'They wouldn't be wasting all that magic on a couple of potential slaves.' He grinned.

'What is it?' said Twoflower.

'Well, the disc itself would have been created by

Fresnel's Wonderful Concentrator,' said Rincewind, authoritatively. 'That calls for many rare and unstable ingredients, such as demon's breath and so forth, and it takes at least eight fourth-grade wizards a week to envision. Then there's those wizards on it, who must all be gifted hydrophobes—'

'You mean they hate water?' said Twoflower.

'No, that wouldn't work,' said Rincewind. 'Hate is an attracting force, just like love. They really *loathe* it, the very idea of it revolts them. A really good hydrophobe has to be trained on dehydrated water from birth. I mean, that costs a fortune in magic alone. But they make great weather magicians. Rain clouds just give up and go away.'

'It sounds terrible,' said the water troll behind them.

'And they all die young,' said Rincewind, ignoring him. 'They just can't live with themselves.'

'Sometimes I think a man could wander across the disc all his life and not see everything there is to see,' said Twoflower. 'And now it seems there are lots of other worlds as well. When I think I might die without seeing a hundredth of all there is to see it makes me feel,' he paused, then added, 'well, humble, I suppose. And very angry, of course.'

The flyer halted a few yards hubward of the island, throwing up a sheet of spray. It hung there, spinning slowly. A hooded figure standing by the stubby pillar at the exact centre of the lens beckoned to them.

'You'd better wade out,' said the troll. 'It doesn't do to keep them waiting. It has been nice to make your acquaintance.' He shook them both, wetly, by the hand. As he waded out a little way with them the two nearest loathers on the lens shied away with expressions of extreme disgust.

The hooded figure reached down with one hand and released a rope ladder. In its other hand it held a silver rod, which had about it the unmistakable air of something designed for killing people. Rincewind's first impression was reinforced when the figure raised the stick and waved it carelessly towards the shore. A section of rock vanished, leaving a small grey haze of nothingness.

'That's so you don't think I'm afraid to use it,' said the figure.

'Don't think *you're* afraid?' said Rincewind. The hooded figure snorted.

'We know all about you, Rincewind the magician. You are a man of great cunning and artifice. You laugh in the face of Death. Your affected air of craven cowardice does not fool me.'

It fooled Rincewind. 'I—' he began, and paled as the nothingness-stick was turned towards him. 'I see you know all about me,' he finished weakly, and sat down heavily on the slippery surface. He and Twoflower, under instructions from the hooded commander, strapped themselves down to rings set in the transparent disc.

'If you make the merest suggestion of weaving a spell,' said the darkness under the hood, 'you die. Third quadrant *reconcile*, ninth quadrant *redouble*, *forward all*!'

A wall of water shot into the air behind Rincewind and the disc jerked suddenly. The dreadful presence of the sea troll had probably concentrated the hydrophobes' minds wonderfully, because it then rose at a very steep angle and didn't begin level flight until it was a dozen fathoms above the waves. Rincewind glanced down through the transparent surface and wished he hadn't.

'Well, off again then,' said Twoflower cheerfully. He turned and waved at the troll, now no more than a speck on the edge of the world.

Rincewind glared at him. 'Doesn't *anything* ever worry you?' he asked.

'We're still alive, aren't we?' asked Twoflower. 'And you yourself said they wouldn't be going to all this trouble if we were just going to be slaves. I expect Tethis was exaggerating. I expect it's all a misunderstanding. I expect we'll be sent home. After we've seen Krull, of course. And I must say it all sounds fascinating.'

'Oh yes,' said Rincewind, in a hollow voice. 'Fascinating.' He was thinking: I've seen excitement, and I've seen boredom. And boredom was best.

Had either of them happened to look down at that moment they would have noticed a strange v-shaped wave surging through the water far below them, its apex pointing directly at Tethis' island. But they weren't looking. The twenty-four hydrophobic magicians *were* looking, but to them it was just another piece of dreadfulness, not really any different from the liquid horror around it. They were probably right.

Sometime before all this the blazing pirate ship had hissed under the waves and started the long slow slide towards the distant ooze. It was more distant than average, because directly under the stricken keel was the Gorunna Trench – a chasm in the disc's surface that was so black, so deep and so reputedly evil that even the krakens went there fearfully, and in pairs. In less reputedly evil chasms the fish went about with natural lights on their heads and on the whole managed quite well. In Gorunna they left them unlit and, insofar as it is possible for something without legs to creep, they crept; they tended to bump into things, too. Horrible things.

The water around the ship turned from green to purple, from purple to black, from black to a darkness so complete that blackness itself seemed merely grey in comparison. Most of its timbers had already been crushed into splinters under the intense pressure.

It spiralled past groves of nightmare polyps and drifting forests of seaweed which glowed with faint, diseased colours. *Things* brushed it briefly with soft, cold tentacles as they darted away into the freezing silence.

Something rose up from the murk and ate it in one mouthful.

Some time later the islanders on a little rimward atoll were amazed to find, washed into their little local lagoon, the wave-rocked corpse of a hideous sea monster, all beaks, eyes and tentacles. They were further astonished at its size, since it was rather larger than their village. But their surprise was tiny compared to the huge, stricken expression on the face of the dead monster, which appeared to have been trampled to death.

Somewhat further rimward of the atoll a couple of little boats, trolling a net for the ferocious free-swimming oysters which abounded in those seas, caught something that dragged both vessels for several miles before one captain had the presence of mind to sever the lines.

But even his bewilderment was as nothing compared to that of the islanders on the last atoll in the archipelago. During the following night they were awakened by a terrific crashing and splintering noise coming from their minute jungle; when some of the bolder spirits went to investigate in the morning they found that the trees had been smashed in a broad swathe that started on the hubmost shore of the atoll and made a line of total destruction pointing precisely Edgewise, littered with broken lianas, crushed bushes and a few bewildered and angry oysters.

They were high enough now to see the wide curve of the Rim sweeping away from them, lapped by the fluffy clouds that mercifully hid the waterfall for most of the time. From up here the sea, a deep blue dappled with cloud-shadows, looked almost inviting. Rincewind shuddered.

'Excuse me,' he said. The hooded figure turned from its contemplation of the distant haze and raised its wand threateningly.

'I don't want to use this,' it said.

'You don't?' said Rincewind.

'What is it, anyway?' said Twoflower.

'Ajandurah's Wand of Utter Negativity,' said Rincewind. 'And I wish you'd stop waving it about. It might go off,' he added, nodding at the wand's glittering point. 'I mean, it's all very flattering, all this magic being used just for our benefit, but there's no need to go quite that far. And—'

'*Shut up.*' The figure reached up and pulled back its hood, revealing itself to be a most unusually tinted young woman. Her skin was black. Not the dark brown of Urabewe, or the polished blue-black of monsoon-haunted Klatch, but the deep black of midnight at the bottom of a cave. Her hair and eyebrows were the colour of moonlight. There was the same pale sheen around her lips. She looked about fifteen, and very frightened.

Rincewind couldn't help noticing that the hand holding the wand was shaking; this was because a piece of sudden death, wobbling uncertainly a mere five feet from your nose, is very hard to miss. It dawned on him – very slowly, because it was a completely new sensation – that someone in the world was frightened of him. The complete reverse was so often the case that he had come to think of it as a kind of natural law.

'What is your name?' he said, as reassuringly as he could manage. She might be frightened, but she *did* have the wand. If I had a wand like that, he thought, I wouldn't be frightened of anything. So what in Creation can she imagine I could do?

'My name is immaterial,' she said.

'That's a pretty name,' said Rincewind. 'Where are you taking us, and why? I can't see any harm in your telling us.'

'You are being brought to Krull,' said the girl. 'And

don't mock me, hublander. Else I'll use the wand. I must bring you in alive, but no-one said anything about bringing you in whole. My name is Marchesa, and I am a wizard of the fifth level. Do you understand?'

'Well, since you know all about me then you know that I never even made it to Neophyte,' said Rincewind. 'I'm not even a wizard, really.' He caught Twoflower's astonished expression, and added hastily, 'Just a wizard of sorts.'

'You can't do magic because one of the Eight Great Spells is indelibly lodged in your mind,' said Marchesa, shifting her balance gracefully as the great lens described a wide arc over the sea. 'That's why you were thrown out of Unseen University. We know.'

'But you said just now that he was a magician of great cunning and artifice,' protested Twoflower.

'Yes, because anyone who survives all that he has survived – most of which he brought on himself by his tendency to think of himself as a wizard – well, he must be some kind of a magician,' said Marchesa. 'I warn you, Rincewind. If you give me the merest suspicion that you are intoning the Great Spell I really will kill you.' She scowled at him nervously.

'Seems to me your best course would be to just, you know, drop us off somewhere,' said Rincewind. 'I mean, thanks for rescuing us and everything, so if you'd just let us get on with leading our lives I'm sure we'd all—'

'I hope you're not proposing to enslave us,' said Twoflower.

Marchesa looked genuinely shocked. 'Certainly

not! Whatever could have given you that idea? Your lives in Krull will be rich, full and comfortable—'

'Oh, good,' said Rincewind.

'—just not very long.'

Krull turned out to be a large island, quite mountainous and heavily wooded, with pleasant white buildings visible here and there among the trees. The land sloped gradually up towards the rim, so that the highest point in Krull in fact slightly overhung the Edge. Here the Krullians had built their major city, also called Krull, and since so much of their building material had been salvaged from the Circumfence the houses of Krull had a decidedly nautical persuasion.

To put it bluntly, entire ships had been mortised artfully together and converted into buildings. Triremes, dhows and caravels protruded at strange angles from the general wooden chaos. Painted figureheads and hublandish dragonprows reminded the citizens of Krull that their good fortune stemmed from the sea; barquentines and carracks lent a distinctive shape to the larger buildings. And so the city rose tier on tier between the blue-green ocean of the disc and the soft cloud sea of the Edge, the eight colours of the Rimbow reflected in every window and in the many telescope lenses of the city's multitude of astronomers.

'It's absolutely awful,' said Rincewind gloomily.

The lens was approaching now along the very lip of the rimfall. The island not only got higher as it neared the Edge. It got narrower too, so that the lens was able to remain over water until it was very near the city.

The parapet along the edgewise cliff was dotted with gantries projecting into nothingness. The lens glided smoothly towards one of them and docked with it as smoothly as a boat might glide up to a quay. Four guards, with the same moonlight hair and nightblack faces as Marchesa, were waiting. They did not appear to be armed, but as Twoflower and Rincewind stumbled on to the parapet they were each grabbed by the arms and held quite firmly enough for any thought of escape to be instantly dismissed.

Then Marchesa and the watching hydrophobic wizards were quickly left behind and the guards and their prisoners set off briskly along a lane that wound between the ship-houses. Soon it led downwards, into what turned out to be a palace of some sort, half-hewn out of the rock of the cliff itself. Rincewind was vaguely aware of brightly lit tunnels, and courtyards open to the distant sky. A few elderly men, their robes covered in mysterious occult symbols, stood aside and watched with interest as the sextet passed. Several times Rincewind noticed hydrophobes – their ingrained expressions of self-revulsion at their own body-fluids were distinctive – and here and there trudging men who could only be slaves. He didn't have much time to reflect on all this before a door was opened ahead of them and they were pushed, gently but firmly, into a room. Then the door slammed behind them.

Rincewind and Twoflower regained their balance and stared around the room in which they now found themselves.

'Gosh,' said Twoflower ineffectually, after a pause

during which he had tried unsuccessfully to find a better word.

'This is a prison cell?' wondered Rincewind aloud.

'All that gold and silk and stuff,' Twoflower added. 'I've never seen anything like it!'

In the centre of the richly decorated room, on a carpet that was so deep and furry that Rincewind trod on it gingerly lest it be some kind of shaggy, floor-loving beast, was a long gleaming table laden with food. Most were fish dishes, including the biggest and most ornately prepared lobster Rincewind had ever seen, but there were also plenty of bowls and platters piled with strange creations that he had never seen before. He reached out cautiously and picked up some sort of purple fruit crusted with green crystals.

'Candied sea urchin,' said a cracked, cheerful voice behind him. 'A great delicacy.'

He dropped it quickly and turned around. An old man had stepped out from behind the heavy curtains. He was tall, thin and looked almost benign compared to some of the faces Rincewind had seen recently.

'The purée of sea cucumbers is very good too,' said the face, conversationally. 'Those little green bits are baby starfish.'

'Thank you for telling me,' said Rincewind weakly.

'Actually, they're rather good,' said Twoflower, his mouth full. 'I thought you liked seafood?'

'Yes, I thought I did,' said Rincewind. 'What's this wine – crushed octopus eyeballs?'

'Sea grape,' said the old man.

'Great,' said Rincewind, and swallowed a glassful. 'Not bad. A bit salty, maybe.'

'Sea grape is a kind of small jellyfish,' explained the stranger. 'And now I really think I should introduce myself. Why has your friend gone that strange colour?'

'Culture shock, I imagine,' said Twoflower. 'What did you say your name was?'

'I didn't. It's Garhartra. I'm the Guestmaster, you see. It is my pleasant task to make sure that your stay here is as delightful as possible.' He bowed. 'If there is anything you want you have only to say.'

Twoflower sat down on an ornate mother-of-pearl chair with a glass of oily wine in one hand and a crystallized squid in the other. He frowned.

'I think I've missed something along the way,' he said. 'First we were told we were going to be slaves—'

'A base canard!' interrupted Garhartra.

'What's a canard?' said Twoflower.

'I think it's a kind of duck,' said Rincewind from the far end of the long table. 'Are these biscuits made of something really nauseating, do you suppose?'

'—and then we were rescued at great magical expense—'

'They're made of pressed seaweed,' snapped the Guestmaster.

'—but then we're threatened, also at a vast expenditure of magic—'

'Yes, I thought it would be something like seaweed,' agreed Rincewind. 'They certainly taste like seaweed would taste if anyone was masochistic enough to eat seaweed.'

'—and then we're manhandled by guards and thrown in here—'

'Pushed gently,' corrected Garhartra.

'—which turned out to be this amazingly rich room and there's all this food and a man saying he's devoting his life to making us happy,' Twoflower concluded. 'What I'm getting at is this sort of lack of consistency.'

'Yar,' said Rincewind. 'What he means is, are you about to start being generally unpleasant again? Is this just a break for lunch?'

Garhartra held up his hands reassuringly.

'Please, please,' he protested. 'It was just necessary to get you here as soon as possible. We certainly do not want to enslave you. Please be reassured on that score.'

'Well, fine,' said Rincewind.

'Yes, you will in fact be sacrificed,' Garhartra continued placidly.

'*Sacrificed?* You're going to kill us?' shouted the wizard.

'Kill? Yes, of course. Certainly! It would hardly be a sacrifice if we didn't, would it? But don't worry – it'll be comparatively painless.'

'Comparatively? Compared to what?' said Rincewind. He picked up a tall green bottle that was full of sea grape jellyfish wine and hurled it hard at the Guestmaster, who flung up a hand as if to protect himself.

There was a crackle of octarine flame from his fingers and the air suddenly took on the thick, greasy feel that indicated a powerful magical discharge. The flung bottle slowed and then stopped in mid-air, rotating gently.

At the same time an invisible force picked Rincewind up and hurled him down the length of the room, pinning him awkwardly halfway up the far wall with no breath left in his body. He hung there with his mouth open in rage and astonishment.

Garhartra lowered his hand and brushed it slowly on his robe.

'I didn't enjoy doing that, you know,' he said.

'I could tell,' muttered Rincewind.

'But what do you want to sacrifice us for?' asked Twoflower. 'You hardly know us!'

'That's rather the point, isn't it? It's not very good manners to sacrifice a friend. Besides, you were, um, *specified*. I don't know a lot about the god in question, but He was quite clear on that point. Look, I must be running along now. So much to organize, you know how it is,' the Guestmaster opened the door, and then peered back around it. 'Please make yourselves comfortable, and don't worry.'

'But you haven't actually *told* us anything!' wailed Twoflower.

'It's not really worth it, is it? What with you being sacrificed in the morning,' said Garhartra, 'it's hardly worth the bother of knowing, really. Sleep well. Comparatively well, anyway.'

He shut the door. A brief octarine flicker of balefire around it suggested that it had now been sealed beyond the skills of any earthly locksmith.

Gling, clang, tang went the bells along the Circumfence in the moonlit, rimfall-roaring night.

Terton, lengthman of the 45th Length, hadn't heard

such a clashing since the night a giant kraken had been swept into the Fence five years ago. He leaned out of his hut, which for the lack of any convenient eyot on this Length had been built on wooden piles driven into the sea bed, and stared into the darkness. Once or twice he thought he could see movement, far off. Strictly speaking, he should row out to see what was causing the din. But here in the clammy darkness it didn't seem like an astoundingly good idea, so he slammed the door, wrapped some sacking around the madly jangling bells, and tried to get back to sleep.

That didn't work, because even the top strand of the Fence was thrumming now, as if something big and heavy was bouncing on it. After staring at the ceiling for a few minutes, and trying hard not to think of great long tentacles and pond-sized eyes, Terton blew out the lantern and opened the door a crack.

Something *was* coming along the Fence, in giant loping bounds that covered metres at a time. It loomed up at him and for a moment Terton saw something rectangular, multi-legged, shaggy with seaweed and – although it had absolutely no features from which he could have deduced this – it was also very angry indeed.

The hut was smashed to fragments as the monster charged through it, although Terton survived by clinging to the Circumfence; some weeks later he was picked up by a returning salvage fleet, subsequently escaped from Krull on a hijacked lens (having developed hydrophobia to an astonishing degree) and after a number of adventures eventually found his way to the Great Nef, an area of the disc so dry that it actually has negative rainfall, which he nevertheless considered uncomfortably damp.

'Have you tried the door?'

'Yes,' said Twoflower. 'And it isn't any less locked than it was last time you asked. There's the window, though.'

'A great way of escape,' muttered Rincewind, from his perch halfway up the wall. 'You said it looks out over the Edge. Just step out, eh, and plunge through space and maybe freeze solid or hit some other world at incredible speeds or plunge wildly into the burning heart of a sun?'

'Worth a try,' said Twoflower. 'Want a seaweed biscuit?'

'No!'

'When are you coming down?'

Rincewind snarled. This was partly in embarrassment. Garhartra's spell had been the little-used and hard-to-master Atavarr's Personal Gravitational Upset, the practical result of which was that until it wore off Rincewind's body was convinced that 'down' lay at ninety degrees to that direction normally accepted as of a downward persuasion by the majority of the disc's inhabitants. He was in fact standing on the wall.

Meanwhile the flung bottle hung supportless in the air a few yards away. In its case time had – well, not actually been stopped, but had been slowed by several orders of magnitude, and its trajectory had so far occupied several hours and a couple of inches as far as Twoflower and Rincewind were concerned. The glass gleamed in the moonlight. Rincewind sighed and tried to make himself comfortable on the wall.

'Why don't you ever *worry*?' he demanded petulantly. 'Here we are, going to be sacrificed to some god or other in the morning, and you just sit there eating barnacle canapés.'

'I expect something will turn up,' said Twoflower.

'I mean, it's not as if we know *why* we're going to be killed,' the wizard went on.

You'd like to, would you?

'Did you say that?' asked Rincewind.

'Say what?'

You're hearing things said the voice in Rincewind's head.

He sat bolt sideways. 'Who are you?' he demanded.

Twoflower gave him a worried look.

'I'm Twoflower,' he said. 'Surely you remember?'

Rincewind put his head in his hands.

'It's happened at last,' he moaned. 'I'm going out of my mind.'

Good idea said the voice. *It's getting pretty crowded in here*

The spell pinning Rincewind to the wall vanished with a faint 'pop'. He fell forward and landed in a heap on the floor.

Careful – you nearly squashed me

Rincewind struggled to his elbows and reached into the pocket of his robe. When he withdrew his hand the green frog was sitting on it, its eyes oddly luminous in the half-light.

'You?' said Rincewind.

Put me down on the floor and stand back The frog blinked.

The wizard did so, and dragged a bewildered Twoflower out of the way.

The room darkened. There was a windy, roaring sound. Streamers of green, purple and octarine cloud appeared out of nowhere and began to spiral rapidly towards the recumbent amphibian, shedding small bolts of lightning as they whirled. Soon the frog was lost in a golden haze which began to elongate upwards, filling the room with a warm yellow light. Within it was a darker, indistinct shape, which wavered and changed even as they watched. And all the time there was the high, brain-curdling whine of a huge magical field . . .

As suddenly as it had appeared, the magical tornado vanished. And there, occupying the space where the frog had been, was a frog.

'Fantastic,' said Rincewind.

The frog gazed at him reproachfully.

'Really amazing,' said Rincewind sourly. 'A frog magically transformed into a frog. Wondrous.'

'Turn around,' said a voice behind them. It was a soft, feminine voice, almost an inviting voice, the sort of voice you could have a few drinks with, but it was coming from a spot where there oughtn't to be a voice at all. They managed to turn without really moving, like a couple of statues revolving on plinths.

There was a woman standing in the pre-dawn light. She looked – she was – she had a – in point of actual fact she . . .

Later Rincewind and Twoflower couldn't quite agree on any single fact about her, except that she had appeared to be beautiful (precisely what physical features made her beautiful they could not, definitively, state) and that she had green eyes. Not the pale green of ordinary eyes, either – these were the green of fresh emeralds and as iridescent as a dragonfly. And one of the few genuinely magical facts that Rincewind knew was that no god or goddess, contrary and volatile as they might be in all other respects, could change the colour or nature of their eyes . . .

'L—' he began. She raised a hand.

'You know that if you say my name I must depart,' she hissed. 'Surely you recall that I am the one goddess who comes only when not invoked?'

'Uh. Yes, I suppose I do,' croaked the wizard, trying not to look at the eyes. 'You're the one they call the Lady?'

'Yes.'

'Are you a goddess then?' said Twoflower excitedly. 'I've always wanted to meet one.'

Rincewind tensed, waiting for the explosion of rage. Instead, the Lady merely smiled.

'Your friend the wizard should introduce us,' she said.

Rincewind coughed. 'Uh, yar,' he said. 'This is Twoflower, Lady, he's a tourist—'

'—I have attended him on a number of occasions—'

'—and, Twoflower, this is the Lady. *Just* the Lady, right? Nothing else. Don't try and give her any other name, OK?' he went on desperately, his eyes darting meaningful glances that were totally lost on the little man.

Rincewind shivered. He was not, of course, an atheist; on the disc the gods dealt severely with atheists. On the few occasions when he had some spare change he had always made a point of dropping a few coppers into a temple coffer, somewhere, on the principle that a man needed all the friends he could get. But usually he didn't bother the Gods, and he hoped the Gods wouldn't bother him. Life was quite complicated enough.

There were two gods, however, who were really terrifying. The rest of the gods were usually only sort of large-scale humans, fond of wine and war and whoring. But Fate and the Lady were chilling.

In the Gods' Quarter, in Ankh-Morpork, Fate had a small, heavy, leaden temple, where hollow-eyed and gaunt worshippers met on dark nights for their predestined and fairly pointless rites. There were no temples at all to the Lady, although she was arguably the most powerful goddess in the entire history of Creation. A few of the more daring members of the Gamblers' Guild had once experimented with a form of worship, in the deepest cellars of Guild headquarters, and had all died of penury, murder or just Death within the week. She was the Goddess Who Must Not Be Named; those who sought her never found her, yet she was known to come to the aid of those in greatest need. And, then again, sometimes she didn't. She was like that. She didn't like the clicking of rosaries, but was attracted to the sound of dice. No man knew what She looked like, although there were many times when a man who was gambling his life on the turn of the cards would pick up the hand he had been dealt and stare Her full in the face. Of course, sometimes he didn't. Among all the gods she was at one and the same time the most courted and the most cursed.

'We don't have gods where I come from,' said Twoflower.

'You do, you know,' said the Lady. 'Everyone has gods. You just don't think they're gods.'

Rincewind shook himself mentally.

'Look,' he said. 'I don't want to sound impatient, but in a few minutes some people are going to come through that door and take us away and kill us.'

'Yes,' said the Lady.

'I suppose you wouldn't tell us *why*?' said Twoflower.

'Yes,' said the Lady. 'The Krullians intend to launch a bronze vessel over the edge of the disc. Their prime purpose is to learn the sex of A'Tuin the World Turtle.'

'Seems rather pointless,' said Rincewind.

'No. Consider. One day Great A'Tuin may encounter another member of the species *chelys galactica*, somewhere in the vast night in which we move. Will they fight? Will they mate? A little imagination will show you that the sex of Great A'Tuin could be very important to us. At least, so the Krullians say.'

Rincewind tried not to think of World Turtles mating. It wasn't completely easy.

'So,' continued the goddess, 'they intend to launch this ship of space, with two voyagers aboard. It will be the culmination of decades of research. It will also be very dangerous for the travellers. And so, in an attempt to reduce the risks, the Arch-astronomer of Krull has bargained with Fate to sacrifice two men at the moment of launch. Fate, in His turn, has agreed to smile on the space ship. A neat barter, is it not?'

'And we're the sacrifices,' said Rincewind.

'Yes.'

'I thought Fate didn't go in for that sort of bargaining. I thought Fate was implacable,' said Rincewind.

'Normally, yes. But you two have been thorns in his side for some time. He specified that the sacrifices should be you. He allowed you to escape from the pirates. He allowed you to drift into the Circumfence. Fate can be one mean god at times.'

There was a pause. The frog sighed and wandered off under the table.

'But you can help us?' prompted Twoflower.

'You amuse me,' said the Lady. 'I have a sentimental streak. You'd know that, if you were gamblers. So for a little while I rode in a frog's mind and you kindly rescued me, for, as we all know, no-one likes to see pathetic and helpless creatures swept to their death.'

'Thank you,' said Rincewind.

'The whole mind of Fate is bent against you,' said the Lady. 'But all I can do is give you one chance. Just one, small chance. The rest is up to you.'

She vanished.

'Gosh,' said Twoflower, after a while. 'That's the first time I've ever seen a goddess.'

The door swung open. Garhartra entered, holding a wand in front of him. Behind him were two guards, armed more conventionally with swords.

'Ah,' he said conversationally. 'You are ready, I see.'

Ready, said a voice inside Rincewind's head.

The bottle that the wizard had flung some eight hours earlier had been hanging in the air, imprisoned by magic in its own personal time-field. But during all those hours the original mana of the spell had been slowly leaking away until the total magical energy was no longer sufficient to hold it against the Universe's own powerful normality field, and when that happened Reality snapped back in a matter of microseconds. The visible sign of this was that the bottle suddenly completed the last part of its parabola and burst against the side of the Guestmaster's head, showering the guards with glass and jellyfish wine.

Rincewind grabbed Twoflower's arm, kicked the nearest guard in the groin, and dragged the startled tourist into the corridor. Before the stunned Garhartra had sunk to the floor his two guests were already pounding across distant flagstones.

Rincewind skidded around a corner and found himself on a balcony that ran around the four sides of a courtyard. Below them, most of the floor of the yard was taken up by an ornamental pond in which a few terrapins sunbathed among the lily leaves.

And ahead of Rincewind were a couple of very surprised wizards wearing the distinctive dark blue and black robes of trained hydrophobes. One of them, quicker on the uptake than his companion, raised a hand and began the first words of a spell.

There was a short sharp noise by Rincewind's side. Twoflower had spat. The hydrophobe screamed and dropped his hand as though it had been stung.

The other didn't have time to move before Rincewind was on him, fists swinging wildly. One stiff punch with the weight of terror behind it sent the man tumbling over the balcony rail and into the pond, which did a very strange thing: the water smacked aside as though a large invisible balloon had been dropped into it, and the hydrophobe hung screaming in his own revulsion field.

Twoflower watched him in amazement until Rincewind snatched at his shoulder and indicated a likely-looking passage. They hurried down it, leaving the remaining hydrophobe writhing on the floor and snatching at his damp hand.

For a while there was some shouting behind them, but they scuttled along a cross corridor and another courtyard and soon left the sounds of pursuit behind. Finally Rincewind picked a safe-looking door, peered around it, found the room beyond to be unoccupied, dragged Twoflower inside, and slammed it behind him. Then he leaned against it, wheezing horribly.

'We're totally lost in a palace on an island we haven't a hope of leaving,' he panted. 'And what's more we—hey!' he finished, as the sight of the contents of the room filtered up his deranged optic nerves.

Twoflower was already staring at the walls.

Because what was so odd about the room was, it contained the whole Universe.

Death sat in His garden, running a whetstone along the edge of His scythe. It was already so sharp that any passing breeze that blew across it was sliced smoothly into two puzzled zephyrs, although breezes were rare indeed in Death's silent garden. It lay on a sheltered plateau overlooking the discworld's complex dimensions, and behind it loomed the cold, still, immensely high and brooding mountains of Eternity.

Swish! went the stone. Death hummed a dirge, and tapped one bony foot on the frosty flagstones.

Someone approached through the dim orchard where the nightapples grew, and there came the sickly sweet smell of crushed lilies. Death looked up angrily, and found Himself staring into eyes that were black as the inside of a cat and full of distant stars that had no counterpart among the familiar constellations of the Realtime universe.

Death and Fate looked at each other. Death grinned – He had no alternative, of course, being made of implacable bone. The whetstone sang rhythmically along the blade as He continued His task.

'I have a task for you,' said Fate. His words drifted across Death's scythe and split tidily into two ribbons of consonants and vowels.

I HAVE TASKS ENOUGH THIS DAY, said Death in a voice as heavy as neutronium. THE WHITE PLAGUE ABIDES EVEN NOW IN PSEUDOPOLIS AND I AM BOUND THERE TO RESCUE MANY OF ITS CITIZENS FROM HIS GRASP. SUCH A ONE HAS NOT BEEN SEEN THESE HUNDRED YEARS. I AM EXPECTED TO STALK THE STREETS, AS IS MY DUTY.

'I refer to the matter of the little wanderer and the rogue wizard,' said Fate softly, seating himself beside Death's black-robed form and staring down at the distant, multifaceted jewel which was the disc universe as seen from this extra-dimensional vantage point.

The scythe ceased its song.

'They die in a few hours,' said Fate. 'It is fated.'

Death stirred, and the stone began to move again.

'I thought you would be pleased,' said Fate.

Death shrugged, a particularly expressive gesture for someone whose visible shape was that of a skeleton.

I DID INDEED CHASE THEM MIGHTILY, ONCE, he said, BUT AT LAST THE THOUGHT CAME TO ME THAT SOONER OR LATER ALL MEN MUST DIE. EVERYTHING DIES IN THE END. I CAN BE ROBBED BUT NEVER DENIED, I TOLD MYSELF. WHY WORRY?

'I too cannot be cheated,' snapped Fate.

SO I HAVE HEARD, said Death, still grinning.

'Enough!' shouted Fate, jumping to his feet. 'They will die!' He vanished in a sheet of blue fire.

Death nodded to Himself and continued at His work. After some minutes the edge of the blade seemed to be finished to His satisfaction. He stood up and levelled the scythe at the fat and noisome candle that burned on the edge of the bench and then, with two deft sweeps, cut the flame into three bright slivers. Death grinned.

A short while later he was saddling his white stallion, which lived in a stable at the back of Death's cottage. The beast snuffled at him in a friendly fashion; though it was crimson-eyed and had flanks like oiled silk, it was nevertheless a real flesh-and-blood horse and, indeed, was in all probability better treated than most beasts of burden on the disc. Death was not an unkind master. He weighed very little and, although He often rode back with His saddlebags bulging, they weighed nothing whatsoever.

'All those worlds!' said Twoflower. 'It's fantastic!'

Rincewind grunted, and continued to prowl warily

around the star-filled room. Twoflower turned to a complicated astrolabe, in the centre of which was the entire Great A'Tuin-Elephant-Disc system wrought in brass and picked out with tiny jewels. Around it stars and planets wheeled on fine silver wires.

'Fantastic!' he said again. On the walls around him constellations made of tiny phosphorescent seed pearls had been picked out on vast tapestries made of jet-black velvet, giving the room's occupants the impression of floating in the interstellar gulf. Various easels held huge sketches of Great A'Tuin as viewed from various parts of the Circumfence, with every mighty scale and cratered pock-mark meticulously marked in. Twoflower stared about him with a far-away look in his eyes.

Rincewind was deeply troubled. What troubled him most of all were the two suits that hung from supports in the centre of the room. He circled them uneasily.

They appeared to be made of fine white leather, hung about with straps and brass nozzles and other highly unfamiliar and suspicious contrivances. The leggings ended in high, thick-soled boots, and the arms were shoved into big supple gauntlets. Strangest of all were the big copper helmets that were obviously supposed to fit on heavy collars around the neck of the suits. The helmets were almost certainly useless for protection – a light sword would have no difficulty in splitting them, even if it didn't hit the ridiculous little glass windows in the front. Each helmet had a crest of white feathers on top, which went absolutely no way at all towards improving their overall appearance.

Rincewind was beginning to have the glimmerings of a suspicion about those suits.

In front of them was a table covered with celestial charts and scraps of parchment covered with figures. Whoever would be wearing those suits, Rincewind decided, was expecting to boldly go where no man – other than the occasional luckless sailor, who didn't really count – had boldly gone before, and he was now beginning to get not just a suspicion but a horrible premonition.

He turned round and found Twoflower looking at him with a speculative expression.

'No—' began Rincewind, urgently. Twoflower ignored him.

'The goddess said two men were going to be sent over the Edge,' he said, his eyes gleaming, 'and you remember Tethis the troll saying you'd need some kind of protection? The Krullians have got over that. These are suits of *space* armour.'

'They don't look very roomy to me,' said Rincewind hurriedly, and grabbed the tourist by the arm, 'so if you'd just come on, no sense in staying here—'

'Why must you always *panic*?' asked Twoflower petulantly.

'Because the whole of my future life just flashed in front of my eyes, and it didn't take very long, and if you don't move now I'm going to leave without you because any second now you're going to suggest that we put on—'

The door opened.

Two husky young men stepped into the room. All they were wearing was a pair of woollen pants apiece.

One of them was still towelling himself briskly. They both nodded at the two escapees with no apparent surprise.

The taller of the two men sat down on one of the benches in front of the seats. He beckoned to Rincewind, and said:

'? Tyø yur åtl hø sooten gåtrunen?'

And this was awkward, because although Rincewind considered himself an expert in most of the tongues of the hubwards segments of the disc it was the first time that he had ever been addressed in Krullian, and he did not understand one word of it. Neither did Twoflower, but that did not stop him stepping forward and taking a breath.

The speed of light through a magical aura such as the one that surrounded the disc was quite slow, being about the speed of sound in less highly tuned universes. But it was still the fastest thing around with the exception, in moments like this, of Rincewind's mind.

In an instant he became aware that the tourist was about to try his own peculiar brand of linguistics, which meant that he would speak loudly and slowly in his own language.

Rincewind's elbow shot back, knocking the breath from Twoflower's body. When the little man looked up in pain and astonishment Rincewind caught his eye and pulled an imaginary tongue out of his mouth and cut it with an imaginary pair of scissors.

The second chelonaut – for such was the profession of the men whose fate it would shortly be to voyage to Great A'Tuin – looked up from the chart table and watched this in puzzlement. His big heroic brow wrinkled with the effort of speech.

'? Hør yu latruin nør u?' he said.

Rincewind smiled and nodded and pushed Twoflower in his general direction. With an inward sigh of relief he saw the tourist pay sudden attention to a big brass telescope that lay on the table.

'! Sooten u!' commanded the seated chelonaut. Rincewind nodded and smiled and took one of the big copper helmets from the rack and brought it down on the man's head as hard as he possibly could. The chelonaut fell forward with a soft grunt.

The other man took one startled step before Twoflower hit him amateurishly but effectively with the telescope. He crumpled on top of his colleague.

Rincewind and Twoflower looked at each other over the carnage.

'All *right*!' snapped Rincewind, aware that he had lost some kind of contest but not entirely certain what it was. 'Don't bother to say it. Someone out there is expecting these two guys to come out in the suits in a minute. I suppose they thought we were slaves. Help me hide these behind the drapes and then, and then—'

'—we'd better suit up,' said Twoflower, picking up the second helmet.

'Yes,' said Rincewind. 'You know, as soon as I saw the suits I just *knew* I'd end up wearing one. Don't ask me how I knew – I suppose it was because it was just about the worst possible thing that was likely to happen.'

'Well, you said yourself we have no way of

escaping,' said Twoflower, his voice muffled as he pulled the top half of a suit over his head. 'Anything's better than being sacrificed.'

'As soon as we get a chance we run for it,' said Rincewind. 'Don't get any ideas.'

He thrust an arm savagely into his suit and banged his head on the helmet. He reflected briefly that someone up there was watching over him.

'Thanks a lot,' he said bitterly.

At the very edge of the city and country of Krull was a large semi-circular amphitheatre, with seating for several tens of thousands of people. The arena was only semi-circular for the very elegant reason that it overlooked the cloud sea that boiled up from the Rimfall, far below, and now every seat was occupied. And the crowd was growing restive. It had come to see a double sacrifice and also the launching of the great bronze space ship. Neither event had yet materialized.

The Arch-astronomer beckoned the Master Launchcontroller to him.

'Well?' he said, filling a mere four letters with a full lexicon of anger and menace. The Master Launchcontroller went pale.

'No news, lord,' said the Launchcontroller, and added with a brittle brightness, 'except that your prominence will be pleased to hear that Garhartra has recovered.'

'That is a fact he may come to regret,' said the Arch-astronomer.

'Yes, lord.'

'How much longer do we have?'

The Launchcontroller glanced at the rapidly climbing sun.

'Thirty minutes, your prominence. After that Krull will have revolved away from Great A'Tuin's tail and the *Potent Voyager* will be doomed to spin away into the interterrapene gulf. I have already set the automatic controls, so—'

'All right, all right,' the Arch-astronomer said, waving him away. 'The launch must go ahead. Maintain the watch on the harbour, of course. When the wretched pair are caught I will personally take a great deal of pleasure in executing them myself.'

'Yes, lord. Er—'

The Arch-astronomer frowned. 'What else have you got to say, man?'

The Launchcontroller swallowed. All this was very unfair on him, he was a practical magician rather than a diplomat, and that was why some wiser brains had seen to it that he would be the one to pass on the news.

'A monster has come out of the sea and it's attacking the ships in the harbour,' he said. 'A runner just arrived from there.'

'A big monster?' said the Arch-astronomer.

'Not particularly, although it is said to be exceptionally fierce, lord.'

The ruler of Krull and the Circumfence considered this for a moment, then shrugged.

'The sea is full of monsters,' he said. 'It is one of its prime attributes. Have it dealt with. And – Master Launchcontroller?'

'Lord?'

'If I am further vexed, you will recall that two people are due to be sacrificed. I may feel generous and increase the number.'

'Yes, lord.' The Master Launchcontroller scuttled away, relieved to be out of the autocrat's sight.

The *Potent Voyager*, no longer the blank bronze shell that had been smashed from the mould a few days earlier, rested in its cradle on top of a wooden tower in the centre of the arena. In front of it a railway ran down towards the Edge, where for the space of a few yards it turned suddenly upwards.

The late Dactylos Goldeneyes, who had designed the launching pad as well as the *Potent Voyager* itself, had claimed that this last touch was merely to ensure that the ship would not snag on any rocks as it began its long plunge. Maybe it was merely coincidental that it would also, because of that little twitch in the track, leap like a salmon and shine theatrically in the sunlight before disappearing into the cloud sea.

There was a fanfare of trumpets at the edge of the arena. The chelonauts' honour guard appeared, to much cheering from the crowd. Then the white-suited explorers themselves stepped out into the light.

It immediately dawned on the Arch-astronomer that something was wrong. Heroes always walked in a certain way, for example. They certainly didn't waddle, and one of the chelonauts was definitely waddling.

The roar of the assembled people of Krull was deafening. As the chelonauts and their guards crossed the great arena, passing between the many altars that had been set up for the various wizards and priests of

Krull's many sects to ensure the success of the launch, the Arch-astronomer frowned. By the time the party was halfway across the floor his mind had reached a conclusion. By the time the chelonauts were standing at the foot of the ladder that led to the ship – and was there more than a hint of reluctance about them? – the Arch-astronomer was on his feet, his words lost in the noise of the crowd. One of his arms shot out and back, fingers spread dramatically in the traditional spell-casting position, and any passing lip-reader who was also familiar with the standard texts on magic would have recognized the opening words of Vestcake's Floating Curse, and would then have prudently run away.

Its final words remained unsaid, however. The Arch-astronomer turned in astonishment as a commotion broke out around the big arched entrance to the arena. Guards were running out into the daylight, throwing down their weapons as they scuttled among the altars or vaulted the parapet into the stands.

Something emerged behind them, and the crowd around the entrance ceased its raucous cheering and began a silent, determined scramble to get out of the way.

The *something* was a low dome of seaweed, moving slowly but with a sinister sense of purpose. One guard overcame his horror sufficiently to stand in its path and hurl his spear, which landed squarely among the weeds. The crowd cheered – then went deathly silent as the dome surged forward and engulfed the man completely.

The Arch-astronomer dismissed the half-formed shape of Vestcake's famous Curse with a sharp wave of his hand, and quickly spoke the words of one of the most powerful spells in his repertoire: the Infernal Combustion Enigma.

Octarine fire spiralled around and between his fingers as he shaped the complex rune of the spell in mid-air and sent it, screaming and trailing blue smoke, towards the shape.

There was a satisfying explosion and a gout of flame shot up into the clear morning sky, shedding flakes of burning seaweed on the way. A cloud of smoke and steam concealed the monster for several minutes, and when it cleared the dome had completely disappeared.

There was a large charred circle on the flagstones, however, in which a few clumps of kelp and bladderwrack still smouldered.

And in the centre of the circle was a perfectly ordinary, if somewhat large, wooden chest. It was not even scorched. Someone on the far side of the arena started to laugh, but the sound was broken off abruptly as the chest rose up on dozens of what could only be legs and turned to face the Arch-astronomer. A perfectly ordinary if somewhat large wooden chest does not, of course, have a face with which to face, but this one was quite definitely facing. In precisely the same way as he understood that, the Arch-astronomer was also horribly aware that this perfectly normal box was in some indescribable way narrowing its eyes.

It began to move resolutely towards him. He shuddered.

'*Magicians!*' he screamed. '*Where are my magicians?*'

Around the arena pale-faced men peeped out from behind altars and under benches. One of the bolder ones, seeing the expression on the Arch-astronomer's face, raised an arm tremulously and essayed a hasty thunderbolt. It hissed towards the chest and struck it squarely in a shower of white sparks.

That was the signal for every magician, enchanter and thaumaturgist in Krull to leap up eagerly and, under the terrified eyes of their master, unleash the first spell that came to each desperate mind. Charms curved and whistled through the air.

Soon the chest was lost to view again in an expanding cloud of magical particles, which billowed out and wreathed it in twisting, disquieting shapes. Spell after spell screamed into the mêlée. Flame and lightning bolts of all eight colours stabbed out brightly from the seething *thing* that now occupied the space where the box had been.

Not since the Mage Wars had so much magic been concentrated on one small area. The air itself wavered and glittered. Spell ricocheted off spell, creating short-lived wild spells whose brief half-life was both weird and uncontrolled. The stones under the heaving mass began to buckle and split. One of them in fact turned into something best left undescribed and slunk off into some dismal dimension. Other strange side-effects began to manifest themselves. A shower of small lead cubes bounced out of the storm and rolled across the heaving floor, and eldritch shapes gibbered and beckoned obscenely; four-sided triangles and double-ended circles existed momentarily before merging again into the booming, screaming tower of runaway raw magic that boiled up from the molten flagstones and spread out over Krull. It no longer mattered that most of the magicians had ceased their spell-casting and fled – the *thing* was now feeding on the stream of octarine particles that were always at their thickest near the Edge of the disc. Throughout the island of Krull every magical activity failed as all the available mana in the area was sucked into the cloud, which was already a quarter of a mile high and streaming out into mind-curdling shapes; hydrophobes on their sea-skimming lenses crashed screaming into the waves, magic potions turned to mere impure water in their phials, magic swords melted and dripped from their scabbards.

But none of this in any way prevented the *thing* at the base of the cloud, now gleaming mirror-bright in the intensity of the power storm around it, from moving at a steady walking pace towards the Arch-astronomer.

Rincewind and Twoflower watched in awe from the shelter of *Potent Voyager*'s launch tower. The honour party had long since vanished, leaving their weapons scattered behind them.

'Well,' sighed Twoflower at last, 'there goes the Luggage.' He sighed.

'Don't you believe it,' said Rincewind. 'Sapient pearwood is totally impervious to all known forms of magic. It's been constructed to follow you anywhere. I mean, when you die, if you go to Heaven, you'll at least have a clean pair of socks in the afterlife. But I don't want to die yet, so let's just get going, shall we?'

'Where?' said Twoflower.

Rincewind picked up a crossbow and a handful of quarrels. 'Anywhere that isn't here,' he said.

'What about the Luggage?'

'Don't worry. When the storm has used up all the free magic in the vicinity it'll just die out.'

In fact that was already beginning to happen. The billowing cloud was still flowing up from the arena but now it had a tenuous, harmless look about it. Even as Twoflower stared, it began to flicker uncertainly.

Soon it was a pale ghost. The Luggage was now visible as a squat shape among the almost invisible flames. Around it the rapidly cooling stones began to crack and buckle.

Twoflower called softly to his Luggage. It stopped its stolid progression across the tortured flags and appeared to be listening intently; then, moving its dozens of feet in an intricate pattern, it turned on its length and headed towards the *Potent Voyager*. Rincewind watched it sourly. The Luggage had an elemental nature, absolutely no brain, a homicidal attitude towards anything that threatened its master, and he wasn't quite sure that its inside occupied the same space-time framework as its outside.

'Not a mark on it,' said Twoflower cheerfully, as the box settled down in front of him. He pushed open the lid.

'This is a fine time to change your underwear,' snarled Rincewind. 'In a minute all those guards and priests are going to come back, and they're going to be *upset*, man!'

'Water,' murmured Twoflower. 'The whole box is full of water!'

Rincewind peered over his shoulder. There was no sign of clothes, moneybags, or any other of the tourist's belongings. The whole box was full of water.

A wave sprang up from nowhere and lapped over the edge. It hit the flagstones but, instead of spreading out, began to take the shape of a foot. Another foot and the bottom half of a pair of legs followed as more water streamed down as if filling an invisible mould. A moment later Tethis the sea troll was standing in front of them, blinking.

'I see,' he said at last. 'You two. I suppose I shouldn't be surprised.'

He looked around, ignoring their astonished expressions.

'I was just sitting outside my hut, watching the sun set, when this thing came roaring up out of the water and swallowed me,' he said. 'I thought it was rather strange. Where is this place?'

'Krull,' said Rincewind. He stared hard at the now closed Luggage, which was managing to project a smug expression. Swallowing people was something it did quite frequently, but always when the lid was next opened there was nothing inside but Twoflower's laundry. Savagely he wrenched the lid up. There was nothing inside but Twoflower's laundry. It was perfectly dry.

'Well, well,' said Tethis. He looked up.

'Hey!' he said. 'Isn't this the ship they're going to

send over the Edge? Isn't it? It must be!'

An arrow zipped through his chest, leaving a faint ripple. He didn't appear to notice. Rincewind did. Soldiers were beginning to appear at the edge of the arena, and a number of them were peering around the entrances.

Another arrow bounced off the tower behind Twoflower. At this range the bolts did not have a lot of force, but it would only be a matter of time . . .

'Quick!' said Twoflower. 'Into the ship! They won't dare fire at that!'

'I *knew* you were going to suggest that,' groaned Rincewind. 'I just *knew* it!'

He aimed a kick at the Luggage. It backed off a few inches, and opened its lid threateningly.

A spear arced out of the sky and trembled to a halt in the woodwork by the wizard's ear. He screamed briefly and scrambled up the ladder after the others.

Arrows whistled around them as they came out on to the narrow catwalk that led along the spine of the *Potent Voyager*. Twoflower led the way, jogging along with what Rincewind considered to be too much suppressed excitement.

Atop the centre of the ship was a large round bronze hatch with hasps around it. The troll and the tourist knelt down and started to work on them.

In the heart of the Potent Voyager *fine sand had been trickling into a carefully designed cup for several hours. Now the cup was filled by exactly the right amount to dip down and upset a carefully balanced weight. The weight swung away, pulling a pin from an intricate little mechanism. A chain began to move. There was a clonk . . .*

'What was that?' said Rincewind urgently. He looked down.

The hail of arrows had stopped. The crowd of priests and soldiers were standing motionless, staring intently at the ship. A small worried man elbowed his way through them and started to shout something.

'What was what?' said Twoflower, busy with a wing-nut.

'I thought I heard something,' said Rincewind. 'Look,' he said, 'we'll threaten to damage the thing if they don't let us go, right? That's all we're going to do, right?'

'Yah,' said Twoflower vaguely. He sat back on his heels. 'That's it,' he said. 'It ought to lift off now.'

Several muscular men were swarming up the ladder to the ship. Rincewind recognized the two chelonauts among them. They were carrying swords.

'I—' he began.

The ship lurched. Then, with infinite slowness, it began to move along the rails.

In that moment of black horror Rincewind saw that Twoflower and the troll had managed to pull the hatch up. A metal ladder inside led into the cabin below. The troll disappeared.

'We've got to get off,' whispered Rincewind. Twoflower looked at him, a strange mad smile on his face.

'Stars,' said the tourist. 'Worlds. The whole damn sky full of worlds. Places no-one will ever see. Except me.' He stepped through the hatchway.

'You're totally mad,' said Rincewind hoarsely, trying to keep his balance as the ship began to speed up. He turned as one of the chelonauts tried to leap the gap between the *Voyager* and the tower, landed on the curving flank of the ship, scrabbled for an instant for purchase, failed to find any, and dropped away with a shriek.

The *Voyager* was travelling quite fast now. Rincewind could see past Twoflower's head to the sunlit cloud sea and the impossible Rimbow, floating tantalizingly beyond it, beckoning fools to venture too far . . .

He also saw a gang of men climbing desperately over the lower slopes of the launching ramp and manhandling a large baulk of timber on to the track, in a frantic attempt to derail the ship before it vanished over the Edge. The wheels slammed into it, but the only effect was to make the ship rock, Twoflower to lose his grip on the ladder and fall into the cabin, and the hatch to slam down with the horrible sound of a dozen fiddly little catches snapping into place. Rincewind dived forward and scrabbled at them, whimpering.

The cloud sea was much nearer now. The Edge itself, a rocky perimeter to the arena, was startlingly close.

Rincewind stood up. There was only one thing to do now, and he did it. He panicked blindly, just as the ship's bogeys hit the little upgrade and flung it, sparkling like a salmon, into the sky and over the Edge.

A few seconds later there was a thunder of little feet

and the Luggage cleared the rim of the world, legs still pumping determinedly, and plunged down into the Universe.

THE END

Rincewind woke up and shivered. He was freezing cold.

So this is it, he thought. When you die you go to a cold, damp, misty freezing place. Hades, where the mournful spirits of the Dead troop for ever across the sorrowful marshes, corpse-lights flickering fitfully in the encircling—hang on a minute . . .

Surely Hades wasn't this uncomfortable? And he was very uncomfortable indeed. His back ached where a branch was pressing into it, his legs and arms hurt where the twigs had lacerated them and, judging by the way his head was feeling, something hard had recently hit it. If this was Hades it sure was hell—hang on a minute . . .

Tree. He concentrated on the word that floated up from his mind, although the buzzing in his ears and the flashing lights in front of his eyes made this an unexpected achievement. Tree. Wooden thing. That was it. Branches and twigs and things. And Rincewind, lying in it. Tree. Dripping wet. Cold white cloud all around. Underneath, too. Now that was odd.

He was alive and lying covered in bruises in a small thorn tree that was growing in a crevice in a rock that projected out of the foaming white wall that was the

Rimfall. The realization hit him in much the same way as an icy hammer. He shuddered. The tree gave a warning creak.

Something blue and blurred shot past him, dipped briefly into the thundering waters, and whirred back and settled on a branch near Rincewind's head. It was a small bird with a tuft of blue and green feathers. It swallowed the little silver fish that it had snatched from the Fall and eyed him curiously.

Rincewind became aware that there were lots of similar birds around.

They hovered, darted and swooped easily across the face of the water, and every so often one would raise an extra plume of spray as it stole another doomed morsel from the waterfall. Several of them were perching in the tree. They were as iridescent as jewels. Rincewind was entranced.

He was in fact the first man ever to see the rimfishers, the tiny creatures who had long ago evolved a lifestyle quite unique even for the disc. Long before the Krullians had built the Circumfence the rimfishers had devised their own efficient method of policing the edge of the world for a living.

They didn't seem bothered about Rincewind. He had a brief but chilling vision of himself living the rest of his life out in this tree, subsisting on raw birds and such fish as he could snatch as they plummeted past.

The tree moved distinctly. Rincewind gave a whimper as he found himself sliding backwards, but managed to grab a branch. Only, sooner or later, he would fall asleep . . .

There was a subtle change of scene, a slight

purplish tint to the sky. A tall, black-cloaked figure was standing on the air next to the tree. It had a scythe in one hand. Its face was hidden in the shadows of the hood.

I HAVE COME FOR THEE, said the invisible mouth, in tones as heavy as a whale's heartbeat.

The trunk of the tree gave another protesting creak, and a pebble bounced off Rincewind's helmet as one root tore loose from the rock.

Death Himself always came in person to harvest the souls of wizards.

'What am I going to die of?' said Rincewind.

The tall figure hesitated.

PARDON? it said.

'Well, I haven't broken anything, and I haven't drowned, so what am I about to die of? You can't just be killed by Death; there has to be a reason,' said Rincewind. To his utter amazement he didn't feel terrified any more. For about the first time in his life he wasn't frightened. Pity the experience didn't look like lasting for long.

Death appeared to reach a conclusion.

YOU COULD DIE OF TERROR, the hood intoned. The voice still had its graveyard ring, but there was a slight tremor of uncertainty.

'Won't work,' said Rincewind smugly.

THERE DOESN'T HAVE TO BE A REASON, said Death, I CAN JUST KILL YOU.

'Hey, you can't do that! It'd be murder!'

The cowled figure sighed and pulled back its hood. Instead of the grinning death's head that Rincewind had been expecting he found himself looking up into the pale and slightly transparent face of a rather worried demon, of sorts.

'I'm making rather a mess of this, aren't I?' it said wearily.

'You're not Death! Who are you?' cried Rincewind.

'Scrofula.'

'*Scrofula?*'

'Death couldn't come,' said the demon wretchedly. 'There's a big plague on in Pseudopolis. He had to go and stalk the streets. So he sent me.'

'No-one dies of scrofula! I've got rights. I'm a wizard!'

'All right, all right. This was going to be my big chance,' said Scrofula, 'but look at it this way – if I hit you with this scythe you'll be just as dead as you would be if Death had done it. Who'd know?'

'I'd know!' snapped Rincewind.

'You wouldn't. You'd be dead,' said Scrofula logically.

'Piss off,' said Rincewind.

'That's all very well,' said the demon, hefting the scythe, 'but why not try to see things from my point of view? This means a lot to me, and you've got to admit that your life isn't all that wonderful. Reincarnation can only be an improvement – uh.'

His hand flew to his mouth but Rincewind was already pointing a trembling finger at him.

'Reincarnation!' he said excitedly. 'So it is true what the mystics say!'

'I'm admitting nothing,' said Scrofula testily. 'It was a slip of the tongue. Now – are you going to die willingly or not?'

'No,' said Rincewind.

'Please yourself,' replied the demon. He raised the scythe. It whistled down in quite a professional way, but Rincewind wasn't there. He was in fact several metres below, and the distance was increasing all the time, because the branch had chosen that moment to snap and send him on his interrupted journey towards the interstellar gulf.

'Come back!' screamed the demon.

Rincewind didn't answer. He was lying belly down in the rushing air, staring down into the clouds that even now were thinning.

They vanished.

Below, the whole Universe twinkled at Rincewind. There was Great A'Tuin, huge and ponderous and pocked with craters. There was the little disc moon. There was a distant gleam that could only be the *Potent Voyager*. And there were all the stars, looking remarkably like powdered diamonds spilled on black velvet, the stars that lured and ultimately called the boldest towards them . . .

The whole Creation was waiting for Rincewind to drop in.

He did so.

There didn't seem to be any alternative.

THE END

THE LIGHT FANTASTIC

Terry Pratchett

CORGI BOOKS

THE SUN ROSE SLOWLY, as if it wasn't sure it was worth all the effort.

Another Disc day dawned, but very gradually, and this is why.

When light encounters a strong magical field it loses all sense of urgency. It slows right down. And on the Discworld the magic was embarrassingly strong, which meant that the soft yellow light of dawn flowed over the sleeping landscape like the caress of a gentle lover or, as some would have it, like golden syrup. It paused to fill up valleys. It piled up against mountain ranges. When it reached Cori Celesti, the ten mile spire of grey stone and green ice that marked the hub of the Disc and was the home of its gods, it built up in heaps until it finally crashed in great lazy tsunami as silent as velvet, across the dark landscape beyond.

It was a sight to be seen on no other world.

Of course, no other world was carried through the starry infinity on the backs of four giant elephants, who were themselves perched on the shell of a giant turtle. His name – or Her name, according to another school of thought – was Great A'Tuin; he – or, as it might be, she – will not take a central role in what follows but it is vital to an understanding of the Disc that he – or she – is there, down below the mines and sea ooze and fake fossil bones put there by a Creator with nothing better to do than upset archaeologists and give them silly ideas.

Great A'Tuin the star turtle, shell frosted with frozen methane, pitted with meteor craters, and scoured with asteroidal dust. Great A'Tuin, with eyes like ancient seas and a brain the size of a continent through which thoughts moved like little glittering glaciers. Great A'Tuin of the great slow sad flippers and star-polished carapace, labouring through the galactic night under the weight of the Disc. As large as worlds. As old as Time. As patient as a brick.

Actually, the philosophers have got it all wrong. Great A'Tuin is in fact having a great time.

Great A'Tuin is the only creature in the entire universe that knows exactly where it is going.

Of course, philosophers have debated for years about where Great A'Tuin might be going, and have often said how worried they are that they might never find out.

They're due to find out in about two months. And then they're *really* going to worry . . .

Something else that has long worried the more imaginative philosophers on the Disc is the question of Great A'Tuin's sex, and quite a lot of time and trouble has been spent in trying to establish it once and for all.

In fact, as the great dark shape drifts past like an endless tortoiseshell hairbrush, the results of the latest effort are just coming into view.

Tumbling past, totally out of control, is the bronze shell of the *Potent Voyager*, a sort of neolithic spaceship built and pushed over the edge by the astronomer-priests of Krull, which is conveniently situated on the very rim of the world and proves, whatever people say, that there *is* such a thing as a free launch.

Inside the ship is Twoflower, the Disc's first tourist. He had recently spent some months exploring it and is now rapidly leaving it for reasons that are rather complicated but have to do with an attempt to escape from Krull.

This attempt has been one thousand per cent successful.

But despite all the evidence that he may be the Disc's *last* tourist as well, he is enjoying the view.

Plunging along some two miles above him is Rincewind the wizard, in what on the Disc passes for a spacesuit. Picture it as a diving suit designed by men who have never seen the sea. Six months ago he was a perfectly ordinary failed wizard. Then he met Twoflower, was employed at an outrageous salary as his guide, and has spent most of the intervening time being shot at, terrorized, chased and hanging from high places with no hope of salvation or, as is now the case, dropping from high places.

He isn't looking at the view because his past life keeps flashing in front of his eyes and getting in the way. He is learning why it is that when you put on a spacesuit it is vitally important not to forget the helmet.

A lot more could be included now to explain why these two are dropping out of the world, and why Twoflower's Luggage, last seen desperately trying to follow him on hundreds of little legs, is no ordinary suitcase, but such questions take time and could be more trouble than they are worth. For example, it is said that someone at a party once asked the famous philosopher Ly Tin Weedle 'Why are you here?' and the reply took three years.

What is far more important is an event happening way overhead, far above A'Tuin, the elephants and the rapidly-expiring wizard. The very fabric of time and space is about to be put through the wringer.

The air was greasy with the distinctive feel of magic, and acrid with the smoke of candles made of a black wax whose precise origin a wise man wouldn't enquire about.

There was something very strange about this room deep in the cellars of Unseen University, the Disc's premier college of magic. For one thing it seemed to have too many dimensions, not exactly visible, just hovering out of eyeshot. The walls were covered with occult symbols, and most of the floor was taken up by the Eightfold Seal of Stasis, generally agreed in magical circles to have all the stopping power of a well-aimed halfbrick.

The only furnishing in the room was a lectern of dark wood, carved into the shape of a bird – well, to be frank, into the shape of a winged thing it is probably best not to examine too closely – and on the lectern, fastened to it by a heavy chain covered in padlocks, was a book.

A large, but not particularly impressive, book. Other books in the University's libraries had covers inlaid with rare jewels and fascinating wood, or bound with dragon skin. This one was just a rather tatty leather. It looked the sort of book described in library catalogues as 'slightly foxed', although it would be more honest to admit that it looked as though it had been badgered, wolved and possibly beared as well.

Metal clasps held it shut. They weren't decorated, they were just very heavy – like the chain, which didn't so much attach the book to the lectern as tether it.

They looked like the work of someone who had a pretty definite aim in mind, and who had spent most of his life making training harnesses for elephants.

The air thickened and swirled. The pages of the book began to crinkle in a quite horrible, deliberate way, and blue light spilled out from between them. The silence of the room crowded in like a fist, slowly being clenched.

Half a dozen wizards in their nightshirts were taking turns to peer in through the little grille in the door. No wizard could sleep with this sort of thing going on – the build-up of raw magic was rising through the University like a tide.

'Right,' said a voice. 'What's going on? And why wasn't I summoned?'

Galder Weatherwax, Supreme Grand Conjuror of the Order of the Silver Star, Lord Imperial of the Sacred Staff, Eighth Level Ipsissimus and 304th Chancellor of Unseen University, wasn't simply an impressive sight even in his red nightshirt with the hand-embroidered mystic runes, even in his long cap with the bobble on, even with the Wee Willie Winkie candlestick in his hand. He even managed to very nearly pull it off in fluffy pompom slippers as well.

Six frightened faces turned towards him.

'Um, you *were* summoned, lord,' said one of the under-wizards. 'That's why you're here,' he added helpfully.

'I mean why wasn't I summoned *before*?' snapped Galder, pushing his way to the grille.

'Um, before who, lord?' said the wizard.

Galder glared at him, and ventured a quick glance through the grille.

The air in the room was now sparkling with tiny flashes as dust motes incinerated in the flow of raw magic. The Seal of Stasis was beginning to blister and curl up at the edges.

The book in question was called the Octavo and, quite obviously, it was no ordinary book.

There are of course many famous books of magic. Some may talk of the Necrotelicomnicon, with its pages made of ancient lizard skin; some may point to the Book of Going Forth Around Elevenish, written by a mysterious and rather lazy Llamaic sect; some may recall that the Bumper Fun Grimoire reputedly contains the one original joke left in the universe. But they are all mere pamphlets when compared with the Octavo, which the Creator of the Universe reputedly left behind – with characteristic absent-mindedness – shortly after completing his major work.

The eight spells imprisoned in its pages led a secret and complex life of their own, and it was generally believed that—

Galder's brow furrowed as he stared into the troubled room. Of course, there were only seven spells now. Some young idiot of a student wizard had stolen a look at the book one day and one of the spells had escaped and lodged in his mind. No one had ever managed to get to the bottom of how it had happened. What was his name, now? Winswand?

Octarine and purple sparks glittered on the spine of the book. A thin curl of smoke was beginning to rise from the lectern, and the heavy metal clasps that held the book shut were definitely beginning to look strained.

'Why are the spells so restless?' said one of the younger wizards.

Galder shrugged. He couldn't show it, of course, but he was beginning to be really worried. As a skilled eighth-level wizard he could see the half-imaginary shapes that appeared momentarily in the vibrating air, wheedling and beckoning. In much the same way that gnats appear before a thunderstorm, really heavy build-ups of magic always attracted things from the chaotic Dungeon Dimensions – nasty Things, all mis-placed organs and spittle, forever searching for any gap through which they might sidle into the world of men.*

This had to be stopped.

'I shall need a volunteer,' he said firmly.

There was a sudden silence. The only sound came from behind the door. It was the nasty little noise of metal parting under stress.

'Very well, then,' he said. 'In that case I shall need some silver tweezers, about two pints of cat's blood, a small whip and a chair—'

It is said that the opposite of noise is silence. This isn't true. Silence is only the absence of noise. Silence would have been a terrible din compared to the sudden soft implosion of noiselessness that hit the wizards with the force of an exploding dandelion clock.

A thick column of spitting light sprang up from the book, hit the ceiling in a splash of flame, and disappeared.

Galder stared up at the hole, ignoring the smouldering patches in his beard. He pointed dramatically.

'To the upper cellars!' he cried, and bounded up the stone stairs. Slippers flapping and nightshirts billowing the other wizards followed him, falling over one another in their eagerness to be last.

* They won't be described, since even the pretty ones looked like the offspring of an octopus and a bicycle. It is well known that *things* from undesirable universes are always seeking an entrance into this one, which is the psychic equivalent of handy for the buses and closer to the shops.

Nevertheless, they were all in time to see the fireball of occult potentiality disappear into the ceiling of the room above.

'Urgh,' said the youngest wizard, and pointed to the floor.

The room had been part of the library until the magic had drifted through, violently reassembling the possibility particles of everything in its path. So it was reasonable to assume that the small purple newts had been part of the floor and the pineapple custard may once have been some books. And several of the wizards later swore that the small sad orang outang sitting in the middle of it all looked very much like the head librarian.

Galder stared upwards. 'To the kitchen!' he bellowed, wading through the custard to the next flight of stairs.

No one ever found out what the great cast-iron cooking range had been turned into, because it had broken down a wall and made good its escape before the dishevelled party of wild-eyed mages burst into the room. The vegetable chef was found much later hiding in the soup cauldron, gibbering unhelpful things like 'The knuckles! The horrible knuckles!'

The last wisps of magic, now somewhat slowed, were disappearing into the ceiling.

'To the Great Hall!'

The stairs were much wider here, and better lit. Panting and pineapple-flavoured, the fitter wizards got to the top by the time the fireball had reached the middle of the huge draughty chamber that was the University's main hall. It hung motionless, except for the occasional small prominence that arched and spluttered across its surface.

Wizards smoke, as everyone knows. That probably explained the chorus of coffin coughs and sawtooth wheezes that erupted behind Galder as he stood appraising the situation and wondering if he dare look for somewhere to hide. He grabbed a frightened student.

'Get me seers, farseers, scryers and within-lookmen!' he barked. 'I want this studied!'

Something was taking shape inside the fireball. Galder shielded his eyes and peered at the shape forming in front of him. There was no mistaking it. It was the universe.

He was quite sure of this, because he had a model of it in his study and it was generally agreed to be far more impressive than the real thing. Faced with the possibilities offered by seed pearls and silver filigree, the Creator had been at a complete loss.

But the tiny universe inside the fireball was uncannily – well, real. The only thing missing was colour. It was all in translucent misty white.

There was Great A'Tuin, and the four elephants, and the Disc itself. From this angle Galder couldn't see the surface very well, but he knew with cold certainty that it would be absolutely accurately modelled. He could, though, just make out a miniature replica of Cori Celesti, upon whose utter peak the world's quarrelsome and somewhat bourgeois gods lived in a palace of marble, alabaster and uncut moquette three-piece suites they had chosen to call Dunmanifestin. It was always a considerable annoyance to any Disc citizen with pretensions to culture that they were ruled by gods whose idea of an uplifting artistic experience was a musical doorbell.

The little embryo universe began to move slowly, tilting . . .

Galder tried to shout, but his voice refused to come out.

Gently, but with the unstoppable force of an explosion, the shape expanded.

He watched in horror, and then in astonishment, as it passed through him as lightly as a thought. He held out a hand and watched the pale ghosts of rock strata stream through his fingers in busy silence.

Great A'Tuin had already sunk peacefully below floor level, larger than a house.

The wizards behind Galder were waist deep in seas. A boat smaller than a thimble caught Galder's eye for a moment before the rush carried it through the walls and away.

'To the roof!' he managed, pointing a shaking finger skywards.

Those wizards with enough marbles left to think with and enough breath to run followed him, running through continents that sleeted smoothly through the solid stone.

It was a still night, tinted with the promise of dawn. A crescent moon was just setting. Ankh-Morpork, largest city in the lands around the Circle Sea, slept.

That statement is not really true.

On the one hand, those parts of the city which normally concerned themselves with, for example, selling vegetables, shoeing horses, carving exquisite small jade ornaments, changing money and making tables, on the whole, slept. Unless they had insomnia. Or had got up in the night, as it might be, to go to the lavatory. On the other hand, many of the less law-abiding citizens were wide awake and, for instance, climbing through windows that didn't belong to them, slitting throats, mugging one another, listening to loud music in smoky cellars and generally having a lot more fun. But most of the animals were asleep, except for the rats. And the bats, too, of course. As far as the insects were concerned . . .

The point is that descriptive writing is very rarely entirely accurate and during the reign of Olaf Quimby II as Patrician of Ankh some legislation was passed in a determined attempt to put a stop to this sort of thing and introduce some honesty into reporting. Thus, if a legend said of a notable hero that 'all men spoke of his prowess' any bard who valued his life would add hastily 'except for a couple of people in his home village who thought he was a liar, and quite a lot of other people who had never really heard of him.' Poetic simile was strictly limited to statements like 'his mighty steed was as fleet as the wind on a fairly calm day, say about Force Three,' and any loose talk about a beloved having a face that launched a thousand ships would have to be backed by evidence that the object of desire did indeed look like a bottle of champagne.

Quimby was eventually killed by a disgruntled poet during an experiment conducted in the palace grounds to prove the disputed accuracy of the proverb 'The pen is mightier than the sword,' and in his memory it was amended to include the phrase 'only if the sword is very small and the pen is very sharp.'

So. Approximately sixty-seven, maybe sixty-eight, per cent of the city slept. Not that the other citizens creeping about on their generally unlawful occasions noticed the pale tide streaming through the streets. Only the wizards, used to seeing the invisible, watched it foam across the distant fields.

The Disc, being flat, has no real horizon. Any adventurous sailors who got funny ideas from staring at eggs and oranges for too long and set out for the antipodes soon learned that the reason why distant ships sometimes looked as though they were disappearing over the edge of the world was that they *were* disappearing over the edge of the world.

But there was still a limit even to Galder's vision in the mist-swirled, dust-filled air. He looked up. Looming high over the University was the grim and ancient Tower of Art, said to be the oldest building on the Disc, with its famous spiral staircase of eight thousand, eight hundred and eighty-eight steps. From its crenelated roof, the haunt of ravens and disconcertingly alert gargoyles, a wizard might see to the very edge of the Disc. After spending ten minutes or so coughing horribly, of course.

'Sod that,' he muttered. 'What's the good of being a wizard, after all? Avyento, thessalous! I would fly! To me, spirits of air and darkness!'

He spread a gnarled hand and pointed to a piece of crumbling parapet. Octarine fire sprouted from under his nicotine-stained nails and burst against the rotting stone far above.

It fell. By a finely calculated exchange of velocities Galder rose, nightshirt flapping around his bony legs. Higher and higher he soared, hurtling through the pale light like a, like a – all right, like an elderly but powerful wizard being propelled upwards by an expertly judged thumb on the scales of the universe.

He landed in a litter of old nests, caught his balance, and stared down at the vertiginous view of a Disc dawn.

At this time of the long year the Circle Sea was almost on the sunset side of Cori Celesti, and as the daylight sloshed down into the lands around Ankh-Morpork the shadow of the mountain scythed across the landscape like the gnomon of God's sundial. But nightwards, racing the slow light towards the edge of the world, a line of white mist surged on.

There was a crackling of dry twigs behind him. He turned to see Ymper Trymon, second in command of the Order, who had been the only other wizard able to keep up.

Galder ignored him for the moment, taking care only to keep a firm grip on the stonework and strengthen his personal spells of protection. Promotion was slow in a profession that traditionally bestowed long life, and it was accepted that younger wizards would frequently seek advancement via dead men's curly shoes, having previously emptied them of their occupants. Besides, there was something disquieting about young Trymon. He didn't smoke, only drank boiled water, and Galder had the nasty suspicion that he was clever. He didn't smile often enough, and he liked figures and the sort of organization charts that show lots of squares with arrows pointing to other squares. In short, he was the sort of man who could use the word 'personnel' and mean it.

The whole of the visible Disc was now covered with a shimmering white skin that fitted it perfectly.

Galder looked down at his own hands and saw them covered with a pale network of shining threads that followed every movement.

He recognized this kind of spell. He'd used them himself. But his had been smaller – much smaller.

'It's a Change spell,' said Trymon. 'The whole world is being changed.'

Some people, thought Galder grimly, would have had the decency to put an exclamation mark on the end of a statement like that.

There was the faintest of pure sounds, high and sharp, like the breaking of a mouse's heart.

'What was that?' he said.

Trymon cocked his head.

'C sharp, I think,' he said.

Galder said nothing. The white shimmer had vanished, and the first sounds of the waking city began to filter up to the two wizards. Everything seemed exactly the same as it had before. All that, just to make things stay the same?

He patted his nightshirt pockets distractedly and finally found what he was looking for lodged behind his ear. He put the soggy dogend in his mouth, called up mystical fire from between his fingers, and dragged hard on the wretched rollup until little blue lights flashed in front of his eyes. He coughed once or twice.

He was thinking very hard indeed.

He was trying to remember if any gods owed him any favours.

In fact the gods were as puzzled by all this as the wizards were, but they were powerless to do anything and in any case were engaged in an eons-old battle with the Ice Giants, who had refused to return the lawnmower.

But some clue as to what actually had happened might be found in the fact that Rincewind, whose past life had just got up to a quite interesting bit when he was fifteen, suddenly found himself not dying after all but hanging upside down in a pine tree.

He got down easily by dropping uncontrollably from branch to branch until he landed on his head in a pile of pine needles, where he lay gasping for breath and wishing he'd been a better person.

Somewhere, he knew, there had to be a perfectly logical connection. One minute one happens to be dying, having dropped off the rim of the world, and the next one is upside down in a tree.

As always happened at times like this, the Spell rose up in his mind.

Rincewind had been generally reckoned by his tutors to be a natural wizard in the same way that fish are natural mountaineers. He probably would have been thrown out of Unseen University anyway – he couldn't remember spells and smoking made him feel ill – but what had really caused trouble was all that stupid business about sneaking into the room where the Octavo was chained and opening it.

And what made the trouble even *worse* was that no one could figure out why all the locks had temporarily become unlocked.

The Spell wasn't a demanding lodger. It just sat there like an old toad at the bottom of a pond. But whenever Rincewind was feeling really tired or very afraid it tried to get itself said. No one knew what would happen if one of the Eight Great Spells was said by itself, but the general agreement was that the best place from which to watch the effects would be the next universe.

It was a weird thought to have, lying on a heap of pine needles after just falling off the edge of the world, but Rincewind had a feeling that the Spell wanted to keep him alive.

'Suits me,' he thought.

He sat up and looked at the trees. Rincewind was a city wizard and, although he was aware that there were various differences among types of tree by which their nearest and dearest could tell them apart, the only thing he knew for certain was that the end without the leaves on fitted into the ground. There were far too many of them, arranged with absolutely no sense of order. The place hadn't been swept for ages.

He remembered something about being able to tell where you were by looking at which side of a tree the moss grew on. These trees had moss everywhere, and wooden warts, and scrabbly old branches; if trees were people, these trees would be sitting in rocking chairs.

Rincewind gave the nearest one a kick. With unerring aim it dropped an acorn on him. He said 'Ow.' The tree, in a voice like a very old door swinging open, said, 'Serves you right.'

There was a long silence.

Then Rincewind said, 'Did you say that?'

'Yes.'

'And that too?'

'Yes.'

'Oh.' He thought for a bit. Then he tried, 'I suppose you wouldn't happen to know the way out of the forest, possibly, by any chance?'

'No. I don't get about much,' said the tree.

'Fairly boring life, I imagine,' said Rincewind.

'I wouldn't know. I've never been anything else,' said the tree.

Rincewind looked at it closely. It seemed pretty much like every other tree he'd seen.

'Are you magical?' he said.

'No one's ever said,' said the tree. 'I suppose so.'

Rincewind thought: I can't be talking to a tree. If I was talking to a tree I'd be mad, and I'm not mad, so trees can't talk.

'Goodbye,' he said firmly.

'Hey, don't go,' the tree began, and then realized the hopelessness of it all. It watched him stagger off through the bushes, and settled down to feeling the sun on its leaves, the slurp and gurgle of the water in its roots, and the very ebb and flow of its sap in response to the natural tug of the sun and moon. Boring, it thought. What a strange thing to say. Trees can be bored, of course, beetles do it all the time, but I don't think that was what he was trying to mean. And: can you actually be anything else?

In fact Rincewind never spoke to this particular tree again, but from that brief conversation it spun the basis of the first tree religion which, in time, swept the forests of the world. Its tenet of faith was this: a tree that was a good tree, and led a clean, decent and upstanding life, could be assured of a future life after death. If it was very good indeed it would eventually be reincarnated as five thousand rolls of lavatory paper.

A few miles away Twoflower was also getting over his surprise at finding himself back on the Disc. He was sitting on the hull of the *Potent Voyager* as it gurgled gradually under the dark waters of a large lake, surrounded by trees.

Strangely enough, he was not particularly worried.

Twoflower was a tourist, the first of the species to evolve on the Disc, and fundamental to his very existence was the rock-hard belief that nothing bad could really happen to him because he was *not involved*; he also believed that anyone could understand anything he said provided he spoke loudly and slowly, that people were basically trustworthy and that anything could be sorted out among men of goodwill if they just acted sensibly.

On the face of it this gave him a survival value marginally less than, say, a soap herring, but to Rincewind's amazement it all seemed to work and the little man's total obliviousness to all forms of danger somehow made danger so discouraged that it gave up and went away.

Merely being faced with drowning stood no chance. Twoflower was quite certain that in a well-organized society people would not be allowed to go around getting drowned.

He was a little bothered, though, about where his Luggage had got to. But he comforted himself with the knowledge that it was made of sapient pearwood, and ought to be intelligent enough to look after itself . . .

In yet another part of the forest a young shaman was undergoing a very essential part of his training. He had eaten of the sacred toadstool, he had smoked the holy rhizome, he had carefully powdered up and inserted into various orifices the mystic mushroom and now, sitting crosslegged under a pine tree, he was concentrating firstly on making contact with the strange and wonderful secrets at the heart of Being but mainly on stopping the top of his head from unscrewing and floating away.

Blue four-side triangles pinwheeled across his vision. Occasionally he smiled knowingly at nothing very much and said things like 'Wow' and 'Urgh'.

There was a movement in the air and what he later described as 'like, a sort of explosion only backwards, you know?', and suddenly where there had only been nothing there was a large, battered, wooden chest.

It landed heavily on the leafmould, extended dozens of little legs, and turned around ponderously to look at the shaman. That is to say, it had no face, but even through the mycological haze he was horribly aware that it was looking at him. And not a nice look, either. It was amazing how baleful a keyhole and a couple of knotholes could be.

To his intense relief it gave a sort of wooden shrug, and set off through the trees at a canter.

With superhuman effort the shaman recalled the correct sequence of movements for standing up and even managed a couple of steps before he looked down and gave up, having run out of legs.

Rincewind, meanwhile, had found a path. It wound about a good deal, and he would have been happier if it had been cobbled, but following it gave him something to do.

Several trees tried to strike up a conversation, but Rincewind was nearly certain that this was not normal behaviour for trees and ignored them.

The day lengthened. There was no sound but the murmur of nasty little stinging insects, the occasional crack of a falling branch, and the whispering of the trees discussing religion and the trouble with squirrels. Rincewind began to feel very lonely. He imagined himself living in the woods forever, sleeping on leaves and eating . . . and eating . . . whatever there was to eat in woods. Trees, he supposed, and nuts and berries. He would have to . . .

'Rincewind!'

There, coming up the path, was Twoflower – dripping wet, but beaming with delight. The Luggage trotted along behind him (anything made of the wood would follow its owner anywhere and it was often used to make luggage for the grave goods of very rich dead kings who wanted to be sure of starting a new life in the next world with clean underwear).

Rincewind sighed. Up to now, he'd thought the day couldn't possibly get worse.

It began to rain a particularly wet and cold rain. Rincewind and Twoflower sat under a tree and watched it.

'Rincewind?'

'Um?'

'Why are we here?'

'Well, some say that the Creator of the Universe made the Disc and everything on it, others say that it's all a very complicated story involving the testicles of the Sky God and the milk of the Celestial Cow, and some even hold that we're all just due to the total random accretion of probability particles. But if you mean why are we *here* as opposed to falling off the Disc, I haven't the faintest idea. It's probably all some ghastly mistake.'

'Oh. Do you think there's anything to eat in this forest?'

'Yes,' said the wizard bitterly, 'us.'

'I've got some acorns, if you like,' said the tree helpfully.

They sat in damp silence for some moments.

'Rincewind, the tree said—'

'Trees can't talk,' snapped Rincewind. 'It's very important to remember that.'

'But you just heard—'

Rincewind sighed. 'Look,' he said. 'It's all down to simple biology, isn't it? If you're going to talk you need the right equipment, like lungs and lips and, and—'

'Vocal chords,' said the tree.

'Yeah, them,' said Rincewind. He shut up and stared gloomily at the rain.

'*I* thought wizards knew all about trees and wild food and things,' said Twoflower reproachfully. It was very seldom that anything in his voice suggested that he thought of Rincewind as anything other than a magnificent enchanter, and the wizard was stung into action.

'I do, I do,' he snapped.

'Well, what kind of tree is this?' said the tourist. Rincewind looked up.

'Beech,' he said firmly.

'Actually—' began the tree, and shut up quickly. It had caught Rincewind's look.

'Those things up there look like acorns,' said Twoflower.

'Yes, well, this is the sessile or heptocarpic variety,' said Rincewind. 'The nuts look very much like acorns, in fact. They can fool practically anybody.'

'Gosh,' said Twoflower, and, 'What's that bush over there, then?'

'Mistletoe.'

'But it's got thorns and red berries!'

'Well?' said Rincewind sternly, and stared hard at him. Twoflower broke first.

'Nothing,' he said meekly. 'I must have been misinformed.'

'Right.'

'But there's some big mushrooms under it. Can you eat them?'

Rincewind looked at them cautiously. They were, indeed, very big, and had red and white spotted caps. They were in fact a variety that the local shaman (who at this point was some miles away, making friends with a rock) would only eat after first attaching one leg to a large stone with a rope. There was nothing for it but to go out in the rain and look at them.

He knelt down in the leafmould and peered under the cap. After a while he said weakly, 'No, no good to eat at all.'

'Why?' called Twoflower. 'Are the gills the wrong shade of yellow?'

'No, not really . . .'

'I expect the stems haven't got the right kind of fluting, then.'

'They look okay, actually.'

'The cap, then, I expect the cap is the wrong colour,' said Twoflower.

'Not sure about that.'

'Well then, why can't you eat them?'

Rincewind coughed. 'It's the little doors and windows,' he said wretchedly, 'it's a dead giveaway.'

Thunder rolled across Unseen University. Rain poured over its roofs and gurgled out of its gargoyles, although one or two of the more cunning ones had scuttled off to shelter among the maze of tiles.

Far below, in the Great Hall, the eight most powerful wizards on the Discworld gathered at the angles of a ceremonial octogram. Actually they probably weren't the most powerful, if the truth were known, but they certainly had great powers of survival which, in the highly competitive world of magic, was pretty much the same thing. Behind every wizard of the eighth rank were half a dozen seventh rank wizards trying to bump him off, and senior wizards had to develop an enquiring attitude to, for example, scorpions in their bed. An ancient proverb summed it up: when a wizard is tired of looking for broken glass in his dinner, it ran, he is tired of life.

The oldest wizard, Greyhald Spold of the Ancient and Truly Original Sages of the Unbroken Circle, leaned heavily on his carven staff and spake thusly:

'Get on with it, Weatherwax, my feet are giving me gyp.'

Galder, who had merely paused for effect, glared at him.

'Very well, then, I will be brief—'

'Jolly good.'

'We all sought guidance as to the events of this morning. Can anyone among us say he received it?'

The wizards looked sidelong at one another. Nowhere outside a trades union conference fraternal benefit night can so much mutual distrust and suspicion be found as among a gathering of senior enchanters. But the plain fact was that the day had gone very badly. Normally informative demons, summoned abruptly from the Dungeon Dimensions, had looked sheepish and sidled away when questioned. Magic mirrors had cracked. Tarot cards had mysteriously become blank. Crystal balls had gone all cloudy. Even tealeaves, normally scorned by wizards as frivolous and unworthy of contemplation, had clustered together at the bottom of cups and refused to move.

In short, the assembled wizards were at a loss. There was a general murmur of agreement.

'And therefore I propose that we perform the Rite of AshkEnte,' said Galder dramatically.

He had to admit that he had hoped for a better response, something on the lines of, well, 'No, not the Rite of AshkEnte! Man was not meant to meddle with such things!'

In fact there was a general mutter of approval.

'Good idea.'

'Seems reasonable.'

'Get on with it, then.'

Slightly put out, he summoned a procession of lesser wizards who carried various magical implements into the hall.

It has already been hinted that around this time there was some disagreement among the fraternity of wizards about how to practise magic.

Younger wizards in particular went about saying that it was time that magic started to update its image and that they should all stop mucking about with bits of wax and bone and put the whole thing on a properly-organized basis, with research programmes and three-day conventions in good hotels where they could read papers with titles like 'Whither Geomancy?' and 'The role of Seven League Boots in a caring society.'

Trymon, for example, hardly ever did any magic these days but ran the Order with hourglass efficiency and wrote lots of memos and had a big chart on his office wall, covered with coloured blobs and flags and lines that no one else really understood but which looked very impressive.

The other type of wizard thought all this was so much marsh gas and wouldn't have anything to do with an image unless it was made of wax and had pins stuck in it.

The heads of the eight orders were all of this persuasion, traditionalists to a mage, and the utensils that were heaped around the octogram had a definite, no-nonsense occult look about them. Rams horns, skulls, baroque metalwork and heavy candles were much in evidence, despite the discovery by younger wizards that the Rite of AshkEnte could perfectly well be performed with three small bits of wood and 4 cc of mouse blood.

The preparation normally took several hours, but the combined powers of the senior wizards shortened it considerably and, after a mere forty minutes, Galder chanted the final words of the spell. They hung in front of him for a moment before dissolving.

The air in the centre of the octogram shimmered and thickened, and suddenly contained a tall, dark figure. Most of it was hidden by a black robe and hood and this was probably just as well. It held a long scythe in one hand and one couldn't help noticing that what should have been fingers were simply white bone.

The other skeletal hand held small cubes of cheese and pineapple on a stick.

WELL? said Death, in a voice with all the warmth and colour of an iceberg. He caught the wizards' gaze, and glanced down at the stick.

I WAS AT A PARTY, he added, a shade reproachfully.

'O Creature of Earth and Darkness, we do charge thee to abjure from—' began Galder in a firm, commanding voice. Death nodded.

YES, YES, I KNOW ALL THAT, he said. WHY HAVE YOU SUMMONED ME?

'It is said that you can see both the past and future,' said Galder a little sulkily, because the big speech of binding and conjuration was one he rather liked and people had said he was very good at it.

THAT IS ABSOLUTELY CORRECT.

'Then perhaps you can tell us what exactly it was that happened this morning?' said Galder. He pulled himself together, and added loudly, 'I command this by Azimrothe, by T'chikel, by—'

ALL RIGHT, YOU'VE MADE YOUR POINT, said Death. WHAT PRECISELY WAS IT YOU WISHED TO KNOW? QUITE A LOT OF THINGS HAPPENED THIS MORNING, PEOPLE WERE BORN, PEOPLE DIED, ALL THE TREES GREW A BIT TALLER, RIPPLES MADE INTERESTING PATTERNS ON THE SEA—

'I mean about the Octavo,' said Galder coldly.

THAT? OH, THAT WAS JUST A READJUSTMENT OF REALITY. I UNDERSTAND THE OCTAVO WAS ANXIOUS NOT TO LOSE THE EIGHTH SPELL. IT WAS DROPPING OFF THE DISC, APPARENTLY.

'Hold on, hold on,' said Galder. He scratched his chin. 'Are we talking about the one inside the head of Rincewind? Tall thin man, bit scraggy? The one—'

—THAT HE HAS BEEN CARRYING AROUND ALL THESE YEARS, YES.

Galder frowned. It seemed a lot of trouble to go to. Everyone knew that when a wizard died all the spells in his head would go feee, so why bother to save Rincewind? The Spell would just float back eventually.

'Any idea why?' he said without thinking and then, remembering himself in time, added hastily, 'By Yrriph and Kcharla I do abjure thee and—'

I WISH YOU WOULDN'T KEEP DOING THAT, said Death.

ALL THAT I KNOW IS THAT ALL THE SPELLS HAVE TO BE SAID TOGETHER NEXT HOGSWATCHNIGHT OR THE DISC WILL BE DESTROYED.

'Speak up there!' demanded Greyhald Spold.

'Shut up!' said Galder.

ME?

'No, him. Daft old—'

'I heard that!' snapped Spold. 'You young people—' He stopped. Death was looking at him thoughtfully, as if he was trying to remember his face.

'Look,' said Galder, 'just repeat that bit again, will you? The Disc will be what?'

DESTROYED, said Death. CAN I GO NOW? I LEFT MY DRINK.

'Hang on,' said Galder hurriedly. 'By Cheliliki and Orizone and so forth, what do you mean, destroyed?'

IT'S AN ANCIENT PROPHECY WRITTEN ON THE INNER WALLS OF THE GREAT PYRAMID OF TSORT. THE WORD DESTROYED SEEMS QUITE SELF-EXPLANATORY TO ME.

'That's all you can tell us?'

YES.

'But Hogswatchnight is only two months away!'

YES.

'At least you can tell us where Rincewind is now!'

Death shrugged. It was a gesture he was particularly well built for.

THE FOREST OF SKUND, RIMWARDS OF THE RAMTOP MOUNTAINS.

'What is he doing there?'

FEELING VERY SORRY FOR HIMSELF.

'Oh.'

NOW MAY I GO?

Galder nodded distractedly. He had been thinking wistfully of the banishment ritual, which started 'Begone, foul shade' and had some rather impressive passages which he had been practising, but somehow he couldn't work up any enthusiasm.

'Oh, yes,' he said. 'Thank you, yes.' And then, because it's as well not to make enemies even among the creatures of night, he added politely, 'I hope it is a good party.'

Death didn't answer. He was looking at Spold in the same way that a dog looks at a bone, only in this case things were more or less the other way around.

'I said I hope it is a good party,' said Galder, loudly.

AT THE MOMENT IT IS, said Death levelly. I THINK IT MIGHT GO DOWNHILL VERY QUICKLY AT MIDNIGHT.

'Why?'

THAT'S WHEN THEY THINK I'LL BE TAKING MY MASK OFF.

He vanished, leaving only a cocktail stick and a short paper streamer behind.

There had been an unseen observer of all this. It was of course entirely against the rules, but Trymon knew all about rules and had always considered they were for making, not obeying.

Long before the eight mages had got down to some serious arguing about what the apparition had meant he was down in the main levels of the University library.

It was an awe-inspiring place. Many of the books were magical, and the important thing to remember about grimoires is that they are deadly in the hands of any librarian who cares about order, because he's bound to stick them all on the same shelf. This is not a good idea with books that tend to leak magic, because more than one or two of them together form a critical Black Mass. On top of that, many of the lesser spells are quite particular about the company they keep, and tend to express any objections by hurling their books viciously across the room. And, of course, there is always the half-felt presence of the Things from the Dungeon Dimensions, clustering around the magical leakage and constantly probing the walls of reality.

The job of magical librarian, who has to spend his working days in this sort of highly charged atmosphere, is a high-risk occupation.

The Head Librarian was sitting on top of his desk, quietly peeling an orange, and was well aware of that.

He glanced up when Trymon entered.

'I'm looking for anything we've got on the Pyramid of Tshut,' said Trymon. He had come prepared: he took a banana out of his pocket.

The librarian looked at it mournfully, and then flopped down heavily on the floor. Trymon found a soft hand poked gently into his and the librarian led the way, waddling sadly between the bookshelves. It was like holding a little leather glove.

Around them the books sizzled and sparked, with the occasional discharge of undirected magic flashing over to the carefully-placed earthing rods nailed to the shelves. There was a tinny, blue smell and, just at the very limit of hearing, the horrible chittering of the dungeon creatures.

Like many other parts of Unseen University the library occupied rather more space than its outside dimensions would suggest, because magic distorts space in strange ways, and it was probably the only library in the universe with Mobius shelves. But the librarian's mental catalogue was ticking over perfectly. He stopped by a soaring stack of musty books and swung himself up into the darkness. There was the sound of rustling paper, and a cloud of dust floated down to Trymon. Then the librarian was back, a slim volume in his hands.

'Oook,' he said.

Trymon took it gingerly.

The cover was scratched and very dog-eared, the gold of its lettering had long ago curled off, but he could just make out, in the old magic tongue of the Tsort Valley, the words: *Iyt Gryet Teymple hyte Tsort, Y Hiystory Myistical.*

'Oook?' said the librarian, anxiously.

Trymon turned the pages cautiously. He wasn't very good at languages, he'd always found them highly inefficient things which by rights ought to be replaced by some sort of easily understood numerical system, but this seemed exactly what he was looking for. There were whole pages covered with meaningful hieroglyphs.

'Is this the only book you've got about the pyramid of Tsort?' he said slowly.

'Oook.'

'You're quite sure?'

'Oook.'

Trymon listened. He could hear, a long way off, the sound of approaching feet and arguing voices. But he had been prepared for that, too.

He reached into a pocket.

'Would you like another banana?' he said.

The Forest of Skund was indeed enchanted, which was nothing unusual on the Disc, and was also the only forest in the whole universe to be called – in the local language – Your Finger You Fool, which was the literal meaning of the word Skund.

The reason for this is regrettably all too common. When the first explorers from the warm lands around the Circle Sea travelled into the chilly hinterland they filled in the blank spaces on their maps by grabbing the nearest native, pointing at some distant landmark, speaking very clearly in a loud voice, and writing down whatever the bemused man told them. Thus were immortalized in generations of atlases such geographical oddities as Just A Mountain, I Don't Know, What? and, of course, Your Finger You Fool.

Rainclouds clustered around the bald heights of Mt. Oolskunrahod ('Who is this Fool who does Not Know what a Mountain Is') and the Luggage settled itself more comfortably under a dripping tree, which tried unsuccessfully to strike up a conversation.

Twoflower and Rincewind were arguing. The

person they were arguing about sat on his mushroom and watched them with interest. He looked like someone who smelled like someone who lived in a mushroom, and that bothered Twoflower.

'Well, why hasn't he got a red hat?'

Rincewind hesitated, desperately trying to imagine what Twoflower was getting at.

'What?' he said, giving in.

'He should have a red hat,' said Twoflower. 'And he certainly ought to be cleaner and more, more sort of jolly. He doesn't look like any sort of gnome to me.'

'What are you going on about?'

'Look at that beard,' said Twoflower sternly. 'I've seen better beards on a piece of cheese.'

'Look, he's six inches high and lives in a mushroom,' snarled Rincewind. 'Of course he's a bloody gnome.'

'We've only got his word for it.'

Rincewind looked down at the gnome.

'Excuse me,' he said. He took Twoflower to the other side of the clearing.

'Listen,' he said between his teeth. 'If he was fifteen feet tall and said he was a giant we'd only have his word for that too, wouldn't we?'

'He could be a goblin,' said Twoflower defiantly.

Rincewind looked back at the tiny figure, which was industriously picking its nose.

'Well?' he said. 'So what? Gnome, goblin, pixie – so what?'

'Not a pixie,' said Twoflower firmly. 'Pixies, they wear these sort of green combinations and they have pointy caps and little knobbly antenna thingies sticking out of their heads. I've seen pictures.'

'Where?'

Twoflower hesitated, and looked at his feet. 'I think it was called the "mutter, mutter, mutter." '

'The what? Called the what?'

The little man took a sudden interest in the backs of his hands.

'*The Little Folks' Book of Flower Fairies*,' he muttered.

Rincewind looked blank.

'It's a book on how to avoid them?' he said.

'Oh no,' said Twoflower hurriedly. 'It tells you where to look for them. I can remember the pictures now.' A dreamy look came over his face, and Rincewind groaned inwardly. 'There was even a special fairy that came and took your teeth away.'

'What, came and pulled out your actual teeth—?'

'No, no, you're wrong. I mean after they'd fallen out, what you did was, you put the tooth under your pillow and the fairy came and took it away and left a *rhinu* piece.'

'Why?'

'Why what?'

'Why did it collect teeth?'

'It just did.'

Rincewind formed a mental picture of some strange entity living in a castle made of teeth. It was the kind of mental picture you tried to forget. Unsuccessfully.

'Urgh,' he said.

Red hats! He wondered whether to enlighten the tourist about what life was really like when a frog was a good meal, a rabbit hole a useful place to shelter out of the rain, and an owl a drifting, silent terror in the night. Moleskin trousers sounded quaint unless you personally had to remove them from their original owner when the vicious little sod was cornered in his burrow. As for red hats, anyone who went around a forest looking bright and conspicuous would only do so very, very briefly.

He wanted to say: look, the life of gnomes and goblins is nasty, brutish and short. So are they.

He wanted to say all this, and couldn't. For a man with an itch to see the whole of infinity, Twoflower never actually moved outside his own head. Telling him the truth would be like kicking a spaniel.

'Swee whee weedle wheet,' said a voice by his foot. He looked down. The gnome, who had introduced himself as Swires, looked up. Rincewind had a very good ear for languages. The gnome had just said, 'I've got some newt sorbet left over from yesterday.'

'Sounds wonderful,' said Rincewind

Swires gave him another prod in the ankle.

'The other bigger, is he all right?' he said solicitously.

'He's just suffering from reality shock,' said Rincewind. 'You haven't got a red hat, by any chance?'

'Wheet?'

'Just a thought.'

'I know where there's some food for biggers,' said the gnome, 'and shelter, too. It's not far.'

Rincewind looked at the lowering sky. The daylight

was draining out of the landscape and the clouds looked as if they had heard about snow and were considering the idea. Of course, people who lived in mushrooms couldn't necessarily be trusted, but right now a trap baited with a hot meal and clean sheets would have had the wizard hammering to get in.

They set off. After a few seconds the Luggage got carefully to its feet and started to follow.

'Psst!'

It turned carefully, little legs moving in a complicated pattern, and appeared to look up.

'Is it good, being joinery?' said the tree, anxiously. 'Did it hurt?'

The Luggage seemed to think about this. Every brass handle, every knothole, radiated extreme concentration.

Then it shrugged its lid and waddled away.

The tree sighed, and shook a few dead leaves out of its twigs.

The cottage was small, tumbledown and as ornate as a doily. Some mad whittler had got to work on it, Rincewind decided, and had created terrible havoc before he could be dragged away. Every door, every shutter had its clusters of wooden grapes and half-moon cutouts, and there were massed outbreaks of fretwork pinecones all over the walls. He half expected a giant cuckoo to come hurtling out of an upper window.

What he also noticed was the characteristic greasy

feel in the air. Tiny green and purple sparks flashed from his fingernails.

'Strong magical field,' he muttered. 'A hundred millithaums* at least.'

'There's magic all over the place,' said Swires. 'An old witch used to live around here. She went a long time ago but the magic still keeps the house going.'

'Here, there's something odd about that door,' said Twoflower.

'Why should a house need magic to keep it going?' said Rincewind. Twoflower touched a wall gingerly.

'It's all sticky!'

'Nougat,' said Swires.

'Good grief! A real gingerbread cottage! Rincewind, a real—'

Rincewind nodded glumly. 'Yeah, the Confectionery School of Architecture,' he said. 'It never caught on.'

He looked suspiciously at the liquorice door-knocker.

'It sort of regenerates,' said Swires. 'Marvellous, really. You just don't get this sort of place nowadays, you just can't get the gingerbread.'

'Really?' said Rincewind, gloomily.

'Come on in,' said the gnome, 'but mind the doormat.'

* A Thaum is the basic unit of magical strength. It has been universally established as the amount of magic needed to create one small white pigeon or three normal sized billiard balls.

'Why?'

'Candyfloss.'

The great Disc spun slowly under its toiling sun, and daylight pooled in hollows and finally drained away as night fell.

In his chilly room in Unseen University, Trymon pored over the book, his lips moving as his finger traced the unfamiliar, ancient script. He read that the Great Pyramid of Tsort, now long vanished, was made of one million, three thousand and ten limestone blocks. He read that ten thousand slaves had been worked to death in its building. He learned that it was a maze of secret passages, their walls reputedly decorated with the distilled wisdom of ancient Tsort. He read that its height plus its length divided by half its width equalled exactly 1.67563, or precisely 1,237.98712567 times the difference between the distance to the sun and the weight of a small orange. He learned that sixty years had been devoted entirely to its construction.

It all seemed, he thought, to be rather a lot of trouble to go to just to sharpen a razor blade.

And in the Forest of Skund Twoflower and Rincewind settled down to a meal of gingerbread mantlepiece and thought longingly of pickled onions.

And far away, but set as it were on a collision course, the greatest hero the Disc ever produced rolled himself a cigarette, entirely unaware of the role that lay in store for him.

It was quite an interesting tailormade that he twirled expertly between his fingers because, like many of the wandering wizards from whom he had picked up the art, he was in the habit of saving dogends in a leather bag and rolling them into fresh smokes. The implacable law of averages therefore dictated that some of that tobacco had been smoked almost continuously for many years now. The thing he was trying unsuccessfully to light was, well, you could have coated roads with it.

So great was the reputation of this person that a group of nomadic barbarian horsemen had respectfully invited him to join them as they sat around a horseturd fire. The nomads of the Hub regions usually migrated rimwards for the winter, and these were part of a tribe who had pitched their felt tents in the sweltering heatwave of a mere –3 degrees and were going around with peeling noses and complaining about heatstroke.

The barbarian chieftain said: 'What then are the greatest things that a man may find in life?' This is the sort of thing you're supposed to say to maintain steppe-cred in barbarian circles.

The man on his right thoughtfully drank his cocktail of mare's milk and snowcat blood, and spoke thus: 'The crisp horizon of the steppe, the wind in your hair, a fresh horse under you.'

The man on his left said: 'The cry of the white eagle in the heights, the fall of snow in the forest, a true arrow in your bow.'

The chieftain nodded, and said: 'Surely it is the

sight of your enemy slain, the humiliation of his tribe and the lamentation of his women.'

There was a general murmur of whiskery approval at this outrageous display.

Then the chieftain turned respectfully to his guest, a small figure carefully warming his chilblains by the fire, and said: 'But our guest, whose name is legend, must tell us truly: what are they that a man may call the greatest things in life?'

The guest paused in the middle of another unsuccessful attempt to light up.

'What shay?' he said, toothlessly.

'I said: what are they that a man may call the greatest things in life?'

The warriors leaned closer. This should be worth hearing.

The guest thought long and hard and then said, with deliberation: 'Hot water, good dentishtry and shoft lavatory paper.'

Brilliant octarine light flared in the forge. Galder Weatherwax, stripped to the waist, his face hidden by a mask of smoked glass, squinted into the glow and brought a hammer down with surgical precision. The magic squealed and writhed in the tongs but still he worked it, drawing it into a line of agonized fire.

A floorboard creaked. Galder had spent many hours tuning them, always a wise precaution with an ambitious assistant who walked like a cat.

D flat. That meant he was just to the right of the door.

'Ah, Trymon,' he said, without turning, and noted with some satisfaction the faint indrawing of breath behind him. 'Good of you to come. Shut the door, will you?'

Trymon pushed the heavy door, his face expressionless. On the high shelf above him various bottled impossibilities wallowed in their pickle jars and watched him with interest.

Like all wizards' workshops, the place looked as though a taxidermist had dropped his stock in a foundry and then had a fight with a maddened glass-blower, braining a passing crocodile in the process (it hung from the ceiling and smelt strongly of camphor). There were lamps and rings that Trymon itched to rub, and mirrors that looked as though they could repay a second glance. A pair of seven league boots stirred restlessly in a cage. A whole library of grimoires, not of course as powerful as the Octavo but still heavy with spells, creaked and rattled their chains as they sensed the wizard's covetous glance on them. The naked power of it all stirred him as nothing else could, but he deplored the scruffiness and Galder's sense of theatre.

For example, he happened to know that the green liquid bubbling mysteriously through a maze of contorted pipework on one of the benches was just green dye with soap in it, because he'd bribed one of the servants.

One day, he thought, it's all going to go. Starting

with that bloody alligator. His knuckles whitened . . .

'Well now,' said Galder cheerfully, hanging up his apron and sitting back in his chair with the lion paw arms and duck legs. 'You sent me this memmy-thing.'

Trymon shrugged. 'Memo. I merely pointed out, lord, that the other Orders have all sent agents to Skund Forest to recapture the Spell, while you do nothing,' he said. 'No doubt you will reveal your reasons in good time.'

'Your faith shames me,' said Galder.

'The wizard who captures the Spell will bring great honour on himself and his order,' said Trymon. 'The others have used boots and all manner of elsewhere spells. What do you propose using, master?'

'Did I detect a hint of sarcasm there?'

'Absolutely not, master.'

'Not even a smidgeon?'

'Not even the merest smidgeon, master.'

'Good. Because I don't propose to go.' Galder reached down and picked up an ancient book. He mumbled a command and it creaked open; a bookmark suspiciously like a tongue flicked back into the binding.

He fumbled down beside his cushion and produced a little leather bag of tobacco and a pipe the size of an incinerator. With all the skill of a terminal nicotine addict he rubbed a nut of tobacco between his hands and tamped it into the bowl. He snapped his fingers and fire flared. He sucked deep, sighed with satisfaction . . .

. . . looked up.

'Still here, Trymon?'

'You summoned me, master,' said Trymon levelly. At least, that's what his voice said. Deep in his grey eyes was the faintest glitter that said he had a list of every slight, every patronizing twinkle, every gentle reproof, every knowing glance, and for every single one Galder's living brain was going to spend a year in acid.

'Oh, yes, so I did. Humour the deficiencies of an old man,' said Galder pleasantly. He held up the book he had been reading.

'I don't hold with all this running about,' he said. 'It's all very dramatic, mucking about with magic carpets and the like, but it isn't true magic to my mind. Take seven league boots, now. If men were meant to walk twenty-one miles at a step I am sure God would have given us longer legs . . . Where was I?'

'I am not sure,' said Trymon coldly.

'Ah, yes. Strange that we could find nothing about the Pyramid of Tsort in the Library, you would have thought there'd be something, wouldn't you?'

'The librarian will be disciplined, of course.'

Galder looked sideways at him. 'Nothing drastic,' he said. 'Withold his bananas, perhaps.'

They looked at each other for a moment.

Galder broke off first – looking hard at Trymon always bothered him. It had the same disconcerting effect as gazing into a mirror and seeing no one there.

'Anyway,' he said, 'strangely enough, I found assistance elsewhere. In my own modest bookshelves, in fact. The journal of Skrelt Changebasket, the founder of our Order. You, my keen young man who would rush off so soon, do you know what happens when a wizard dies?'

'Any spells he has memorized say themselves,' said Trymon. 'It is one of the first things we learn.'

'In fact it is not true of the original Eight Great Spells. By dint of close study Skrelt learned that a Great Spell will simply take refuge in the nearest mind open and ready to receive it. Just push the big mirror over here, will you?'

Galder got to his feet and shuffled across to the forge, which was now cold. The strand of magic still writhed, though, at once present and not present, like a slit cut into another universe full of hot blue light. He picked it up easily, took a longbow from a rack, said a word of power, and watched with satisfaction as the magic grasped the ends of the bow and then tightened until the wood creaked. Then he selected an arrow.

Trymon had tugged a heavy, full-length mirror into the middle of the floor. When I am head of the Order, he told himself, I certainly won't shuffle around in carpet slippers.

Trymon, as mentioned earlier, felt that a lot could be done by fresh blood if only the dead wood could be removed – but, just for the moment, he was genuinely interested in seeing what the old fool would do next.

He may have derived some satisfaction if he had known that Galder and Skrelt Changebasket were both absolutely wrong.

Galder made a few passes in front of the glass,

which clouded over and then cleared to show an aerial view of the Forest of Skund. He looked at it intently while holding the bow with the arrow pointing vaguely at the ceiling. He muttered a few words like 'allow for wind speed of, say, three knots' and 'adjust for temperature' and then, with a rather disappointing movement, released the arrow.

If the laws of action and reaction had anything to do with it, it should have flopped to the ground a few feet away. But no one was listening to them.

With a sound that defies description, but which for the sake of completeness can be thought of basically as 'spang!' plus three days' hard work in any decently equipped radiophonic workshop, the arrow vanished.

Galder threw the bow aside and grinned.

'Of course, it'll take about an hour to get there,' he said. 'Then the Spell will simply follow the ionized path back here. To me.'

'Remarkable,' said Trymon, but any passing telepath would have read in letters ten yards high: if you, then why not me? He looked down at the cluttered workbench, where a long and very sharp knife looked tailormade for what he suddenly had in mind.

Violence was not something he liked to be involved in except at one remove. But the Pyramid of Tsort had been quite clear about the rewards for whoever brought all eight spells together at the right time, and Trymon was not about to let years of painstaking work go for nothing because some old fool had a bright idea.

'Would you like some cocoa while we're waiting?' said Galder, hobbling across the room to the servants' bell.

'Certainly,' said Trymon. He picked up the knife, weighing it for balance and accuracy. 'I must congratulate you, master. I can see that we must all get up very early in the morning to get the better of you.'

Galder laughed. And the knife left Trymon's hand at such speed that (because of the somewhat sluggish nature of Disc light) it actually grew a bit shorter and a little more massive as it plunged, with unerring aim, towards Galder's neck.

It didn't reach it. Instead, it swerved to one side and began a fast orbit – so fast that Galder appeared suddenly to be wearing a metal collar. He turned around, and to Trymon it seemed that he had suddenly grown several feet taller and much more powerful.

The knife broke away and shuddered into the door a mere shadow's depth from Trymon's ear.

'Early in the morning?' said Galder pleasantly. 'My dear lad, you will need to stay up all night.'

'Have a bit more table,' said Rincewind.

'No thanks, I don't like marzipan,' said Twoflower. 'Anyway, I'm sure it's not right to eat other people's furniture.'

'Don't worry,' said Swires. 'The old witch hasn't been seen for years. They say she was done up good and proper by a couple of young tearaways.'

'Kids of today,' commented Rincewind.

'I blame the parents,' said Twoflower.

Once you had made the necessary mental adjustments, the gingerbread cottage was quite a pleasant place. Residual magic kept it standing and it was shunned by such local wild animals who hadn't already died of terminal tooth decay. A bright fire of liquorice logs burned rather messily in the fireplace; Rincewind had tried gathering wood outside, but had given up. It's hard to burn wood that talks to you.

He belched.

'This isn't very healthy,' he said. 'I mean, why sweets? Why not crispbread and cheese? Or salami, now – I could just do with a nice salami sofa.'

'Search me,' said Swires. 'Old Granny Whitlow just did sweets. You should have seen her meringues—'

'I have,' said Rincewind, 'I looked at the mattresses . . .'

'Gingerbread is more traditional,' said Twoflower.

'What, for mattresses?'

'Don't be silly,' said Twoflower reasonably. 'Whoever heard of a gingerbread mattress?'

Rincewind grunted. He was thinking of food – more accurately, of food in Ankh-Morpork. Funny how the old place seemed more attractive the further he got from it. He only had to close his eyes to picture, in dribbling detail, the food stalls of a hundred different cultures in the market places. You could eat *squishi* or shark's fin soup so fresh that swimmers wouldn't go near it, and—

'Do you think I could buy this place?' said

Twoflower. Rincewind hesitated. He'd found it always paid to think very carefully before answering Twoflower's more surprising questions.

'What for?' he said, cautiously.

'Well, it just reeks of ambience.'

'Oh.'

'What's ambience?' said Swires, sniffing cautiously and wearing the kind of expression that said that he hadn't done it, whatever it was.

'I think it's a kind of frog,' said Rincewind. 'Anyway, you can't buy this place because there isn't anyone to buy it *from*—'

'I think I could probably arrange that, on behalf of the forest council of course,' interrupted Swires, trying to avoid Rincewind's glare.

'—and anyway you couldn't take it with you, I mean, you could hardly pack it in the Luggage, could you?' Rincewind indicated the Luggage, which was lying by the fire and managing in some quite impossible way to look like a contented but alert tiger, and then looked back at Twoflower. His face fell.

'Could you?' he repeated.

He had never quite come to terms with the fact that the inside of the Luggage didn't seem to inhabit quite the same world as the outside. Of course, this was simply a byproduct of its essential weirdness, but it was disconcerting to see Twoflower fill it full of dirty shirts and old socks and then open the lid again on a pile of nice crisp laundry, smelling faintly of lavender. Twoflower also bought a lot of quaint native artifacts or, as Rincewind would put it, junk, and even a seven-foot ceremonial pig tickling pole seemed to fit inside quite easily without sticking out *anywhere.*

'I don't know,' said Twoflower. 'You're a wizard, you know about these things.'

'Yes, well, of course, but baggage magic is a highly specialized art,' said Rincewind. 'Anyway, I'm sure the gnomes wouldn't really want to sell it, it's, it's—,' he groped through what he knew of Twoflower's mad vocabulary – 'it's a tourist attraction.'

'What's that?' said Swires, interestedly.

'It means that lots of people like him will come and look at it,' said Rincewind.

'Why?'

'Because—' Rincewind groped for words – 'it's quaint. Um, oldey worldey. Folkloresque. Er, a delightful example of a vanished folk art, steeped in the traditions of an age long gone.'

'It is?' said Swires, looking at the cottage in bewilderment.

'Yes.'

'All that?'

''Fraid so.'

'I'll help you pack.'

And the night wears on, under a blanket of lowering clouds which covers most of the Disc – which is fortuitous, because when it clears and the astrologers get a good view of the sky they are going to get angry and upset.

And in various parts of the forest parties of wizards are getting lost, and going around in circles, and hiding from each other, and getting upset because whenever they bump into a tree it apologizes to them. But, unsteadily though it may be, many of them are getting quite close to the cottage . . .

Which is a good time to get back to the rambling buildings of Unseen University and in particular the apartments of Greyhald Spold, currently the oldest wizard on the Disc and determined to keep it that way.

He has just been extremely surprised and upset.

For the last few hours he has been very busy. He may be deaf and a little hard of thinking, but elderly wizards have very well-trained survival instincts, and they know that when a tall figure in a black robe and the latest in agricultural handtools starts looking thoughtfully at you it is time to act fast. The servants have been dismissed. The doorways have been sealed with a paste made from powdered mayflies, and protective octograms have been drawn on the windows. Rare and rather smelly oils have been poured in complex patterns on the floor, in designs which hurt the eyes and suggest the designer was drunk or from some other dimension or, possibly, both; in the very centre of the room is the eightfold octogram of Witholding, surrounded by red and green candles. And in the centre of that is a box made from wood of the curlyfern pine, which grows to a great age, and it is lined with red silk and yet more protective amulets. Because Greyhald Spold knows that Death is looking for him, and has spent many years designing an impregnable hiding place.

He has just set the complicated clockwork of the

lock and shut the lid, lying back in the knowledge that here at last is the perfect defence against the most ultimate of all his enemies, although as yet he has not considered the important part that airholes must play in an enterprise of this kind.

And right beside him, very close to his ear, a voice has just said: DARK IN HERE, ISN'T IT?

It began to snow. The barleysugar windows of the cottage showed bright and cheerful against the blackness.

At one side of the clearing three tiny red points of light glowed momentarily and there was the sound of a chesty cough, abruptly silenced.

'Shut up!' hissed a third rank wizard. 'They'll hear us!'

'Who will? We gave the lads from the Brotherhood of the Hoodwink the slip in the swamp, and those idiots from the Venerable Council of Seers went off the wrong way anyway.'

'Yeah,' said the most junior wizard, 'but who keeps talking to us? They say this is a magic wood, it's full of goblins and wolves and—'

'Trees,' said a voice out of the darkness, high above. It possessed what can only be described as timbre.

'Yeah,' said the youngest wizard. He sucked on his dogend, and shivered.

The leader of the party peered over the rock and watched the cottage.

'Right then,' he said, knocking out his pipe on the

heel of his seven league boot, who squeaked in protest. 'We rush in, we grab them, we're away. Okay?'

'You sure it's just people?' said the youngest wizard, nervously.

'Of course I'm sure,' snarled the leader. 'What do you expect, three bears?'

'There could be monsters. This is the sort of wood that has monsters.'

'And trees,' said a friendly voice from the branches.

'Yeah,' said the leader, cautiously.

Rincewind looked carefully at the bed. It was quite a nice little bed, in a sort of hard toffee inlaid with caramel, but he'd rather eat it than sleep in it and it looked as though someone already had.

'Someone's been eating my bed,' he said.

'I like toffee,' said Twoflower defensively.

'If you don't watch out the fairy will come and take all your teeth away,' said Rincewind.

'No, that's elves,' said Swires from the dressing table. 'Elves do that. Toenails, too. Very touchy at times, elves can be.'

Twoflower sat down heavily on his bed.

'You've got it wrong,' he said. 'Elves are noble and beautiful and wise and fair; I'm sure I read that somewhere.'

Swires and Rincewind's kneecap exchanged glances.

'I think you must be thinking about different elves,' the gnome said slowly. 'We've just got the other sort around here. Not that you could call them quick-tempered,' he added hastily. 'Not if you didn't want to take your teeth home in your hat, anyway.'

There was the tiny, distinctive sound of a nougat door opening. At the same time, from the other side of the cottage, came the faintest of tinkles, like a rock smashing a barley sugar window as delicately as possible.

'What was that?' said Twoflower.

'Which one?' said Rincewind.

There was the clonk of a heavy branch banging against the window sill. With a cry of 'Elves!' Swires scuttled across the floor to a mousehole and vanished.

'What shall we do?' said Twoflower.

'Panic?' said Rincewind hopefully. He always held that panic was the best means of survival; back in the olden days, his theory went, people faced with hungry sabre-toothed tigers could be divided very simply into those who panicked and those who stood there saying 'What a magnificent brute!' and 'Here, pussy.'

'There's a cupboard,' said Twoflower, pointing to a narrow door that was squeezed between the wall and the chimneybreast. They scrambled into sweet, musty darkness.

There was the creak of a chocolate floorboard outside. Someone said 'I heard voices.'

Someone else said, 'Yeah, downstairs. I think it's the Hoodwinkers.'

'I thought you said we'd given them the slip!'

'Hey, you two, you can eat this place! Here, look you can—'

'*Shut up!*'

There was a lot more creaking, and a muffled scream from downstairs where a Venerable Seer, creeping carefully through the darkness from the broken window, had trodden on the fingers of a Hoodwinker who was hiding under the table. There was the sudden zip and zing of magic.

'Bugger!' said a voice outside. 'They've got him! Let's go!'

There was more creaking, and then silence. After a while Twoflower said, 'Rincewind, I think there's a broomstick in this cupboard.'

'Well, what's so unusual about that?'

'This one's got handlebars.'

There was a piercing shriek from below. In the darkness a wizard had tried to open the Luggage's lid. A crash from the scullery indicated the sudden arrival of a party of Illuminated Mages of the Unbroken Circle.

'What do you think they're after?' whispered Twoflower.

'I don't know, but I think it might be a good idea not to find out,' said Rincewind thoughtfully.

'You could be right.'

Rincewind pushed open the door gingerly. The room was empty. He tiptoed across to the window, and looked down into the upturned faces of three Brothers of the Order of Midnight.

'That's him!'

He drew back hurriedly and rushed for the stairs.

The scene below was indescribable but since that

statement would earn the death penalty in the reign of Olaf Quimby II the attempt better be made. Firstly, most of the struggling wizards were trying to illuminate the scene by various flames, fireballs and magical glows, so the overall lighting gave the impression of a disco in a strobelight factory; each man was trying to find a position from which he could see the rest of the room without being attacked himself, and absolutely everyone was trying to keep out of the way of the Luggage, which had two Venerable Seers pinned in a corner and was snapping its lid at anyone who approached. But one wizard did happen to look up.

'It's him!'

Rincewind jerked back, and something bumped into him. He looked around hurriedly, and stared when he saw Twoflower sitting on the broomstick – which was floating in mid-air.

'The witch must have left it behind!' said Twoflower. 'A genuine magic broomstick!'

Rincewind hesitated. Octarine sparks were spitting off the broomstick's bristles and he hated heights almost more than anything else, but what he really hated more than anything at all was a dozen very angry and bad-tempered wizards rushing up the stairs towards him, and this was happening.

'All right,' he said, 'but I'll drive.'

He lashed out with a boot at a wizard who was halfway through a Spell of Binding and jumped onto the broomstick, which bobbed down the stairwell and then turned upside down so that Rincewind was horribly eye to eye with a Brother of Midnight.

He yelped and gave the handlebars a convulsive twist.

Several things happened at once. The broomstick shot forward and broke through the wall in a shower of crumbs: the Luggage surged forward and bit the Brother in the leg: and with a strange whistling sound an arrow appeared from nowhere, missed Rincewind by inches, and struck the Luggage's lid with a very solid thud.

The Luggage vanished.

In a little village deep in the forest an ancient shaman threw a few more twigs on his fire and stared through the smoke at his shamefaced apprentice.

'A box with legs on?' he said.

'Yes, master. It just appeared out of the sky and looked at me,' said the apprentice.

'It had eyes then, this box?'

'N—,' began the apprentice and stopped, puzzled. The old man frowned.

'Many have seen Topaxci, God of the Red Mushroom, and they earn the name of shaman,' he said. 'Some have seen Skelde, spirit of the smoke, and they are called sorcerers. A few have been privileged to see Umcherrel, the soul of the forest, and they are known as spirit masters. But none have seen a box with hundreds of legs that looked at them without eyes, and they are known as idio—'

The interruption was caused by a sudden

screaming noise and a flurry of snow and sparks that blew the fire across the dark hut; there was a brief blurred vision and then the opposite wall was blasted aside and the apparition vanished.

There was a long silence. Then a slightly shorter silence. Then the old shaman said carefully, 'You didn't just see two men go through upside down on a broomstick, shouting and screaming at each other, did you?'

The boy looked at him levelly. 'Certainly not,' he said.

The old man heaved a sigh of relief. 'Thank goodness for that,' he said. 'Neither did I.'

The cottage was in turmoil, because not only did the wizards want to follow the broomstick, they also wanted to prevent each other from doing so, and this led to several regrettable incidents. The most spectacular, and certainly the most tragic, happened when one Seer attempted to use his seven league boots without the proper sequence of spells and preparations. Seven league boots, as has already been intimated, are a tricksy form of magic at best, and he remembered too late that the utmost caution must be taken in using a means of transport which, when all is said and done, relies for its effectiveness on trying to put one foot twenty-one miles in front of the other.

* * *

The first snowstorms of winter were raging, and in fact there was a suspiciously heavy covering of cloud over most of the Disc. And yet, from far above and by the silver light of the Discworld's tiny moon, it presented one of the most beautiful sights in the multiverse.

Great streamers of cloud, hundreds of miles along, swirled from the waterfall at the Rim to the mountains of the Hub. In the cold crystal silence the huge white spiral glittered frostily under the stars, imperceptibly turning, very much as though God had stirred His coffee and then poured the cream in.

Nothing disturbed the glowing scene, which—

Something small and distant broke through the cloud layer, trailing shreds of vapour. In the stratospheric calm the sounds of bickering came sharp and clear.

'You said you could fly one of these things!'

'No I didn't; I just said *you* couldn't!'

'But I've never been on one before!'

'What a coincidence!'

'Anyway, you said— *look at the sky!*'

'No I didn't!'

'What's happened to the stars?'

And so it was that Rincewind and Twoflower became the first two people on the Disc to see what the future held.

A thousand miles behind them the Hub mountain of Cori Celesti stabbed the sky and cast a knife-bright shadow across the broiling clouds, so that gods ought to have noticed too – but the gods don't normally look at the sky and in any case were engaged in litigation with the Ice Giants, who had refused to turn their radio down.

Rimwards, in the direction of Great A'Tuin's travel, the sky had been swept of stars.

In that circle of blackness there was just one star, a red and baleful star, a star like the glitter in the eye-socket of a rabid mink. It was small and horrible and uncompromising. And the Disc was being carried straight towards it.

Rincewind knew precisely what to do in these circumstances. He screamed and pointed the broomstick straight down.

Galder Weatherwax stood in the centre of the octogram and raised his hands.

'Urshalo, dileptor, c'hula, do my bidding!'

A small mist formed over his head. He glanced sideways at Trymon, who was sulking at the edge of the magic circle.

'This next bit's quite impressive,' he said. 'Watch. *Kot-b'hai! Kot-sham!* To me, o spirits of small isolated rocks and worried mice not less than three inches long!'

'What?' said Trymon.

'That bit took quite a lot of research,' agreed Galder, 'especially the mice. Anyway, where was I? Oh, yes . . .'

He raised his arms again. Trymon watched him, and licked his lips distractedly. The old fool was really concentrating, bending his mind entirely to the Spell and hardly paying any attention to Trymon.

Words of power rolled around the room, bouncing off the walls and scuttling out of sight behind shelves and jars. Trymon hesitated.

Galder shut his eyes momentarily, his face a mask of ecstasy as he mouthed the final word.

Trymon tensed, his fingers curling around the knife again. And Galder opened one eye, nodded at him and sent a sideways blast of power that picked the younger man up and sent him sprawling against the wall.

Galder winked at him and raised his arms again.

'To me, o spirits of—'

There was a thunderclap, an implosion of light and a moment of complete physical uncertainty during which even the walls seemed to turn in on themselves. Trymon heard a sharp intake of breath and then a dull, solid thump.

The room was suddenly silent.

After a few minutes Trymon crawled out from behind a chair and dusted himself off. He whistled a few bars of nothing much and turned towards the door with exaggerated care, looking at the ceiling as if he had never seen it before. He moved in a way that suggested he was attempting the world speed record for the nonchalant walk.

The Luggage squatted in the centre of the circle and opened its lid.

Trymon stopped. He turned very, very carefully, dreading what he might see.

The Luggage seemed to contain some clean laundry,

smelling slightly of lavender. Somehow it was quite the most terrifying thing the wizard had ever seen.

'Well, er,' he said. 'You, um, wouldn't have seen another wizard around here, by any chance?'

The Luggage contrived to look more menacing.

'Oh,' said Trymon. 'Well, fine. It doesn't matter.'

He pulled vaguely at the hem of his robe and took a brief interest in the detail of its stitching. When he looked up the horrible box was still there.

'Goodbye,' he said, and ran. He managed to get through the door just in time.

'Rincewind?'

Rincewind opened his eyes. Not that it helped much. It just meant that instead of seeing nothing but blackness he saw nothing but whiteness which, surprisingly, was worse.

'Are you all right?'

'No.'

'Ah.'

Rincewind sat up. He appeared to be on a rock speckled with snow, but it didn't seem to be everything a rock ought to be. For example, it shouldn't be moving.

Snow blew around him. Twoflower was a few feet away, a look of genuine concern on his face.

Rincewind groaned. His bones were very angry at the treatment they had recently received and were queuing up to complain.

'What now?' he said.

'You know when we were flying and I was worried we might hit something in the storm and you said the only thing we could possibly hit at this height was a cloud stuffed with rocks?'

'Well?'

'How did you know?'

Rincewind looked around, but for all the variety and interest in the scene around him they might as well have been in the inside of a pingpong ball.

The rock underneath was – well, rocking. He ran his hands over it, and felt the scoring of chisels. When he put an ear to the cold wet stone he fancied he could hear a dull, slow thumping, like a heartbeat. He crawled forward until he came to an edge, and peered very cautiously over it.

At that moment the rock must have been passing over a break in the clouds, because he caught a dim but horribly distant view of jagged-edged mountain peaks. They were a long way down.

He gurgled incoherently and inched his way backwards.

'This is ridiculous,' he told Twoflower. 'Rocks don't fly. They're noted for not doing it.'

'Maybe they would if they could,' said Twoflower. 'Perhaps this one just found out how.'

'Let's just hope it doesn't forget again,' said Rincewind. He huddled up in his soaking robe and looked glumly at the cloud around him. He supposed there were some people somewhere who had some control over their lives; they got up in the morning, and went to bed at night in the reasonable certainty of not falling over the edge of the world or being attacked by lunatics or waking up on a rock with ideas above its station. He dimly remembered leading a life like that once.

Rincewind sniffed. This rock smelt of frying. The smell seemed to be coming from up ahead, and appealed straight to his stomach.

'Can you smell anything?' he said.

'I think it's bacon,' said Twoflower.

'I hope it's bacon,' said Rincewind, 'because I'm going to eat it.' He stood up on the trembling stone and tottered forward into the clouds, peering through the wet gloom.

At the front or leading edge of the rock a small druid was sitting crosslegged in front of a small fire. A square of oilskin was tied across his head and knotted under his chin. He was poking at a pan of bacon with an ornamental sickle.

'Um,' said Rincewind. The druid looked up, and dropped the pan into the fire. He leapt to his feet and gripped the sickle aggressively, or at least as aggressively as anyone can look in a long wet white nightshirt and a dripping headscarf.

'I warn you, I shall deal harshly with hijackers,' he said, and sneezed violently.

'We'll help,' said Rincewind, looking longingly at the burning bacon. This seemed to puzzle the druid who, to Rincewind's mild surprise, was quite young; he supposed there had to be such things as young druids, theoretically, it was just that he had never imagined them.

'You're not trying to steal the rock?' said the druid, lowering the sickle a fraction.

'I didn't even know you could steal rocks,' said Rincewind wearily.

'Excuse me,' said Twoflower politely, 'I think your breakfast is on fire.'

The druid glanced down and flailed ineffectually at the flames. Rincewind hurried forward to help, there was a fair amount of smoke, ash and confusion, and the shared triumph of actually rescuing a few pieces of rather charred bacon did more good than a whole book on diplomacy.

'How did you get here, actually?' said the druid. 'We're five hundred feet up, unless I've got the runes wrong again.'

Rincewind tried not to think about height. 'We sort of dropped in as we were passing,' he said.

'On our way to the ground,' Twoflower added.

'Only your rock broke our fall,' said Rincewind. His back complained. 'Thanks,' he added.

'I thought we'd run into some turbulence a while back,' said the druid, whose name turned out to be Belafon. 'That must have been you.' He shivered. 'It must be morning by now,' he said. 'Sod the rules, I'm taking us up. Hang on.'

'What to?' said Rincewind.

'Well, just indicate a general unwillingness to fall off,' said Belafon. He took a large iron pendulum out of his robe and swung it in a series of baffling sweeps over the fire.

Clouds whipped around them, there was a horrible

feeling of heaviness, and suddenly the rock burst into sunlight.

It levelled off a few feet above the clouds, in a cold but bright blue sky. The clouds that had seemed chillingly distant last night and horribly clammy this morning were now a fleecy white carpet, stretching away in all directions; a few mountain peaks stood out like islands. Behind the rock the wind of its passage sculpted the clouds into transient whirls. The rock—

It was about thirty feet long and ten feet wide, and blueish.

'What an amazing panorama,' said Twoflower, his eyes shining.

'Um, what's keeping us up?' said Rincewind.

'Persuasion,' said Belafon, wringing out the hem of his robe.

'Ah,' said Rincewind sagely.

'Keeping them up is easy,' said the druid, holding up a thumb and squinting down the length of his arm at a distant mountain. 'The hard part is landing.'

'You wouldn't think so, would you?' said Twoflower.

'Persuasion is what keeps the whole universe together,' said Belafon. 'It's no good saying it's all done by magic.'

Rincewind happened to glance down through the thinning cloud to a snowy landscape a considerable distance below. He knew he was in the presence of a madman, but he was used to that; if listening to this madman meant he stayed up here, he was all ears.

Belafon sat down with his feet dangling over the edge of the rock.

'Look, don't worry,' he said. 'If you keep thinking the rock shouldn't be flying it might hear you and become persuaded and you will turn out to be right, okay? It's obvious you aren't up to date with modern thinking.'

'So it would seem,' said Rincewind weakly. He was trying not to think about rocks on the ground. He was trying to think about rocks swooping like swallows, bounding across landscapes in the sheer joy of levity, zooming skywards in a—

He was horribly aware he wasn't very good at it.

The druids of the Disc prided themselves on their forward-looking approach to the discovery of the mysteries of the Universe. Of course, like druids everywhere they believed in the essential unity of all life, the healing power of plants, the natural rhythm of the seasons and the burning alive of anyone who didn't approach all this in the right frame of mind, but they had also thought long and hard about the very basis of creation and had formulated the following theory:

The universe, they said, depended for its operation on the balance of four forces which they identified as charm, persuasion, uncertainty and bloody-mindedness.

Thus it was that the sun and moon orbited the Disc because they were persuaded not to fall down, but didn't actually fly away because of uncertainty. Charm allowed trees to grow and bloody-mindedness kept them up, and so on.

Some druids suggested that there were certain flaws in this theory, but senior druids explained very pointedly that there was indeed room for informed argument, the cut and thrust of exciting scientific debate, and basically it lay on top of the next solstice bonfire.

'Ah, so you're an astronomer?' said Twoflower.

'Oh no,' said Belafon, as the rock drifted gently around the curve of a mountain, 'I'm a computer hardware consultant.'

'What's a computer hardware?'

'Well, this is,' said the druid, tapping the rock with a sandalled foot. 'Part of one, anyway. It's a replacement. I'm delivering it. They're having trouble with the big circles up on the Vortex Plains. So they say, anyway; I wish I had a bronze torc for every user who didn't read the manual.' He shrugged.

'What use is it, then, exactly?' asked Rincewind. Anything to keep his mind off the drop below.

'You can use it to – to tell you what time of year it is,' said Belafon.

'Ah. You mean if it's covered in snow then it must be winter?'

'Yes. I mean no. I mean, supposing you wanted to know when a particular star is going to rise—'

'Why?' said Twoflower, radiating polite interest.

'Well, maybe you want to know when to plant your crops,' said Belafon, sweating a little, 'or maybe—'

'I'll lend you my almanac, if you like,' said Twoflower.

'Almanac?'

'It's a book that tells you what day it is,' said Rincewind wearily. 'It'd be right up your leyline.'

Belafon stiffened. 'Book?' he said. 'Like, with paper?'

'Yes.'

'That doesn't sound very reliable to *me*,' said the druid nastily. 'How can a book know what day it is? Paper can't count.'

He stamped off to the front of the rock, causing it to wallow alarmingly. Rincewind swallowed hard and beckoned Twoflower closer.

'Have you ever heard of culture shock?' he hissed.

'What's that?'

'It's what happens when people spend five hundred years trying to get a stone circle to work properly and then someone comes up with a little book with a page for every day and little chatty bits saying things like "Now is a good time to plant broad beans" and "Early to rise, early to bed, makes a man healthy, wealthy and dead," and do you know what the most important thing to remember about culture shock,' Rincewind paused for breath, and moved his lips silently trying to remember where the sentence had got to, 'is?' he concluded.

'What?'

'Don't give it to a man flying a thousand ton rock.'

'Has it gone?'

Trymon peered cautiously over the battlements of the Tower of Art, the great spire of crumbling masonry that loomed over Unseen University. The cluster of students and instructors of magic, far below, nodded.

'Are you sure?'

The bursar cupped his hands and shouted.

'It broke down the hubward door and escaped an hour ago, sir,' he yelled.

'Wrong,' said Trymon. 'It left, we escaped. Well, I'll be getting down, then. Did it get anyone?'

The bursar swallowed. He was not a wizard, but a kind, good-natured man who should not have had to see the things he had witnessed in the past hour. Of course, it wasn't unknown for small demons, coloured lights and various half-materialized imaginings to wander around the campus, but there had been something about the implacable onslaught of the Luggage that had unnerved him. Trying to stop it would have been like trying to wrestle a glacier.

'It – it swallowed the Dean of Liberal Studies, sir,' he shouted.

Trymon brightened. 'It's an ill wind,' he murmured.

He started down the long spiral staircase. After a while he smiled, a thin, tight smile. The day was definitely improving.

There was a lot of organizing to do. And if there was something Trymon really liked, it was organizing.

The rock swooped across the high plains, whipping snow from the drifts a mere few feet below. Belafon scuttled about urgently, smearing a little mistletoe ointment here, chalking a rune there, while Rincewind cowered in terror and exhaustion and Twoflower worried about his Luggage.

'Up ahead!' screamed the druid above the noise of the slipstream. 'Behold, the great computer of the skies!'

Rincewind peered between his fingers. On the distant skyline was an immense construction of grey and black slabs, arranged in concentric circles and mystic avenues, gaunt and forbidding against the snow. Surely men couldn't have moved those nascent mountains – surely a troop of giants had been turned to stone by some . . .

'It looks like a lot of rocks,' said Twoflower.

Belafon hesitated in mid-gesture.

'What?' he said.

'It's very nice,' added the tourist hurriedly. He sought for a word. 'Ethnic,' he decided.

The druid stiffened. '*Nice?*' he said. 'A triumph of the silicon chunk, a miracle of modern masonic technology – *nice*?'

'Oh, yes,' said Twoflower, to whom sarcasm was merely a seven letter word beginning with S.

'What does ethnic mean?' said the druid.

'It means terribly impressive,' said Rincewind

hurriedly, 'and we seem to be in danger of landing, if you don't mind—'

Belafon turned around, only slightly mollified. He raised his arms wide and shouted a series of untranslatable words, ending with '*nice!*' in a hurt whisper.

The rock slowed, drifted sideways in a billow of snow, and hovered over the circle. Down below a druid waved two bunches of mistletoe in complicated patterns, and Belafon skilfully brought the massive slab to rest across two giant uprights with the faintest of clicks.

Rincewind let his breath out in a long sigh. It hurried off to hide somewhere.

A ladder banged against the side of the slab and the head of an elderly druid appeared over the edge. He gave the two passengers a puzzled glance, and then looked up at Belafon.

'About bloody time,' he said. 'Seven weeks to Hogswatchnight and it's gone down on us again.'

'Hallo, Zakriah,' said Belafon. 'What happened this time?'

'It's all totally fouled up. Today it predicted sunrise three minutes early. Talk about a klutz, boy, this is it.'

Belafon clambered onto the ladder and disappeared from view. The passengers looked at each other, and then stared down into the vast open space between the inner circle of stones.

'What shall we do now?' said Twoflower.

'We could go to sleep?' suggested Rincewind.

Twoflower ignored him, and climbed down the ladder.

Around the circle druids were tapping the megaliths with little hammers and listening intently. Several of the huge stones were lying on their sides, and each was surrounded by another crowd of druids who were examining it carefully and arguing amongst themselves. Arcane phrases floated up to where Rincewind sat:

'It can't be software incompatibility – the Chant of the Trodden Spiral was *designed* for concentric rings, idiot . . .'

'I say fire it up again and try a simple moon ceremony . . .'

'. . . all right, all right, nothing's wrong with the stones, it's just that the universe has gone wrong, right? . . .'

Through the mists of his exhausted mind Rincewind remembered the horrible star they'd seen in the sky. Something *had* gone wrong with the universe last night.

How had he come to be back on the Disc?

He had a feeling that the answers were somewhere inside his head. And an even more unpleasant feeling began to dawn on him that something else was watching the scene below – watching it from behind his eyes.

The Spell had crept from its lair deep in the untrodden dirtroads of his mind, and was sitting bold as brass in his forebrain, watching the passing scene and doing the mental equivalent of eating popcorn.

He tried to push it back – and the world vanished . . .

He was in darkness; a warm, musty darkness, the darkness of the tomb, the velvet blackness of the mummy case.

There was a strong smell of old leather and the sourness of ancient paper. The paper rustled.

He felt that the darkness was full of unimaginable horrors – and the trouble with unimaginable horrors was that they were only too easy to imagine . . .

'Rincewind,' said a voice. Rincewind had never heard a lizard speak, but if one did it would have a voice like that.

'Um,' he said. 'Yes?'

The voice chuckled – a strange sound, rather papery.

'You ought to say "Where am I?" ' it said.

'Would I like it if I knew?' said Rincewind. He stared hard at the darkness. Now that he was accustomed to it, he could see something. Something vague, hardly bright enough to be anything at all, just the merest tracery in the air. Something strangely familiar.

'All right,' he said. 'Where am I?'

'You're dreaming.'

'Can I wake up now, please?'

'No,' said another voice, as old and dry as the first but still slightly different.

'We have something very important to tell you,' said a third voice, if anything more corpse-dry than the others. Rincewind nodded stupidly. In the back of his mind the Spell lurked and peered cautiously over his mental shoulder.

'You've caused us a lot of trouble, young Rincewind,' the voice went on. 'All this dropping over the edge of the world with no thought for other people. We had to seriously distort reality, you know.'

'Gosh.'

'And now you have a very important task ahead of you.'

'Oh. Good.'

'Many years ago we arranged for one of our number to hide in your head, because we could foresee a time coming when you would need to play a very important role.'

'Me? Why?'

'You run away a lot,' said one of the voices. 'That is good. You are a survivor.'

'Survivor? I've nearly been killed dozens of times!'

'Exactly.'

'Oh.'

'But try not to fall off the Disc again. We really can't have that.'

'Who are *we*, exactly?' said Rincewind.

There was a rustling in the darkness.

'In the beginning was the word,' said a dry voice right behind him.

'It was the Egg,' corrected another voice. 'I distinctly remember. The Great Egg of the Universe. Slightly rubbery.'

'You're both wrong, in fact. I'm sure it was the primordial slime.'

A voice by Rincewind's knee said: 'No, that came afterwards. There was firmament first. Lots of firmament. Rather sticky, like candyfloss. Very syrupy, in fact—'

'*In case anyone's interested*,' said a crackly voice on Rincewind's left, 'you're all wrong. In the beginning was the Clearing of the Throat—'

'—then the word—'

'Pardon me, the slime—'

'Distinctly rubbery, I thought—'

There was a pause. Then a voice said carefully, 'Anyway, whatever it was, we remember it distinctly.'

'Quite so.'

'Exactly.'

'And our task is to see that nothing dreadful happens to it, Rincewind.'

Rincewind squinted into the blackness. 'Would you kindly explain what you're talking about?'

There was a papery sigh. 'So much for metaphor,' said one of the voices. 'Look, it is very important you safeguard the Spell in your head and bring it back to us at the right time, you understand, so that when the moment is precisely right we can be said. Do you understand?'

Rincewind thought: we can be *said*?

And it dawned on him what the tracery was, ahead of him. It was writing on a page, seen from underneath.

'I'm *in* the Octavo?' he said.

'In certain metaphysical respects,' said one of the voices in offhand tones. It came closer. He could feel the dry rustling right in front of his nose . . .

He ran away.

* * *

The single red dot glowed in its patch of darkness. Trymon, still wearing the ceremonial robes from his inauguration as head of the Order, couldn't rid himself of the feeling that it had grown slightly while he watched. He turned away from the window with a shudder.

'Well?' he said.

'It's a star,' said the Professor of Astrology, 'I think.'

'You think?'

The astrologer winced. They were standing in Unseen University's observatory, and the tiny ruby pinpoint on the horizon wasn't glaring at him any worse than his new master.

'Well, you see, the point is that we've always believed stars to be pretty much the same as our sun—'

'You mean balls of fire about a mile across?'

'Yes. But this new one is, well – big.'

'Bigger than the sun?' said Trymon. He'd always considered a mile-wide ball of fire quite impressive, although he disapproved of stars on principle. They made the sky look untidy.

'A lot bigger,' said the astrologer slowly.

'Bigger than Great A'Tuin's head, perhaps?'

The astrologer looked wretched.

'Bigger than Great A'Tuin and the Disc together,' he said. 'We've checked,' he added hurriedly, 'and we're quite sure.'

'That is big,' agreed Trymon. 'The word "huge" comes to mind.'

'Massive,' agreed the astrologer hurriedly.

'Hmm.'

Trymon paced the broad mosaic floor of the observatory, which was inlaid with the signs of the Disc zodiac. There were sixty-four of them, from Wezen the Double-headed Kangaroo to Gahoolie, the Vase of Tulips (a constellation of great religious significance whose meaning, alas, was now lost).

He paused on the blue and gold tilework of Mubbo the Hyaena, and turned suddenly.

'We're going to hit it?' he asked.

'I am afraid so, sir,' said the astrologer.

'Hmm.' Trymon walked a few paces forward, stroking his beard thoughtfully. He paused on the cusp of Okjock the Salesman and The Celestial Parsnip.

'I'm not an expert in these matters,' he said, 'but I imagine this would not be a good thing?'

'No, sir.'

'Very hot, stars?'

The astrologer swallowed. 'Yes, sir.'

'We'd be burned up?'

'Eventually. Of course, before that there would be discquakes, tidal waves, gravitational disruption and probably the atmosphere would be stripped away.'

'Ah. In a word, lack of decent organization.'

The astrologer hesitated, and gave in. 'You could say so, sir.'

'People would panic?'

'Fairly briefly, I'm afraid.'

'Hmm,' said Trymon, who was just passing over

The Perhaps Gate and orbiting smoothly towards the Cow of Heaven. He squinted up again at the red gleam on the horizon. He appeared to reach a decision.

'We can't find Rincewind,' he said, 'and if we can't find Rincewind we can't find the eighth spell of the Octavo. But we believe that the Octavo must be read to avert catastrophe – otherwise why did the Creator leave it behind?'

'Perhaps He was just forgetful,' suggested the astrologer.

Trymon glared at him.

'The other Orders are searching all the lands between here and the Hub,' he continued, counting the points on his fingers, 'because it seems unreasonable that a man can fly into a cloud and not come out . . .'

'Unless it was stuffed with rocks,' said the astrologer, in a wretched and, as it turned out, entirely unsuccessful attempt to lighten the mood.

'But come down he must – somewhere. Where? we ask ourselves.'

'Where?' said the astrologer loyally.

'And immediately a course of action suggests itself to us.'

'Ah,' said the astrologer, running in an attempt to keep up as the wizard stalked across The Two Fat Cousins.

'And that course is . . .?'

The astrologer looked up into two eyes as grey and bland as steel.

'Um. We stop looking?' he ventured.

'Precisely! We use the gifts the Creator has given us, to whit, we look down and what is it we see?'

The astrologer groaned inwardly. He looked down.

'Tiles?' he hazarded.

'Tiles, yes, which together make up the . . . ?' Trymon looked expectant.

'Zodiac?' ventured the astrologer, a desperate man.

'Right! And therefore all we need do is cast Rincewind's precise horoscope and we will know exactly where he is!'

The astrologer grinned like a man who, having tap-danced on quicksand, feels the press of solid rock under his feet.

'I shall need to know his precise place and time of birth,' he said.

'Easily done. I copied them out of the University files before I came up here.'

The astrologer looked at the notes, and his forehead wrinkled. He crossed the room and pulled out a wide drawer full of charts. He read the notes again. He picked up a complicated pair of compasses and made some passes across the charts. He picked up a small brass astrolobe and cranked it carefully. He whistled between his teeth. He picked up a piece of chalk and scribbled some numbers on a blackboard.

Trymon, meanwhile, had been staring out at the new star. He thought: the legend in the Pyramid of Tsort says that whoever says the Eight Spells together when the Disc is in danger will obtain all that he truly desires. And it will be so soon!

And he thought: I remember Rincewind, wasn't he the scruffy boy who always came bottom of the class when we were training? Not a magical bone in his body. Let me get him in front of me, and we'll see if we can't get all eight—

The astrologer said 'Gosh' under his breath. Trymon spun around.

'Well?'

'Fascinating chart,' said the astrologer, breathlessly. His forehead wrinkled. 'Bit strange, really,' he said.

'How strange?'

'He was born under The Small Boring Group of Faint Stars which, as you know, lies between The Flying Moose and The Knotted String. It is said that even the ancients couldn't find anything interesting to say about the sign, which—'

'Yes, yes, get on with it,' said Trymon irritably.

'It's the sign traditionally associated with chess board makers, sellers of onions, manufacturers of plaster images of small religious significance, and people allergic to pewter. Not a wizard's sign at all. And at the time of his birth the shadow of Cori Celesti—'

'I don't want to know all the mechanical details,' growled Trymon. 'Just give me his horoscope.'

The astrologer, who had been rather enjoying himself, sighed and made a few additional calculations.

'Very well,' he said. 'It reads as follows: "Today is a good time for making new friends. A good deed may have unforeseen consequences. Don't upset any druids. You will soon be going on a very strange journey. Your lucky food is small cucumbers. People pointing knives at you are probably up to no good. PS, we really mean it about druids." '

'Druids?' said Trymon. 'I wonder . . .'

'Are you all right?' said Twoflower.

Rincewind opened his eyes.

The wizard sat up hurriedly and grabbed Twoflower by the shirt.

'I want to leave here!' he said urgently. 'Right now!'

'But there's going to be an ancient and traditional ceremony!'

'I don't care how ancient! I want the feel of honest cobbles under my feet, I want the old familiar smell of cesspits, I want to go where there's lots of people and fires and roofs and walls and friendly things like that! I want to go *home*!'

He found that he had this sudden desperate longing for the fuming, smoky streets of Ankh-Morpork, which was always at its best in the spring, when the gummy sheen on the turbid waters of the Ankh River had a special iridescence and the eaves were full of birdsong, or at least birds coughing rhythmically.

A tear sprang to his eye as he recalled the subtle play of light on the Temple of Small Gods, a noted local landmark, and a lump came to his throat when he remembered the fried fish stall on the junction of Midden Street and The Street of Cunning Artificers. He thought of the gherkins they sold there, great green things lurking at the bottom of their jar like drowned whales. They called to Rincewind across the miles, promising to introduce him to the pickled eggs in the next jar.

He thought of the cosy livery stable lofts and warm gratings where he spent his nights. Foolishly, he had sometimes jibbed at this way of life. It seemed incredible now, but he had found it boring.

Now he'd had enough. He was going home. Pickled gherkins, I hear you calling . . .

He pushed Twoflower aside, gathered his tattered robe around him with great dignity, set his face towards that area of horizon he believed to contain the city of his birth, and with intense determination and considerable absent-mindedness stepped right off the top of a thirty-foot trilithon.

Some ten minutes later, when a worried and rather contrite Twoflower dug him out of the large snowdrift at the base of the stones, his expression hadn't changed. Twoflower peered at him.

'Are you all right?' he said. 'How many fingers am I holding up?'

'I want to go home!'

'Okay.'

'No, don't try and talk me out of it, I've had enough, I'd like to say it's been great fun but I can't, and – what?'

'I said okay,' said Twoflower. 'I'd quite like to see Ankh-Morpork again. I expect they've rebuilt quite a lot of it by now.'

It should be noted that the last time the two of them had seen the city it was burning quite fiercely, a fact which had a lot to do with Twoflower introducing the concept of fire insurance to a venial but ignorant populace. But devastating fires were a regular feature of Morporkian life and it had always been cheerfully and meticulously rebuilt, using the traditional local materials of tinder-dry wood and thatch waterproofed with tar.

'Oh,' said Rincewind, deflating a bit. 'Oh, right. Right then. Good. Perhaps we'd better be off, then.'

He scrambled up and brushed the snow off himself.

'Only I think we should wait until morning,' added Twoflower.

'Why?'

'Well, because it's freezing cold, we don't really know where we are, the Luggage has gone missing, it's getting dark—'

Rincewind paused. In the deep canyons of his mind he thought he heard the distant rustle of ancient paper. He had a horrible feeling that his dreams were going to be very repetitive from now on, and he had much better things to do than be lectured by a bunch of ancient spells who couldn't even agree on how the Universe began—

A tiny dry voice at the back of his brain said: *What things*?

'Oh, shut up,' he said.

'I only said it's freezing cold and—' Twoflower began.

'I didn't mean you, I meant me.'

'What?'

'Oh, shut up,' said Rincewind wearily. 'I don't suppose there's anything to eat around here?'

The giant stones were black and menacing against the dying green light of sunset. The inner circle was full of druids, scurrying around by the light of several bonfires and tuning up all the necessary peripherals of a stone computer, like rams' skulls on poles topped with mistletoe, banners embroidered with twisted snakes and so on. Beyond the circles of firelight a large number of plains people had gathered; druidic festivals were always popular, especially when things went wrong.

Rincewind stared at them.

'What's going on?'

'Oh, well,' said Twoflower enthusiastically, 'apparently there's this ceremony dating back for thousands of years to celebrate the, um, rebirth of the moon, or possibly the sun. No, I'm pretty certain it's the moon. Apparently it's very solemn and beautiful and invested with a quiet dignity.'

Rincewind shivered. He always began to worry when Twoflower started to talk like that. At least he hadn't said 'picturesque' or 'quaint' yet; Rincewind had never found a satisfactory translation for those words, but the nearest he had been able to come was 'trouble'.

'I wish the Luggage was here,' said the tourist regretfully. 'I could use my picture box. It sounds very quaint and picturesque.'

The crowd stirred expectantly. Apparently things were about to start.

'Look,' said Rincewind urgently. 'Druids are priests. You must remember that. Don't do anything to upset them.'

'But—'

'Don't offer to buy the stones.'

'But I—'

'Don't start talking about quaint native folkways.'

'I thought—'

'*Really* don't try to sell them insurance, that always upsets them.'

'But they're priests!' wailed Twoflower. Rincewind paused.

'Yes,' he said. 'That's the whole point, isn't it?'

At the far side of the outer circle some sort of procession was forming up.

'But priests are good, kind men,' said Twoflower. 'At home they go around with begging bowls. It's their only possession,' he added.

'Ah,' said Rincewind, not certain he understood. 'This would be for putting the blood in, right?'

'Blood?'

'Yes, from sacrifices.' Rincewind thought about the priests he had known at home. He was, of course, anxious not to make an enemy of any god and had attended any number of temple functions and, on the whole, he thought that the most accurate definition of any priest in the Circle Sea Regions was someone who spent quite a lot of time gory to the armpits.

Twoflower looked horrified.

'Oh no,' he said. 'Where I come from priests are holy men who have dedicated themselves to lives of poverty, good works and the study of the nature of God.'

Rincewind considered this novel proposition.

'No sacrifices?' he said.

'Absolutely not.'

Rincewind gave up. 'Well,' he said, 'they don't sound very holy to *me*.'

There was a loud blarting noise from a band of bronze trumpets. Rincewind looked around. A line of druids marched slowly past, their long sickles hung with sprays of mistletoe. Various junior druids and apprentices followed them, playing a variety of percussion instruments that were traditionally supposed to drive away evil spirits and quite probably succeeded.

Torchlight made excitingly dramatic patterns on the stones, which stood ominously against the green-lit sky. Hubwards, the shimmering curtains of the aurora coriolis began to wink and glitter among the stars as a million ice crystals danced in the Disc's magical field.

'Belafon explained it all to me,' whispered Twoflower. 'We're going to see a time-honoured ceremony that celebrates the Oneness of Man with the Universe, that was what he said.'

Rincewind looked sourly at the procession. As the druids spread out around a great flat stone that dominated the centre of the circle he couldn't help noticing the attractive if rather pale young lady in their midst. She wore a long white robe, a gold torc around her neck, and an expression of vague apprehension.

'Is she a druidess?' said Twoflower.

'I don't think so,' said Rincewind slowly.

The druids began to chant. It was, Rincewind felt, a particularly nasty and rather dull chant which sounded very much as if it was going to build up to an abrupt crescendo. The sight of the young woman lying down on the big stone didn't do anything to derail his train of thought.

'I want to stay,' said Twoflower. 'I think ceremonies like this hark back to a primitive simplicity which—'

'Yes, yes,' said Rincewind, 'but they're going to sacrifice her, if you must know.'

Twoflower looked at him in astonishment.

'What, kill her?'

'Yes.'

'Why?'

'Don't ask me. To make the crops grow or the moon rise or something. Or maybe they're just keen on killing people. That's religion for you.'

He became aware of a low humming sound, not so much heard as felt. It seemed to be coming from the stone next to them. Little points of light flickered under its surface, like mica specks.

Twoflower was opening and shutting his mouth.

'Can't they just use flowers and berries and things?' he said. 'Sort of symbolic?'

'Nope.'

'Has anyone ever tried?'

Rincewind sighed. 'Look,' he said. 'No self-respecting High Priest is going to go through all the business with the trumpets and the processions and the banners and everything, and then shove his knife into a daffodil and a couple of plums. You've got to face it, all this stuff about golden boughs and the cycles of nature and stuff just boils down to sex and violence, usually at the same time.'

To his amazement Twoflower's lip was trembling. Twoflower didn't just look at the world through rose-tinted spectacles, Rincewind knew – he looked at it through a rose-tinted brain, too, and heard it through rose-tinted ears.

The chant was rising inexorably to a crescendo. The head druid was testing the edge of his sickle and all eyes were turned to the finger of stone on the snowy hills beyond the circle where the moon was due to make a guest appearance.

'It's no use you—'

But Rincewind was talking to himself.

However, the chilly landscape outside the circle was not entirely devoid of life. For one thing a party of wizards was even now drawing near, alerted by Trymon.

But a small and solitary figure was also watching from the cover of a handy fallen stone. One of the Disc's greatest 1egends watched the events in the stone circle with considerable interest.

He saw the druids circle and chant, saw the chief druid raise his sickle . . .

Heard the voice.

'I say! Excuse me! Can I have a word?'

* * *

Rincewind looked around desperately for a way of escape. There wasn't one. Twoflower was standing by the altar stone with one finger in the air and an attitude of polite determination.

Rincewind remembered one day when Twoflower had thought a passing drover was beating his cattle too hard, and the case he had made for decency towards animals had left Rincewind severely trampled and lightly gored.

The druids were looking at Twoflower with the kind of expression normally reserved for mad sheep or the sudden appearance of a rain of frogs. Rincewind couldn't quite hear what Twoflower was saying, but a few phrases like 'ethnic folkways' and 'nuts and flowers' floated acoss the hushed circle.

Then fingers like a bunch of cheese straws clamped over the wizard's mouth and an extremely sharp cutting edge pinked his Adam's apple and a damp voice right by his ear said, 'Not a shound, or you ish a dead man.'

Rincewind's eyes swivelled in their sockets as if trying to find a way out.

'If you don't want me to say anything, how will you know I understand what you just said?' he hissed.

'Shut up and tell me what that other idiot ish doing!'

'No, but look, if I've got to shut up, how can I—' The knife at his throat became a hot streak of pain and Rincewind decided to give logic a miss.

'His name's Twoflower. He isn't from these parts.'

'Doeshn't look like it. Friend of yoursh?'

'We've got this sort of hate-hate relationship, yes.'

Rincewind couldn't see his captor, but by the feel of it he had a body made of coathangers. He also smelt strongly of peppermints.

'He hash got guts, I'll give him that. Do exshactly what I shay and it ish just poshible he won't end up with them wrapped around a shtone.'

'Urrr.'

'They're not very ecumenical around here, you shee.'

It was at that moment that the moon, in due obedience to the laws of persuasion, rose, although in deference to the laws of computing it wasn't anywhere near where the stones said it should be.

But what was there, peeking through ragged clouds, was a glaring red star. It hung exactly over the circle's holiest stone, glittering away like the sparkle in the eyesocket of Death. It was sullen and awful and, Rincewind couldn't help noticing, just a little bit bigger than it was last night.

A cry of horror went up from the assembled priests. The crowd on the surrounding banks pressed forward; this looked quite promising.

Rincewind felt a knife handle slip into his hand, and the squelchy voice behind him said, 'You ever done this short of thing before?'

'What sort of thing?'

'Rushed into a temple, killed the prieshts, shtolen the gold and reshcued the girl.'

'No, not in so many words.'

'You do it like thish.'

Two inches from Rincewind's left ear a voice broke into a sound like a baboon with its foot trapped in an echo canyon, and a small but wiry shape rushed past him.

By the light of the torches he saw that it was a very old man, the skinny variety that generally gets called 'spry', with a totally bald head, a beard almost down to his knees, and a pair of matchstick legs on which varicose veins had traced the street map of quite a large city. Despite the snow he wore nothing more than a studded leather holdall and a pair of boots that could have easily accommodated a second pair of feet.

The two druids closest to him exchanged glances and hefted their sickles. There was a brief blur and they collapsed into tight balls of agony, making rattling noises.

In the excitement that followed Rincewind sidled along towards the altar stone, holding his knife gingerly so as not to attract any unwelcome comment. In fact no one was paying a great deal of attention to him; the druids that hadn't fled the circle, generally the younger and more muscular ones, had congregated around the old man in order to discuss the whole subject of sacrilege as it pertained to stone circles, but judging by the cackling and sounds of gristle he was carrying the debate.

Twoflower was watching the fight with interest. Rincewind grabbed him by the shoulder.

'Let's go,' he said.

'Shouldn't we help?'

'I'm sure we'd only get in the way,' said Rincewind hurriedly. 'You know what it's like to have people looking over your shoulder when you're busy.'

'At least we must rescue the young lady,' said Twoflower firmly.

'All right, but get a move on!'

Twoflower took the knife and hurried up to the altar stone. After several inept slashes he managed to cut the ropes that bound the girl, who sat up and burst into tears.

'It's all right—' he began.

'It bloody well isn't!' she snapped, glaring at him through two red-rimmed eyes. 'Why do people always go and spoil things?' She blew her nose resentfully on the edge of her robe.

Twoflower looked up at Rincewind in embarrassment.

'Um, I don't think you quite understand,' he said. 'I mean, we just saved you from absolutely certain death.'

'It's not easy around here,' she said. 'I mean, keeping yourself—' she blushed, and twisted the hem of her robe wretchedly. 'I mean, staying . . . not letting yourself . . . not losing your qualifications . . .'

'Qualifications?' said Twoflower, earning the Rincewind Cup for the slowest person on the uptake in the entire multiverse. The girl's eyes narrowed.

'I could have been up there with the Moon Goddess by now, drinking mead out of a silver bowl,' she said petulantly. 'Eight years of staying home on Saturday nights right down the drain!'

She looked up at Rincewind and scowled.

Then he sensed something. Perhaps it was a barely heard footstep behind him, perhaps it was movement reflected in her eyes – but he ducked.

Something whistled through the air where his neck had been and glanced off Twoflower's bald head. Rincewind spun round to see the archdruid readying his sickle for another swing and, in the absence of any hope of running away, lashed out desperately with a foot.

It caught the druid squarely on the kneecap. As the man screamed and dropped his weapon there was a nasty little fleshy sound and he fell forward. Behind him the little man with the long beard pulled his sword from the body, wiped it with a handful of snow, and said, 'My lumbago is giving me gyp. You can carry the treashure.'

'Treasure?' said Rincewind weakly.

'All the necklashes and shtuff. All the gold collarsh. They've got lotsh of them. Thatsh prieshts for you,' said the old man wetly. 'Nothing but torc, torc, torc. Who'she the girl?'

'She won't let us rescue her,' said Rincewind. The girl looked at the old man defiantly through her smudged eyeshadow.

'Bugger that,' he said, and with one movement picked her up, staggered a little, screamed at his arthritis and fell over.

After a moment he said, from his prone position, 'Don't just shtand there, you daft bitcsh – help me up.' Much to Rincewind's amazement, and almost certainly to hers as well, she did so.

Rincewind, meanwhile, was trying to rouse Twoflower. There was a graze across his temple which didn't look too deep, but the little man was unconscious with a faintly worried smile plastered across his face. His breathing was shallow and – strange.

And he felt light. Not simply underweight, but weightless. The wizard might as well have been holding a shadow.

Rincewind remembered that it was said that druids used strange and terrible poisons. Of course, it was often said, usually by the same people, that crooks always had close-set eyes, lightning never struck twice in the same place and if the gods had wanted men to fly they'd have given them an airline ticket. But something about Twoflower's lightness frightened Rincewind. Frightened him horribly.

He looked up at the girl. She had the old man slung over one shoulder, and gave Rincewind an apologetic half-smile. From somewhere around the small of her back a voice said, 'Got everything? Letsh get out of here before they come back.'

Rincewind tucked Twoflower under one arm and jogged along after them. It seemed the only thing to do.

The old man had a large white horse tethered to a withered tree in a snow-filled gully some way from the circles. It was sleek, glossy and the general effect of a superb battle charger was only very slightly spoiled by the haemorrhoid ring tied to the saddle.

'Okay, put me down. There'sh a bottle of shome linament shtuff in the shaddle bag, if you wouldn't mind . . .'

Rincewind propped Twoflower as nicely as possible against the tree, and by moonlight – and, he realized, by the faint red light of the menacing new star – took the first real look at his rescuer.

The man had only one eye; the other was covered by a black patch. His thin body was a network of scars and, currently, twanging white-hot with tendonitis. His teeth had obviously decided to quit long ago.

'Who are you?' he said.

'Bethan,' said the girl, rubbing a handful of nasty-smelling green ointment into the old man's back. She wore the air of one who, if asked to consider what sort of events might occur after being rescued from virgin sacrifice by a hero with a white charger, would probably not have mentioned linament, but who, now linament was apparently what did happen to you after all, was determined to be good at it.

'I meant him,' said Rincewind.

One star-bright eye looked up at him.

'Cohen ish my name, boy.' Bethan's hands stopped moving.

'Cohen?' she said. 'Cohen the Barbarian?'

'The very shame.'

'Hang on, hang on,' said Rincewind. 'Cohen's a great big chap, neck like a bull, got chest muscles like a sack of footballs. I mean, he's the Disc's greatest warrior, a legend in his own lifetime. I remember my grandad telling me he saw him . . . my grandad telling me he . . . my grandad . . .'

He faltered under the gimlet gaze.

'Oh,' he said. 'Oh. Of course. Sorry.'

'Yesh,' said Cohen, and sighed. 'Thatsh right, boy. I'm a lifetime in my own legend.'

'Gosh,' said Rincewind. 'How old are you, exactly?'

'Eighty-sheven.'

'But you were the greatest!' said Bethan. 'Bards still sing songs about you.'

Cohen shrugged, and gave a little yelp of pain.

'I never get any royaltiesh,' he said. He looked moodily at the snow. 'That'sh the shaga of my life. Eighty yearsh in the bushiness and what have I got to show for it? Backache, pilesh, bad digeshtion and a hundred different recipesh for shoop. Shoop! I hate shoop!'

Bethan's forehead wrinkled. 'Shoop?'

'Soup,' explained Rincewind.

'Yeah, shoop,' said Cohen, miserably. 'It'sh my teeths, you shee. No one takes you sheriously when you've got no teeths, they shay "Shit down by the fire, grandad, and have shome shoo—"' Cohen looked sharply at Rincewind. 'That'sh a nashty cough you have there, boy.'

Rincewind looked away, unable to look Bethan in the face. Then his heart sank. Twoflower was still leaning against the tree, peacefully unconscious, and looking as reproachful as was possible in the circumstances.

Cohen appeared to remember him, too. He got unsteadily to his feet and shuffled over to the tourist. He thumbed both eyes open, examined the graze, felt the pulse.

'He'sh gone,' he said.

'Dead?' said Rincewind. In the debating chamber of his mind a dozen emotions got to their feet and started shouting. Relief was in full spate when Shock cut in on a point of order and then Bewilderment, Terror and Loss started a fight which was ended only when Shame slunk in from next door to see what all the row was about.

'No,' said Cohen thoughtfully, 'not exshactly. Just – gone.'

'Gone where?'

'I don't know,' said Cohen, 'but I think I know shomeone who might have a map.'

Far out on the snowfield half a dozen pinpoints of red light glowed in the shadows.

'He's not far away,' said the leading wizard, peering into a small crystal sphere.

There was general mutter from the ranks behind him which roughly meant that however far away Rincewind was he couldn't be further than a nice hot bath, a good meal and a warm bed.

Then the wizard who was tramping along in the rear stopped and said, 'Listen!'

They listened. There were the subtle sounds of winter beginning to close its grip on the land, the creak of rocks, the muted scuffling of small creatures in their tunnels under the blanket of snow. In a distant forest a wolf howled, felt embarrassed when no one joined in, and stopped. There was the silver sleeting sound of moonlight. There was also the wheezing noise of half a dozen wizards trying to breathe quietly.

'I can't hear a thing—' one began.

'Ssshh!'

'All right, all right—'

Then they all heard it; a tiny distant crunching, like something moving very quickly over the snow crust.

'Wolves?' said a wizard. They all thought about hundreds of lean, hungry bodies leaping through the night.

'N-no,' said the leader. 'It's too regular. Perhaps it's a messenger?'

It was louder now, a crisp rhythm like someone eating celery very fast.

'I'll send up a flare,' said the leader. He picked up a handful of snow, rolled it into a ball, threw it up into the air and ignited it with a stream of octarine fire from his fingertips. There was a brief, fierce blue glare.

There was silence. Then another wizard said, 'You daft bugger, I can't see a thing now.'

That was the last thing they heard before something fast, hard and noisy cannoned into them out of the darkness and vanished into the night.

When they dug one another out of the snow all they could find was a tight pressed trail of little footprints. Hundreds of little footprints, all very close together and heading across the snow as straight as a searchlight.

'A necromancer!' said Rincewind.

The old woman across the fire shrugged and pulled a pack of greasy cards from some unseen pocket.

Despite the deep frost outside, the atmosphere inside the yurt was like a blacksmith's armpit and the wizard was already sweating heavily. Horse dung made a good fuel, but the Horse People had a lot to learn about air conditioning, starting with what it meant.

Bethan leaned sideways.

'What's neck romance?' she whispered.

'Necromancy. Talking to the dead,' he explained.

'Oh,' she said, vaguely disappointed.

They had dined on horse meat, horse cheese, horse black pudding, horse d'oeuvres and a thin beer that Rincewind didn't want to speculate about. Cohen (who'd had horse soup) explained that the Horse Tribes of the Hubland steppes were born in the saddle, which Rincewind considered was a gynaecological impossibility, and they were particularly adept at natural magic, since life on the open steppe makes you realize how neatly the sky fits the land all around the edges and this naturally inspires the mind to deep thoughts like 'Why?', 'When?' and 'Why don't we try beef for a change?'

The chieftain's grandmother nodded at Rincewind and spread the cards in front of her.

Rincewind, as it has already been noted, was the

worst wizard on the Disc: no other spells would stay in his mind once the Spell had lodged in there, in much the same way that fish don't hang around in a pike pool. But he still had his pride, and wizards don't like to see women perform even simple magic. Unseen University had never admitted women, muttering something about problems with the plumbing, but the real reason was an unspoken dread that if women were allowed to mess around with magic they would probably be embarrassingly good at it . . .

'Anyway, I don't believe in Caroc cards,' he muttered. 'All that stuff about it being the distilled wisdom of the universe is a load of rubbish.'

The first card, smoke-yellowed and age-crinkled, was . . .

It should have been The Star. But instead of the familar round disc with crude little rays, it had become a tiny red dot. The old woman muttered and scratched at the card with a fingernail, then looked sharply at Rincewind.

'Nothing to do with me,' he said.

She turned up the Importance of Washing the Hands, the Eight of Octograms, the Dome of the Sky, the Pool of Night, the Four of Elephants, the Ace of Turtles, and – Rincewind had been expecting it – Death.

And something was wrong with Death, too. It should have been a fairly realistic drawing of Death on his white horse, and indeed He was still there. But the sky was red lit, and coming over a distant hill was a tiny figure, barely visible by the light of the horsefat lamps. Rincewind didn't have to identify it, because behind it was a box on hundreds of little legs.

The Luggage would follow its owner anywhere.

Rincewind looked across the tent to Twoflower, a pale shape on a pile of horsehides.

'He's really dead?' he said. Cohen translated for the old woman, who shook her head. She reached down to a small wooden chest beside her and rummaged around in a collection of bags and bottles until she found a tiny green bottle which she tipped into Rincewind's beer. He looked at it suspiciously.

'She shays it's sort of medicine,' said Cohen. 'I should drink it if I were you, theshe people get a bit upshet if you don't accshept hoshpitality.'

'It's not going to blow my head off?' said Rincewind.

'She shays it's esshential you drink it.'

'Well, if you're sure it's okay. It can't make the beer taste any worse.'

He took a swig, aware of all eyes on him.

'Um,' he said. 'Actually, it's not at all ba—'

Something picked him up and threw him into the air. Except that in another sense he was still sitting by the fire – he could see himself there, a dwindling figure in the circle of firelight that was rapidly getting smaller. The toy figures around it were looking intently at his body. Except for the old woman. She was looking right up at *him*, and grinning.

* * *

The Circle Sea's senior wizards were not grinning at all. They were becoming aware that they were confronted with something entirely new and fearsome: a young man on the make.

Actually none of them was quite sure how old Trymon really was, but his sparse hair was still black and his skin had a waxy look to it that could be taken, in a poor light, to be the bloom of youth.

The six surviving heads of the Eight Orders sat at the long, shiny and new table in what had been Galder Weatherwax's study and each one wondered precisely what it was about Trymon that made them want to kick him.

It wasn't that he was ambitious and cruel. Cruel men were stupid; they all knew how to use cruel men, and they certainly knew how to bend other men's ambitions. You didn't stay an Eighth Level magus for long unless you were adept at a kind of mental judo.

It wasn't that he was bloodthirsty, power-hungry or especially wicked. These things were not necessarily drawbacks in a wizard. The wizards were, on the whole, no more wicked than, say, the committee of the average Rotary Club, and each had risen to pre-eminence in his chosen profession not so much by skill at magic but by never neglecting to capitalize on the weaknesses of opponents.

It wasn't that he was particularly wise. Every wizard considered himself a fairly hot property, wisewise; it went with the job.

It wasn't even that he had charisma. They all knew

charisma when they encountered it, and Trymon had all the charisma of a duck egg.

That was it, in fact . . .

He wasn't good or evil or cruel or extreme in any way but one, which was that he had elevated greyness to the status of a fine art and cultivated a mind that was as bleak and pitiless and logical as the slopes of Hell.

And what was so strange was that each of the wizards, who had in the course of their work encountered many a fire-spitting, bat-winged, tiger-taloned entity in the privacy of a magical octogram, had never before had quite the same uncomfortable feeling as they had when, ten minutes late, Trymon strode into the room.

'Sorry I'm late, gentlemen,' he lied, rubbing his hands briskly. 'So many things to do, so much to organize, I'm sure you know how it is.'

The wizards looked sidelong at one another as Trymon sat down at the head of the table and shuffled busily through some papers.

'What happened to old Galder's chair, the one with the lion arms and the chicken feet?' said Jiglad Wert. It had gone, along with most of the other familiar furniture, and in its place were a number of low leather chairs that appeared to be incredibly comfortable until you'd sat in them for five minutes.

'That? Oh, I had it burnt,' said Trymon, not looking up.

'Burnt? But it was a priceless magical artifact, a genuine—'

'Just a piece of junk, I'm afraid,' said Trymon, treating him to a fleeting smile. 'I'm sure real wizards don't really need that sort of thing. Now if I may draw your attention to the business of the day—'

'What's this paper?' said Jiglad Wert, of the Hoodwinkers, waving the document that had been left in front of him, and waving it all the more forcefully because his own chair, back in his cluttered and comfortable tower, was if anything more ornate than Galder's had been.

'It's an agenda, Jiglad,' said Trymon, patiently.

'And what does a gender do?'

'It's just a list of the things we've got to discuss. It's very simple, I'm sorry if you feel that—'

'We've never needed one before!'

'I think perhaps you *have* needed one, you just haven't used one,' said Trymon, his voice resonant with reasonableness.

Wert hesitated. 'Well, all right,' he said sullenly, looking around the table for support, 'but what's this here where it says—' he peered closely at the writing, ' "Successor to Greyhald Spold". It's going to be old Rhunlet Vard, isn't it? He's been waiting for years.'

'Yes, but is he sound?' said Trymon.

'What?'

'I'm sure we all realize the importance of proper leadership,' said Trymon. ' Now, Vard is – well, worthy, of course, in his way, but—'

'It's not our business,' said one of the other wizards.

'No, but it could be,' said Trymon.

There was silence.

'Interfere with the affairs of another Order?' said Wert.

'Of course not,' said Trymon. 'I merely suggest that we could offer ... advice. But let us discuss this later ...'

The wizards had never heard of the words 'power base', otherwise Trymon would never have been able to get away with all this. But the plain fact was that helping others to achieve power, even to strengthen your own hand, was quite alien to them. As far as they were concerned, every wizard stood alone. Never mind about hostile paranormal entities, an ambitious wizard had quite enough to do fighting his enemies in his own Order.

'I think we should now consider the matter of Rincewind,' said Trymon.

'And the star,' said Wert. 'People are noticing, you know.'

'Yes, they say *we* should be doing something,' said Lumuel Panter, of the Order of Midnight. 'What, I should like to know?'

'Oh, that's easy,' said Wert. 'They say we should read the Octavo. That's what they always say. Crops bad? Read the Octavo. Cows ill? Read the Octavo. The Spells will make everything all right.'

'There could be something in that,' said Trymon. 'My, er, late predecessor made quite a study of the Octavo.'

'We all have,' said Panter, sharply, 'but what's the use? The Eight Spells have to work together. Oh, I agree, if all else fails maybe we should risk it, but the

Eight have to be said together or not at all – and one of them is inside this Rincewind's head.'

'And we cannot find him,' said Trymon. 'That is the case, isn't it? I'm sure we've all tried, privately.'

The wizards looked at one another, embarrassed. Eventually Wert said, 'Yes. All right. Cards on the table. I can't seem to locate him.'

'I've tried scrying,' said another. 'Nothing.'

'I've sent familiars,' said a third. The others sat up. If confessing failure was the order of the day, then they were damn well going to make it clear that they had failed heroically.

'Is that all? *I've* sent demons.'

'*I've* looked into the Mirror of Oversight.'

'Last night I sought him out in the Runes of M'haw.'

'I'd like to make it clear that I tried both the Runes and the Mirror *and* the entrails of a manicreach.'

'*I've* spoken to the beasts of the field and the birds of the air.'

'Any good?'

'Nah.'

'Well, I've questioned the very bones of the country, yea, and the deep stones and the mountains thereof.'

There was a sudden chilly silence. Everyone looked at the wizard who had spoken. It was Ganmack Treehallet, of the Venerable Seers, who shifted uneasily in his seat.

'Yes, with bells on, I expect,' said someone.

'I never said they answered, did I?'

Trymon looked along the table.

'*I've* sent someone to find him,' he said.

Wert snorted. 'That didn't work out so well the last two times, did it?'

'That was because we relied on magic, but it is obvious that Rincewind is somehow hidden from magic. But he can't hide his footprints.'

'You've set a tracker?'

'In a manner of speaking.'

'A *hero*?' Wert managed to pack a lot of meaning into the one word. In such a tone of voice, in another universe, would a Southerner say 'damnyankee'.

The wizards looked at Trymon, open-mouthed.

'Yes,' he said calmly.

'On whose authority?' demanded Wert. Trymon turned his grey eyes on him.

'Mine. I needed no other.'

'It's – it's highly irregular! Since when have wizards needed to hire heroes to do their work for them?'

'Ever since wizards found their magic wouldn't work,' said Trymon.

'A temporary setback, nothing more.'

Trymon shrugged. 'Maybe,' he said, 'but we haven't the time to find out. Prove me wrong. Find Rincewind by scrying or talking to birds. But as for me, I know I'm meant to be wise. And wise men do what the times demand.'

It is a well known fact that warriors and wizards do not get along, because one side considers the other side to be a collection of bloodthirsty idiots who can't walk and think at the same time, while the other side is naturally suspicious of a body of men who mumble a lot and wear long dresses. Oh, say the wizards, if we're going to be like that, then, what about all those studded collars and oiled muscles down at the Young Men's Pagan Association? To which the heroes reply, that's a pretty good allegation coming from a bunch of wimpsoes who won't go near a woman on account, can you believe it, of their mystical power being sort of drained out. Right, say the wizards, that just about does it, you and your leather posing pouches. Oh yeah, say the heroes, why don't you . . .

And so on. This sort of thing has been going on for centuries, and caused a number of major battles which have left large tracts of land uninhabitable because of magical harmonics.

In fact, the hero, even at this moment galloping towards the Vortex Plains, didn't get involved in this kind of argument because they didn't take it seriously but mainly because this particular hero was a heroine. A red-headed one.

Now, there is a tendency at a point like this to look over one's shoulder at the cover artist and start going on at length about leather, thighboots and naked blades.

Words like 'full', 'round' and even 'pert' creep into the narrative, until the writer has to go and have a cold shower and a lie down.

Which is all rather silly, because any woman setting out to make a living by the sword isn't about to go around looking like something off the cover of the more advanced kind of lingerie catalogue for the specialized buyer.

Oh well, all right. The point that must be made is that although Herrena the Henna-Haired Harridan would look quite stunning after a good bath, a heavy-duty manicure, and the pick of the leather racks in Woo Hun Ling's Oriental Exotica and Martial Aids on Heroes Street, she was currently quite sensibly dressed in light chain mail, soft boots, and a short sword.

All right, maybe the boots were leather. But not black.

Riding with her were a number of swarthy men that will certainly be killed before too long anyway, so a description is probably not essential. There was absolutely nothing pert about any of them.

Look, they can wear leather if you like.

Herrena wasn't too happy about them, but they were all that was available for hire in Morpork. Many of the citizens were moving out and heading for the hills, out of fear of the new star.

But Herrena was heading for the hills for a different reason. Just turnwise and rimwards of the Plains were the bare Trollbone Mountains. Herrena, who had for many years availed herself of the uniquely equal opportunities available to any woman who could make a sword sing, was trusting to her instincts.

This Rincewind, as Trymon had described him, was a rat, and rats like cover. Anyway, the mountains were a long way from Trymon and, for all that he was currently her employer, Herrena was very happy about that. There was something about his manner that made her fists itch.

* * *

Rincewind knew he ought to be panicking, but that was difficult because, although he wasn't aware of it, emotions like panic and terror and anger are all to do with stuff sloshing around in glands and all Rincewind's glands were still in his body.

It was difficult to be certain where his real body was, but when he looked down he could see a fine blue line trailing from what for the sake of sanity he would still call his ankle into the blackness around him, and it seemed reasonable to assume that his body was on the other end.

It was not a particularly good body, he'd be the first to admit, but one or two bits of it had sentimental value and it dawned on him that if the little blue line snapped he'd have to spend the rest of his li— his existence hanging around ouija boards pretending to be people's dead aunties and all the other things lost souls do to pass the time.

The sheer horror of this so appalled him he hardly felt his feet touch the ground. *Some* ground, anyway; he decided that it almost certainly wasn't *the* ground, which as far as he could remember wasn't black and didn't swirl in such a disconcerting way.

He took a look around.

Sheer sharp mountains speared up around him into a frosty sky hung with cruel stars, stars which appeared on no celestial chart in the multiverse, but right in there amongst them was a malevolent red disc. Rincewind shivered, and looked away. The land ahead of him sloped down sharply, and a dry wind whispered across the frost-cracked rocks.

It really did whisper. As grey eddies caught at his robe and tugged at his hair Rincewind thought he could hear voices, faint and far off, saying things like 'Are you sure those were mushrooms in the stew? I feel a bit—,' and 'There's a lovely view if you lean over this—,' and 'Don't fuss, it's only a scratch—,' and 'Watch where you're pointing that bow, you nearly—' and so on.

He stumbled down the slope, with his fingers in his ears, until he saw a sight seen by very few living men.

The ground dipped sharply until it became a vast funnel, fully a mile across, into which the whispering wind of the souls of the dead blew with a vast, echoing susurration, as though the Disc itself was breathing. But a narrow spur of rock arched out and over the hole, ending in an outcrop perhaps a hundred feet across. There was a garden up there, with orchards and flower-beds, and a quite small black cottage.

A little path led up to it.

Rincewind looked behind him. The shiny blue line was still there.

So was the Luggage.

It squatted on the path, watching him.

Rincewind had never got on with the Luggage, it had always given him the impression that it thoroughly disapproved of him. But just for once it wasn't glaring at him. It had a rather pathetic look, like a dog that's just come home after a pleasant roll in the cowpats to find that the family has moved to the next continent.

'All right,' said Rincewind. 'Come on.'

It extended its legs and followed him up the path.

Somehow Rincewind had expected the garden on the outcrop to be full of dead flowers, but it was in fact well kept and had obviously been planted by someone with an eye for colour, always provided the colour was deep purple, night black or shroud white. Huge lilies perfumed the air. There was a sundial without a gnomon in the middle of a freshly-scythed lawn.

With the Luggage trailing behind him Rincewind crept along a path of marble chippings until he was at the rear of the cottage, and pushed open a door.

Four horses looked at him over the top of their nosebags. They were warm and alive, and some of the best kept beasts Rincewind had ever seen. A big white one had a stall all to itself, and a silver and black harness hung over the door. The other three were tethered in front of a hay rack on the opposite wall, as if visitors had just dropped by. They regarded Rincewind with vague animal curiosity.

The Luggage bumped into his ankle. He spun around and hissed, 'Push off, you!'

The Luggage backed away. It looked abashed.

Rincewind tiptoed to the far door and cautiously pushed it open. It gave onto a stone-flagged passage-way, which in turn opened onto a wide entrance hall.

He crept forward with his back pressed tightly against a wall. Behind him the Luggage rose up on tiptoes and skittered along nervously.

The hall itself . . .

Well, it wasn't the fact that it was considerably bigger than the whole cottage had appeared from the outside that worried Rincewind; the way things were these days, he'd have laughed sarcastically if anyone had said you couldn't get a quart into a pint pot. And it wasn't the decor, which was Early Crypt and ran heavily to black drapes.

It was the clock. It was very big, and occupied a space between two curving wooden staircases covered with carvings of things that normal men only see after a heavy session on something illegal.

It had a very long pendulum, and the pendulum swung with a slow tick-tock that set his teeth on edge, because it was the kind of deliberate, annoying ticking that wanted to make it abundantly clear that every tick and every tock was stripping another second off your life. It was the kind of sound that suggested very pointedly that in some hypothetical hourglass, somewhere, another few grains of sand had dropped out from under you.

Needless to say, the weight on the pendulum was knife-edged and razor sharp.

Something tapped him in the small of the back. He turned angrily.

'Look, you son of a suitcase, I told you—'

It wasn't the Luggage. It was a young woman – silver haired, silver eyed, rather taken aback.

'Oh,' said Rincewind. 'Um. Hallo?'

'Are you alive?' she said. It was the kind of voice associated with beach umbrellas, suntan oil and long cool drinks.

'Well, I hope so,' said Rincewind, wondering if his glands were having a good time wherever they were. 'Sometimes I'm not so sure. What is this place?'

'This is the house of Death,' she said.

'Ah,' said Rincewind. He ran a tongue over his dry lips. 'Well, nice to meet you. I think I ought to be getting along—'

She clapped her hands. 'Oh, you mustn't go!' she said. 'We don't often have living people here. Dead people are so boring, don't you think?'

'Uh, yes,' Rincewind agreed fervently, eyeing the doorway. 'Not much conversation, I imagine.'

'It's always "When I was alive—" and "We really knew how to breathe in my day—"', she said, laying a small white hand on his arm and smiling at him. 'They're always so set in their ways, too. No fun at all. So formal.'

'Stiff?' suggested Rincewind. She was propelling him towards an archway.

'Absolutely. What's your name? My name is Ysabell.'

'Um, Rincewind. Excuse me, but if this *is* the house of Death, what are you doing here? You don't look dead to me.'

'Oh, I live here.' She looked intently at him. 'I say, you haven't come to rescue your lost love, have you? That always annoys Daddy, he says it's a good job he never sleeps because if he did he'd be kept awake by the tramp, tramp, tramp of young heroes coming down here to carry back a lot of silly girls, he says.'

'Goes on a lot, does it?' said Rincewind weakly, as they walked along a black-hung corridor.

'All the time. I think it's very romantic. Only when you leave, it's very important not to look back.'

'Why not?'

She shrugged. 'I don't know. Perhaps the view isn't very good. Are you a hero, actually?'

'Um, no. Not as such. Not at all, really. Even less than that, in fact. I just came to look for a friend of mine,' he said wretchedly. 'I suppose you haven't seen him? Little fat man, talks a lot, wears eyeglasses, funny sort of clothes?'

As he spoke he was aware that he may have missed something vital. He shut his eyes and tried to recall the last few minutes of conversation. Then it hit him like a sandbag.

'*Daddy?*'

She looked down demurely. 'Adopted, actually,' she said. 'He found me when I was a little girl, he says. It was all rather sad.' She brightened. 'But come and meet him – he's got his friends in tonight, I'm sure he'll be interested to see you. He doesn't meet many people socially. Nor do I, actually,' she added.

'Sorry,' said Rincewind. 'Have I got it right? We're talking about Death, yes? Tall, thin, empty eye-sockets, handy in the scythe department?'

She sighed. 'Yes. His looks are against him, I'm afraid.'

While it was true that, as has already been indicated, Rincewind was to magic what a bicycle is to a bumblebee, he nevertheless retained one privilege available to practitioners of the art, which was that at the point of death it would be Death himself who turned up to claim him (instead of delegating the job to a lesser mythological anthropomorphic personification, as is usually the case). Owing largely to inefficiency Rincewind had consistently failed to die at the right time, and if there is one thing that Death does not like it is unpunctuality.

'Look, I expect my friend has just wandered off somewhere,' he said. 'He's always doing that, story of his life, nice to have met you, must be going—'

But she had already stopped in front of a tall door padded with purple velvet. There were voices on the other side – eldritch voices, the sort of voices that mere typography will remain totally unable to convey until someone can make a linotype machine with echo-reverb and, possibly, a typeface that looks like something said by a slug.

This is what the voices were saying:

WOULD YOU KIND EXPLAINING THAT AGAIN?

'Well, if you return anything *except* a trump, South will be able to get in his two ruffs, losing only one Turtle, one Elephant and one Major Arcana, then—'

'That's Twoflower!' hissed Rincewind. 'I'd know that voice anywhere!'

JUST A MINUTE – PESTILENCE IS SOUTH?

'*Oh, come on, Mort. He explained that. What if Famine had played a – what was it – a trump return?*' It was a breathy, wet voice, practically contagious all by itself.

'Ah, then you'd only be able to ruff one Turtle instead of two,' said Twoflower enthusiastically.

'But if War had chosen a trump lead originally,

then the contract would have gone two down?'

'Exactly!'

I DIDN'T QUITE FOLLOW THAT. TELL ME ABOUT PSYCHIC BIDS AGAIN, I THOUGHT I WAS GETTING THE HANG OF THAT. It was a heavy, hollow voice, like two large lumps of lead smashing together.

'That's when you make a bid primarily to deceive your opponents, but of course it might cause problems for your partner—'

Twoflower's voice rambled on in its enthusiastic way. Rincewind looked blankly at Ysabell as words like 'rebiddable suit', 'double finesse' and 'grand slam' floated through the velvet.

'Do you understand any of that?' she asked.

'Not a word,' he said.

'It sounds awfully complicated.'

On the other side of the door the heavy voice said: DID YOU SAY HUMANS PLAY THIS FOR FUN?

'Some of them get to be very good at it, yes. I'm only an amateur, I'm afraid.'

BUT THEY ONLY LIVE EIGHTY OR NINETY YEARS!

'You should know, Mort,' said a voice that Rincewind hadn't heard before and certainly never wanted to hear again, especially after dark.

'*It's certainly very – intriguing.*'

DEAL AGAIN AND LET'S SEE IF I'VE GOT THE HANG OF IT.

'Do you think perhaps we should go in?' said Ysabell. A voice behind the door said, I BID . . . THE KNAVE OF TERRAPINS.

'No, sorry, I'm sure you're wrong, let's have a look at your—'

Ysabell pushed the door open.

It was, in fact, a rather pleasant study, perhaps a little on the sombre side, possibly created on a bad day by an interior designer who had a headache and a craving for putting large hourglasses on every flat surface and also a lot of large, fat, yellow and extremely runny candles he wanted to get rid of.

The Death of the Disc was a traditionalist who prided himself on his personal service and spent most of the time being depressed because this was not appreciated. He would point out that no one feared death itself, just pain and separation and oblivion, and that it was quite unreasonable to take against someone just because he had empty eye-sockets and a quiet pride in his work. He still used a scythe, he'd point out, while the Deaths of other worlds had long ago invested in combine harvesters.

Death sat at one side of a black baize table in the centre of the room, arguing with Famine, War and Pestilence. Twoflower was the only one to look up and notice Rincewind.

'Hey, how did you get here?' he said.

'Well, some say the Creator took a handful – oh, I see, well, it's hard to explain but I—'

'Have you got the Luggage?'

The wooden box pushed past Rincewind and settled down in front of its owner, who opened its lid and rummaged around inside until he came up with a small, leatherbound book which he handed to War, who was hammering the table with a mailed fist.

'It's "Nosehinger on the Laws of Contract",' he said.

'It's quite good, there's a lot in it about double finessing and how to—'

Death snatched the book with a bony hand and flipped through the pages, quite oblivious to the presence of the two men.

RIGHT, he said, PESTILENCE, OPEN ANOTHER PACK OF CARDS. I'M GOING TO GET TO THE BOTTOM OF THIS IF IT KILLS ME, FIGURATIVELY SPEAKING OF COURSE.

Rincewind grabbed Twoflower and pulled him out of the room. As they jogged down the corridor with the Luggage galloping behind them he said:

'What was all that about?'

'Well, they've got lots of time and I thought they might enjoy it,' panted Twoflower.

'What, playing with cards?'

'It's a special kind of playing,' said Twoflower. 'It's called—' he hesitated. Language wasn't his strong point. 'In your language it's called a thing you put across a river, for example,' he concluded, 'I think.'

'Aqueduct?' hazarded Rincewind. 'Fishing line? Weir? Dam?'

'Yes, possibly.'

They reached the hallway, where the big clock still shaved the seconds off the lives of the world.

'And how long do you think that'll keep them occupied?'

Twoflower paused. 'I'm not sure,' he said thoughtfully. 'Probably until the last trump – what an amazing clock . . .'

'Don't try to buy it,' Rincewind advised. 'I don't think they'd appreciate it around here.'

'Where is here, exactly?' said Twoflower, beckoning the Luggage and opening its lid.

Rincewind looked around. The hall was dark and deserted, its tall narrow windows whorled with ice. He looked down. There was the faint blue line stretching away from his ankle. Now he could see that Twoflower had one too.

'We're sort of informally dead,' he said. It was the best he could manage.

'Oh.' Twoflower continued to rummage.

'Doesn't that worry you?'

'Well, things tend to work out in the end, don't you think? Anyway, I'm a firm believer in reincarnation. What would you like to come back as?'

'I don't want to go,' said Rincewind firmly. 'Come on, let's get out of— oh, no. Not that.'

Twoflower had produced a box from the depths of the Luggage. It was large and black and had a handle on one side and a little round window in front and a strap so that Twoflower could put it around his neck, which he did.

There was a time when Rincewind had quite liked the iconoscope. He believed, against all experience, that the world was fundamentally understandable, and that if he could only equip himself with the right mental toolbox he could take the back off and see how it worked. He was, of course, dead wrong. The iconoscope didn't take pictures by letting light fall onto specially treated paper, as he had surmised, but by the far simpler method of imprisoning a small demon with a good eye for colour and a speedy hand with a paintbrush. He had been very upset to find that out.

'You haven't got time to take pictures!' he hissed.

'It won't take long,' said Twoflower firmly, and rapped on the side of the box. A tiny door flew open and the imp poked his head out.

'Bloody hell,' it said. 'Where are we?'

'It doesn't matter,' said Twoflower. 'The clock first, I think.'

The demon squinted.

'Poor light,' he said. 'Three bloody years at f8, if you ask me.' He slammed the door shut. A second later there was the tiny scraping noise of his stool being dragged up to his easel.

Rincewind gritted his teeth.

'You don't need to take pictures, you can just remember it!' he shouted.

'It's not the same,' said Twoflower calmly.

'It's better! It's more real!'

'It isn't really. In years to come, when I'm sitting by the fire—'

'You'll be sitting by the fire forever if we don't get out of here!'

'Oh, I do hope you're not going.'

They both turned. Ysabell was standing in the archway, smiling faintly. She held a scythe in one hand, a scythe with a blade of proverbial sharpness. Rincewind tried not to look down at his blue lifeline; a girl holding a scythe shouldn't smile in that unpleasant, knowing and slightly deranged way.

'Daddy seems a little preoccupied at the moment but I'm sure he wouldn't dream of letting you go off just like that,' she added. 'Besides, I'd have no one to talk to.'

'Who's this?' said Twoflower.

'She sort of lives here,' mumbled Rincewind. 'She's a sort of girl,' he added.

He grabbed Twoflower's shoulder and tried to shuffle imperceptibly towards the door into the dark, cold garden. It didn't work, largely because Twoflower wasn't the sort of person who went in for nuances of expression and somehow never assumed that anything bad might apply to him.

'Charmed, I'm sure,' he said. 'Very nice place, you have here. Interesting baroque effect with the bones and skulls.'

Ysabell smiled. Rincewind thought: if Death ever does hand over the family business, she'll be better at it than he is – she's bonkers.

'Yes, but we must be going,' he said.

'I really won't hear of it,' she said. 'You must stay and tell me all about yourselves. There's plenty of time and it's so boring here.'

She darted sideways and swung the scythe at the shining threads. It screamed through the air like a neutered tomcat – and stopped sharply.

There was the creak of wood. The Luggage had snapped its lid shut on the blade.

Twoflower looked up at Rincewind in astonishment. And the wizard, with great deliberation and a certain amount of satisfaction, hit him smartly on the chin. As the little man fell backwards Rincewind caught him, threw him over a shoulder and ran.

Branches whipped at him in the starlit garden, and small, furry and probably horrible things scampered away as he pounded desperately along the faint lifeline that shone eerily on the freezing grass.

From the building behind him came a shrill scream of disappointment and rage. He cannoned off a tree and sped on.

Somewhere there was a path, he remembered. But in this maze of silver light and shadows, tinted now with red as the terrible new star made its presence felt even in the netherworld, nothing looked right. Anyway, the lifeline appeared to be going in quite the wrong direction.

There was the sound of feet behind him. Rincewind wheezed with effort; it sounded like the Luggage, and at the moment he didn't want to meet the Luggage, because it might have got the wrong idea about him hitting its master, and generally the Luggage bit people it didn't like. Rincewind had never had the nerve to ask where it was they actually *went* when the heavy lid slammed shut on them, but they certainly weren't there when it opened again.

In fact he needn't have worried. The Luggage overtook him easily, its little legs a blur of movement. It seemed to Rincewind to be concentrating very heavily on running, as if it had some inkling of what was coming up behind it and didn't like the idea at all.

Don't look back, he remembered. The view probably isn't very nice.

The Luggage crashed through a bush and vanished.

A moment later Rincewind saw why. It had careened over the edge of the outcrop and was dropping towards the great hole underneath, which he could now see was faintly red lit at the bottom. Stretching from Rincewind, out over the edge of the rocks and down into the hole, were two shimmering blue lines.

He paused uncertainly, although that isn't precisely true because he was totally certain of several things, for example that he didn't want to jump, and that he certainly didn't want to face whatever it was coming up behind him, and that in the spirit world Twoflower was quite heavy, and that there were worse things than being dead.

'Name two,' he muttered, and jumped.

A few seconds later the horsemen arrived and didn't stop when they reached the edge of the rock but simply rode into the air and reined their horses over nothingness.

Death looked down.

THAT ALWAYS ANNOYS ME, he said. I MIGHT AS WELL INSTALL A REVOLVING DOOR.

'*I wonder what they wanted?*' said Pestilence.

'Search me,' said War. 'Nice game, though.'

'Right,' agreed Famine. 'Compelling, I thought.'

WE'VE GOT TIME FOR ANOTHER FONDLE, said Death.

'Rubber,' corrected War.

RUBBER WHAT?

'You call them rubbers,' said War.

RIGHT, RUBBERS, said Death. He looked up at the new star, puzzled as to what it might mean.

I think we've got time, he repeated, a trifle uncertainly.

Mention has already been made of an attempt to inject a little honesty into reporting on the Disc, and how poets and bards were banned on pain of – well, pain – from going on about babbling brooks and rosy-fingered dawn and could only say, for example, that a face had launched a thousand ships if they were able to produce certified dockyard accounts.

And therefore, out of a passing respect for this tradition, it will not be said of Rincewind and Twoflower that they became an ice-blue sinewave arcing through the dark dimensions, or that there was a sound like the twanging of a monstrous tusk, or that their lives passed in front of their eyes (Rincewind had in any case seen his past life flash in front of his eyes so many times that he could sleep through the boring bits) or that the universe dropped on them like a large jelly.

It will be said, because experiment has proven it to be true, that there was a noise like a wooden ruler being struck heavily with a C sharp tuning fork, possibly B flat, and a sudden sensation of absolute stillness.

This was because they were absolutely still, and it was absolutely dark.

It occurred to Rincewind that something had gone wrong.

Then he saw the faint blue tracery in front of him.

He was inside the Octavo again. He wondered what

would happen if anyone opened the book; would he and Twoflower appear like a colour plate?

Probably not, he decided. The Octavo they were in was something a bit different from the mere book chained to its lectern deep in Unseen University, which was merely a three-dimensional representation of a multidimensional reality, and—

Hold on, he thought. I don't think like this. Who's thinking for me?

'Rincewind,' said a voice like the rustle of old pages.

'Who? Me?'

'Of course you, you daft sod.'

A flicker of defiance flared very briefly in Rincewind's battered heart.

'Have you managed to recall how the Universe started yet?' he said nastily. 'The Clearing of the Throat, wasn't it, or the Drawing of the Breath, or the Scratching of the Head and Trying to Remember It, It was On the Tip of the Tongue?'

Another voice, dry as tinder, hissed, 'You would do well to remember where you are.' It should be impossible to hiss a sentence with no sibilants in it, but the voice made a very good attempt.

'Remember where I am? Remember where I am?' shouted Rincewind. 'Of course I remember where I am, I'm inside a bloody book talking to a load of voices I can't see. Why do you think I'm screaming?'

'I expect you're wondering why we brought you here again,' said a voice by his ear.

'No.'

'No?'

'What did he say?' said another disembodied voice.

'He said no.'

'He really said no?'

'Yes.'

'Oh.'

'Why?'

'This sort of thing happens to me all the time,' said Rincewind. 'One minute I'm falling off the world, then I'm inside a book, then I'm on a flying rock, then I'm watching Death learn how to play Weir or Dam or whatever it was, why should I wonder about anything?'

'Well, we imagine you will be wondering why we don't want anyone to say us,' said the first voice, aware that it was losing the initiative.

Rincewind hesitated. The thought had crossed his mind, only very fast and looking nervously from side to side in case it got knocked over.

'Why should anyone want to say you?'

'It's the star,' said the Spell. 'The red star. Wizards are already looking for you; when they find you they want to say all eight Spells together to change the future. They think the Disc is going to collide with the star.'

Rincewind thought about this. 'Is it?'

'Not exactly, but in a – *what's that*?'

Rincewind looked down. The Luggage padded out of the darkness. There was a long sliver of scytheblade in its lid.

'It's just the Luggage,' he said.

'But we didn't summon it here!'

'No one summons it anywhere,' said Rincewind. 'It just turns up. Don't worry about it.'

'Oh. What were we talking about?'

'This red star thing.'

'Right. It's very important that you—'

'Hallo? Hallo? Anyone out there?'

It was a small and squeaky voice and came from the picture box still slung around Twoflower's inert neck.

The picture imp opened his hatch and squinted up at Rincewind.

'Where's this, squire?' it said.

'I'm not sure.'

'We still dead?'

'Maybe.'

'Well, let's hope we go somewhere where we don't need too much black, because I've run out.' The hatch slammed shut.

Rincewind had a fleeting vision of Twoflower handing around his pictures and saying things like 'This is me being tormented by a million demons' and 'This is me with that funny couple we met on the freezing slopes of the Underworld.' Rincewind wasn't certain about what happened to you after you really died, the authorities were a little unclear on the subject; a swarthy sailor from the Rimward lands had said that he was confident of going to a paradise where there was sherbet and houris. Rincewind wasn't certain what a houri was, but after some thought he came to the conclusion that it was a little liquorice tube for sucking up the sherbet. Anyway, sherbet made him sneeze.

'Now that interruption is over,' said a dry voice firmly, 'perhaps we can get on. It is most important that you don't let the wizards take the Spell from you. Terrible things will happen if all eight spells are said too soon.'

'I just want to be left in peace,' said Rincewind.

'Good, good. We knew we could trust you from the day you first opened the Octavo.'

Rincewind hesitated. 'Hang on a minute,' he said. 'You want me to run around keeping the wizards from getting all the spells together?'

'Exactly.'

'That's why one of you got into my head?'

'Precisely.'

'You totally ruined my life, you know that?' said Rincewind hotly. 'I could have really made it as a wizard if you hadn't decided to use me as a sort of portable spellbook. I can't remember any other spells, they're too frightened to stay in the same head as you!'

'We're sorry.'

'I just want to go home! I want to go back to where—' a trace of moisture appeared in Rincewind's eye – 'to where there's cobbles under your feet and some of the beer isn't too bad and you can get quite a good piece of fried fish of an evening, with maybe a couple of big green gherkins, and even an eel pie and a dish of whelks, and there's always a warm stable somewhere to sleep in and in the morning you are always in the same place as you were the night before and there wasn't all this weather all over the place. I mean, I don't mind about the magic, I'm probably not, you know, the right sort of material for a wizard, I just want to go *home*!—'

'But you must—' one of the spells began.

It was too late. Homesickness, the little elastic band in the subconscious that can wind up a salmon and propel it three thousand miles through strange seas, or send a million lemmings running joyfully back to an ancestral homeland which, owing to a slight kink in the continental drift, isn't there any more – homesickness rose up inside Rincewind like a late-night prawn biriani, flowed along the tenuous thread linking his tortured soul to his body, dug its heels in and tugged . . .

The spells were alone inside their Octavo.

Alone, at any rate, apart from the Luggage.

They looked at it, not with eyes, but with consciousness as old as the Discworld itself.

'And you can bugger off too,' they said.

'—bad.'

Rincewind knew it was himself speaking, he recognized the voice. For a moment he was looking out through his eyes not in any normal way, but as a spy might peer through the cut-out eyes of a picture. Then he was back.

'You okay, Rinshwind?' said Cohen. 'You looked a bit gone there.'

'You did look a bit white,' agreed Bethan. 'Like someone had walked over your grave.'

'Uh, yes, it was probably me,' he said. He held up his

fingers and counted them. There appeared to be the normal amount.

'Um, have I moved at all?' he said.

'You just looked at the fire as if you had seen a ghost,' said Bethan.

There was a groan behind them. Twoflower was sitting up, holding his head in his hands.

His eyes focused on them. His lips moved soundlessly.

'That was a really strange . . . dream,' he said. 'What's this place? Why am I here?'

'Well,' said Cohen, 'shome shay the Creator of the Univershe took a handful of clay and—'

'No, I mean *here*,' said Twoflower. 'Is that you, Rincewind?'

'Yes,' said Rincewind, giving it the benefit of the doubt.

'There was this . . . a clock that . . . and these people who . . .' said Twoflower. He shook his head. 'Why does everything smell of horses?'

'You've been ill,' said Rincewind. 'Hallucinating.'

'Yes . . . I suppose I was.' Twoflower looked down at his chest. 'But in that case, why have I—'

Rincewind jumped to his feet.

'Sorry, very close in here, got to have a breath of fresh air,' he said. He removed the picture box's strap from Twoflower's neck, and dashed for the tent flap.

'I didn't notice that when he came in,' said Bethan. Cohen shrugged.

Rincewind managed to get a few yards from the yurt before the ratchet of the picture box began to click. Very slowly, the box extruded the last picture that the imp had taken.

Rincewind snatched at it.

What it showed would have been quite horrible even in broad daylight. By freezing starlight, tinted red with the fires of the evil new star, it was a lot worse.

'No,' said Rincewind softly. 'No, it wasn't like that, there was a house, and this girl, and . . .'

'You see what you see and I paint what I see,' said the imp from its hatch. 'What I see is real. I was bred for it. I only see what's really there.'

A dark shape crunched over the snowcrust towards Rincewind. It was the Luggage. Rincewind, who normally hated and distrusted it, suddenly felt it was the most refreshingly normal thing he had ever seen.

'I see you made it, then,' said Rincewind. The Luggage rattled its lid.

'Okay, but what did *you* see?' said Rincewind. 'Did you look behind?'

The Luggage said nothing. For a moment they were silent, like two warriors who have fled the field of carnage and have paused for a return of breath and sanity.

Then Rincewind said, 'Come on, there's a fire inside.' He reached out to pat the Luggage's lid. It snapped irritably at him, nearly catching his fingers. Life was back to normal again.

The next day dawned bright and clear and cold. The sky became a blue dome stuck on the white sheet of the world, and the whole effect would have been as fresh and clean as a toothpaste advert if it wasn't for the pink dot on the horizon.

'You can shee it in daylight now,' said Cohen. 'What is it?'

He looked hard at Rincewind, who reddened.

'Why does everyone look at me?' he said. 'I don't know what it is, maybe it's a comet or something.'

'Will we all be burned up?' said Bethan.

'How should I know? I've never been hit by a comet before.'

They were riding in single file across the brilliant snowfield. The Horse people, who seemed to hold Cohen in high regard, had given them their mounts and directions to the River Smarl, a hundred miles rimward, where Cohen reckoned Rincewind and Twoflower could find a boat to take them to the Circle Sea. He had announced that he was coming with them, on account of his chilblains.

Bethan had promptly announced that she was going to come too, in case Cohen wanted anything rubbed. Rincewind was vaguely aware of some sort of chemistry bubbling away. For one thing, Cohen had made an effort to comb his beard.

'I think she's rather taken with you,' he said. Cohen sighed.

'If I wash twenty yearsh younger,' he said wistfully.

'Yes?'

'I'd be shixty-sheven.'

'What's that got to do with it?'

'Well – how can I put it? When I wash a young man,

carving my name in the world, well, then I liked my women red-haired and fiery.'

'Ah.'

'And then I grew a little older and for preference I looked for a woman with blonde hair and the glint of the world in her eye.'

'Oh? Yes?'

'But then I grew a little older again and I came to see the point of dark women of a sultry nature.'

He paused. Rincewind waited.

'And?' he said. 'Then what? What is it that you look for in a woman now?'

Cohen turned one rheumy blue eye on him.

'Patience,' he said.

'I can't believe it!' said a voice behind them. 'Me riding with Cohen the Barbarian!'

It was Twoflower. Since early morning he had been like a monkey with the key to the banana plantation after discovering he was breathing the same air as the greatest hero of all time.

'Is he perhapsh being sharcashtic?' said Cohen to Rincewind.

'No. He's always like that.'

Cohen turned in his saddle. Twoflower beamed at him, and waved proudly. Cohen turned back, and grunted.

'He's got eyesh, hashn't he?'

'Yes, but they don't work like other people's. Take it from me. I mean – well, you know the Horse people's yurt, where we were last night?'

'Yesh.'

'Would you say it was a bit dark and greasy and smelt like a very ill horse?'

'Very accurate deshcription, I'd shay.'

'He wouldn't agree. He'd say it was a magnificent barbarian tent, hung with the pelts of the great beasts hunted by the lean-eyed warriors from the edge of civilization, and smelt of the rare and curious resins plundered from the caravans as they crossed the trackless – well, and so on. I mean it,' he added.

'He'sh mad?'

'Sort of mad. But mad with lots of money.'

'Ah, then he can't be mad. I've been around; if a man hash lotsh of money he'sh just ecshentric.'

Cohen turned in his saddle again. Twoflower was telling Bethan how Cohen had single-handedly defeated the snake warriors of the witch lord of S'belinde and stolen the sacred diamond from the giant statue of Offler the Crocodile God.

A weird smile formed among the wrinkles of Cohen's face.

'I could tell him to shut up, if you like,' said Rincewind.

'Would he?'

'No, not really.'

'Let him babble,' said Cohen. His hand fell to the handle of his sword, polished smooth by the grip of decades.

'Anyway, I *like* his eyes,' he said. 'They can see for fifty years.'

A hundred yards behind them, hopping rather awkwardly through the soft snow, came the

Luggage. No one ever asked its opinion about anything.

By evening they had come to the edge of the high plains, and rode down through gloomy pine forests that had only been lightly dusted by the snowstorm. It was a landscape of huge cracked rocks, and valleys so narrow and deep that the days only lasted about twenty minutes. A wild, windy country, the sort where you might expect to find—

'Trollsh,' said Cohen, sniffing the air.

Rincewind stared around him in the red evening light. Suddenly rocks that had seemed perfectly normal looked suspiciously alive. Shadows that he wouldn't have looked at twice now began to look horribly occupied.

'I like trolls,' said Twoflower.

'No you don't,' said Rincewind firmly. 'You can't. They're big and knobbly and they eat people.'

'No they don't,' said Cohen, sliding awkwardly off his horse and massaging his knees. 'Well-known mishapprehenshion, that ish. Trolls never ate anybody.'

'No?'

'No, they alwaysh spit the bitsh out. Can't digesht people, see? Your average troll don't want any more out of life than a nice lump of granite, maybe, with perhapsh a nice slab of limeshtone for aftersh. I heard someone shay it's becosh they're a shilicashe – a shillycaysheou—' Cohen paused, and wiped his beard, 'made out of rocks.'

Rincewind nodded. Trolls were not unknown in Ankh-Morpork, of course, where they often got employment as bodyguards. They tended to be a bit expensive to keep until they learned about doors and didn't simply leave the house by walking aimlessly through the nearest wall.

As they gathered firewood Cohen went on, 'Trollsh teeth, that'sh the thingsh.'

'Why?' said Bethan.

'Diamonds. Got to be, you shee. Only thing that can shtand the rocksh, and they shtill have to grow a new shet every year.'

'Talking of teeth—' said Twoflower.

'Yesh?'

'I can't help noticing—'

'Yesh?'

'Oh, nothing,' said Twoflower.

'Yesh? Oh. Let'sh get thish fire going before we loshe the light. And then,' Cohen's face fell, 'I supposhe we'd better make some shoop.'

'Rincewind's good at that,' said Twoflower enthusiastically. 'He knows all about herbs and roots and things.'

Cohen gave Rincewind a look which suggested that he, Cohen, didn't believe that.

'Well, the Horshe people gave us shome horse jerky,' he said. 'If you can find shome wild onionsh and stuff, it might make it tashte better.'

'But I—' Rincewind began, and gave up. Anyway, he reasoned, I know what an onion looks like, it's a sort of saggy white thing with a green bit sticking out of the top, should be fairly conspicuous.

'I'll just go and have a look, shall I?' he said.

'Yesh.'

'Over there in all that thick, shadowy undergrowth?'

'Very good playshe, yesh.'

'Where all the deep gullies and things are, you mean?'

'Ideal shpot, I'd shay.'

'Yes, I thought so,' said Rincewind bitterly. He set off, wondering how you attracted onions. After all, he thought, although you see them hanging in ropes on market stalls they probably don't grow like that, perhaps peasants or whatever use onion hounds or something, or sing songs to attract onions.

There were a few early stars out as he started to poke aimlessly among the leaves and grass. Luminous fungi, unpleasantly organic and looking like marital aids for gnomes, squished under his feet. Small flying things bit him. Other things, fortunately invisible, hopped or slithered away under the bushes and croaked reproachfully at him.

'Onions?' whispered Rincewind. 'Any onions here?'

'There's a patch of them by that old yew tree,' said a voice beside him.

'Ah,' said Rincewind. 'Good.'

There was a long silence, except for the buzzing of the mosquitoes around Rincewind's ears.

He was standing perfectly still. He hadn't even moved his eyes.

Eventually he said, 'Excuse me.'

'Yes?'

'Which one's the yew?'

'Small gnarly one with the little dark green needles.'

'Oh, yes. I see it. Thanks again.'

He didn't move. Eventually the voice said conversationally, 'Anything more I can do for you?'

'You're not a tree, are you?' said Rincewind, still staring straight ahead.

'Don't be silly. Trees can't talk.'

'Sorry. It's just that I've been having a bit of difficulty with trees lately, you know how it is.'

'Not really. I'm a rock.'

Rincewind's voice hardly changed.

'Fine, fine,' he said slowly. 'Well, I'll just be getting those onions, then.'

'Enjoy them.'

He walked forward in a careful and dignified fashion, spotted a clump of stringy white things huddling in the undergrowth, uprooted them carefully, and turned around.

There was a rock a little way away. But there were rocks everywhere, the very bones of the Disc were near the surface here.

He looked hard at the yew tree, just in case it had been speaking. But the yew, being a fairly solitary tree, hadn't heard about Rincewind the arborial saviour, and in any case was asleep.

'If that was you, Twoflower, I knew it was you all along,' said Rincewind. His voice sounded suddenly clear and very alone in the gathering dusk.

Rincewind remembered the only fact he knew for

sure about trolls, which was that they turned to stone when exposed to sunlight, so that anyone who employed trolls to work during daylight had to spend a fortune on barrier cream.

But now that he came to think about it, it didn't say *anywhere* what happened to them after the sun had gone down again . . .

The last of the daylight trickled out of the landscape. And there suddenly seemed to be a great many rocks about.

'He's an awful long time with those onions,' said Twoflower. 'Do you think we'd better go and look for him?'

'Wishards know how to look after themselves,' said Cohen. 'Don't worry.' He winced. Bethan was cutting his toenails.

'He's not a terribly good wizard, actually,' said Twoflower, drawing nearer the fire. 'I wouldn't say this to his face, but' – he leaned towards Cohen – 'I've never actually seen him do any magic.'

'Right, let's have the other one,' said Bethan.

'Thish is very kind of you.'

'You'd have quite nice feet if only you'd look after them.'

'Can't sheem to bend down like I used to,' said Cohen, sheepishly. 'Of courshe, you don't get to meet many chiropodishts in my line of work. Funny, really. I've met any amount of snake prieshts, mad godsh, warlordsh, never any chiropodishts. I shupposhe it wouldn't look right, really – Cohen Against the Chiropodishts . . .'

'Or Cohen And The Chiropractors of Doom,' suggested Bethan. Cohen cackled

'Or Cohen And The Mad Dentists!' laughed Twoflower.

Cohen's mouth snapped shut.

'What'sh sho funny about that?' he asked, and his voice had knuckles in it.

'Oh, er, well,' said Twoflower. 'Your teeth, you see . . .'

'What about them?' snapped Cohen.

Twoflower swallowed. 'I can't help noticing that they're, um, not in the same geographical location as your mouth.'

Cohen glared at him. Then he sagged, and looked very small and old.

'True, of corsh,' he muttered. 'I don't blame you. It'sh hard to be a hero with no teethsh. It don't matter what elsh you loosh, you can get by with one eye even, but you show 'em a mouth full of gumsh and no one hash any reshpect.'

'I do,' said Bethan loyally.

'Why don't you get some more?' said Twoflower brightly.

'Yesh, well, if I wash a shark or something, yesh, I'd grow shome,' said Cohen sarcastically.

'Oh, no, you buy them,' said Twoflower. 'Look, I'll show you – er, Bethan, do you mind looking the other way?' He waited until she had turned around and then put his hand to his mouth.

'You shee?' he said.

Bethan heard Cohen gasp.

'You can take yoursh out?'

'Oh yesh. I've got sheveral shets. Excushe me—' There was a swallowing noise, and then in a more normal voice Twoflower said, 'It's very convenient, of course.'

Cohen's very voice radiated awe, or as much awe as is possible without teeth, which is about the same amount as with teeth but sounds a great deal less impressive.

'I should think show,' he said. 'When they ache, you jusht take them out and let them get on with it, yesh? Teach the little buggersh a lesshon, shee how they like being left to ache all by themshelvesh!'

'That's not quite right,' said Twoflower carefully. 'They're not mine, they just *belong* to me.'

'You put shomeone elshe's teethsh in your mouth?'

'No, someone made them, lots of people wear them where I come from, it's a—'

But Twoflower's lecture on dental appliances went ungiven, because somebody hit him.

The Disc's little moon toiled across the sky. It shone by its own light, owing to the cramped and rather inefficient astronomical arrangements made by the Creator, and was quite crowded with assorted lunar goddesses who were not, at this particular time, paying much attention to what went on in the Disc but were getting up a petition about the Ice Giants.

Had they looked down, they would have seen Rincewind talking urgently to a bunch of rocks.

Trolls are one of the oldest lifeforms in the multiverse, dating from an early attempt to get the whole life thing on the road without all that squashy protoplasm. Individual trolls live for a long time, hibernating during the summertime and sleeping during the day, since heat affects them and makes them slow. They have a fascinating geology. One could talk about tribology, one could mention the semiconductor effects of impure silicon, one could talk about the giant trolls of prehistory who make up most of the Disc's major mountain ranges and will cause some real problems if they ever awake, but the plain fact is that without the Disc's powerful and pervasive magical field trolls would have died out a long time ago.

Psychiatry hadn't been invented on the Disc. No one had ever shoved an inkblot under Rincewind's nose to see if he had any loose toys in the attic. So the only way he'd have been able to describe the rocks turning back into trolls was by gabbling vaguely about how pictures suddenly form when you look at the fire, or clouds.

One minute there'd be a perfectly ordinary rock, and suddenly a few cracks that had been there all along took on the definite appearance of a mouth or a pointed ear. A moment later, and without anything actually changing at all, a troll would be sitting there, grinning at him with a mouth full of diamonds.

They wouldn't be able to digest me, he told himself. I'd make them awfully ill.

It wasn't much of a comfort.

'So you're Rincewind the wizard,' said the nearest one. It sounded like someone running over gravel. 'I dunno. I thought you'd be taller.'

'Perhaps he's eroded a bit,' said another one. 'The legend is awfully old.'

Rincewind shifted awkwardly. He was pretty certain the rock he was sitting on was changing shape, and a tiny troll – hardly any more than a pebble – was sitting companionably on his foot and watching him with extreme interest.

'Legend?' he said. 'What legend?'

'It's been handed down from mountain to gravel since the sunset* of time,' said the first troll. ' "When the red star lights the sky Rincewind the wizard will come looking for onions. Do not bite him. It is very important that you help him stay alive." '

There was a pause.

'That's it?' said Rincewind.

'Yes,' said the troll. 'We've always been puzzled about it. Most of our legends are much more exciting. It was more interesting being a rock in the old days.'

'It was?' said Rincewind weakly.

'Oh yes. No end of fun. Volcanoes all over the place. It really *meant* something, being a rock then. There was none of this sedimentary nonsense, you were igneous or nothing. Of course, that's all gone now. People call themselves trolls today, well, sometimes

* An interesting metaphor. To nocturnal trolls, of course, the dawn of time lies in the future.

they're hardly more than slate. Chalk even. I wouldn't give myself airs if you could use me to draw with, would you?'

'No,' said Rincewind quickly. 'Absolutely not, no. This, er, this legend thing. It said you shouldn't bite me?'

'That's right!' said the little troll on his foot. 'And it was me who told you where the onions were!'

'We're rather glad you came along,' said the first troll, which Rincewind couldn't help noticing was the biggest one there. 'We're a bit worried about this new star. What does it mean?'

'I don't know,' said Rincewind. 'Everyone seems to think I know about it, but I don't—'

'It's not that we would mind being melted down,' said the big troll. 'That's how we all started, anyway. But we thought, maybe, it might mean the end of everything and that doesn't seem a very good thing.'

'It's getting bigger,' said another troll. 'Look at it now. Bigger than last night.'

Rincewind looked. It was *definitely* bigger than last night.

'So we thought you might have some suggestions?' said the head troll, as meekly as it is possible to sound with a voice like a granite gargle.

'You could jump over the Edge,' said Rincewind. 'There must be lots of places in the universe that could do with some extra rocks.'

'We've heard about that,' said the troll. 'We've met rocks that tried it. They say you float about for millions of years and then you get very hot and burn away and end up at the bottom of a big hole in the scenery. That doesn't sound very bright.'

It stood up with a noise like coal rattling down a chute, and stretched its thick, knobbly arms.

'Well, we're supposed to help you,' it said. 'Anything you want doing?'

'I was supposed to be making some soup,' said Rincewind. He waved the onions vaguely. It was probably not the most heroic or purposeful gesture ever made.

'Soup?' said the troll. 'Is that all?'

'Well, maybe some biscuits too.'

The trolls looked at one another, exposing enough mouth jewellery to buy a medium-sized city.

Eventually the biggest troll said, 'Soup it is, then.' It shrugged grittily. 'It's just that we imagined that the legend would, well, be a little more – I don't know, somehow I thought – still, I expect it doesn't matter.'

It extended a hand like a bunch of fossil bananas.

'I'm Kwartz,' it said. 'That's Krysoprase over there, and Breccia, and Jasper, and my wife Beryl – she's a bit metamorphic, but who isn't these days? Jasper, get off his foot.'

Rincewind took the hand gingerly, bracing himself for the crunch of crushed bone. It didn't come. The troll's hand was rough and a bit lichenous around the fingernails.

'I'm sorry,' said Rincewind. 'I never really met trolls before.'

'We're a dying race,' said Kwartz sadly, as the party set off under the stars. 'Young Jasper's the only pebble in our tribe. We suffer from philosophy, you know.'

'Yes?' said Rincewind, trying to keep up. The troll band moved very quickly, but also very quietly, big round shapes moving like wraiths through the night. Only the occasional flat squeak of a night creature who hadn't heard them approaching marked their passage.

'Oh, yes. Martyrs to it. It comes to all of us in the end. One evening, they say, you start to wake up and then you think "Why bother?" and you just don't. See those boulders over there?'

Rincewind saw some huge shapes lying in the grass.

'The one on the end's my aunt. I don't know what she's thinking about, but she hasn't moved for two hundred years. '

'Gosh, I'm sorry.'

'Oh, it's no problem with us around to look after them,' said Kwartz. 'Not many humans around here, you see. I know it's not your fault, but you don't seem to be able to spot the difference between a thinking troll and an ordinary rock. My great-uncle was actually *quarried*, you know.'

'That's terrible!'

'Yes, one minute he was a troll, the next he was an ornamental fireplace.'

They paused in front of a familiar-looking cliff. The scuffed remains of a fire smouldered in the darkness.

'It looks like there's been a fight,' said Beryl.

'They're all gone!' said Rincewind. He ran to the end of the clearing. 'The horses, too! Even the Luggage!'

'One of them's leaked,' said Kwartz, kneeling down. 'That red watery stuff you have in your insides. Look.'

'Blood!'

'Is that what it's called? I've never really seen the point of it.'

Rincewind scuttled about in the manner of one totally at his wits' end, peering behind bushes in case anyone was hiding there. That was why he tripped over a small green bottle.

'Cohen's linament!' he moaned. 'He never goes anywhere without it!'

'Well,' said Kwartz, 'you humans have something you can do, I mean like when we slow right down and catch philosophy, only you just fall to bits—'

'Dying, it's called!' screamed Rincewind.

'That's it. They haven't done that, because they're not here.'

'Unless they were eaten!' suggested Jasper excitedly.

'Hmm,' said Kwartz, and, 'Wolves?' said Rincewind.

'We flattened all the wolves around here years ago,' said the troll. 'Old Grandad did, anyway.'

'He didn't like them?'

'No, he just didn't used to look where he was going. Hmm.' The trolls looked at the ground again.

'There's a trail,' he said. 'Quite a lot of horses.' He looked up at the nearby hills, where sheer cliffs and dangerous crags loomed over the moonlit forests.

'Old Grandad lives up there,' he said quietly.

There was something about the way he said it that

made Rincewind decide that he didn't ever want to meet Old Grandad.

'Dangerous, is he?' he ventured.

'He's very old and big and mean. We haven't seen him about for years,' said Kwartz.

'Centuries,' corrected Beryl.

'He'll squash them all flat!' added Jasper, jumping up and down on Rincewind's toes.

'It just happens sometimes that a really old and big troll will go off by himself into the hills, and – um – the rock takes over, if you follow me.'

'No?'

Kwartz sighed. 'People sometimes act like animals, don't they? And sometimes a troll will start thinking like a rock, and rocks don't like people much.'

Breccia, a skinny troll with a sandstone finish, rapped on Kwartz's shoulder.

'Are we going to follow them, then?' he said. 'The legend says we should help this Rincewind squashy.'

Kwartz stood up, thought for a moment, then picked Rincewind up by the scruff of his neck and with a big gritty movement placed him on his shoulders.

'We go,' he said firmly. 'If we meet Old Grandad I'll try to explain . . .'

Two miles away a string of horses trotted through the night. Three of them carried captives, expertly gagged and bound. A fourth pulled a rough *travois* on which the Luggage lay trussed and netted and silent.

Herrena softly called the column to a halt and beckoned one of her men to her.

'Are you quite sure?' she said. 'I can't hear anything.'

'I saw troll shapes,' he said flatly.

She looked around. The trees had thinned out here, there was a lot of scree, and ahead of them the track led towards a bald, rocky hill that looked especially unpleasant by red starlight.

She was worried about that track. It was extremely old, but something had made it, and trolls took a lot of killing.

She sighed. Suddenly it looked as though that secretarial career was not such a bad option, at that.

Not for the first time she reflected that there were many drawbacks to being a swordswoman, not least of which was that men didn't take you seriously until you'd actually killed them, by which time it didn't really matter anyway. Then there was all the leather, which brought her out in a rash but seemed to be unbreakably traditional. And then there was the ale. It was all right for the likes of Hrun the Barbarian or Cimbar the Assassin to carouse all night in low bars, but Herrena drew the line at it unless they sold proper drinks in small glasses, preferably with a cherry in. As for the toilet facilities . . .

But she was too big to be a thief, too honest to be an assassin, too intelligent to be a wife, and too proud to enter the only other female profession generally available.

So she'd become a swordswoman and had been a good one, amassing a modest fortune that she was carefully husbanding for a future that she hadn't quite worked out yet but which would certainly include a bidet if she had anything to say about it.

There was a distant sound of splintering timber. Trolls had never seen the point of walking around trees.

She looked up at the hill again. Two arms of high ground swept away to right and left, and up ahead was a large outcrop with – she squinted – some caves in it?

Troll caves. But maybe a better option than blundering around at night. And come sunup, there'd be no problem.

She leaned across to Gancia, leader of the gang of Morpork mercenaries. She wasn't very happy about him. It was true that he had the muscles of an ox and the stamina of an ox, the trouble was that he seemed to have the brains of an ox. And the viciousness of a ferret. Like most of the lads in downtown Morpork he'd have cheerfully sold his granny for glue, and probably had.

'We'll head for the caves and light a big fire in the entrance,' she said. 'Trolls don't like fire.'

He gave her a look which suggested he had his own ideas about who should be giving the orders, but his lips said, 'You're the boss.'

'Right.'

Herrena looked back at the three captives. That was the box all right – Trymon's description had been absolutely accurate. But neither of the men looked like a wizard. Not even a failed wizard.

* * *

'Oh, dear,' said Kwartz

The trolls halted. The night closed in like velvet. An owl hooted eerily – at least Rincewind assumed it was an owl, he was a little hazy on ornithology. Perhaps a nightingale hooted, unless it was a thrush. A bat flittered overhead. He was quite confident about that.

He was also very tired and quite bruised.

'Why oh dear?' he said.

He peered into the gloom. There was a distant speck in the hills that might have been a fire.

'Oh,' he said. 'You don't like fires, do you?'

Kwartz nodded. 'It destroys the superconductivity of our brains,' he said, 'but a fire that small wouldn't have much effect on Old Grandad.'

Rincewind looked around cautiously, listening for the sound of a rogue troll. He'd seen what normal trolls could do to a forest. They weren't naturally destructive, they just treated organic matter as a sort of inconvenient fog.

'Let's hope he doesn't find it then,' he said fervently.

Kwartz sighed. 'Not much chance of that,' he said. 'They've lit it in his mouth.'

'It'sh a judgeshment on me!' moaned Cohen. He tugged ineffectually at his bonds.

Twoflower peered at him muzzily. Gancia's slingshot had raised quite a lump on the back of his head and he was a little uncertain about things, starting with his name and working upwards.

'I should have been lisshening out,' said Cohen. 'I

should have been paying attenshion and not being shwayed by all this talk about your wosshnames, your *din-chewers.* I mussht be getting shoft.'

He levered himself up by his elbows. Herrena and the rest of the gang were standing around the fire in the cave mouth. The Luggage was still and silent under its net in a corner.

'There's something funny about this cave,' said Bethan.

'What?' said Cohen.

'Well, look at it. Have you ever seen rocks like those before?'

Cohen had to agree that the semi-circle of stones around the cave entrance was unusual; each one was higher than a man, heavily worn, and surprisingly shiny. There was a matching semi-circle on the ceiling. The whole effect was that of a stone computer built by a druid with a vague idea of geometry and no sense of gravity.

'Look at the walls, too.'

Cohen squinted at the wall next to him. There were veins of red crystal in it. He couldn't be quite certain, but it was almost as if little points of light kept flashing on and off deep within the rock itself.

It was also extremely drafty. A steady breeze blew out of the black depths of the cave.

'I'm sure it was blowing the other way when we came in,' whispered Bethan. 'What do you think, Twoflower?'

'Well, I'm not a cave expert,' he said, 'but I was just thinking, that's a very interesting stalag-thingy hanging from the ceiling up there. Sort of bulbous, isn't it?'

They looked at it.

'I can't quite put my finger on why,' said Twoflower, 'but I think it might be a rather good idea to get out of here.'

'Oh yesh,' said Cohen sarcastically, 'I shupposhe we'd jusht better ashk theesh people to untie ush and let us go, eh?'

Cohen hadn't spent much time in Twoflower's company, otherwise he would not have been surprised when the little man nodded brightly and said, in the loud, slow and careful voice he employed as an alternative to actually speaking other people's languages: 'Excuse me? Could you please untie us and let us go? It's rather damp and drafty here. Sorry.'

Bethan looked sidelong at Cohen.

'Was he supposed to say that?'

'It'sh novel, I'll grant you.'

And, indeed, three people detached themselves from the group around the fire and came towards them. They did not look as if they intended to untie anyone. The two men, in fact, looked the sort of people who, when they see other people tied up, start playing around with knives and making greasy suggestions and leering a lot.

Herrena introduced herself by drawing her sword and pointing it at Twoflower's heart.

'Which one of you is Rincewind the wizard?' she said. 'There were four horses. Is he here?'

'Um, I don't know where he is,' said Twoflower. 'He was looking for some onions.'

'Then you are his friends and he will come looking for you,' said Herrena. She glanced at Cohen and Bethan, then looked closely at the Luggage.

Trymon had been emphatic that they shouldn't touch the Luggage. Curiosity may have killed the cat, but Herrena's curiosity could have massacred a pride of lions.

She slit the netting and grasped the lid of the box.

Twoflower winced.

'Locked,' she said eventually. 'Where is the key, fat one?'

'It – it hasn't got a key,' said Twoflower.

'There is a keyhole,' she pointed out.

'Well, yes, but if it wants to stay locked, it stays locked,' said Twoflower uncomfortably.

Herrena was aware of Gancia's grin. She snarled.

'I want it open,' she said. 'Gancia, see to it.' She strode back to the fire.

Gancia drew a long thin knife and leaned down close to Twoflower's face.

'She wants it open,' he said. He looked up at the other man and grinned.

'She wants it open, Weems.'

'Yah.'

Gancia waved the knife slowly in front of Twoflower's face.

'Look,' said Twoflower patiently, 'I don't think you understand. No one can open the Luggage if it's feeling in a locked mood.'

'Oh yes, I forgot,' said Gancia thoughtfully. 'Of course, it's a magic box, isn't that right? With little legs, they say. I say, Weems, any legs your side? No?'

He held his knife to Twoflower's throat.

'I'm really upset about that,' he said. 'So's Weems. He doesn't say much but what he does is, he tears bits off people. So open – the – box!'

He turned and planted a kick on the side of the box, leaving a nasty gash in the wood.

There was a tiny little click.

Gancia grinned. The lid swung up slowly, ponderously. The distant firelight gleamed off gold – lots of gold, in plate, chain, and coin, heavy and glistening in the flickering shadows.

'All right,' said Gancia softly.

He looked back at the unheeding men around the fire, who seemed to be shouting at someone outside the cave. Then he looked speculatively at Weems. His lips moved soundlessly with the unaccustomed effort of mental arithmetic.

He looked down at his knife.

Then the floor moved.

'I heard someone,' said one of the men. 'Down there. Among the – uh – rocks.'

Rincewind's voice floated up out of the darkness.

'I say,' he said.

'Well?' said Herrena.

'You're in great danger!' shouted Rincewind. 'You must put the fire out!'

'No, no,' said Herrena. 'You've got it wrong, *you're* in great danger. And the fire stays.'

'There's this big old troll—'

'Everyone knows trolls keep away from fire,' said Herrena. She nodded. A couple of men drew their swords and slipped out into the darkness.

'Absolutely true!' shouted Rincewind desperately. 'Only this specific troll can't, you see.'

'Can't?' Herrena hesitated. Something of the terror in Rincewind's voice hit her.

'Yes, because, you see, you've lit it on his tongue.'

Then the floor moved.

Old Grandad awoke very slowly from his centuries-old slumber. He nearly didn't awake at all, in fact a few decades later none of this could have happened. When a troll gets old and starts to think seriously about the universe it normally finds a quiet spot and gets down to some hard philosophizing, and after a while starts to forget about its extremities. It begins to crystallize around the edges until nothing remains except a tiny flicker of life inside quite a large hill with some unusual rock strata.

Old Grandad hadn't quite got that far. He awoke from considering quite a promising line of enquiry about the meaning of truth and found a hot ashy taste in what, after a certain amount of thought, he remembered as being his mouth.

He began to get angry. Commands skittered along neural pathways of impure silicon. Deep within his silicaceous body stone slipped smoothly along special fracture lines. Trees toppled, turf split, as fingers the size of ships unfolded and gripped the ground. Two enormous rockslides high on his cliff face marked the opening of eyes like great crusted opals.

Rincewind couldn't see all this, of course, since his own eyes were daylight issue only, but he did see the whole dark landscape shake itself slowly and then begin to rise impossibly against the stars.

The sun rose.

However, the sunlight didn't. What did happen was that the famous Discworld sunlight which, as has already been indicated, travels very slowly through the Disc's powerful magical field, sloshed gently over the lands around the Rim and began its soft, silent battle against the retreating armies of the night. It poured like molten gold* across the sleeping landscape – bright, clean and, above all, slow.

Herrena didn't hesitate. With great presence of mind she ran to the edge of Old Grandad's bottom lip and jumped, rolling as she hit the earth. The men followed her, cursing as they landed among the debris.

* Not precisely, of course. Trees didn't burst into flame, people didn't suddenly become very rich and extremely dead, and the seas didn't flash into steam. A better simile, in fact, would be 'not like molten gold'.

Like a fat man trying to do press-ups the old troll pushed himself upwards.

This wasn't apparent from where the prisoners were lying. All they knew was that the floor kept rolling under them and that there was a lot of noise going on, most of it unpleasant.

Weems grabbed Gancia's arm.

'It's a herthquake,' he said. 'Let's get out of here!'

'Not without that gold,' said Gancia.

'What?'

'The gold, the gold. Man, we could be as rich as Creosote!'

Weems might have had a room-temperature IQ, but he knew idiocy when he saw it. Gancia's eyes gleamed more than gold, and he appeared to be staring at Weems's left ear.

Weems looked desperately at the Luggage. It was still open invitingly, which was odd – you'd have thought all this shaking would have slammed the lid shut.

'We'd never carry it,' he suggested. 'It's too heavy,' he added.

'We'll damn well carry some of it!' shouted Gancia, and leapt towards the chest as the floor shook again.

The lid snapped shut. Gancia vanished.

And just in case Weems thought it was accidental the Luggage's lid snapped open again, just for a second, and a large tongue as red as mahogany licked across broad teeth as white as sycamore. Then it slammed shut again.

To Weems's further horror hundreds of little legs

extruded from the underside of the box. It rose very deliberately and, carefully arranging its feet, shuffled around to face him. There was a particularly malevolent look about its keyhole, the sort of look that says 'Go on – make my day . . .'

He backed away and looked imploringly at Twoflower.

'I think it might be a good idea if you untied us,' suggested Twoflower. 'It's really quite friendly once it gets to know you.'

Licking his lips nervously, Weems drew his knife. The Luggage gave a warning creak.

He slashed through their bonds and stood back quickly.

'Thank you,' said Twoflower.

'I think my back'sh gone again,' complained Cohen, as Bethan helped him to his feet.

'What do we do with this man?' said Bethan.

'We take hish knife and tell him to bugger off,' said Cohen. 'Right?'

'Yes, sir! Thank you, sir!' said Weems, and bolted towards the cavemouth. For a moment he was outlined against the grey pre-dawn sky, and then he vanished. There was a distant cry of 'aaargh'.

The sunlight roared silently across the land like surf. Here and there, where the magic field was slightly weaker, tongues of morning raced ahead of the day, leaving isolated islands of night that contracted and vanished as the bright ocean flowed onwards.

The uplands around the Vortex Plains stood out ahead of the advancing tide like a great grey ship.

It is possible to stab a troll, but the technique takes practice and no one ever gets a chance to practise more than once. Herrena's men saw the trolls loom out of the darkness like very solid ghosts. Blades shattered as they hit silica skins, there were one or two brief, flat screams, and then nothing more but shouts far away in the forest as they put as much distance as they could between themselves and the avenging earth.

Rincewind crept out from behind a tree and looked around. He was alone, but the bushes behind him rustled as the trolls lumbered after the gang.

He looked up.

High above him two great crystalline eyes focused in hatred of everything soft and squelchy and, above all, warm. Rincewind cowered in horror as a hand the size of a house rose, curled into a fist, and dropped towards him.

Day came with a silent explosion of light. For a moment the huge terrifying bulk of Old Grandad was a breakwater of shadow as the daylight streamed past. There was a brief grinding noise.

There was silence.

Several minutes passed. Nothing happened.

A few birds started singing. A bumble-bee buzzed over the boulder that was Old Grandad's fist and alighted on a patch of thyme that had grown under a stone fingernail.

There was a scuffling down below. Rincewind slid awkwardly out of the narrow gap between the fist and the ground like a snake leaving a burrow.

He lay on his back, staring up at the sky past the frozen shape of the troll. It hadn't changed in any way, apart from the stillness, but already the eye started to play tricks. Last night Rincewind had looked at cracks in stone and seen them become mouths and eyes; now he looked at the great cliff face and saw the features become, like magic, mere blemishes in the rock.

'Wow!' he said.

That didn't seem to help. He stood up, dusted himself off, and looked around. Apart from the bumble-bee, he was completely alone.

After poking around for a bit he found a rock that, from certain angles, looked like Beryl.

He was lost and lonely and a long way from home. He—

There was a crunch high above him, and shards of rock spattered into the earth. High up on the face of Old Grandad a hole appeared; there was a brief sight of the Luggage's backside as it struggled to regain its footing, and then Twoflower's head poked out of the mouth cave.

'Anyone down there? I say?'

'Hey!' shouted the wizard. 'Am I glad to see you!'

'I don't know. Are you?' said Twoflower.

'Am I what?'

'Gosh, there's a wonderful view from up here!'

* * *

It took them half an hour to get down. Fortunately Old Grandad had been quite craggy with plenty of handholds, but his nose would have presented a tricky obstacle if it hadn't been for the luxuriant oak tree that flourished in one nostril.

The Luggage didn't bother to climb. It just jumped, and bounced its way down with no apparent harm.

Cohen sat in the shade, trying to catch his breath and waiting for his sanity to catch up with him. He eyed the Luggage thoughtfully.

'The horses have all gone,' said Twoflower.

'We'll find 'em,' said Cohen. His eyes bored into the Luggage, which began to look embarrassed.

'They were carrying all our food,' said Rincewind.

'Plenty of food in the foreshts.'

'I have some nourishing biscuits in the Luggage,' said Twoflower. 'Traveller's Digestives. Always a comfort in a tight spot.'

'I've tried them,' said Rincewind. 'They've got a mean edge on them, and—'

Cohen stood up, wincing.

'Excushe me,' he said flatly. 'There'sh shomething I've got to know.'

He walked over to the Luggage and gripped its lid. The box backed away hurriedly, but Cohen stuck out a skinny foot and tripped up half its legs. As it twisted to snap at him he gritted his teeth and heaved, jerking the Luggage onto its curved lid where it rocked angrily like a maddened tortoise.

'Hey, that's my Luggage!' said Twoflower. 'Why's he attacking my Luggage?'

'I think I know,' said Bethan quietly. 'I think it's because he's scared of it.'

Twoflower turned to Rincewind, open-mouthed. Rincewind shrugged.

'Search me,' he said. 'I run away from things I'm scared of, myself.'

With a snap of its lid the Luggage jerked into the air and came down running, catching Cohen a crack on the shins with one of its brass corners. As it wheeled around he got a grip on it just long enough to send it galloping full tilt into a rock.

'Not bad,' said Rincewind, admiringly.

The Luggage staggered back, paused for a moment, then came at Cohen waving its lid menacingly. He jumped and landed on it, with both his hands and feet caught in the gap between the box and the lid.

This severely puzzled the Luggage. It was even more astonished when Cohen took a deep breath and heaved, muscles standing out on his skinny arms like a sock full of coconuts.

They stood locked there for some time, tendon versus hinge. Occasionally one or other would creak.

Bethan elbowed Twoflower in the ribs.

'Do something,' she said.

'Um,' said Twoflower. 'Yes. That's about enough, I think. Put him down, please.'

The Luggage gave a creak of betrayal at the sound of its master's voice. Its lid flew up with such force that Cohen tumbled backwards, but he scrambled to his feet and flung himself towards the box.

Its contents lay open to the skies.

Cohen reached inside.

The Luggage creaked a bit, but had obviously weighed up the chances of being sent to the top of that Great Wardrobe in the Sky. When Rincewind dared to peek through his fingers Cohen was peering into the Luggage and cursing under his breath.

'Laundry?' he shouted. 'Is that it? Just laundry?' He was shaking with rage.

'I think there's some biscuits too,' said Twoflower in a small voice.

'But there wash gold! And I shaw it eat shomebody!' Cohen looked imploringly at Rincewind.

The wizard sighed. 'Don't ask me,' he said. 'I don't own the bloody thing.'

'I bought it in a shop,' said Twoflower defensively. 'I said I wanted a travelling trunk.'

'That's what you got, all right,' said Rincewind.

'It's very loyal,' said Twoflower.

'Oh yes,' agreed Rincewind. 'If loyalty is what you look for in a suitcase.'

'Hold on,' said Cohen, who had sagged onto a rock. 'Wash it one of thoshe shopsh – I mean, I bet you hadn't noticed it before and when you went back again it washn't there?'

Twoflower brightened. 'That's right!'

'Shopkeeper a little wizened old guy? Shop full of strange shtuff?'

'Exactly! Never could find it again, I thought I must have got the wrong street, nothing but a brick wall where I thought it was. I remember thinking at the time it was rather—'

Cohen shrugged. 'One of *those* shops*,' he said. 'That explainsh it, then.' He felt his back, and grimaced. 'Bloody horshe ran off with my linament!'

Rincewind remembered something, and fumbled in the depths of his torn and now very grubby robe. He held up a green bottle.

'That'sh the shtuff!' said Cohen. 'You're a marvel.' He looked sideways at Twoflower.

'I would have beaten it,' he said quietly, 'even if you hadn't called it off, I would have beaten it in the end.'

'That's right,' said Bethan.

'You two can make yourshelf usheful,' he added. 'That Luggage broke through a troll tooth to get ush out. That wash diamond. Shee if you can find the bitsh. I've had an idea about them.'

As Bethan rolled up her sleeves and uncorked the bottle Rincewind took Twoflower to one side. When they were safely hidden behind a shrub he said, 'He's gone barmy.'

'That's Cohen the Barbarian you're talking about!' said Twoflower, genuinely shocked. 'He is the greatest warrior that—'

'*Was*,' said Rincewind urgently. 'All that stuff with

* No one knows why, but all the most truly mysterious and magical items are bought from shops that appear and, after a trading life even briefer than a double-glazing company, vanish like smoke. There have been various attempts to explain this, all of which don't fully account for the observed facts. These shops turn up anywhere in the universe, and their immediate non-existence in any particular city can normally be deduced from crowds of people wandering the streets clutching defunct magical items, ornate guarantee cards, and looking very suspiciously at brick walls.

the warrior priests and man-eating zombies was years ago. All he's got now is memories and so many scars you could play noughts-and-crosses on him.'

'He is rather more elderly than I imagined, yes,' said Twoflower. He picked up a fragment of diamond.

'So we ought to leave them and find our horses and move on,' said Rincewind.

'That's a bit of a mean trick, isn't it?'

'They'll be all right,' said Rincewind heartily. 'The point is, would you feel happy in the company of someone who would attack the Luggage with his bare hands ?'

'That is a point,' said Twoflower.

'They'll probably be better off without us anyway.'

'Are you sure?'

'Positive,' said Rincewind.

They found the horses wandering aimlessly in the scrub, breakfasted on badly-dried horse jerky, and set off in what Rincewind believed was the right direction. A few minutes later the Luggage emerged from the bushes and followed them.

The sun rose higher in the sky, but still failed to blot out the light of the star.

'It's got bigger overnight,' said Twoflower. 'Why isn't anybody doing something?'

'Such as what?'

Twoflower thought. 'Couldn't somebody tell Great A'Tuin to avoid it?' he said. 'Sort of go around it?'

'That sort of thing has been tried before,' said

Rincewind. 'Wizards tried to tune in to Great A'Tuin's mind.'

'It didn't work?'

'Oh, it worked all right,' said Rincewind. 'Only . . .'

Only there had been certain unforeseen risks in reading a mind as great as the World Turtle's, he explained. The wizards had trained up on tortoises and giant sea turtles first, to get the hang of the chelonian frame of mind, but although they knew that Great A'Tuin's mind would be big they hadn't realized that it would be *slow*.

'There's a bunch of wizards that have been reading it in shifts for thirty years,' said Rincewind. 'All they've found out is that Great A'Tuin is looking forward to something.'

'What?'

'Who knows?'

They rode in silence for a while through a rough country where huge limestone blocks lined the track. Eventually Twoflower said, 'We ought to go back, you know.'

'Look, we'll reach the Smarl tomorrow,' said Rincewind. 'Nothing will happen to them out here, I don't see why—'

He was talking to himself. Twoflower had wheeled his horse and was trotting back, demonstrating all the horsemanship of a sack of potatoes.

Rincewind looked down. The Luggage regarded him owlishly.

'What are you looking at?' said the wizard. 'He can go back if he wants, why should I bother?'

The Luggage said nothing.

'Look, he's not my responsibility,' said Rincewind. 'Let's be absolutely clear about that.'

The Luggage said nothing, but louder this time.

'Go on – follow him. You're nothing to do with me.'

The Luggage retracted its little legs and settled down on the track.

'Well, I'm going,' said Rincewind. 'I mean it,' he added.

He turned the horse's head back towards the new horizon, and glanced down. The Luggage sat there.

'It's no good trying to appeal to my better nature. You can stay there all day for all I care. I'm just going to ride off, okay?'

He glared at the Luggage. The Luggage looked back.

'I thought you'd come back,' said Twoflower.

'I don't want to talk about it,' said Rincewind.

'Shall we talk about something else?'

'Yeah, well, discussing how to get these ropes off would be favourite,' said Rincewind. He wrenched at the bonds around his wrists.

'I can't imagine why you're so important,' said Herrena. She sat on a rock opposite them, sword across her knees. Most of the gang lay among the rocks high above, watching the road. Rincewind and Twoflower had been a pathetically easy ambush.

'Weems told me what your box did to Gancia,' she added. 'I can't say that's a great loss, but I hope it understands that if it comes within a mile of us I will personally cut both your throats, yes?'

Rincewind nodded violently.

'Good,' said Herrena. 'You're wanted dead or alive, I'm not really bothered which, but some of the lads might want to have a little discussion with you about those trolls. If the sun hadn't come up when it did—'

She left the words hanging, and walked away.

'Well, here's another fine mess,' said Rincewind. He had another pull at the ropes that bound him. There was a rock behind him, and if he could bring his wrists up – yes, as he thought, it lacerated him while at the same time being too blunt to have any effect on the rope.

'But why us?' said Twoflower. 'It's to do with that star, isn't it?'

'I don't know anything about the star,' said Rincewind. 'I never even attended astrology lessons at the University!'

'I expect everything will turn out all right in the end,' said Twoflower.

Rincewind looked at him. Remarks like that always threw him.

'Do you really believe that?' he said. 'I mean, really?'

'Well, things generally do work out satisfactorily, when you come to think about it.'

'If you think the total disruption of my life for the last year is satisfactory then you might be right. I've lost count of the times I've nearly been killed—'

'Twenty-seven,' said Twoflower.

'What?'

'Twenty-seven times,' said Twoflower helpfully. 'I worked it out. But you never actually *have*.'

'What? Worked it out?' said Rincewind, who was beginning to have the familiar feeling that the conversation had been mugged.

'No. Been killed. Doesn't that seem a bit suspicious?'

'I've never objected to it, if that's what you mean,' said Rincewind. He glared at his feet. Twoflower was right, of course. The Spell was keeping him alive, it was obvious. No doubt if he jumped over a cliff a passing cloud would cushion his fall.

The trouble with that theory, he decided, was that it only worked if he didn't believe it was true. The moment he thought he was invulnerable he'd be dead.

So, on the whole it was wisest not to think about it at all.

Anyway, he might be wrong.

The only thing he could be certain of was that he was getting a headache. He hoped that the Spell was somewhere in the area of the headache and really suffering.

When they rode out of the hollow both Rincewind and Twoflower were sharing a horse with one of their captors. Rincewind perched uncomfortably in front of Weems, who had sprained an ankle and was not in a good mood. Twoflower sat in front of Herrena which, since he was fairly short, meant that at least he kept his ears warm. She rode with a drawn knife and a sharp eye out for any walking boxes; Herrena hadn't quite worked out what the Luggage was, but she was bright enough to know that it wouldn't let Twoflower be killed.

After about ten minutes they saw it in the middle of the road. Its lid lay open invitingly. It was full of gold.

'Go round it,' said Herrena.

'But—'

'It's a trap.'

'That's right,' said Weems, white-faced. 'You take it from me.'

Reluctantly they reined their horses around the glittering temptation and trotted on along the track. Weems glanced back fearfully, dreading to see the chest coming after him.

What he saw was almost worse. It had gone.

Far off to one side of the path the long grass moved mysteriously and was still.

Rincewind wasn't much of a wizard and even less of a fighter, but he was an expert at cowardice and he knew fear when he smelt it. He said, quietly, 'It'll follow you, you know.'

'What?' said Weems, distractedly. He was still peering at the grass.

'It's very patient and it never gives up. That's sapient pearwood you're dealing with. It'll let you think it's forgotten you, then one day you'll be walking along a dark street and you'll hear these little footsteps behind you – shlup, shlup, they'll go, then you'll start running and they'll speed up, shlupshlupSHLUP—'

'Shut up!' shouted Weems.

'It's probably already recognized you, so—'

'I said shut up!'

Herrena turned around in her saddle and glared at them. Weems scowled and pulled Rincewind's ear until it was right in front of his mouth, and said hoarsely, 'I'm afraid of nothing, understand? This wizard stuff, I spit on it.'

'They all say that until they hear the footsteps,' said Rincewind. He stopped. A knifepoint was pricking his ribs.

Nothing happened for the rest of the day but, to Rincewind's satisfaction and Weems's mounting paranoia, the Luggage showed itself several times. Here it would be perched incongruously on a crag, there it would be half-hidden in a ditch with moss growing over it.

By late afternoon they came to the crest of a hill and looked down on the broad valley of the upper Smarl, the longest river on the Disc. It was already half a mile across, and heavy with the silt that made the lower valley the most fertile area on the continent. A few wisps of early mist wreathed its banks.

'Shlup,' said Rincewind. He felt Weems jerk upright in the saddle.

'Eh?'

'Just clearing my throat,' said Rincewind, and grinned. He had put a lot of thought into that grin. It was the sort of grin people use when they stare at your left ear and tell you in an urgent tone of voice that they are being spied on by secret agents from the next galaxy. It was not a grin to inspire confidence. More horrible grins had probably been seen, but only on the sort of grinner that is orange with black stripes, has a long tail and hangs around in jungles looking for victims to grin at.

'Wipe that off,' said Herrena, trotting up.

Where the track led down to the river bank there was a crude jetty and a big bronze gong.

'It'll summon the ferryman,' said Herrena. 'If we cross here we can cut off a big bend in the river. Might even make it to a town tonight.'

Weeems looked doubtful. The sun was getting fat and red, and the mists were beginning to thicken.

'Or maybe you want to spend the night this side of the water?'

Weems picked up the hammer and hit the gong so hard that it spun right around on its hanger and fell off.

They waited in silence. Then with a wet clinking sound a chain sprang out of the water and pulled taut against an iron peg set into the bank. Eventually the slow flat shape of the ferry emerged from the mist, its hooded ferryman heaving on a big wheel set in its centre as he winched his way towards the shore

The ferry's flat bottom grated on the gravel, and the hooded figure leaned against the wheel, panting.

'Two at a time,' it muttered. 'That'sh all. Jusht two, with horshesh.'

Rincewind swallowed, and tried not to look at Twoflower. The man would probably be grinning and mugging like an idiot. He risked a sideways glance.

Twoflower was sitting with his mouth open.

'You're not the usual ferryman,' said Herrena. 'I've been here before, the usual man is a big fellow, sort of—'

'It'sh hish day off.

'Well, okay,' she said doubtfully. 'In that case – *what's he laughing at*?'

Twoflower's shoulders were shaking, his face had gone red, and he was emitting muffled snorts. Herrena glared at him, then looked hard at the ferryman.

'Two of you – grab him!'

There was a pause. Then one of the men said, 'What, the ferryman?'

'Yes!'

'Why?'

Herrena looked blank. This sort of thing wasn't supposed to happen. It was accepted that when someone yelled something like 'Get him!' or 'Guards!' people jumped to it, they weren't supposed to sit around discussing things.

'Because I said so!' was the best she could manage. The two men nearest to the bowed figure looked at each other, shrugged, dismounted, and each took a shoulder. The ferryman was about half their size.

'Like this?' said one of them. Twoflower was choking for breath.

'Now I want to see what he's got under that robe.'

The two men exchanged glances.

'I'm not sure that—' said one.

He got no further because a knobbly elbow jerked into his stomach like a piston. His companion looked down incredulously and got the other elbow in the kidneys.

Cohen cursed as he struggled to untangle his sword from his robe while hopping crabwise towards Herrena. Rincewind groaned, gritted his teeth, and jerked his head backwards hard. There was a scream from Weems and Rincewind rolled sideways, landed heavily in the mud, scrambled up madly and looked around for somewhere to hide.

With a cry of triumph Cohen managed to free his sword and waved it triumphantly, severely wounding a man who had been creeping up behind him.

Herrena pushed Twoflower off her horse and fumbled for her own blade. Twoflower tried to stand up and caused the horse of another man to rear, throwing him off and bringing his head down to the right level for Rincewind to kick it as hard as possible. Rincewind would be the first to call himself a rat, but even rats fight in a corner.

Weems's hands dropped onto his shoulder and a fist like a medium-sized rock slammed into his head.

As he went down he heard Herrena say, quite quietly, 'Kill them both. I'll deal with this old fool.'

'Roight!' said Weems, and turned towards Twoflower with his sword drawn.

Rincewind saw him hesitate. There was a moment of silence, and then even Herrena could hear the splashing as the Luggage surged ashore, water pouring from it.

Weems stared at it in horror. His sword fell from his hand. He turned and ran into the mists. A moment later the Luggage bounded over Rincewind and followed him.

Herrena lunged at Cohen, who parried the thrust and grunted as his arm twinged. The blades clanged wetly, and then Herrena was forced to back away as a cunning upward sweep from Cohen nearly disarmed her.

Rincewind staggered towards Twoflower and tugged at him ineffectually.

'Time to be going,' he muttered.

'This is great!' said Twoflower. 'Did you see the way he—'

'Yes, yes, come on.'

'But I want – I say, well done!'

Herrena's sword spun out of her hand and stood quivering in the dirt. With a snort of satisfaction Cohen brought his own sword back, went momentarily crosseyed, gave a little yelp of pain, and stood absolutely motionless.

Herrena looked at him, puzzled. She made an experimental move in the direction of her own sword and when nothing happened she grasped it, tested its balance, and stared at Cohen. Only his agonized eyes moved to follow her as she circled him cautiously.

'His back's gone again!' whispered Twoflower. 'What can we do?'

'We can see if we can catch the horses?'

'Well,' said Herrena, 'I don't know who you are or why you're here, and there's nothing personal about this, you understand.'

She raised her sword in both hands.

There was a sudden movement in the mists and the dull thud of a heavy piece of wood hitting a head. Herrena looked bewildered for a moment, and then fell forward.

Bethan dropped the branch she had been holding and looked at Cohen. Then she grabbed him by the shoulders, stuck her knee in the small of his back, gave a businesslike twist and let him go.

An expression of bliss passed across his face. He gave an experimental bend.

'It's gone!' he said. 'The back! Gone!'

Twoflower turned to Rincewind.

'My father used to recommend hanging from the top of a door,' he said conversationally.

Weems crept very cautiously through the scrubby, mist-laden trees. The pale damp air muffled all sounds, but he was certain that there had been nothing to hear for the past ten minutes. He turned around very slowly, and then allowed himself the luxury of a long, heartfelt sigh. He stepped back into the cover of the bushes.

Something nudged the back of his knees, very gently. Something angular.

He looked down. There seemed to be more feet down there than there ought to be.

There was a short, sharp snap.

The fire was a tiny dot of light in a dark landscape. The

moon wasn't up yet, but the star was a lurking glow on the horizon.

'It's circular now,' said Bethan. 'It looks like a tiny sun. I'm sure it's getting hotter, too.'

'Don't,' said Rincewind. 'As if I hadn't got enough to worry about.'

'What I don't undershtand,' said Cohen, who was having his back massaged, 'ish how they captured you without ush hearing it. We wouldn't have known at all if your Luggage hadn't kept jumping up and down.'

'And whining,' said Bethan. They all looked at her.

'Well, it *looked* as if it was whining,' she said. 'I think it's rather sweet, really.'

Four pairs of eyes turned towards the Luggage, which was squatting on the other side of the fire. It got up, and very pointedly moved back into the shadows.

'Eashy to feed,' said Cohen.

'Hard to lose' agreed Rincewind.

'Loyal,' suggested Twoflower.

'Roomy,' said Cohen.

'But I wouldn't say sweet,' said Rincewind.

'I shuppose you wouldn't want to shell it?' said Cohen.

Twoflower shook his head. 'I don't think it would understand,' he said.

'No, I shupposhe not,' said Cohen. He sat up, and bit his lip. 'I wash looking for a preshent for Bethan, you shee. We're getting married.'

'We thought you ought to be the first to know,' said Bethan, and blushed.

Rincewind didn't catch Twoflower's eye.

'Well, that's very, er—'

'Just as soon as we find a town where there's a priest,' said Bethan. 'I want it done properly.'

'That's very important,' said Twoflower seriously. 'If there were more morals about we wouldn't be crashing into stars.'

They considered this for a moment. Then Twoflower said brightly, 'This calls for a celebration. I've got some biscuits and water, if you've still got some of that jerky.'

'Oh, good,' said Rincewind weakly. He beckoned Cohen to one side. With his beard trimmed the old man could easily have passed for seventy on a dark night.

'This is, uh, serious?' he said. 'You're really going to marry her?'

'Shure thing. Any objections?'

'Well, no, of course not, but – I mean, she's seventeen and you're, you're how can I put it, you're of the elderly persuasion.'

'Time I shettled down, you mean?'

Rincewind groped for words. 'You're seventy years older than her, Cohen. Are you sure that—'

'I have been married before, you know. I've got quite a good memory,' said Cohen reproachfully.

'No, what I mean is, well, I mean physically, the point is, what about, you know, the age difference and everything. It's a matter of health, isn't it, and—'

'Ah,' said Cohen slowly, 'I shee what you mean. The strain. I hadn't looked at it like that.'

'No,' said Rincewind, straightening up. 'No, well, that's only to be expected.'

'You've given me something to think about and no mishtake,' said Cohen.

'I hope I haven't upset anything.'

'No, no,' said Cohen vaguely. 'Don't apologishe. You were right to point it out.'

He turned and looked at Bethan, who waved at him, and then he looked up at the star that glared through the mists.

Eventually he said, 'Dangerous times, these.'

'That's a fact.'

'Who knows what tomorrow may bring?'

'Not me.'

Cohen clapped Rincewind on the shoulder. 'Shometimesh we jusht have to take rishks,' he said. 'Don't be offended, but I think we'll go ahead with the wedding anyway and, well,' he looked at Bethan and sighed, 'we'll just have to hope she's shtrong enough.'

Around noon the following day they rode into a small, mud-walled city surrounded by fields still lush and green. There seemed to be a lot of traffic going the other way, though. Huge carts rumbled past them. Herds of livestock ambled along the crown of the road. Old ladies stomped past carrying entire households and haystacks on their backs.

'Plague?' said Rincewind, stopping a man pushing a handcart full of children.

He shook his head. 'It's the star, friend,' he said. 'Haven't you seen it in the sky?'

'We couldn't help noticing it, yes.'

'They say that it'll hit us on Hogswatchnight and the seas will boil and the countries of the Disc will be broken and kings will be brought down and the cities will be as lakes of glass,' said the man. 'I'm off to the mountains.'

'That'll help, will it?' said Rincewind doubtfully.

'No, but the view will be better.'

Rincewind rode back to the others.

'Everyone's worried about the star,' he said. 'Apparently there's hardly anyone left in the cities, they're all frightened of it.'

'I don't want to worry anyone,' said Bethan, 'but hasn't it struck you as unseasonably hot?'

'That's what I said last night,' said Twoflower. 'Very warm, I thought.'

'I shuspect it'll get a lot hotter,' said Cohen. 'Let'sh get on into the city.'

They rode through echoing streets that were practically deserted. Cohen kept peering at merchants' signs until he reined his horse and said, 'Thish ish what I've been looking for. You find a temple and a priesht, I'll join you shortly.'

'A jeweller?' said Rincewind.

'It's a shuprishe.'

'I could do with a new dress, too,' said Bethan.

'I'll shteal you one.'

There was something very oppressive about the city, Rincewind decided. There was also something very odd.

Almost every door was painted with a large red star.

'It's creepy,' said Bethan. 'As if people wanted to bring the star here.'

'Or keep it away,' said Twoflower.

'That won't work. It's too big,' said Rincewind. He saw their faces turned towards him.

'Well, it stands to reason, doesn't it?' he said lamely.

'No,' said Bethan.

'Stars are small lights in the sky,' said Twoflower. 'One fell down near my home once – big white thing, size of a house, glowed for weeks before it went out.'

'This star is different,' said a voice. 'Great A'Tuin has climbed the beach of the universe. This is the great ocean of space.'

'How do you know?' said Twoflower.

'Know what?' said Rincewind.

'What you just said. About beaches and oceans.'

'I didn't say anything!'

'Yes you did, you silly man!' yelled Bethan. 'We saw your lips going up and down and everything!'

Rincewind shut his eyes. Inside his mind he could feel the Spell scuttling off to hide behind his conscience, and muttering to itself.

'All right, all right,' he said. 'No need to shout. I – I don't know how I know, I just *know*—'

'Well, I wish you'd tell us.'

They turned the corner.

All the cities around the Circle Sea had a special area set aside for the gods, of which the Disc had an elegant sufficiency. Usually they were crowded and not very attractive from an architectural point of view. The most senior gods, of course, had large and splendid temples, but the trouble was that later gods demanded equality and soon the holy areas were sprawling with lean-to's, annexes, loft conversions, sub-basements, bijou flatlets, ecclesiastical infilling and trans-temporal timesharing, since no god would dream of living outside the holy quarter or, as it had become, three-eighths. There were usually three hundred different types of incense being burned and the noise was normally at pain threshold because of all the priests vying with each other to call their share of the faithful to prayer.

But this street was deathly quiet, that particularly unpleasant quiet that comes when hundreds of frightened and angry people are standing very still.

A man at the edge of the crowd turned around and scowled at the newcomers. He had a red star painted on his forehead.

'What's—' Rincewind began, and stopped as his voice seemed far too loud, 'what's this?'

'You're strangers?' said the man.

'Actually we know one another quite—' Twoflower began, and fell silent. Bethan pointed up the street.

Every temple had a star painted on it. There was a particularly big one daubed across the stone eye outside the temple of Blind Io, leader of the gods.

'Urgh,' said Rincewind. 'Io is going to be really pissed when he sees that. I don't think we ought to hang around here, friends.'

The crowd was facing a crude platform that had

been built in the centre of the wide street. A big banner had been draped across the front of it.

'I always heard that Blind Io can see everything that happens everywhere,' said Bethan quietly. 'Why hasn't—'

'Quiet!' said the man beside them. 'Dahoney speaks!'

A figure had stepped up on the platform, a tall thin man with hair like a dandelion. There was no cheer from the crowd, just a collective sigh. He began to speak.

Rincewind listened in mounting horror. Where were the gods? said the man. They had gone. Perhaps they had never been. Who, actually, could remember seeing them? And now the star had been sent—

It went on and on, a quiet, clear voice that used words like 'cleanse' and 'scouring' and 'purify' and drilled into the brain like a hot sword. Where were the wizards? Where was magic? Had it ever really worked, or had it all been a dream?

Rincewind began to be really afraid that the gods might get to hear about this and be so angry that they'd take it out on anyone who happened to have been around at the time.

But somehow even the wrath of the gods would have been better than the sound of that voice. The star was coming, it seemed to say, and its fearful fire could only be averted by – by – Rincewind couldn't be certain, but he had visions of swords and banners and blank-eyed warriors. The voice didn't believe in gods, which in Rincewind's book was fair enough, but it didn't believe in people either.

A tall hooded stranger on Rincewind's left jostled him. He turned – and looked up into a grinning skull under a black hood.

Wizards, like cats, can see Death.

Compared to the sound of that voice, Death seemed almost pleasant. He leaned against a wall, his scythe propped up beside him. He nodded at Rincewind.

'Come to gloat?' whispered Rincewind. Death shrugged.

I HAVE COME TO SEE THE FUTURE, he said.

'This is the future?'

A FUTURE, said Death.

'It's horrible,' said Rincewind.

I'M INCLINED TO AGREE, said Death.

'I would have thought you'd be all for it!'

NOT LIKE THIS. THE DEATH OF THE WARRIOR OR THE OLD MAN OR THE LITTLE CHILD, THIS I UNDERSTAND, AND I TAKE AWAY THE PAIN AND END THE SUFFERING. I DO NOT UNDERSTAND THIS DEATH-OF-THE-MIND.

'Who are you talking to?' said Twoflower. Several members of the congregation had turned around and were looking suspiciously at Rincewind.

'Nobody,' said Rincewind. 'Can we go away? I've got a headache.'

Now a group of people at the edge of the crowd were muttering and pointing to them. Rincewind grabbed the other two and hurried them around the corner.

'Mount up and let's go,' he said. 'I've got a bad feeling that—'

A hand landed on his shoulder. He turned around.

A pair of cloudy grey eyes set in a round bald head on top of a large muscular body were staring hard at his left ear. The man had a star painted on his forehead.

'You look like a wizard,' he said, in a tone of voice that suggested this was very unwise and quite possibly fatal.

'Who, me? No, I'm – a clerk. Yes. A clerk. That's right,' said Rincewind.

He gave a little laugh.

The man paused, his lips moving soundlessly, as though he was listening to a voice in his head. Several other star people had joined him. Rincewind's left ear began to be widely regarded.

'I think you're a wizard,' said the man.

'Look,' said Rincewind, 'if I was a wizard I'd be able to do magic, right? I'd just turn you into something, and I haven't, so I'm not.'

'We killed all our wizards,' said one of the men. 'Some ran away, but we killed quite a lot. They waved their hands and nothing came out.'

Rincewind stared at him.

'And we think you're a wizard too,' said the man holding Rincewind in an ever-tightening grip. 'You've got the box on legs and you look like a wizard.'

Rincewind became aware that the three of them and the Luggage had somehow become separated from their horses, and that they were now in a contracting circle of grey-faced, solemn people.

Bethan had gone pale. Even Twoflower, whose ability to recognize danger was as good as Rincewind's ability to fly, was looking worried.

Rincewind took a deep breath.

He raised his hands in the classic pose he'd learned years before, and rasped, 'Stand back! Or I'll fill you full of magic!'

'The magic has faded,' said the man. 'The star has taken it away. All the false wizards said their funny words and then nothing happened and they looked at their hands in horror and very few of them, in fact, had the sense to run away.'

'I mean it!' said Rincewind.

He's going to kill me, he thought. That's it. I can't even bluff any more. No good at magic, no good at bluffing, I'm just a—

The Spell stirred in his mind. He felt it trickle into his brain like iced water and brace itself. A cold tingle coursed down his arm.

His arm raised of its own volition, and he felt his own mouth opening and shutting and his own tongue moving as a voice that wasn't his, a voice that sounded old and dry, said syllables that puffed into the air like steam clouds.

Octarine fire flashed from under his fingernails. It wrapped itself around the horrified man until he was lost in a cold, spitting cloud that rose above the street, hung there for a long moment, and then exploded into nothingness.

There wasn't even a wisp of greasy smoke.

Rincewind stared at his hand in horror.

Twoflower and Bethan each grabbed him by an arm and hustled him through the shocked crowd until they reached the open street. There was a painful moment as they each chose to run down a different alley, but they hurried on with Rincewind's feet barely touching the cobbles.

'Magic,' he mumbled excitedly, drunk with power. 'I did magic . . .'

'That's right,' said Twoflower soothingly.

'Would you like me to do a spell?' said Rincewind. He pointed a finger at a passing dog and said 'Wheeee!' It gave him a hurt look.

'Making your feet run a lot faster'd be favourite,' said Bethan grimly.

'Sure!' slurred Rincewind. 'Feet! Run faster! Hey, look, they're doing it!'

'They've got more sense than you,' said Bethan. 'Which way now?'

Twoflower peered at the maze of alleyways around them. There was a lot of shouting going on, some way off.

Rincewind lurched out of their grasp, and tottered uncertainly down the nearest alley.

'I can do it!' he shouted wildly. 'Just you all watch out—'

'He's in shock,' said Twoflower.

'Why?'

'He's never done a spell before.'

'But he's a wizard!'

'It's all a bit complicated,' said Twoflower, running after Rincewind. 'Anyway, I'm not sure that was actually him. It certainly didn't sound like him. Come along, old fellow.'

Rincewind looked at him with wild, unseeing eyes.

'I'll turn *you* into a rosebush,' he said.

'Yes, yes, jolly good. Just come along,' said Twoflower soothingly, pulling gently at his arm.

There was a pattering of feet from several alleyways and suddenly a dozen star people were advancing on them.

Bethan grabbed Rincewind's limp hand and held it up threateningly.

'That's far enough!' she screamed.

'Right!' shouted Twoflower. 'We've got a wizard and we're not afraid to use him!'

'I mean it!' screamed Bethan, spinning Rincewind around by his arm, like a capstan.

'Right! We're heavily armed! What?' said Twoflower.

'I said, where's the Luggage?' hissed Bethan behind Rincewind's back.

Twoflower looked around. The Luggage was missing.

Rincewind was having the desired effect on the star people, though. As his hand waved vaguely around they treated it like a rotary scythe and tried to hide behind one another.

'Well, where's it gone?'

'How should I know?' said Twoflower.

'It's *your* Luggage!'

'I often don't know where my Luggage is, that's what being a tourist is all about,' said Twoflower. 'Anyway, it often wanders off by itself. It's probably best not to ask why.'

It began to dawn on the mob that nothing was actually happening, and that Rincewind was in no condition to hurl insults, let alone magical fire. They advanced, watching his hands cautiously.

Twoflower and Bethan backed away. Twoflower looked around.

'Bethan?'

'What?' said Bethan, not taking her eyes off the advancing figures.

'This is a dead end.'

'Are you sure?'

'I think I know a brick wall when I see one,' said Twoflower reproachfully.

'That's about it, then,' said Bethan.

'Do you think perhaps if I explain—?'

'No.'

'Oh.'

'I don't think these are the sort of people who listen to explanations,' Bethan added.

Twoflower stared at them. He was, as has been mentioned, usually oblivious to personal danger. Against the whole of human experience Twoflower believed that if only people would talk to each other, have a few drinks, exchange pictures of their grand-children, maybe take in a show or something, then everything could be sorted out. He also believed that people were basically good but sometimes had their bad days. What was coming down the street was having about the same effect on him as a gorilla in a glass factory.

There was the faintest of sounds behind him, not so much a sound in fact as a change in the texture of the air.

The faces in front of him gaped open, turned, and disappeared rapidly down the alley.

'Eh?' said Bethan, still propping up the now unconscious Rincewind.

Twoflower was looking the other way, at a big glass window full of strange wares, and a beaded doorway, and a large sign above it all which now said, after its characters had finished writhing into position:

'Skillet, Wang, Yrxle!yt, Bunglestiff,
Cwmlad and Patel'
'Estblshd: various'
PURVEYORS

The jeweller turned the gold slowly over the tiny anvil, tapping the last strangely-cut diamond into place.

'From a troll's tooth, you say?' he muttered, squinting closely at his work.

'Yesh,' said Cohen, 'and as I shay, you can have all the resht.' He was fingering a tray of gold rings.

'Very generous,' murmured the jeweller, who was dwarvish and knew a good deal when he saw one. He sighed.

'Not much work lately?' said Cohen. He looked out through the tiny window and watched a group of empty-eyed people gathered on the other side of the narrow street.

'Times are hard, yes.'

'Who are all theshe guysh with the starsh painted on?' said Cohen.

The dwarf jeweller didn't look up.

'Madmen,' he said. 'They say I should do no work because the star comes. I tell them stars have never hurt me, I wish I could say the same about people.'

Cohen nodded thoughtfully as six men detached themselves from the group and came towards the shop. They were carrying an assortment of weapons, and had a driven, determined look about them.

'Strange,' said Cohen.

'I am, as you can see, of the dwarvish persuasion,' said the jeweller. 'One of the magical races, it is said. The star people believe that the star will not destroy the Disc if we turn aside from magic. They're probably going to beat me up a bit. So it goes.'

He held up his latest work in a pair of tweezers.

'The strangest thing I have ever made,' he said, 'but practical, I can see that. What did you say they were called again?'

'Din-chewersh,' said Cohen. He looked at the horseshoe shapes nestling in the wrinkled palm of his hand, then opened his mouth and made a series of painful grunting noises.

The door burst open. The men strode in and took up positions around the walls. They were sweating and uncertain, but their leader pushed Cohen aside disdainfully and picked up the dwarf by his shirt.

'We tole you yesterday, small stuff,' he said. 'You go out feet down or feet up, we don't mind. So now we gonna get really—'

Cohen tapped him on the shoulder. The man looked around irritably.

'What do you want, grandad?' he snarled.

Cohen paused until he had the man's full attention, and then he smiled. It was a slow, lazy smile, unveiling about 300 carats of mouth jewellery that seemed to light up the room.

'I will count to three,' he said, in a friendly tone of voice. 'One. Two.' His bony knee came up and buried itself in the man's groin with a satisfyingly meaty noise, and he half-turned to bring the full force of an elbow into the kidneys as the leader collapsed around his private universe of pain.

'Three,' he told the ball of agony on the floor. Cohen had heard of fighting fair, and had long ago decided he wanted no part of it.

He looked up at the other men, and flashed his incredible smile.

They ought to have rushed him. Instead one of them, secure in the knowledge that he had a broad-sword and Cohen didn't, sidled crabwise towards him.

'Oh, no,' said Cohen, waving his hands. 'Oh, come on, lad, not like that.'

The man looked sideways at him.

'Not like what?' he asked suspiciously.

'You never held a sword before?'

The man half-turned to his colleagues for reassurance.

'Not a lot, no,' he said. 'Not often.' He waved his sword menacingly.

Cohen shrugged. 'I may be going to die, but I should hope I could be killed by a man who could hold his sword like a warrior,' he said.

The man looked at his hands. 'Looks all right,' he said, doubtfully.

'Look, lad, I know a little about these things. I mean, come here a minute and – do you mind? – right, your left hand goes *here*, around the pommel, and your right hand goes – that's right, just *here* – and the blade goes right into your leg.'

As the man screamed and clutched at his foot Cohen kicked his remaining leg away and turned to the room at large.

'This is getting fiddly,' he said. 'Why don't you rush me?'

'That's right,' said a voice by his waist. The jeweller had produced a very large and dirty axe, guaranteed to add tetanus to all the other terrors of warfare.

The four men gave these odds some consideration, and backed towards the door.

'And wipe those silly stars off,' said Cohen. 'You can tell everyone that Cohen the Barbarian will be very angry if he sees stars like that again, right?'

The door slammed shut. A moment later the axe thumped into it, bounced off, and took a sliver of leather off the toe of Cohen's sandal.

'Sorry,' said the dwarf. 'It belonged to my grandad. I only use it for splitting firewood.'

Cohen felt his jaw experimentally. The dine chewers seemed to be settling in quite well.

'If I was you, I'd be getting out of here anyway,' he said. But the dwarf was already scuttling around the room, tipping trays of precious metal and gems into a leather sack. A roll of tools went into one pocket, a packet of finished jewellery went into another, and with a grunt the dwarf stuck his arms through handles on either side of his little forge and heaved it bodily onto his back.

'Right,' he said. 'I'm ready.'

'You're coming with me?'

'As far as the city gates, if you don't mind,' he said. 'You can't blame me, can you?'

'No. But leave the axe behind.'

They stepped out into the afternoon sun and a deserted street. When Cohen opened his mouth little pinpoints of bright light illuminated all the shadows.

'I've got some friends around here to pick up,' he said, and added, 'I hope they're all right. What's your name?'

'Lackjaw.'

'Is there anywhere around here where I can—' Cohen paused lovingly, savouring the words, 'where I can get a steak?'

'The star people have closed all the inns. They said it's wrong to be eating and drinking when—'

'I know, I know,' said Cohen. 'I think I'm beginning to get the hang of it. Don't they approve of anything?'

Lackjaw was lost in thought for a moment. 'Setting fire to things,' he said at last. 'They're quite good at that. Books and stuff. They have these great big bonfires.'

Cohen was shocked.

'Bonfires of books?'

'Yes. Horrible, isn't it?'

'Right,' said Cohen. He thought it was appalling.

Someone who spent his life living rough under the sky knew the value of a good thick book, which ought to outlast at least a season of cooking fires if you were careful how you tore the pages out. Many a life had been saved on a snowy night by a handful of sodden kindling and a really dry book. If you felt like a smoke and couldn't find a pipe, a book was your man every time.

Cohen realized people wrote things in books. It had always seemed to him to be a frivolous waste of paper.

'I'm afraid if your friends met them they might be in trouble,' said Lackjaw sadly as they walked up the street.

They turned the corner and saw the bonfire. It was in the middle of the street. A couple of star people were feeding it with books from a nearby house, which had had its door smashed in and had been daubed with stars.

News of Cohen hadn't spread too far yet. The book burners took no notice as he wandered up and leaned against the wall. Curly flakes of burnt paper bounced in the hot air and floated away over the rooftops.

'What are you doing?' he said.

One of the star people, a woman, pushed her hair out of her eyes with a soot-blackened hand, gazed intently at Cohen's left ear, and said, 'Ridding the Disc of wickedness.'

Two men came out of the building and glared at Cohen, or at least at his ear.

Cohen reached out and took the heavy book the woman was carrying. Its cover was crusted with strange red and black stones that spelled out what Cohen was sure was a word. He showed it to Lackjaw.

'The Necrotelecomnicon,' said the dwarf. 'Wizards use it. It's how to contact the dead, I think.'

'That's wizards for you,' said Cohen. He felt a page between finger and thumb; it was thin, and quite soft. The rather unpleasant organic-looking writing didn't worry him at all. Yes, a book like this could be a real friend to a man—

'Yes? You want something?' he said to one of the star men, who had gripped his arm.

'All books of magic must be burned,' said the man, but a little uncertainly, because something about Cohen's teeth was giving him a nasty feeling of sanity.

'Why?' said Cohen.

'It has been revealed to us.' Now Cohen's smile was as wide as all outdoors, and rather more dangerous.

'I think we ought to be getting along,' said Lackjaw nervously. A party of star people had turned into the street behind them.

'*I* think I would like to kill someone,' said Cohen, still smiling.

'The star directs that the Disc must be cleansed,' said the man, backing away.

'Stars can't talk,' said Cohen, drawing his sword.

'If you kill me a thousand will take my place,' said the man, who was now backed against the wall.

'Yes,' said Cohen, in a reasonable tone of voice, 'but that isn't the point, is it? The point is, *you'll* be dead.'

The man's Adam's apple began to bob like a yoyo. He squinted down at Cohen's sword.

'There is that, yes,' he conceded. 'Tell you what – how about if we put the fire out?'

'Good idea,' said Cohen.

Lackjaw tugged at his belt. The other star people were running towards them. There were a lot of them, many of them were armed, and it began to look as though things would become a little more serious,

Cohen waved his sword at them defiantly, and turned and ran. Even Lackjaw had difficulty in keeping up.

'Funny,' he gasped, as they plunged down another alley, 'I thought – for a minute – you'd want to stand – and fight them.'

'Blow that – for a – lark.'

As they came out into the light at the other end of the alley Cohen flung himself against the wall, drew his sword, stood with his head on one side as he judged the approaching footsteps, and then brought the blade around in a dead flat sweep at stomach height. There was an unpleasant noise and several screams, but by then Cohen was well away up the street, moving in the unusual shambling run that spared his bunions.

With Lackjaw pounding along grimly beside him he turned off into an inn painted with red stars, jumped onto a table with only a faint whimper of pain, ran along it – while, with almost perfect choreography, Lackjaw ran straight underneath without ducking – jumped down at the other end, kicked his way through the kitchens, and came out into another alley.

They scurried around a few more turnings and piled into a doorway. Cohen clung to the wall and wheezed until the little blue and purple lights went away.

'Well,' he panted, 'what did you get?'

'Um, the cruet,' said Lackjaw.

'Just that?'

'Well, I had to go *under* the table, didn't I? You didn't do so well yourself.'

Cohen looked disdainfully at the small melon he had managed to skewer in his flight.

'This must be pretty tough here,' he said, biting through the rind.

'Want some salt on it?' said the dwarf.

Cohen said nothing. He just stood holding the melon, with his mouth open.

Lackjaw looked around. The cul de sac they were in was empty, except for an old box someone had left against a wall.

Cohen was staring at it. He handed the melon to the dwarf without looking at him and walked out into the sunlight. Lackjaw watched him creep stealthily around the box, or as stealthily as is possible with joints that creaked like a ship under full sail, and prod it once or twice with his sword, but very gingerly, as if he half-expected it to explode.

'It's just a box,' the dwarf called out. 'What's so special about a box?'

Cohen said nothing. He squatted down painfully and peered closely at the lock on the lid.

'What's in it?' said Lackjaw.

'You wouldn't want to know,' said Cohen. 'Help me up, will you?'

'Yes, but this box—'

'This box,' said Cohen, 'this box is—' he waved his arms vaguely.

'Oblong?'

'*Eldritch*,' said Cohen mysteriously.

'Eldritch?'

'Yup.'

'Oh,' said the dwarf. They stood looking at the box for a moment.

'Cohen?'

'Yes?'

'What does eldritch mean?'

'Well, eldritch is—' Cohen paused and looked down irritably. 'Give it a kick and you'll see.'

Lackjaw's steel-capped dwarfboot whammed into the side of the box. Cohen flinched. Nothing else happened.

'I see,' said the dwarf. 'Eldritch means wooden?'

'No,' said Cohen. 'It – it oughtn't to have done that.'

'I see,' said Lackjaw, who didn't, and was beginning to wish Cohen hadn't gone out into all this hot sunlight. 'It ought to have run away, you think?'

'Yes. Or bitten your leg off.'

'Ah,' said the dwarf. He took Cohen gently by the arm. 'It's nice and shady over here,' he said. 'Why don't you just have a little—'

Cohen shook him off.

'It's watching that wall,' he said. 'Look, that's why it's not taking any notice of us. It's staring at the wall.'

'Yes, that's right,' said Lackjaw soothingly. 'Of course it's watching that wall with its little eyes—'

'Don't be an idiot, it hasn't got any eyes,' snapped Cohen.

'Sorry, sorry,' said Lackjaw hurriedly. 'It's watching the wall without eyes, sorry.'

'I think it's worried about something,' said Cohen.

'Well, it would be, wouldn't it,' said Lackjaw. 'I expect it just wants us to go off somewhere and leave it alone.'

'I think it's very puzzled,' Cohen added.

'Yes, it certainly looks puzzled,' said the dwarf. Cohen glared at him.

'How can *you* tell?' he snapped.

It struck Lackjaw that the roles were unfairly reversing. He looked from Cohen to the box, his mouth opening and shutting.

'How can *you* tell?' he said. But Cohen wasn't listening anyway. He sat down in front of the box, assuming that the bit with the keyhole was the front, and watched it intently. Lackjaw backed away. Funny, said his mind, but the damn thing *is* looking at me.

'All right,' said Cohen, 'I know you and me don't see eye to eye, but we're all trying to find someone we care for, okay?'

'I'm—' said Lackjaw, and realized that Cohen was talking to the box.

'So tell me where they've gone.'

As Lackjaw looked on in horror the Luggage extended its little legs, braced itself, and ran full tilt at the nearest wall. Clay bricks and dusty mortar exploded around it.

Cohen peered through the hole. There was a small grubby storeroom on the other side. The Luggage stood in the middle of the floor, radiating extreme bafflement.

'Shop!' said Twoflower.

'Anyone here?' said Bethan.

'Urrgh,' said Rincewind.

'I think we ought to sit him down somewhere and get him a glass of water,' said Twoflower. 'If there's one here.'

'There's everything else,' said Bethan.

The room was full of shelves, and the shelves were full of everything. Things that couldn't be accommodated on them hung in bunches from the dark and shadowy ceiling; boxes and sacks of everything spilled onto the floor.

There was no sound from outside. Bethan looked around and found out why.

'I've never seen so much stuff,' said Twoflower.

'There's one thing it's out of stock of,' said Bethan, firmly.

'How can you tell?'

'You just have to look. It's fresh out of exits.'

Twoflower turned around. Where the door and window had been there were shelves stacked with boxes; they looked as though they had been there for a long time.

Twoflower sat Rincewind down on a rickety chair by the counter and poked doubtfully at the shelves. There were boxes of nails, and hairbrushes. There were bars of soap, faded with age. There was a stack of jars containing deliquescent bath salts, to which someone had fixed a rather sad and jaunty little notice announcing, in the face of all the evidence, that one would make an Ideal Gift. There was also quite a lot of dust.

Bethan peered at the shelves on the other wall, and laughed.

'Would you look at this!' she said.

Twoflower looked. She was holding a – well, it was a little mountain chalet, but with seashells stuck all over it, and then the perpetrator had written 'A Special Souvenir' in pokerwork on the roof (which, of course, opened so that cigarettes could be kept in it, and played a tinny little tune).

'Have you ever seen anything like it?' she said.

Twoflower shook his head. His mouth dropped open.

'Are you all right?' said Bethan.

'I think it's the most beautiful thing I've ever seen,' he said.

There was a whirring noise overhead. They looked up.

A big black globe had lowered itself from the darkness of the ceiling. Little red lights flashed on and off on it, and as they stared it spun around and looked at them with a big glass eye. It was menacing, that eye. It seemed to suggest very emphatically that it was watching something distasteful.

'Hallo?' said Twoflower.

A head appeared over the edge of the counter. It looked angry.

'I hope you were intending to pay for that,' it said nastily. Its expression suggested that it expected Rincewind to say yes, and that it wouldn't believe him.

'This?' said Bethan. 'I wouldn't buy this if you threw in a hatful of rubies and—'

'*I'll* buy it. How much?' said Twoflower urgently, reaching into his pockets. His face fell.

'Actually, I haven't got any money,' he said. 'It's in my Luggage, but I—'

There was a snort. The head disappeared from behind the counter, and reappeared from behind a display of toothbrushes.

It belonged to a very small man almost hidden behind a green apron. He seemed very upset.

'No money?' he said. 'You come into my shop—'

'We didn't mean to,' said Twoflower quickly. 'We didn't notice it was there.'

'It wasn't,' said Bethan firmly. 'It's magical, isn't it?'

The small shopkeeper hesitated.

'Yes,' he reluctantly agreed. 'A bit.'

'A bit?' said Bethan. 'A *bit* magical?'

'Quite a bit, then,' he conceded, backing away, and, 'All right,' he agreed, as Bethan continued to glare at him. 'It's magical. I can't help it. The bloody door hasn't been and gone again, has it?'

'Yes, and we're not happy about that thing in the ceiling.'

He looked up, and frowned. Then he disappeared

through a little beaded doorway half-hidden among the merchandise. There was a lot of clanking and whirring, and the black globe disappeared into the shadows. It was replaced by, in succession, a bunch of herbs, a mobile advertising something Twoflower had never heard of but which was apparently a bedtime drink, a suit of armour and a stuffed crocodile with a lifelike expression of extreme pain and surprise.

The shopkeeper reappeared.

'Better?' he demanded.

'It's an improvement,' said Twoflower, doubtfully. 'I liked the herbs best.'

At this point Rincewind groaned. He was about to wake up.

There have been three general theories put forward to explain the phenomenon of the wandering shops or, as they are generically known, *tabernae vagantes.*

The first postulates that many thousands of years ago there evolved somewhere in the multiverse a race whose single talent was to buy cheap and sell dear. Soon they controlled a vast galactic empire or, as they put it, Emporium, and the more advanced members of the species found a way to equip their very shops with unique propulsion units that could break the dark walls of space itself and open up vast new markets. And long after the worlds of the Emporium perished in the heat death of their particular universe, after one last defiant fire sale, the wandering starshops still ply their trade, eating their way through the pages of spacetime like a worm through a three-volume novel.

The second is that they are the creation of a sympathetic Fate, charged with the role of supplying exactly the right thing at the right time.

The third is that they are simply a very clever way of getting around the various Sunday Closing acts.

All these theories, diverse as they are, have two things in common: they explain the observed facts, and they are completely and utterly wrong.

Rincewind opened his eyes and lay for a moment looking up at the stuffed reptile. It was not the best thing to see when awakening from troubled dreams . . .

Magic! So that's what it felt like! No wonder wizards didn't have much truck with sex!

Rincewind knew what orgasms were, of course, he'd had a few in his time, sometimes even in company, but nothing in his experience even approximated to that tight, hot moment when every nerve in his body streamed with blue-white fire and raw magic had blazed forth from his fingers. It filled you and lifted you and you surfed down the rising, curling wave of elemental force. No wonder wizards fought for power . . .

And so on. The Spell in his head had been doing it, though, not Rincewind. He was really beginning to hate that Spell. He was sure that if it hadn't frightened away all the other spells he'd tried to learn he could have been a decent wizard in his own right.

Somewhere in Rincewind's battered soul the worm of rebellion flashed a fang.

Right, he thought. You're going back into the Octavo, first chance I get.

He sat up.

'Where the hell is this?' he said, grabbing his head to stop it exploding.

'A shop,' said Twoflower mournfully.

'I hope it sells knives because I think I'd like to cut my head off,' said Rincewind. Something about the expression of the two opposite him sobered him up.

'That was a joke,' he said. 'Mainly a joke, anyway. Why are we in this shop?'

'We can't get out,' said Bethan.

'The door's disappeared,' added Twoflower helpfully.

Rincewind stood up, a little shakily.

'Oh,' he said. 'One of *those* shops?'

'All right,' said the shopkeeper testily. 'It's magical, yes, it moves around, yes, no, I'm not telling you why—'

'Can I have a drink of water, please?' said Rincewind.

The shopkeeper looked affronted.

'First no money, then they want a glass of water,' he snapped. 'That's just about—'

Bethan snorted and strode across to the little man, who tried to back away. He was too late.

She picked him up by his apron straps and glared at

him eye to eye. Torn though her dress was, disarrayed though her hair was, she became for a moment the symbol of every woman who has caught a man with his thumb on the scales of life.

'Time is money,' she hissed. 'I'll give you thirty seconds to get him a glass of water. I think that's a bargain, don't you?'

'I say,' Twoflower whispered. 'She's a real terror when she's roused, isn't she?'

'Yes,' said Rincewind, without enthusiasm.

'All right, all right,' said the shopkeeper, visibly cowed.

'And then you can let us out,' Bethan added.

'That's fine by me. I wasn't open for business anyway, I just stopped for a few seconds to get my bearings and you barged in!'

He grumbled off through the bead curtains and returned with a cup of water.

'I washed it out special,' he said, avoiding Bethan's gaze.

Rincewind looked at the liquid in the cup. It had probably been clean before it was poured in, now drinking it would be genocide for thousands of innocent germs.

He put it down carefully.

'Now I'm going to have a good wash!' stated Bethan, and stalked off through the curtain.

The shopkeeper waved a hand vaguely and looked appealingly at Rincewind and Twoflower.

'She's not bad,' said Twoflower. 'She's going to marry a friend of ours.'

'Does he know?'

'Things not so good in the starshop business?' said Rincewind, as sympathetically as he could manage.

The little man shuddered. 'You wouldn't believe it,' he said. 'I mean, you learn not to expect much, you make a sale here and there, it's a living, you know what I mean? But these people you've got these days, the ones with these star things painted on their faces, well, I hardly have time to open the store and they're threatening to burn it down. Too magical, they say. So I say, of course magical, what else?'

'Are there a lot of them about, then?' said Rincewind.

'All over the Disc, friend. Don't ask me why.'

'They believe a star is going to crash into the Disc,' said Rincewind.

'Is it?'

'Lots of people think so.'

'That's a shame. I've done good business here. Too magical, they say! What's wrong with magic, that's what I'd like to know?'

'What will you do?' said Twoflower.

'Oh, go to some other universe, there's plenty around,' said the shopkeeper airily. 'Thanks for telling me about the star, though. Can I drop you off somewhere?'

The Spell gave Rincewind's mind a kick.

'Er, no,' he said, 'I think perhaps we'd better stay. To see it through, you know.'

'You're not worried about this star thing, then?'

'The star is life, not death,' said Rincewind.

'How's that?'

'How's what?'

'You did it again!' said Twoflower, pointing an accusing finger. 'You say things and then don't know you've said them!'

'I just said we'd better stay,' said Rincewind.

'You said the star was life, not death,' said Twoflower. 'Your voice went all crackly and far away. Didn't it?' He turned to the shopkeeper for confirmation.

'That's true,' said the little man. 'I thought his eyes crossed a bit, too.'

'It's the Spell, then,' said Rincewind. 'It's trying to take me over. It knows what's going to happen, and I think it wants to go to Ankh-Morpork. I want to go too,' he added defiantly. 'Can you get us there?'

'Is that the big city on the Ankh? Sprawling place, smells of cesspits?'

'It has an ancient and honourable history,' said Rincewind, his voice stiff with injured civic pride.

'That's not how you described it to *me*,' said Twoflower. 'You told me it was the only city that actually started out decadent.'

Rincewind looked embarrassed. 'Yes, but, well, it's my home, don't you see?'

'No,' said the shopkeeper, 'not really. I always say home is where you hang your hat.'

'Um, no,' said Twoflower, always anxious to enlighten. 'Where you hang your hat is a hatstand. A home is—'

'I'll just go and see about setting you on your way,'

said the shopkeeper hurriedly, as Bethan came in. He scooted past her.

Twoflower followed him.

On the other side of the curtain was a room with a small bed, a rather grubby stove, and a three-legged table. Then the shopkeeper did something to the table, there was a noise like a cork coming reluctantly out of a bottle, and the room contained a wall-to-wall universe.

'Don't be frightened,' said the shopkeeper, as stars streamed past.

'I'm not frightened,' said Twoflower, his eyes sparkling.

'Oh,' said the shopkeeper, slightly annoyed. 'Anyway, it's just imagery generated by the shop, it's not real.'

'And you can go anywhere?'

'Oh no,' said the shopkeeper, deeply shocked. 'There's all kinds of fail-safes built in, after all, there'd be no point in going somewhere with insufficient per capita disposable income. And there's got to be a suitable wall, of course. Ah, here we are, this is your universe. Very bijou, I always think. A sort of universette . . .'

Here is the blackness of space, the myriad stars gleaming like diamond dust or, as some people would say, like great balls of exploding hydrogen a very long way off. But then, some people would say anything.

A shadow starts to blot out the distant glitter, and it is blacker than space itself.

From here it also looks a great deal bigger, because space is not really big, it is simply somewhere to be big *in*. Planets are big, but planets are meant to be big and there is nothing clever about being the right size.

But this shape blotting out the sky like the footfall of God isn't a planet.

It is a turtle, ten thousand miles long from its crater-pocked head to its armoured tail.

And Great A'Tuin is *huge*.

Great flippers rise and fall ponderously, warping space into strange shapes. The Discworld slides across the sky like a royal barge. But even Great A'Tuin is struggling now as it leaves the free depths of space and must fight the tormenting pressures of the solar shallows. Magic is weaker here, on the littoral of light. Many more days of this and the Discworld will be stripped away by the pressures of reality.

Great A'Tuin knows this, but Great A'Tuin can recall doing all this before, many thousands of years ago.

The astrochelonian's eyes, glowing red in the light of the dwarf star, are not focused on it but at a little patch of space nearby . . .

'Yes, but where are we?' said Twoflower. The shopkeeper, hunched over his table, just shrugged.

'I don't think we're any*where*,' he said. 'We're in a cotangent incongruity, I believe. I could be wrong. The shop generally knows what it's doing.'

'You mean you don't?'

'I pick a bit up, here and there.' The shopkeeper blew his nose. 'Sometimes I land on a world where they understand these things.' He turned a pair of small, sad eyes on Twoflower. 'You've got a kind face, sir. I don't mind telling you.'

'Telling me what?'

'It's no life, you know, minding the Shop. Never settling down, always on the move, never closing.'

'Why don't you stop, then?'

'Ah, that's it, you see, sir – I can't. I'm under a curse, I am. A terrible thing.' He blew his nose again.

'Cursed to run a shop?'

'Forever, sir, forever. And never closing! For hundreds of years! There was this sorcerer, you see. I did a terrible thing.'

'In a shop?' said Twoflower.

'Oh, yes. I can't remember what it was he wanted, but when he asked for it I – I gave one of those sucking-in noises, you know, like whistling only backwards?' He demonstrated.

Twoflower looked sombre, but he was at heart a kind man and always ready to forgive.

'I see,' he said slowly. 'Even so—'

'That's not all!'

'Oh.'

'I told him there was no demand for it!'

'After making the sucking noise?'

'Yes. I probably grinned, too.'

'Oh, dear. You didn't call him squire, did you?'

'I – I may have done.'

'Um.'

'There's more.'

'Surely not?'

'Yes, I said I could order it and he could come back next day.'

'That doesn't sound too bad,' said Twoflower, who alone of all the people in the multiverse allowed shops to order things for him and didn't object at all to paying quite large sums of money to reimburse the shopkeeper for the inconvenience of having a bit of stock in his store often for several hours.

'It was early closing day,' said the shopkeeper.

'Oh.'

'Yes, and I heard him rattling the doorhandle. I had this sign on the door, you know, it said something like "Closed even for the sale of Necromancer cigarettes," anyway, I heard him banging and I laughed.'

'You laughed?'

'Yes. Like this. Hnufhnufhnufblort.'

'Probably not a wise thing to do,' said Twoflower, shaking his head.

'I know, I know. My father always said, he said, "Do not peddle in the affairs of wizards . . ." Anyway, I heard him shouting something about never closing again, and a lot of words I couldn't understand, and then the shop – the shop – the shop came *alive*.'

'And you've wandered like this ever since?'

'Yes. I suppose one day I might find the sorcerer and perhaps the thing he wanted will be in stock. Until then I must go from place to place—'

'That was a terrible thing to do,' said Twoflower.

The shopkeeper wiped his nose on his apron. 'Thank you,' he said.

'Even so, he shouldn't have cursed you quite so badly,' Twoflower added.

'Oh. Yes, well.' The shopkeeper straightened his apron and made a brave little attempt to pull himself together. 'Anyway, this isn't getting you to Ankh-Morpork, is it?'

'Funny thing is,' said Twoflower, 'that I bought my Luggage in a shop like this, once. Another shop I mean.'

'Oh yes, there's several of us,' said the shopkeeper, turning back to the table. 'That sorcerer was a very impatient man, I understand.'

'Endlessly roaming through the universe,' mused Twoflower.

'That's right. Mind you, there is a saving on the rates.'

'Rates?'

'Yes, they're—' the shopkeeper paused, and wrinkled his forehead. 'I can't quite remember, it was such a long time ago. Rates, rates—'

'Very large mice?'

'That's probably it.'

'Hold on – it's thinking about something,' said Cohen.

Lackjaw looked up wearily. It had been quite nice, sitting here in the shade. He had just worked out that in trying to escape from a city of crazed madmen he appeared to have allowed one mad man to give him his full attention. He wondered whether he would live to regret this.

He earnestly hoped so.

'Oh yes, it's definitely thinking,' he said bitterly. 'Anyone can see that.'

'I think it's found them.'

'Oh, good.'

'Hold on to it.'

'Are you mad?' said Lackjaw.

'I know this thing, trust me. Anyway, would you rather be left with all these star people? They might be interested in having a talk with you.'

Cohen sidled over to the Luggage, and then flung himself astride it. It took no notice.

'Hurry up,' he said. 'I think it's going to go.'

Lackjaw shrugged and climbed on gingerly behind Cohen.

'Oh?' he said, 'and how does it g—'

Ankh-Morpork!

Pearl of cities!

This is not a completely accurate description, of course – it was not round and shiny – but even its worst enemies would agree that if you had to liken Ankh-Morpork to anything, then it might as well be a piece of rubbish covered with the diseased secretions of a dying mollusc.

There have been bigger cities. There have been richer cities. There have certainly been prettier cities. But no city in the multiverse could rival Ankh-Morpork for its smell.

The Ancient Ones, who know everything about all the universes and have smelt the smells of Calcutta and !Xrc—! and dauntocum Marsport, have agreed that even these fine examples of nasal poetry are mere limericks when set against the glory of the Ankh-Morpork smell.

You can talk about tramps. You can talk about garlic. You can talk about France. Go on. But if you haven't smelled Ankh-Morpork on a hot day you haven't smelled anything.

The citizens are proud of it. They carry chairs outside to enjoy it on a really good day. They puff out their cheeks and slap their chests and comment cheerfully on its little distinctive nuances. They have even put up a statue to it, to commemorate the time when the troops of a rival state tried to invade by stealth one dark night and managed to get to the top of the walls before, to their horror, their nose plugs gave out. Rich merchants who have spent many years abroad send back home for specially-stoppered and sealed bottles of the stuff, which brings tears to their eyes.

It has that kind of effect.

There is only really one way to describe the effect the smell of Ankh-Morpork has on the visiting nose, and that is by analogy.

Take a tartan. Sprinkle it with confetti. Light it with strobe lights.

Now take a chameleon.

Put the chameleon on the tartan.

Watch it closely.

See?

Which explains why, when the shop finally materialized in Ankh-Morpork, Rincewind sat bolt upright and said 'We're here,' Bethan went pale and Twoflower, who had no sense of smell, said, 'Really? How can you tell?'

It had been a long afternoon. They had broken into realspace in a number of walls in a variety of cities because, according to the shopkeeper, the Disc's magical field was playing up and upsetting everything.

All the cities were empty of most of their citizens and belonged to roaming gangs of crazed left-ear people.

'Where do they all come from?' said Twoflower, as they fled yet another mob.

'Inside every sane person there's a madman struggling to get out,' said the shopkeeper. 'That's what I've always thought. No one goes mad quicker than a totally sane person.'

'That doesn't make sense,' said Bethan, 'or if it makes sense, I don't like it.'

The star was bigger than the sun. There would be no night tonight. On the opposite horizon the Disc's own sunlet was doing its best to set normally, but the general effect of all that red light was to make the city, never particularly beautiful, look like something painted by a fanatical artist after a bad time on the shoe polish.

But it was *home*. Rincewind peered up and down the empty street and felt almost happy.

At the back of his mind the Spell was kicking up a ruckus, but he ignored it. Maybe it was true that magic was getting weaker as the star got nearer, or perhaps he'd had the Spell in his head for so long he had built up some kind of psychic immunity, but he found he *could* resist it.

'We're in the docks,' he declared. 'Just smell that sea air!'

'Oh,' said Bethan, leaning against the wall, 'yes.'

'That's ozone, that is,' said Rincewind. 'That's air with character, is that.' He breathed deeply.

Twoflower turned to the shopkeeper.

'Well, I hope you find your sorcerer,' he said. 'Sorry we didn't buy anything, but all my money's in my Luggage, you see.'

The shopkeeper pushed something into his hand.

'A little gift,' he said. 'You'll need it.'

He darted back into his shop, the bell jangled, the sign saying Call Again Tomorrow For Spoonfetcher's Leeches, the Little Suckers banged forlornly against the door, and the shop faded into the brickwork as though it had never been. Twoflower reached out gingerly and touched the wall, not quite believing it.

'What's in the bag?' said Rincewind.

It was a thick brown paper bag, with string handles.

'If it sprouts legs I don't want to know about it,' said Bethan.

Twoflower peered inside, and pulled out the contents.

'Is that all?' said Rincewind. 'A little house with shells on?'

'It's very useful,' said Twoflower defensively. 'You can keep cigarettes in it.'

'And they're what you really need, are they?' said Rincewind.

'I'd plump for a bottle of really strong sun-tan oil,' said Bethan.

'Come on,' said Rincewind, and set off down the street. The others followed.

It occurred to Twoflower that some words of comfort were called for, a little tactful small talk to take Bethan out of herself, as he would put it, and generally cheer her up.

'Don't worry,' he said. 'There's just a chance that Cohen might still be alive.'

'Oh, I expect he's alive all right,' she said, stamping along the cobbles as if she nursed a personal grievance against each one of them. 'You don't live to be eighty-seven in his job if you go around dying all the time. But he's not here.'

'Nor is my Luggage,' said Twoflower. 'Of course, that's not the same thing.'

'Do you think the star is going to hit the Disc?'

'No,' said Twoflower confidently.

'Why not?'

'Because Rincewind doesn't think so.'

She looked at him in amazement.

'You see,' the tourist went on, 'you know that thing you do with seaweed?'

Bethan, brought up on the Vortex Plains, had only heard of the sea in stories, and had decided she didn't like it. She looked blank.

'Eat it?'

'No, what you do is, you hang it up outside your door, and it tells you if it's going to rain.'

Another thing Bethan had learned was that there was no real point in trying to understand anything Twoflower said, and that all anyone could do was run alongside the conversation and hope to jump on as it turned a corner.

'I see,' she said.

'Rincewind is like that, you see.'

'Like seaweed.'

'Yes. If there was anything at all to be frightened about, he'd be frightened. But he's not. The star is just about the only thing I've ever seen him not frightened of. If he's not worried, then take it from me, there's nothing to worry about.'

'It's not going to rain?' said Bethan.

'Well, no. Metaphorically speaking.'

'Oh.' Bethan decided not to ask what 'metaphorically' meant, in case it was something to do with seaweed.

Rincewind turned around.

'Come on,' he said. 'Not far now.'

'Where to?' said Twoflower.

'Unseen University, of course.'

'Is that wise?'

'Probably not, but I'm still going—' Rincewind paused, his face a mask of pain. He put his hand to his ears and groaned.

'Spell giving you trouble?'

'Yargh.'

'Try humming.'

Rincewind grimaced. 'I'm going to get rid of this thing,' he said thickly. 'It's going back into the book where it belongs. I want my head back!'

'But then—' Twoflower began, and stopped. They could all hear it – a distant chanting and the stamping of many feet.

'Do you think it's star people?' said Bethan.

It was. The lead marchers came around a corner a hundred yards away, behind a ragged white banner with an eight-pointed star on it.

'Not just star people,' said Twoflower. 'All kinds of people!'

The crowd swept them up in its passage. One moment they were standing in the deserted street, the next they were perforce moving with a tide of humanity that bore them onwards through the city.

Torchlight flickered easily on the damp tunnels far under the University as the heads of the eight Orders of wizardry filed onwards.

'At least it's cool down here,' said one.

'We shouldn't *be* down here.'

Trymon, who was leading the party, said nothing. But he was thinking very hard. He was thinking about the bottle of oil in his belt, and the eight keys the wizards carried – eight keys that would fit the eight locks that chained the Octavo to its lectern. He was thinking that old wizards who sense that magic is draining away are preoccupied with their own problems and are perhaps less alert than they should be. He was thinking that within a few minutes the Octavo, the greatest concentration of magic on the Disc, would be under his hands.

Despite the coolness of the tunnel he began to sweat.

They came to a lead-lined door set in the sheer stone. Trymon took a heavy key – a good, honest iron key, not like the twisted and disconcerting keys that would unlock the Octavo – gave the lock a squirt of oil, inserted the key, turned it. The lock squeaked open protestingly.

'Are we of one resolve?' said Trymon. There was a series of vaguely affirmative grunts.

He pushed at the door.

A warm gale of thick and somehow oily air rolled over them. The air was filled with a high-pitched and unpleasant chittering. Tiny sparks of octarine fire flared off every nose, fingernail and beard.

The wizards, their heads bowed against the storm of randomized magic that blew out of the room, pushed forward. Half-formed shapes giggled and fluttered around them as the nightmare inhabitants of the Dungeon Dimensions constantly probed (with things that passed for fingers only because they were at the ends of their arms) for an unguarded entry into the circle of firelight that passed for the universe of reason and order.

Even at this bad time for all things magical, even in a room designed to damp down all magical vibrations, the Octavo was still crackling with power.

There was no real need for the torches. The Octavo filled the room with a dull, sullen light, which wasn't strictly light at all but the opposite of light; darkness isn't the opposite of light, it is simply its absence, and what was radiating from the book was the light that lies on the far side of darkness, the light fantastic.

It was a rather disappointing purple colour.

As has been noted before, the Octavo was chained to a lectern carved into the shape of something that looked vaguely avian, slightly reptilian and horribly alive. Two glittering eyes regarded the wizards with hooded hatred.

'I saw it move,' said one of them.

'We're safe so long as we don't touch the book,' said Trymon. He pulled a scroll out of his belt and unrolled it.

'Bring that torch here,' he said, '*and put that cigarette out*!'

He waited for the explosion of infuriated pride. But none came. Instead, the offending mage removed the dogend from his lips with trembling fingers and ground it into the floor.

Trymon exulted. So, he thought, they do what I say. Just for now, maybe – but just for now is enough.

He peered at the crabby writing of a wizard long dead.

'Right,' he said, 'let's see: "To Appease Yt, The Thynge That Ys The Guardian . . ." '

* * *

The crowd surged over one of the bridges that linked Morpork with Ankh. Below it the river, turgid at the best of times, was a mere trickle which steamed.

The bridge shook under their feet rather more than it should. Strange ripples ran across the muddy remains of the river. A few tiles slid off the roof of a nearby house.

'What was that?' said Twoflower.

Bethan looked behind them, and screamed.

The star was rising. As the Disc's own sun scurried for safety below the horizon, the great bloated ball of the star climbed slowly into the sky until the whole of it was several degrees above the edge of the world.

They pulled Rincewind into the safety of a doorway. The crowd hardly noticed them, but ran on, terrified as lemmings.

'The star's got spots on,' said Twoflower.

'No,' said Rincewind. 'They're . . . things. Things going around the star. Like the sun goes around the Disc. But they're close in, because, because . . .' he paused. 'I nearly know!'

'Know what?'

'I've got to get rid of this Spell!'

'Which way is the University?' said Bethan.

'This way!' said Rincewind, pointing along the street.

'It must be very popular. That's where everyone's going.'

'I wonder why?' said Twoflower.

'Somehow,' said Rincewind, 'I don't think it's to enroll for evening classes.'

In fact Unseen University was under siege, or at least those parts of it that extruded into the usual, everyday dimensions were under siege. The crowds outside its gates were, generally, making one of two demands. They were demanding that either a) the wizards should stop messing about and get rid of the star or, and this was the demand favoured by the star people, that b) they should cease all magic and commit suicide in good order, thus ridding the Disc of the curse of magic and warding off the terrible threat in the sky.

The wizards on the other side of the walls had no idea how to do a) and no intention of doing b) and many had in fact plumped for c), which largely consisted of nipping out of hidden side doors and having it away on their toes as fast as possible, if not faster.

What reliable magic still remained in the University was being channelled into keeping the great gates secure. The wizards were learning that while it was all very fine and impressive to have a set of gates that were locked by magic, it ought to have occurred to the builders to include some sort of emergency back-up device such as, for example, a pair of ordinary, unimpressive stout iron bolts.

In the square outside the gates several large bonfires had been lit, for effect as much as anything else, because the heat from the star was scorching.

'But you can still see the stars,' said Twoflower, 'the other stars, I mean. The little ones. In a black sky.'

Rincewind ignored him. He was looking at the gates. A group of star people and citizens were trying to batter them down.

'It's hopeless,' said Bethan. 'We'll never get in. Where are you going?'

'For a walk,' said Rincewind. He was setting off determinedly down a side street.

There were one or two freelance rioters here, mostly engaged in wrecking shops. Rincewind took no notice, but followed the wall until it ran parallel to a dark alley that had the usual unfortunate smell of all alleys, everywhere.

Then he started looking very closely at the stonework. The wall here was twenty feet high, and topped with cruel metal spikes.

'I need a knife,' he said.

'You're going to cut your way through?' said Bethan.

'Just find me a knife,' said Rincewind. He started to tap stones.

Twoflower and Bethan looked at each other, and shrugged. A few minutes later they returned with a selection of knives, and Twoflower had even managed to find a sword.

'We just helped ourselves,' said Bethan.

'But we left some money,' said Twoflower. 'I mean, we would have left some money, if we'd had any—'

'So he insisted on writing a note,' said Bethan wearily.

Twoflower drew himself up to his full height, which was hardly worth it.

'I see no reason—' he began, stiffly.

'Yes, yes,' said Bethan, sitting down glumly. 'I know you don't. Rincewind, all the shops have been smashed open. There was a whole bunch of people across the street helping themselves to musical instruments, can you believe that?'

'Yeah,' said Rincewind, picking up a knife and testing its blade thoughtfully. 'Luters, I expect.'

He thrust the blade into the wall, twisted it, and stepped back as a heavy stone fell out. He looked up, counting under his breath, and levered another stone from its socket.

'How did you do that?' said Twoflower.

'Just give me a leg up, will you?' said Rincewind. A moment later, his feet wedged into the holes he had created, he was making further steps halfway up the wall.

'It's been like this for centuries,' his voice floated down. 'Some of the stones haven't got any mortar. Secret entrance, see? Watch out below.'

Another stone cracked into the cobbles.

'Students made it long ago,' said Rincewind. 'Handy way in and out after lights out.'

'Ah,' said Twoflower, 'I *understand*. Over the wall and out to brightly-lit tavernas to drink and sing and recite poetry, yes?'

'Nearly right except for the singing and the poetry, yes,' said Rincewind. 'A couple of these spikes should be loose—' There was a clang.

'There's not much of a drop this side,' came his voice after a few seconds. 'Come on, then. If you're coming.'

And so it was that Rincewind, Twoflower and Bethan entered Unseen University.

Elsewhere on the campus—

The eight wizards inserted their keys and, with many a worried glance at one another, turned them. There was a faint little snicking sound as the lock slid open.

The Octavo was unchained. A faint octarine light played across its bindings.

Trymon reached out and picked it up, and none of the others objected. His arm tingled.

He turned towards the door.

'Now to the Great Hall, brothers,' he said, 'if I may lead the way—'

And there were no objections.

He reached the door with the book tucked under his arm. It felt hot, and somehow prickly.

At every step he expected a cry, a protest, and none came. He had to use every ounce of control to stop himself from laughing. It was easier than he could have imagined.

The others were halfway across the claustrophobic dungeon by the time he was through the door, and perhaps they had noticed something in the set of his shoulders, but it was too late because he had crossed the threshold, gripped the handle, slammed the door, turned the key, smiled the smile.

He walked easily back along the corridor, ignoring the enraged screams of the wizards who had just discovered how impossible it is to pass spells in a room built to be impervious to magic.

The Octavo *squirmed*, but Trymon held it tightly. Now he ran, putting out of his mind the horrible sensations under his arm as the book shape-changed into things hairy, skeletal and spiky. His hand went numb. The faint chittering noises he had been hearing grew in volume, and there were other sounds behind them – leering sounds, beckoning sounds, sounds made by the voices of unimaginable horrors that Trymon found it all too easy to imagine. As he ran across the Great Hall and up the main staircase the shadows began to move and reform and close in around him, and he also became aware that something was following, something with skittery legs moving obscenely fast. Ice formed on the walls. Doorways lunged at him as he barrelled past. Underfoot the stairs began to feel just like a tongue . . .

Not for nothing had Trymon spent long hours in the University's curious equivalent of a gymnasium, building up mental muscle. Don't trust the senses, he knew, because they can be deceived. The stairs are there, somewhere – *will* them to be there, summon them into being as you climb and, boy, you better get good at it. Because this isn't all imagination.

Great A'Tuin slowed.

With flippers the size of continents the skyturtle fought the pull of the star, and waited.

There would not be long to wait . . .

Rincewind sidled into the Great Hall. There were a few torches burning, and it looked as though it had been set up for some sort of magical work. But the ceremonial candlesticks had been overturned, the complex octograms chalked on the floor were scuffed as if something had danced on them, and the air was full of a smell unpleasant even by Ankh-Morpork's broad standards. There was a hint of sulphur to it, but that underlay something worse. It smelt like the bottom of a pond.

There was a distant crash, and a lot of shouting.

'Looks like the gates have gone down,' said Rincewind.

'Let's get out of here,' said Bethan.

'The cellars are this way,' said Rincewind, and set off through an arch.

'Down *there*?'

'Yes. Would you rather stay here?'

He took a torch from its bracket on the wall and started down the steps.

After a few flights the walls stopped being panelled and were bare stone. Here and there heavy doors had been propped open.

'I heard something,' said Twoflower.

Rincewind listened. There did seem to be a noise coming from the depths below. It didn't sound frightening. It sounded like a lot of people hammering on a door and shouting 'Oi!'

'It's not those Things from the Dungeon Dimensions you were telling us about, is it?' said Bethan.

'They don't swear like that,' said Rincewind. 'Come on.'

They hurried along the dripping passages,

following the screamed curses and deep hacking coughs that were somehow reassuring; anything that wheezed like that, the listeners decided, couldn't possibly represent a danger.

At last they came to a door set in an alcove. It looked strong enough to hold back the sea. There was a tiny grille.

'Hey!' shouted Rincewind. It wasn't very useful, but he couldn't think of anything better.

There was a sudden silence. Then a voice from the other side of the door said, very slowly, 'Who is out there?'

Rincewind recognized that voice. It had jerked him from daydreams into terror on many a hot classroom afternoon, years before. It was Lemuel Panter, who had once made it his personal business to hammer the rudiments of scrying and summoning into young Rincewind's head. He remembered the eyes like gimlets in a piggy face and the voice saying 'And now Mister Rincewind will come out here and draw the relevant symbol on the board' and the million mile walk past the waiting class as he tried desperately to remember what the voice had been droning on about five minutes before. Even now his throat was going dry with terror and randomized guilt. The Dungeon Dimensions just weren't in it.

'Please sir, it's me, sir, Rincewind, sir,' he squeaked. He saw Twoflower and Bethan staring at him, and coughed. 'Yes,' he added, in as deep a voice as he could manage. 'That's who it is. Rincewind. Right.'

There was a susurration of whispers on the other side of the door.

'*Rincewind?*'

'*Prince who?*'

'*I remember a boy who wasn't any—*'

'*The Spell, remember?*'

'*Rincewind?*'

There was a pause. Then the voice said, 'I suppose the key isn't in the lock, is it?'

'No,' said Rincewind.

'*What did he say?*'

'*He said no.*'

'*Typical of the boy.*'

'Um, who is in there?' said Rincewind.

'The Masters of Wizardry,' said the voice, haughtily.

'Why?'

There was another pause, and then a conference of embarrassed whispers.

'We, uh, got locked in,' said the voice, reluctantly.

'What, with the Octavo?'

Whisper, whisper.

'The Octavo, in fact, isn't in here, in fact,' said the voice slowly.

'Oh. But you are?' said Rincewind, as politely as possible while grinning like a necrophiliac in a morgue.

'That would appear to be the case.'

'Is there anything we can get you?' said Twoflower anxiously.

'You could try getting us out.'

'Could we pick the lock?' said Bethan.

'No use,' said Rincewind. 'Totally thief-proof.'

'I expect Cohen would have been able to,' said Bethan loyally. 'Wherever he's got to.'

'The Luggage would soon smash it down,' agreed Twoflower.

'Well, that's it then,' said Bethan. 'Let's get out into the fresh air. Fresher air, anyway.' She turned to walk away.

'Hang on, hang on,' said Rincewind. 'That's just typical, isn't it? Old Rincewind won't have any ideas, will he? Oh, no, he's just a makeweight, he is. Kick him as you pass. Don't rely on him, he's—'

'All right,' said Bethan. 'Let's hear it, then.'

'—a nonentity, a failure, just a— what?'

'How are you going to get the door open?' said Bethan.

Rincewind looked at her with his mouth open. Then he looked at the door. It really was very solid, and the lock had a smug air.

But he had got in, once, long ago. Rincewind the student had pushed at the door and it had swung open, and then a moment later the Spell had jumped into his mind and ruined his life.

'Look,' said a voice from behind the grille, as kindly as it could manage, 'just go and find us a wizard, there's a good fellow.'

Rincewind took a deep breath.

'Stand back,' he rasped.

'What?'

'Find something to hide behind,' he barked, with his voice shaking only slightly. 'You too,' he said to Bethan and Twoflower.

'But you can't—'

'I mean it!'

'He means it,' said Twoflower. 'That little vein on the side of his forehead, you know, when it throbs like that, well—'

'Shut up!'

Rincewind raised one arm uncertainly and pointed it at the door.

There was total silence.

Oh gods, he thought, what happens now?

In the blackness at the back of his mind the Spell shifted uneasily.

Rincewind tried to get in tune or whatever with the metal of the lock. If he could sow discord amongst its atoms so that they flew apart—

Nothing happened.

He swallowed hard, and turned his attention to the wood. It was old and nearly fossilized, and probably wouldn't burn even if soaked in oil and dropped into a furnace. He tried anyway, explaining to the ancient molecules that they should try to jump up and down to keep warm–

In the strained silence of his own mind he glared at the Spell, which looked very sheepish.

He considered the air around the door itself, how it might best be twisted into weird shapes so that the door existed in another set of dimensions entirely.

The door sat there, defiantly solid.

Sweating, his mind beginning the endless walk up to the blackboard in front of the grinning class, he turned desperately to the lock again. It must be made of little bits of metal, not very heavy—

From the grille came the faintest of sounds. It was the noise of wizards untensing themselves and shaking their heads.

Someone whispered, '*I told you—*'

There was a tiny grinding noise, and a click.

Rincewind's face was a mask. Perspiration dripped off his chin.

There was another click, and the grinding of reluctant spindles. Trymon had oiled the lock, but the oil had been soaked up by the rust and dust of years, and the only way for a wizard to move something by magic, unless he can harness some external movement, is to use the leverage of his mind itself.

Rincewind was trying very hard to prevent his brain being pushed out of his ears.

The lock rattled. Metal rods flexed in pitted groves, gave in, pushed levers.

Levers clicked, notches engaged. There was a long drawn-out grinding noise that left Rincewind on his knees.

The door swung open on pained hinges. The wizards sidled out cautiously.

Twoflower and Bethan helped Rincewind to his feet. He stood grey-faced and swaying.

'Not bad,' said one of the wizards, looking closely at the lock. 'A little slow, perhaps.'

'Never mind that!' snapped Jiglad Wert. 'Did you three see anyone on the way down here?'

'No,' said Twoflower.

'Someone has stolen the Octavo.'

Rincewind's head jerked up. His eyes focused.

'Who?'

'Trymon—'

Rincewind swallowed. 'Tall man?' he said. 'Fair hair, looks a bit like a ferret?'

'Now that you mention it—'

'He was in my class,' said Rincewind. 'They always said he'd go a long way.'

'He'll go a lot further if he opens the book,' said one of the wizards, who was hastily rolling a cigarette in shaking fingers.

'Why?' said Twoflower. 'What will happen?'

The wizards looked at one another.

'It's an ancient secret, handed down from mage to mage, and we can't pass it on to knowlessmen,' said Wert.

'Oh, go on,' said Twoflower.

'Oh well, it probably doesn't matter any more. One mind can't hold all the spells. It'll break down, and leave a hole.'

'What? In his head?'

'Um. No. In the fabric of the Universe,' said Wert. 'He might think he can control it by himself, but—'

They felt the sound before they heard it. It started off in the stones as a slow vibration, then rose suddenly to a knife-edge whine that bypassed the eardrums and bored straight into the brain. It sounded like a human voice singing, or chanting, or screaming, but there were deeper and more horrible harmonics.

The wizards went pale. Then, as one man, they turned and ran up the steps.

There were crowds outside the building. Some people were holding torches, others had stopped in the act of piling kindling around the walls. But everyone was staring up at the Tower of Art.

The wizards pushed their way through the unheeding bodies, and turned to look up.

The sky was full of moons. Each one was three times bigger than the Disc's own moon, and each was in shadow except for a pink crescent where it caught the light of the star.

But in front of everything the top of the Tower of Art was an incandescent fury. Shapes could be dimly glimpsed within it, but there was nothing reassuring about them. The sound had changed now to the wasp-like buzzing, magnified a million times.

Some of the wizards sank to their knees.

'He's done it,' said Wert, shaking his head. 'He's opened a pathway.'

'Are those things demons?' said Twoflower.

'Oh, *demons*,' said Wert. 'Demons would be a picnic compared with what's trying to come through up there.'

'They're worse than anything we can possibly imagine,' said Panter.

'I can imagine some pretty bad things,' said Rincewind.

'These are worse.'

'Oh.'

'And what do you propose to do about it?' said a clear voice.

They turned. Bethan was glaring at them, arms folded.

'Pardon?' said Wert.

'You're wizards, aren't you?' she said. 'Well, get on with it.'

'What, tackle that?' said Rincewind.

'Know anyone else?'

Wert pushed forward. 'Madam, I don't think you quite understand—'

'The Dungeon Dimensions will empty into our Universe, right?' said Bethan.

'Well, yes—'

'We'll all be eaten by things with tentacles for faces, right?'

'Nothing so pleasant, but—'

'And you're just going to let it happen?'

'Listen,' said Rincewind. 'It's all over, do you see? You can't put the spells back in the book, you can't unsay what's been said, you can't—'

'You can *try*!'

Rincewind sighed, and turned to Twoflower.

He wasn't there. Rincewind's eyes turned inevitably towards the base of the Tower of Art, and he was just in time to see the tourist's plump figure, sword inexpertly in hand, as it disappeared into a door.

Rincewind's feet made their own decision and, from the point of view of his head, got it entirely wrong.

The other wizards watched him go.

'Well?' said Bethan. '*He's* going.'

The wizards tried to avoid one another's eyes.

Eventually Wert said, 'We could try, I suppose. It doesn't seem to be spreading.'

'But we've got hardly any magic to speak of,' said one of the wizards.

'Have you got a better idea, then?'

One by one, their ceremonial robes glittering in the weird light, the wizards turned and trudged towards the tower.

The tower was hollow inside, with the stone treads of its staircase mortared spiral-fashion into the walls. Twoflower was already several turns up by the time Rincewind caught him.

'Hold on,' he said, as cheerfully as he could manage. 'This sort of thing is a job for the likes of Cohen, not you. No offence.'

'Would he do any good?'

Rincewind looked up at the actinic light that lanced down through the distant hole at the top of the staircase.

'No,' he admitted.

'Then I'd be as good as him, wouldn't I?' said Twoflower, flourishing his looted sword.

Rincewind hopped after him, keeping as close to the wall as possible.

'You don't understand!' he shouted. 'There's unimaginable horrors up there!'

'You always said I didn't have any imagination.'

'It's a point, yes,' Rincewind conceded, 'but—'

Twoflower sat down.

'Look,' he said, 'I've been looking forward to something like this ever since I came here. I mean, this is an adventure, isn't it? Alone against the gods, that sort of thing?'

Rincewind opened and shut his mouth for a few seconds before the right words managed to come out.

'Can you use a sword?' he said weakly.

'I don't know. I've never tried.'

'You're mad!'

Twoflower looked at him with his head on one side. 'You're a fine one to talk,' he said. 'I'm here because I don't know any better, but what about you?' He pointed downwards, to where the other wizards were toiling up the stairs. 'What about them?'

Blue light speared down the inside of the tower. There was a peal of thunder.

The wizards reached them, coughing horribly and fighting for breath.

'What's the plan?' said Rincewind.

'There isn't one,' said Wert.

'Right. Fine,' said Rincewind. 'I'll leave you to get on with it, then.'

'You'll come with us,' said Panter.

'But I'm not even a proper wizard. You threw me out, remember?'

'I can't think of any student less able,' said the old wizard, 'but you're here, and that's the only qualification you need. Come on.'

The light flared and went out. The terrible noises died as if strangled.

Silence filled the tower; one of those heavy, pressing silences.

'It's stopped,' said Twoflower.

Something moved, high up against the circle of red sky. It fell slowly, turning over and over and drifting from side to side. It hit the stairs a turn above them.

Rincewind was first to it.

It was the Octavo. But it lay on the stone as limp and lifeless as any other book, its pages fluttering in the breeze that blew up the tower.

Twoflower panted up behind Rincewind, and looked down.

'They're blank,' he whispered. 'Every page is completely blank.'

'Then he did it,' said Wert. 'He's read the spells. Successfully, too. I wouldn't have believed it.'

'There was all that noise,' said Rincewind doubtfully. 'The light, too. Those shapes. That didn't sound so successful to me.'

'Oh, you always get a certain amount of extra-dimensional attention in any great work of magic,' said Panter dismissively. 'It impresses people, nothing more.'

'It looked like monsters up there,' said Twoflower, standing closer to Rincewind.

'Monsters? Show me some monsters!' said Wert.

Instinctively they looked up. There was no sound. Nothing moved against the circle of light.

'I think we should go up and, er, congratulate him,' said Wert.

'Congratulate?' exploded Rincewind. 'He stole the Octavo! He locked you up!'

The wizards exchanged knowing looks.

'Yes, well,' said one of them. 'When you've advanced in the craft, lad, you'll know that there are times when the important thing is success.'

'It's getting there that matters,' said Wert bluntly. 'Not how you travel.'

They set off up the spiral.

Rincewind sat down, scowling at the darkness.

He felt a hand on his shoulder. It was Twoflower, who was holding the Octavo.

'This is no way to treat a book,' he said. 'Look, he's bent the spine right back. People always do that, they've got no idea of how to treat them.'

'Yah,' said Rincewind vaguely.

'Don't worry,' said Twoflower.

'I'm not worried, I'm just angry,' snapped Rincewind. 'Give me the bloody thing!'

He snatched the book and snapped it open viciously.

He rummaged around in the back of his mind, where the Spell hung out.

'All right,' he snarled. 'You've had your fun, you've ruined my life, now get back to where you belong!'

'But I—' protested Twoflower.

'The Spell, I mean the Spell,' said Rincewind. 'Go on, get back on the page!'

He glared at the ancient parchment until his eyes crossed.

'Then I'll say you!' he shouted, his voice echoing up the tower. 'You can join the rest of them and much good may it do you!'

He shoved the book back into Twoflower's arms and staggered off up the steps.

The wizards had reached the top and disappeared from view. Rincewind climbed after them.

'Lad, am I?' he muttered. 'When I'm advanced in

the craft, eh? I just managed to go around with one of the Great Spells in my head for years without going totally insane, didn't I?' He considered the last question from all angles. 'Yes, you did,' he reassured himself. 'You didn't start talking to trees, even when trees started talking to *you*.'

His he ad emerged into the sultry air at the top of the tower.

He had expected to see fire-blackened stones criss-crossed with talon marks, or perhaps something even worse.

Instead he saw the seven senior wizards standing by Trymon, who seemed totally unscathed. He turned and smiled pleasantly at Rincewind.

'Ah, Rincewind. Come and join us, won't you?'

So this is it, Rincewind thought. All that drama for nothing. Maybe I really am not cut out to be a wizard, maybe—

He looked up and into Trymon's eyes.

Perhaps it was the Spell, in its years of living in Rincewind's head, that had affected his eyes. Perhaps his time with Twoflower, who only saw things as they ought to be, had taught him to see things as they are.

But what was certain was that by far the most difficult thing Rincewind did in his whole life was look at Trymon without running in terror or being very violently sick.

The others didn't seem to have noticed.

They also seemed to be standing very still.

Trymon had tried to contain the seven Spells in his mind and it had broken, and the Dungeon

Dimensions had found their hole, all right. Silly to have imagined that the Things would have come marching out of a sort of rip in the sky, waving mandibles and tentacles. That was old-fashioned stuff, far too risky. Even nameless terrors learned to move with the times. All they really needed to enter was one head.

His eyes were empty holes.

Knowledge speared into Rincewind's mind like a knife of ice. The Dungeon Dimensions would be a playgroup compared to what the Things could do in a universe of order. People were craving order, and order they would get – the order of the turning screw, the immutable law of straight lines and numbers. They would beg for the harrow . . .

Trymon was looking at him. *Something* was looking at him. And still the others hadn't noticed. Could he even explain it? Trymon looked the same as he had always done, except for the eyes, and a slight sheen to his skin.

Rincewind stared, and knew that there were far worse things than Evil. All the demons in Hell would torture your very soul, but that was precisely because they valued souls very highly; Evil would always try to steal the universe, but at least it considered the universe worth stealing. But the grey world behind those empty eyes would trample and destroy without even according its victims the dignity of hatred. It wouldn't even notice them.

Trymon held out his hand.

'The eighth spell,' he said. 'Give it to me.'

Rincewind backed away.

'This is disobedience, Rincewind. I am your superior, after all. In fact, I have been voted the supreme head of all the Orders.'

'Really?' said Rincewind hoarsely. He looked at the other wizards. They were immobile, like statues.

'Oh yes,' said Trymon pleasantly. 'Quite without prompting, too. Very democratic.'

'I preferred tradition,' said Rincewind. 'That way even the dead get the vote.'

'You will give me the Spell voluntarily,' said Trymon. 'Do I have to show you what I will do otherwise? And in the end you will still yield it. You will scream for the opportunity to give it to me.'

If it stops anywhere, it stops here, thought Rincewind.

'You'll have to take it,' he said. 'I won't give it to you.'

'I remember you,' said Trymon. 'Not much good as a student, as I recall. You never really trusted magic, you kept on saying there should be a better way to run a universe. Well, you'll see. I have plans. We can—'

'Not we,' said Rincewind firmly.

'Give me the Spell!'

'Try and take it,' said Rincewind, backing away. 'I don't think you can.'

'Oh?'

Rincewind jumped aside as octarine fire flashed from Trymon's fingers and left a bubbling rock puddle on the stones.

He could sense the Spell lurking in the back of his mind. He could sense its fear.

In the silent caverns of his head he reached out for it. It retreated in astonishment, like a dog faced with a maddened sheep. He followed, stamping angrily through the disused lots and inner-city disaster areas of his subconscious, until he found it cowering behind a heap of condemned memories. It roared silent defiance at him, but Rincewind wasn't having any.

Is this it? he shouted at it. When it's time for the showdown, you go and hide? You're frightened?

The Spell said, That's nonsense, you can't possibly believe that, I'm one of the Eight Spells. But Rincewind advanced on it angrily, shouting, Maybe, but the fact is I do believe it and you'd better remember whose head you're in, right? I can believe anything I like in here!

Rincewind jumped aside again as another bolt of fire lanced through the hot night. Trymon grinned, and made another complicated motion with his hands.

Pressure gripped Rincewind. Every inch of his skin felt as though it was being used as an anvil. He flopped onto his knees.

'There are much worse things,' said Trymon pleasantly. 'I can make your flesh burn on the bones, or fill your body with ants. I have the power to—'

'I have a sword, you know.'

The voice was squeaky with defiance.

Rincewind raised his head. Through a purple haze of pain he saw Twoflower standing behind Trymon, holding a sword in exactly the wrong way.

Trymon laughed, and flexed his fingers. For a

moment his attention was diverted. Rincewind was angry. He was angry at the Spell, at the world, at the unfairness of everything, at the fact that he hadn't had much sleep lately, at the fact that he wasn't thinking quite straight. But most of all he was angry with Trymon, standing there full of the magic Rincewind had always wanted but had never achieved, and doing nothing worthwhile with it.

He sprang, striking Trymon in the stomach with his head and flinging his arms around him in desperation. Twoflower was knocked aside as they slid along the stones.

Trymon snarled, and got out the first syllable of a spell before Rincewind's wildly flailing elbow caught him in the neck. A blast of randomized magic singed Rincewind's hair.

Rincewind fought as he always fought, without skill or fairness or tactics but with a great deal of whirlwind effort. The strategy was to prevent an opponent getting enough time to realize that in fact Rincewind wasn't a very good or strong fighter, and it often worked.

It was working now, because Trymon had spent rather too much time reading ancient manuscripts and not getting enough healthy exercise and vitamins. He managed to get several blows in, which Rincewind was far too high on rage to notice, but he only used his hands while Rincewind employed knees, feet and teeth as well.

He was, in fact, winning.

This came as a shock.

It came as more of a shock when, as he knelt on Trymon's chest hitting him repeatedly about the head, the other man's face changed. The skin crawled and waved like something seen through a heat haze, and Trymon spoke.

'Help me!'

For a moment his eyes looked up at Rincewind in fear, pain and entreaty. Then they weren't eyes at all, but multi-faceted things on a head that could be called a head only by stretching the definition to its limits. Tentacles and saw-edged legs and talons unfolded to rip Rincewind's rather sparse flesh from his body.

Twoflower, the tower and the red sky all vanished. Time ran slowly, and stopped.

Rincewind bit hard on a tentacle that was trying to pull his face off. As it uncoiled in agony he thrust out a hand and felt it break something hot and squishy.

They were watching. He turned his head, and saw that now he was fighting on the floor of an enormous amphitheatre. On each side tier upon tier of creatures stared down at him, creatures with bodies and faces that appeared to have been made by crossbreeding nightmares. He caught a glimpse of even worse things behind him, huge shadows that stretched into the overcast sky, before the Trymon-monster lunged at him with a barbed sting the size of a spear.

Rincewind dodged sideways, and then swung around with both hands clasped together into one fist that caught the thing in the stomach, or possibly the thorax, with a blow that ended in the satisfying crunch of chitin.

He plunged forward, fighting now out of terror of what would happen if he stopped. The ghostly arena was full of the chittering of the Dungeon creatures, a wall of rustling sound that hammered at his ears as he struggled. He imagined that sound filling the Disc, and he flung blow after blow to save the world of men, to preserve the little circle of firelight in the dark night of chaos and to close the gap through which the nightmare was advancing. But mainly he hit it to stop it hitting back.

Claws or talons drew white-hot lines across his back, and something bit his shoulder, but he found a nest of soft tubes among all the hairs and scales and squeezed it hard.

An arm barbed with spikes swept him away, and he rolled over in the gritty black dust.

Instinctively he curled into a ball, but nothing happened. Instead of the onslaught of fury he expected he opened his eyes to see the creature limping away from him, various liquids leaking from it.

It was the first time anything had ever run away from Rincewind.

He dived after it, caught a scaly leg, and wrenched. The creature chittered at him and flailed desperately with such appendages as were still working, but Rincewind's grip was unshakeable. He pulled himself up and planted one last satisfying blow into its remaining eye. It screamed, and ran. And there was only one place for it to run to.

The tower and the red sky came back with the click of restored time.

As soon as he felt the press of the flagstones under his feet Rincewind flung his weight to one side and rolled on his back with the frantic creature at arms' length.

'Now!' he yelled.

'Now what?' said Twoflower. 'Oh. Yes. Right!'

He swung the sword inexpertly but with some force, missing Rincewind by inches and burying it deeply in the Thing. There was a shrill buzzing, as though he had smashed a wasps' nest, and the mêlée of arms and legs and tentacles flailed in agony. It rolled again, screaming and thrashing at the flagstones, and then it was thrashing at nothing at all because it had rolled over the edge of the stairway, taking Rincewind with it.

There was a squelching noise as it bounced off a few of the stone steps, and then a distant and disappearing shriek as it tumbled the depth of the tower.

Finally there was a dull explosion and a flash of octarine light.

Then Twoflower was alone on the top of the tower – alone, that is, except for seven wizards who still seemed to be frozen to the spot

He sat bewildered as seven fireballs rose out of the blackness and plunged into the discarded Octavo, which suddenly looked its old self and far more interesting.

'Oh dear,' he said. 'I suppose they're the Spells.'

'Twoflower.' The voice was hollow and echoing, and just recognizable as Rincewind's.

Twoflower stopped with his hand halfway to the book.

'Yes?' he said. 'Is that – is that you, Rincewind?'

'Yes,' said the voice, resonant with the tones of the grave. 'And there is something very important I want you to do for me, Twoflower.'

Twoflower looked around. He pulled himself together. So the fate of the Disc would depend on him, after all.

'I'm ready,' he said, his voice vibrating with pride. 'What is it you want me to do?'

'First, I want you to listen very carefully,' said Rincewind's disembodied voice patiently.

'I'm listening.'

'It's very important that when I tell you what to do you don't say "What do you mean?" or argue or anything, understand?'

Twoflower stood to attention. At least, his mind stood to attention, his body really couldn't. He stuck out several of his chins.

'I'm ready,' he said.

'Good. Now, what I want you to do is—'

'Yes?'

Rincewind's voice rose from the depths of the stairwell.

'I want you to come and help me up before I lose my grip on this stone,' it said.

Twoflower opened his mouth, then shut it quickly. He ran to the square hole and peered down. By the ruddy light of the star he could just make out Rincewind's eyes looking up at him.

Twoflower lay down on his stomach and reached out. Rincewind's hand gripped his wrist in the sort of grip that told Twoflower that if he, Rincewind, wasn't pulled up then there was no possible way in which that grip was going to be relaxed.

'I'm glad you're alive,' he said.

'Good. So am I,' said Rincewind.

He hung around in the darkness for a bit. After the past few minutes it was almost enjoyable, but only almost.

'Pull me up, then,' he hinted.

'I think that might be sort of difficult,' grunted Twoflower. 'I don't actually think I can do it, in fact.'

'What are you holding on to, then?'

'You.'

'I mean besides me.'

'What do you mean, besides you?' said Twoflower.

Rincewind said a word.

'Well, look,' said Twoflower. 'The steps go around in a spiral, right? If I sort of swing you and then you let go—'

'If you're going to suggest I try dropping twenty feet down a pitch dark tower in the hope of hitting a couple of greasy little steps which might not even still be there, you can forget it,' said Rincewind sharply.

'There is an alternative, then.'

'Out with it, man.'

'You could drop five hundred feet down a pitch black tower and hit stones which certainly are there,' said Twoflower.

Dead silence came from below him. Then

Rincewind said, accusingly, 'That was sarcasm.'

'I thought it was just stating the obvious.'

Rincewind grunted.

'I suppose you couldn't do some magic—' Twoflower began.

'No.'

'Just a thought.'

There was a flare of light far below, and a confused shouting, and then more lights, more shouting, and a line of torches starting up the long spiral.

'There's some people coming up the stairs,' said Twoflower, always keen to inform.

'I hope they're running,' said Rincewind. 'I can't feel my arm.'

'You're lucky,' said Twoflower. 'I can feel mine.'

The leading torch stopped its climb and a voice rang out, filling the hollow tower with indecipherable echoes.

'I think,' said Twoflower, aware that he was gradually sliding further over the hole, 'that was someone telling us to hold on.'

Rincewind said another word.

Then he said, in a lower and more urgent tone, 'Actually, I don't think I can hang on any longer.'

'Try.'

'It's no good, I can feel my hand slipping!'

Twoflower sighed. It was time for harsh measures. 'All right, then,' he said. 'Drop, then. See if I care.'

'What?' said Rincewind, so astonished he forgot to let go.

'Go on, die. Take the easy way out.'

'*Easy?*'

'All you have to do is plummet screaming through the air and break every bone in your body,' said Twoflower. 'Anybody can do it. Go on. I wouldn't want you to think that perhaps you ought to stay alive because we need you to say the Spells and save the Disc. Oh, no. Who cares if we all get burned up? Go on, just think of yourself. Drop.'

There was a long, embarrassed silence.

'I don't know why it is,' said Rincewind eventually, in a voice rather louder than necessary, 'but ever since I met you I seem to have spent a lot of time hanging by my fingers over certain depth, have you noticed?'

'Death,' corrected Twoflower.

'Death what?' said Rincewind.

'Certain death,' said Twoflower helpfully, trying to ignore the slow but inexorable slide of his body across the flagstones. 'Hanging over certain death. You don't like heights.'

'Heights I don't mind,' said Rincewind's voice from the darkness. 'Heights I can live with. It's depths that are occupying my attention at the moment. Do you know what I'm going to do when we get out of this?'

'No?' said Twoflower, wedging his toes into a gap in the flagstones and trying to make himself immobile by sheer force of will.

'I'm going to build a house in the flattest country I can find and it's only going to have a ground floor and I'm not even going to wear sandals with thick soles—'

The leading torch came around the last turn of the

spiral and Twoflower looked down on the grinning face of Cohen. Behind him, still hopping awkwardly up the stones, he could make out the reassuring bulk of the Luggage.

'Everything all right?' said Cohen. 'Can I do anything?'

Rincewind took a deep breath.

Twoflower recognized the signs. Rincewind was about to say something like, 'Yes, I've got this itch on the back of my neck, you couldn't scratch it, could you, on your way past?' or 'No, I enjoy hanging over bottomless drops' and he decided he couldn't possibly face that. He spoke very quickly.

'Pull Rincewind back onto the stairs,' he snapped. Rincewind deflated in mid-snarl.

Cohen caught him around the waist and jerked him unceremoniously onto the stones.

'Nasty mess down on the floor down there,' he said conversationally. 'Who was it?'

'Did it—' Rincewind swallowed, 'did it have – you know – tentacles and things?'

'No,' said Cohen. 'Just the normal bits. Spread out a bit, of course.'

Rincewind looked at Twoflower, who shook his head.

'Just a wizard who let things get on top of him,' he said.

Unsteadily, with his arms screaming at him, Rincewind let himself be helped back onto the roof of the tower.

'How did you get here?' he added.

Cohen pointed to the Luggage, which had trotted over to Twoflower and opened its lid like a dog that knows it's been bad and is hoping that a quick display of affection may avert the rolled-up newspaper of authority.

'Bumpy but fast,' he said admiringly. 'I'll tell you this, no one tries to stop you.'

Rincewind looked up at the sky. It was indeed full of moons, huge cratered discs now ten times bigger than the Disc's tiny satellite. He looked at them without much interest. He felt washed out and stretched well beyond breaking point, as fragile as ancient elastic.

He noticed that Twoflower was trying to set up his picture box.

Cohen was looking at the seven senior wizards.

'Funny place to put statues,' he said. 'No one can see them. Mind you, I can't say they're up to much. Very poor work.'

Rincewind staggered across and tapped Wert gingerly on the chest. He was solid stone.

This is it, he thought. I just want to go home.

Hang on, I am home. More or less. So I just want a good sleep, and perhaps it will all be better in the morning.

His gaze fell on the Octavo, which was outlined in tiny flashes of octarine fire. Oh yes, he thought.

He picked it up and thumbed idly through its pages. They were thick with complex and swirling script that changed and reformed even as he looked at it. It seemed undecided as to what it should be; one moment it was an orderly, matter-of-fact printing; the next a series of angular runes. Then it would be curly Kythian spellscript. Then it would be pictograms in some ancient, evil and forgotten writing that seemed to consist exclusively of unpleasant reptilian beings doing complicated and painful things to one another . . .

The last page was empty. Rincewind sighed, and looked in the back of his mind. The Spell looked back.

He had dreamed of this moment, how he would finally evict the Spell and take vacant possession of his own head and learn all those lesser spells which had, up until then, been too frightened to stay in his mind. Somehow he had expected it to be far more exciting.

Instead, in utter exhaustion and in a mood to brook no argument, he stared coldly at the Spell and jerked a metaphorical thumb over his shoulder.

You. Out.

It looked for a moment as though the Spell was going to argue, but it wisely thought better of it.

There was a tingling sensation, a blue flash behind his eyes, and a sudden feeling of emptiness.

When he looked down at the page it was full of words. They were runes again. He was glad about that, the reptilian pictures were not only unspeakable but probably unpronounceable too, and reminded him of things he would have great difficulty in forgetting.

He looked blankly at the book while Twoflower bustled around unheeded and Cohen tried in vain to lever the rings off the stone wizards.

He had to do something, he reminded himself. What was it, now?

He opened the book at the first page and began to read, his lips moving and his forefinger tracing the outline of each letter. As he mumbled each word it appeared soundlessly in the air beside him, in bright colours that streamed away in the night wind.

He turned over the page.

Other people were coming up the steps now – star people, citizens, even some of the Patrician's personal guard. A couple of star people made a half-hearted attempt to approach Rincewind, who was surrounded now by a rainbow swirl of letters and took absolutely no notice of them, but Cohen drew his sword and looked nonchalantly at them and they thought better of it.

Silence spread out from Rincewind's bent form like ripples in a puddle. It cascaded down the tower and spread out through the milling crowds below, flowed over the walls, gushed darkly through the city, and engulfed the lands beyond.

The bulk of the star loomed silently over the Disc. In the sky around it the new moons turned slowly and noiselessly.

The only sound was Rincewind's hoarse whispering as he turned page after page.

'Isn't this exciting!' said Twoflower. Cohen, who was rolling a cigarette from the tarry remnants of its ancestors, looked at him blankly, paper halfway to his lips.

'Isn't *what* exciting?' he said.

'All this magic!'

'It's only lights,' said Cohen critically. 'He hasn't even produced doves out of his sleeves.'

'Yes, but can't you sense the occult potentiality?' said Twoflower.

Cohen produced a big yellow match from somewhere in his tobacco bag, looked at Wert for a moment, and with great deliberation struck the match on his fossilized nose.

'Look,' he said to Twoflower, as kindly as he could manage, 'what do you expect? I've been around a long time, I've seen the whole magical thing, and I can tell you that if you go around with your jaw dropping all the time people hit it. Anyway, wizards die just like anyone else when you stick a—'

There was a loud snap as Rincewind shut the book. He stood up, and looked around.

What happened next was this:

Nothing.

It took a little while for people to realize it. Everyone had ducked instinctively, waiting for the explosion of white light or scintillating fireball or, in the case of Cohen, who had fairly low expectations, a few white pigeons, possibly a slightly crumpled rabbit.

It wasn't even an interesting nothing. Sometimes things can fail to happen in quite impressive ways, but as far as non-events went this one just couldn't compete.

'Is that it?' said Cohen. There was a general muttering from the crowd, and several of the star people were looking angrily at Rincewind.

The wizard stared blearily at Cohen.

'I suppose so,' he said.

'But nothing's happened.'

Rincewind looked blankly at the Octavo.

'Maybe it has a subtle effect?' he said hopefully. 'After all, we don't know exactly what is supposed to happen.'

'We knew it!' shouted one of the star people. 'Magic doesn't work! It's all illusion!'

A stone looped over the roof and hit Rincewind on the shoulder.

'Yeah,' said another star person. 'Let's get him!'

'Let's throw him off the tower!'

'Yeah, let's get him *and* throw him off the tower!'

The crowd surged forward. Twoflower held up his hands.

'I'm sure there's just been a slight mistake—' he began, before his legs were kicked from underneath him.

'Oh bugger,' said Cohen, dropping his dogend and grinding it under a sandalled foot. He drew his sword and looked around for the Luggage.

It hadn't rushed to Twoflower's aid. It was standing in front of Rincewind, who was clutching the Octavo to his chest like a hot-water bottle and looking frantic.

A star man lunged at him. The Luggage raised its lid threateningly.

'I know why it hasn't worked,' said a voice from the back of the crowd. It was Bethan.

'Oh yeah?' said the nearest citizen. 'And why should we listen to you?'

A mere fraction of a second later Cohen's sword was pressed against his neck.

'On the other hand,' said the man evenly, 'perhaps we should pay attention to what this young lady has got to say.'

As Cohen swung around slowly with his sword at the ready, Bethan stepped forward and pointed to the swirling shapes of the spells, which still hung in the air around Rincewind.

'That one can't be right,' she said, indicating a smudge of dirty brown amidst the pulsing, brightly coloured flares. 'You must have mispronounced a word. Let's have a look.'

Rincewind passed her the Octavo without a word.

She opened it and peered at the pages.

'What funny writing,' she said. 'It keeps changing. What's that crocodile thing doing to the octopus?'

Rincewind looked over her shoulder and, without thinking, told her. She was silent for a moment.

'Oh,' she said levelly. 'I didn't know crocodiles could do that.'

'It's just ancient picture writing,' said Rincewind hurriedly. 'It'll change if you wait. The Spells can appear in every known language.'

'Can you remember what you said when the wrong colour appeared?'

Rincewind ran a finger down the page.

'There, I think. Where the two-headed lizard is doing – whatever it's doing.'

Twoflower appeared at her other shoulder. The Spell flowed into another script.

'I can't even pronounce it,' said Bethan. 'Squiggle, squiggle, dot, dash.'

'That's Cupumuguk snow runes,' said Rincewind. 'I think it should be pronounced "zph".'

'It didn't work, though. How about "sph"?'

They looked at the word. It remained resolutely off-colour.

'Or "sff"?' said Bethan.

'It might be "tsff",' said Rincewind doubtfully. If anything the colour became a dirtier shade of brown.

'How about "zsff"?' said Twoflower.

'Don't be silly,' said Rincewind. 'With snow runes the—'

Bethan elbowed him in the stomach and pointed.

The brown shape in the air was now a brilliant red.

The book trembled in her hands. Rincewind grabbed her around the waist, snatched Twoflower by the collar, and jumped backwards.

Bethan lost her grip on the Octavo, which tumbled towards the floor. And didn't reach it.

The air around the Octavo glowed. It rose slowly, flapping its pages like wings.

Then there was a plangent, sweet twanging noise and it seemed to explode in a complicated silent flower of light which rushed outwards, faded, and was gone.

But something was happening much further up in the sky . . .

* * *

Down in the geological depths of Great A'Tuin's huge brain, new thoughts surged along neural pathways the size of arterial roads. It was impossible for a sky turtle to change its expression, but in some indefinable way its scaly, meteor-pocked face looked quite expectant.

It was staring fixedly at the eight spheres endlessly orbiting around the star, on the very beaches of space.

The spheres were cracking.

Huge segments of rock broke away and began the long spiral down to the star. The sky filled with glittering shards.

From the wreckage of one hollow shell a very small sky turtle paddled its way into the red light. It was barely bigger than an asteroid, its shell still shiny with molten yolk.

There were four small world-elephant calves on there, too. And on their backs was a discworld, tiny as yet, covered in smoke and volcanoes.

Great A'Tuin waited until all eight baby turtles had freed themselves from their shells and were treading space and looking bewildered. Then, carefully, so as not to dislodge anything, the old turtle turned and with considerable relief set out on the long swim to the blessedly cool, bottomless depths of space.

The young turtles followed, orbiting their parent.

Twoflower stared raptly at the display overhead. He probably had the best view of anyone on the Disc.

Then a terrible thought occurred to him.

'Where's the picture box?' he asked urgently.

'What?' said Rincewind, eyes fixed on the sky.

'The picture box,' said Twoflower. 'I must get a picture of this!'

'Can't you just remember it?' said Bethan, not looking at him.

'I might forget.'

'*I* won't ever forget,' she said. 'It's the most beautiful thing I've ever seen.'

'Much better than pigeons and billiard balls,' agreed Cohen. 'I'll give you that, Rincewind. How's it done?'

'I dunno,' said Rincewind.

'The star's getting smaller,' said Bethan.

Rincewind was vaguely aware of Twoflower's voice arguing with the demon who lived in the box and painted the pictures. It was quite a technical argument, about field depths and whether or not the demon still had enough red paint.

It should be pointed out that currently Great A'Tuin was very pleased and contented, and feelings like that in a brain the size of several large cities are bound to radiate out. In fact most people on the Disc were currently in a state of mind normally achievable only by a lifetime of dedicated meditation or about thirty seconds of illegal herbage.

That's old Twoflower, Rincewind thought. It's not that he doesn't appreciate beauty, he just appreciates it in his own way. I mean, if a poet sees a daffodil he stares at it and writes a long poem about it, but Twoflower wanders off to find a book on botany. And treads on it. It's right what Cohen said. He just looks at things, but nothing he looks at is ever the same again. Including me, I suspect.

The Disc's own sun rose. The star was already dwindling, and it wasn't quite so much competition. Good reliable Disc light poured across the enraptured landscape, like a sea of gold.

Or, as the more reliable observers generally held, like golden syrup.

That is a nice dramatic ending, but life doesn't work like that and there were other things that had to happen.

There was the Octavo, for example.

As the sunlight hit it the book snapped shut and started to fall back to the tower. And many of the observers realized that dropping towards them was the single most magical thing on the Discworld.

The feeling of bliss and brotherhood evaporated along with the morning dew. Rincewind and Twoflower were elbowed aside as the crowd surged forward, struggling and trying to climb up one another, hands outstretched.

The Octavo dropped into the centre of the shouting mass. There was a snap. A decisive snap, the sort of snap made by a lid that doesn't intend to be opening in a hurry.

Rincewind peered between someone's legs at Twoflower.

'Do you know what I think's going to happen?' he said, grinning.

'What?'

'I think that when you open the Luggage there's just going to be your laundry in there, that's what I think.'

'Oh dear.'

'I think the Octavo knows how to look after itself. Best place for it, really.'

'I suppose so. You know, sometimes I get the feeling that the Luggage knows exactly what it's doing.'

'I know what you mean.'

They crawled to the edge of the milling crowd, stood up, dusted themselves off and headed for the steps. No one paid them any attention.

'What are they doing now?' said Twoflower, trying to see over the heads of the throng.

'It looks as though they're trying to lever it open,' said Rincewind.

There was a snap and a scream.

'I think the Luggage rather enjoys the attention,' said Twoflower, as they began their cautious descent.

'Yes, it probably does it good to get out and meet people,' said Rincewind. 'And now I think it'd do me good to go and order a couple of drinks.'

'Good idea,' said Twoflower 'I'll have a couple of drinks too.'

It was nearly noon when Twoflower awoke. He couldn't remember why he was in a hayloft, or why he was wearing someone else's coat, but he did wake up with one idea right in the forefront of his mind.

He decided it was vitally important to tell Rincewind about it.

He fell out of the hay and landed on the Luggage.

'Oh, you're here, are you?' he said. 'I hope you're ashamed of yourself.'

The Luggage looked bewildered.

'Anyway, I want to comb my hair. Open up,' said Twoflower.

The Luggage obligingly flipped its lid. Twoflower rooted around among the bags and boxes inside until he found a comb and mirror and repaired some of the damage of the night. Then he looked hard at the Luggage.

'I suppose you wouldn't like to tell me what you've done with the Octavo?'

The Luggage's expression could only be described as wooden.

'All right. Come on, then.'

Twoflower stepped out into the sunlight, which was slightly too bright for his current tastes, and wandered aimlessly along the street. Everything seemed fresh and new, even the smells, but there didn't seem to be many people up yet. It had been a long night.

He found Rincewind at the foot of the Tower of Art, supervising a team of workmen who had rigged up a gantry of sorts on the roof and were lowering the stone wizards to the ground. He seemed to be assisted by a monkey, but Twoflower was in no mood to be surprised at anything.

'Will they be able to be turned back?' he said.

Rincewind looked around. 'What? Oh, it's you. No,

probably not. I'm afraid they dropped poor old Wert, anyway. Five hundred feet onto cobbles.'

'Will you be able to do anything about that?'

'Make a nice rockery.' Rincewind turned and waved at the workmen.

'You're very cheerful,' said Twoflower, a shade reproachfully. 'Didn't you go to bed?'

'Funny thing, I couldn't sleep,' said Rincewind. 'I came out for a breath of fresh air, and no one seemed to have any idea what to do, so I just sort of got people together,' he indicated the librarian, who tried to hold his hand, 'and started organizing things. Nice day, isn't it? Air like wine.'

'Rincewind, I've decided that—'

'You know, I think I might re-enroll,' said Rincewind cheerfully. 'I think I could really make a go of things this time. I can really see myself getting to grips with magic and graduating really well. They do say if it's summa cum laude, then the living is easy—'

'Good, because—'

'There's plenty of room at the top, too, now all the big boys will be doing doorstop duty, and—'

'I'm going home.'

'—a sharp lad with a bit of experience of the world could – what?'

'Oook?'

'I said I'm going home,' repeated Twoflower, making polite little attempts to shake off the librarian, who was trying to pick lice off him.

'What home?' said Rincewind, astonished.

'Home home. My home. Where I live,' Twoflower

explained sheepishly. 'Back across the sea. You know. Where I came from. Will you please stop doing that?'

'Oh.'

'Oook?'

There was a pause. Then Twoflower said, 'You see, last night it occurred to me, I thought, well, the thing is, all this travelling and seeing things is fine but there's also a lot of fun to be had from having *been*. You know, sticking all your pictures in a book and remembering things.'

'There is?'

'Oook?'

'Oh, yes. The important thing about having lots of things to remember is that you've got to go somewhere afterwards where you can remember them, you see? You've got to stop. You haven't really been anywhere until you've got back home. I think that's what I mean.'

Rincewind ran the sentence across his mind again. It didn't seem any better second time around.

'Oh,' he said again. 'Well, good. If that's the way you look at it. When are you going, then?'

'Today, I think. There's bound to be a ship going part of the way.'

'I expect so,' said Rincewind awkwardly. He looked at his feet. He looked at the sky. He cleared his throat.

'We've been through some times together, eh?' said Twoflower, nudging him in the ribs.

'Yeah,' said Rincewind, contorting his face into something like a grin.

'You're not upset, are you?'

'Who, me?' said Rincewind. 'Gosh, no. Hundred and one things to do.'

'That's all right, then. Listen, let's go and have breakfast and then we can go down to the docks.'

Rincewind nodded dismally, turned to his assistant, and took a banana out of his pocket.

'You've got the hang of it now, you take over,' he muttered.

'Oook.'

In fact there wasn't any ship going anywhere near the Agatean Empire, but that was an academic point because Twoflower simply counted gold pieces into the hand of the first captain with a halfway clean ship until the man suddenly saw the merits of changing his plans.

Rincewind waited on the quayside until Twoflower had finished paying the man about forty times more than his ship was worth.

'That's settled, then,' said Twoflower. 'He'll drop me at the Brown Islands and I can easily get a ship from there.'

'Great,' said Rincewind.

Twoflower looked thoughtful for a moment. Then he opened the Luggage and pulled out a bag of gold.

'Have you seen Cohen and Bethan?' he said.

'I think they went off to get married,' said Rincewind. 'I heard Bethan say it was now or never.'

'Well, when you see them give them this,' said Twoflower, handing him the bag. 'I know it's expensive, setting up home for the first time.'

Twoflower had never fully understood the gulf in the exchange rate. The bag could quite easily set Cohen up with a small kingdom.

'I'll hand it over first chance I get,' he said, and to his own surprise realized that he meant it.

'Good. I've thought about something to give you, too.'

'Oh, there's no—'

Twoflower rummaged in the Luggage and produced a large sack. He began to fill it with clothes and money and the picture box until finally the Luggage was completely empty. The last thing he put in was his souvenir musical cigarette box with the shell-encrusted lid, carefully wrapped in soft paper.

'It's all yours,' he said, shutting the Luggage's lid. 'I shan't really need it any more, and it won't fit on my wardrobe anyway.'

'What?'

'Don't you want it?'

'Well, I – of course, but – it's yours. It follows you, not me.'

'Luggage,' said Twoflower, 'this is Rincewind. You're his, right?'

The Luggage slowly extended its legs, turned very deliberately and looked at Rincewind.

'I don't think it belongs to anyone but itself, really,' said Twoflower.

'Yes,' said Rincewind uncertainly.

'Well, that's about it, then,' said Twoflower. He held out his hand.

'Goodbye, Rincewind. I'll send you a postcard when I get home. Or something.'

'Yes. Any time you're passing, there's bound to be someone here who knows where I am.'

'Yes. Well. That's it, then.'

'That's it, right enough.'

'Right.'

'Yep.'

Twoflower walked up the gangplank, which the impatient crew hauled up behind him.

The rowing drum started its beat and the ship was propelled slowly out onto the turbid waters of the Ankh, now back to their old level, where it caught the tide and turned towards the open sea.

Rincewind watched it until it was a dot. Then he looked down at the Luggage. It stared back at him.

'Look,' he said. 'Go away. I'm giving you to yourself, do you understand?'

He turned his back on it and stalked away. After a few seconds he was aware of the little footsteps behind him. He spun around.

'I said I don't want you!' he snapped, and gave it a kick.

The Luggage sagged. Rincewind stalked away.

After he had gone a few yards he stopped and listened. There was no sound. When he turned the Luggage was where he had left it. It looked sort of huddled. Rincewind thought for a while.

'All right, then,' he said. 'Come on.'

He turned his back and strode off to the University. After a few minutes the Luggage appeared to make up its mind, extended its legs again and padded after him. It didn't see that it had a lot of choice.

They headed along the quay and into the city, two dots on a dwindling landscape which, as the perspective broadened, included a tiny ship starting out across a wide green sea that was but a part of a bright circling ocean on a cloud-swirled Disc on the back of four giant elephants that themselves stood on the shell of an enormous turtle.

Which soon became a glint among the stars, and disappeared.

THE END

Equal Rites

Terry Pratchett

'Persistently amusing, good-hearted and shrewd'
Sunday Times

They say that a little knowledge is a dangerous thing, but it is not one half so bad as a lot of ignorance.

THERE ARE some situations where the correct response is to display the sort of ignorance which happily and wilfully flies in the face of the facts. In this case, the birth of a baby girl, born a wizard – by mistake. Everybody knows that there's no such thing as a female wizard. But now it's gone and happened, there's nothing much anyone can do about it. Let the battle of the sexes begin...

'Pratchett keeps getting better and better…It's hard to think of any humorist writing in Britain today who can match him'
Time Out

'If you are unfamiliar with Pratchett's unique blend of philosophical badinage, you are on the threshold of a mind-expanding opportunity'
Financial Times

9780552152600

Mort

Terry Pratchett

'He is screamingly funny. He is wise.
He has style'
Sunday Telegraph

Although the scythe isn't pre-eminent among the weapons of war, anyone who has been on the wrong end of, say, a peasants' revolt will know that in skilled hands it is fearsome.

For Mort however, it is about to become one of the tools of his trade. From henceforth, Death is no longer going to be the end, merely the means to an end. He has received an offer he can't refuse. As Death's apprentice he'll have free board, use of the company horse and being dead isn't compulsory. It's the dream job until he discovers that it can be a killer on his love life…

'Pratchett is a comic genius'
Daily Express

'Cracking dialogue, compelling illogic and unchained whimsy…Pratchett has a subject and a style that is very much his own'
Sunday Times

'Pratchett's humour takes logic past the point of absurdity and round again, but it is his unexpected insights into human morality that make the Discworld series stand out'
Times Educational Supplement

9780552152617

Sourcery

Terry Pratchett

'One of the best and funniest English authors alive'
Independent

All this books and stuff, that isn't what it should all be about. What we need is real wizardry.

All is not well within the Unseen University. The endemic politics of the place have ensured that it has finally got what it wished for: the most powerful wizard on the disc. Which could mean that the death of all wizardry is at hand. And the world is going to end, depending on whom you listen to. Unless of course one inept wizard can take the University's most precious artefact, the very embodiment of magic itself, and deliver it halfway across the disc to safety...

'He would be amusing in any form and his spectacular inventiveness makes the Discworld series one of the perennial joys of modern fiction'
Mail on Sunday

'Pratchett is a comic genius'
Daily Express

'May well be considered his masterpiece...Humour such as his is an endangered species'
The Times

9780552152624

THE DISCWORLD MAPP

Devised by Terry Pratchett and Stephen Briggs

Being the Onlie True & Mostlie Accurate
Mappe of the Fantastyk and Magical Dyscworlde

'De Chelonian Mobile'

They said it couldn't be done. Well, it *has* been done, proving them wrong once again. After years of research, cunningly contrived in as many minutes, the Discworld has its map. It takes full account of the historic and much-documented expeditions of the Discworld's feted (or at least fated) explorers: General Sir Roderick Purdeigh, Lars Larsnephew, Llamedos Jones, Lady Alice Venturi, Ponce da Quirm and, of course, Venter Borass.

Now travellers on this circular world can see it all: from Klatch to the Ramtops, from Cori Celesti to the Circle Sea, from genua to Bhangbhangduc. The great cities of Hunghung, Pseudopolis, Al Khali and, of course, Ankh-Morpork are placed with loving care upon this world which is carried through space by Great A'Tuin.

9780552143240

A LIST OF OTHER TERRY PRATCHETT TITLES AVAILABLE FROM CORGI BOOKS

The prices shown below were correct at the time of going to press. However Transworld Publishers reserve the right to show new retail prices on covers which may differ from those previously advertised in the text or elsewhere.

15260 0	EQUAL RITES	£7.99
15261 7	MORT	£7.99
15262 4	SOURCERY	£7.99
15263 1	WYRD SISTERS	£6.99
15264 8	PYRAMIDS	£7.99
15293 8	GUARDS! GUARDS!	£7.99
15294 5	MOVING PICTURES	£7.99
15295 2	REAPER MAN	£6.99
15296 9	WITCHES ABROAD	£6.99
15297 6	SMALL GODS	£7.99
15315 7	LORDS AND LADIES	£6.99
15316 4	MEN AT ARMS	£6.99
15319 5	SOUL MUSIC	£7.99
15321 8	INTERESTING TIMES	£7.99
15323 2	MASKERADE	£7.99
15325 6	FEET OF CLAY	£7.99
15428 4	HOGFATHER	£7.99
15416 1	JINGO	£6.99
15418 5	THE LAST CONTINENT	£6.99
14615 9	CARPE JUGULUM	£7.99
14616 6	THE FIFTH ELEPHANT	£6.99
14768 2	THE TRUTH	£7.99
14840 5	THIEF OF TIME	£7.99
14899 3	NIGHT WATCH	£7.99
14941 9	MONSTROUS REGIMENT	£7.99
14943 3	GOING POSTAL	£7.99
15267 9	THUD!	£6.99
14161 1	THE STREETS OF ANKH-MORPORK (with Stephen Briggs)	£9.99
14324 0	THE DISCWORLD MAPP (with Stephen Briggs)	£9.99
14608 1	A TOURIST GUIDE TO LANCRE (with Stephen Briggs & Paul Kidby)	£6.99
14672 2	DEATH'S DOMAIN (with Paul Kidby)	£9.99
14673 9	NANNY OGG'S COOKBOOK (with Stephen Briggs, Tina Hannan and Paul Kidby)	£9.99
14429 2	MORT – THE PLAY (adapted by Stephen Briggs)	£4.99
14430 8	WYRD SISTERS – THE PLAY (adapted by Stephen Briggs)	£7.99
14431 5	GUARDS! GUARDS! – THE PLAY(adapted by Stephen Briggs)	£6.99
14432 2	MEN AT ARMS – THE PLAY (adapted by Stephen Briggs)	£6.99
14159 8	THE LIGHT FANTASTIC – GRAPHIC NOVEL	£9.99
14556 5	SOUL MUSIC: THE ILLUSTRATED SCREENPLAY	£9.99
14575 6	WYRD SISTERS: THE ILLUSTRATED SCREENPLAY	£9.99
13325 8	STRATA	£6.99
13326 5	THE DARK SIDE OF THE SUN	£7.99
13703 4	GOOD OMENS (with Neil Gaiman)	£7.99

All Transworld titles are available by post from:
Bookpost, P.O.Box 29, Douglas, Isle of Man IM99 1BQ.

Credit cards accepted.
Please telephone +44(0)1624 677237, fax +44(0)1624 670923,
Internet www.bookpost.co.uk or
e-mail: bookshop@enterprise.net for details.

Free postage and packing in the UK.
Overseas customers allow £2 per book (paperbacks) and £3 per book (hardbacks).